get on your knees

M. ROBINSON
Willow Winters

Get ready for forbidden, high stakes, and crackling tension.
It's two for one in this collection.

We've each included a standalone romance plus a never before
seen sneak peek of our co-written work coming soon!

Enjoy!

second chance contract

M. ROBINSON

To all my angst readers!

I wrote this for you!

prologue

Autumn

"I'm sorry, Autumn."

Three little words that left a gaping hole in my heart. I should've listened to my brother. I should've known this man would break me. He didn't just tear me open, no... He shattered me into a million tiny pieces.

"You're sorry?" I countered in a condescending tone. "What exactly are you sorry for, Julian? The fact that you not only pushed me away but also led me on all these years? Or is it the fact that you took my virginity, and now you're telling me you're sorry for it? Which is it? Because I honestly don't know."

"Kid, you know that's not true. I've been back inside of you since I took your virginity months ago."

I scoffed out, shaking my head in disgust. "That's all you've ever seen me as. I'm just a kid to you."

"You think I see you as a child?" He jerked back. Offended was an understatement. "For fuck's sake! Your mouth's been wrapped around my cock, Autumn, so your statement is full of shit."

I couldn't help but remember the first time he'd called me kid. I was six years old, and he was almost thirteen. Even back then I knew I loved him. There we were, almost thirteen years later, and I was no longer a little girl with a crush on her older brother's best friend.

Now I was a woman who was madly in love with him instead.

"I can't do this anymore. *We* can't do this anymore."

It pained me to hear him say that. He sounded so unbelievably defeated which wasn't in his nature. Julian was always determined in whatever he wanted, and he never backed down from a challenge.

"So what? Are we just supposed to pretend like you don't love me?"

With the utmost sincere expression on his face, he argued, "I don't love you, Autumn."

I stumbled back, almost falling to the ground from his cruel response. "You don't mean that."

Our relationship wasn't supposed to be this hard. Today was supposed to be Christian's day. My brother was getting married, and I was in the wedding. We both were. Julian was the best man, standing tall beside my brother who was marrying the love of his life that he'd known since childhood. They were high school sweethearts.

Throughout the entire ceremony Julian and I cautiously locked eyes, and I wondered if his thoughts mirrored mine. Was he was envisioning us standing in front of all our family and friends, sharing our vows to one another?

Our love for each other?

I'd known Julian for as long as I could remember. He was always there, through thick and thin, my brother's best friend. I should have been celebrating with everyone else at the reception, not wallowing in the illusions I'd made up in my mind of a future that existed only in my mind.

"I've never meant anything more in all my life."

I didn't know what to say or how to act. All I could do was feel this powerful pain spiraling inside of me. I closed my eyes as a single tear fell down the side of my face, reminding me of all the times I'd spent crying over him.

Over us.

"Why are you doing this? Is it because I told you I loved you?"

"Autumn, you've been telling me you love me since you were almost seventeen years old."

"Then why are you doing this? You at least owe me that."

I would never forget the expression on his face when he confessed, "At Christian's bachelor party last weekend, I fucked someone else, kid."

Julian

"You're lying!"

"Do I ever lie to you?"

She wrapped her arms around her torso in a comforting gesture while I waited to finally end us once and for all.

"Who?"

"It doesn't matter."

"Then why are you telling me?"

"I'm not good for you. I've never been good enough for you."

"That didn't stop you from sleeping with me, did it?"

"If anything, kid, you should be thankful it was me and not some boy in the back of his car who doesn't even know how to make you come."

"Oh, because you did?"

"Yeah, just ask my soaking wet sheets."

"You arrogant asshole!"

"What do you want from me? You want me to lie and tell you I love you when I don't? You want me to hurt you more than I already am? More than I already have?"

"You know what I want. It's what I've always wanted. It hasn't changed, it never changes. You know it as much as I do. All I've ever wanted is you."

I hated that she was speaking the truth.

"I want you to look me in the eyes and swear to me that you cheated on me, and you're not just telling me that to push me away again."

"We're not together, kid. I didn't cheat on you."

I debated for the last week if I was going to do this. If I truly had the strength to tell her this. I thought about it for hours on end, driving myself fucking insane with what the right or wrong thing to do was when it came to us.

We never had a future.

We barely had a present.

After seeing the look in her eyes during the ceremony, I knew what she was envisioning, and it was the cold, hard reality I needed to witness in order to tell her it was over. The sneaking around and lying to her brother, to her family. The only family I'd ever known. They took me in when I didn't have anyone, and this was how I repaid them.

By fucking over their daughter.

What kind of man was I?

I was hurting her in the worst possible ways, and I had to live with knowing I did that. My hands were firmly placed in the pockets of my slacks, resisting the urge to pull her into my arms and comfort her the only way I knew how.

The second I walked into the church this afternoon, I stopped dead in my tracks just to take her in. She was a vision in her lavender gown. Her red hair was down, framing her beautiful freckled face and her bright green eyes that I lost myself in night after night.

She looked breathtaking, smiling at everyone. Always the center of attention in any room without having to try. I couldn't take my eyes off her. It took everything inside me not to claim her right then and there. In front of her family, her friends, her brother…

My best friend.

There was no controlling the internal battle that surfaced in the forefront of my mind—it was such a wave of emotions.

It wasn't fair.

None of this was fucking fair.

Especially to her.

When she suddenly caught my stare like she'd felt me from across the church, I didn't look away. She was the first to break our connection, gazing at the ground instead of my eyes. Fully aware she couldn't hide her feelings for me.

Her love.

It seared off of her, burning into my skin. Inflicting scars that would never heal—I wouldn't let them. I didn't know if she'd adverted her gaze for my benefit or hers, but I didn't give it too much thought.

I shoved it away as I did with everything when it came to her. Out of respect for her overprotective brother, it was easier to pretend she was just my best friend's little sister and not the woman who had the power to bring me to my knees if I'd let her.

Since she'd turned eighteen almost a year ago, there was no holding back anymore, and I indulged in the sweetest sin that was Autumn Troy. The little girl who used to follow me around with pigtails and her baby doll in her arms was long gone, and in her place stood an adult, a woman.

My feet moved of their own accord as I followed her out to the cove. We exchanged words that would eternally haunt me, only adding to the pile of endless secrets and betrayals I'd let happen to the family that raised me as if I was their own.

For a few seconds, I inhaled the sweet and enticing smell of Autumn. Remembering that the scent of her strawberry shampoo and coconut lotion still lingered on my pillow and sheets was the only comforting thing I had to go home to.

Stepping toward her, I swept the hair away from her face as a few tears slid down the sides of her cheeks. I wiped those away too. Her tears were the only thing I'd ever be worthy of.

Our emotions were running wild, fighting a battle I knew I could never win.

The emotional turmoil ate away at me the closer I got to telling her this would be the last time she would see me. It would be the last time anyone in her family would see me. Including her brother.

I had to leave.

If I stayed, I'd make her mine, and I couldn't do that to them. Not after everything they had done for me.

Gripping onto the back of her neck, I tugged her toward me, and she caught herself on my chest. Her lips were now mere inches away from my mouth.

Leaning in, I rasped, "I'm leaving town."

Autumn's doe eyes widened, and her breathing hitched. "Leaving?" She choked back a sob. "What do you mean leaving? Where are you going?"

"Away from you."

She sucked in a breath. "Julian…" Softly, she pecked my lips, beckoning my mouth to open for her.

"But before I go…" I hesitated for a moment, wanting to remember the feel of her lips against mine. "I just need you to know."

There was no coming back from this.

What I'd say next would break her heart. She'd hate me, but in the end, I did what I had to do.

Looking deep into her eyes, I viciously spewed, "You were nothing more than a fuck to me, kid."

Those were the last words I'd ever said to her before I turned around and left her there.

With nothing but the man she once knew.

one

Autumn

Ten years later

"**W**ELCOME, MISS TROY. WE CAN'T TELL YOU how excited we are to finally have you here in Miami with us."

I smiled, nodding at the women who'd just welcomed me. "Thank you. I'm excited to be here and working with everyone."

She nervously chuckled, quickly playing it off. "Right… We've spoken on the phone several times in the last couple of weeks, and I've given you a brief overview, but I figured it would be best for us to discuss all the details in person and with everyone present."

"Everyone except the most important person," an older man sitting to the right of her informed.

She didn't pay him any mind. "Now that you've signed your nondisclosure, it's best if we begin with introductions before we proceed." She touched her chest. "As you know, I'm Claire, the head of human resources, and I've been with Mr. Locke for the last four years. This is Mr. Locke's assistant, Erin." She gestured to the younger woman sitting beside her who appeared anxious and a bit shy.

"Erin will be citing our entire meeting, so please don't be alarmed as she types away on her computer. Mr. Locke prefers all meetings to be noted for future reference and, of course, to avoid any indiscretions that may arise."

"I understand."

Claire nodded toward the older man who had just spoken. "This is Carl, and he is the Vice President here at Locke Enterprises. He's been with Mr. Locke the longest out of everyone in this board meeting."

"And because I've been with him the longest, I know we're all wasting our time. He's never going to go for this."

"He doesn't have a choice in the matter. We're announcing and going public in ten days, Carl."

"I understand the severity, Claire, but we both know he's a private person."

She ignored his statement, gesturing toward the man who sat in front of her at the rectangular mahogany table where we were all sitting at.

"That's Robert. He's our chief financial officer." She pointed to the woman next to him. "This is Julia. She's our senior marketing officer, and the man sitting to her right is Adam. He's the head of our public relations department. The woman sitting beside him is Sylvia, and she's one of our board members who is accompanied by James and Andrew, who are also board members. Last, but certainly not least is Marcus." She nodded toward the man sitting parallel to her. "He's one of our chief executives."

I smiled at the room. "Nice to meet everyone."

"Great, now that we have that out of the way, I can share some history on Locke Enterprises with you. I'm sure you Googled the company, but even the internet doesn't know much about our CEO. As Carl stated, Mr. Locke is an extremely private man and is adamant about staying so. However, we're in the process of transitioning from a private business to a public one as we discussed on the phone. We've all come to the mutual agreement that Mr. Locke must remain the face of the company, and with that, there are a few concerns."

"There aren't a few concerns," Carl interrupted, only looking at me. "There's only one, Miss Troy, and it's why you're here."

She glared at him. "We're not trying to scare her away, Carl. She's the best at what she does. It's why she's here."

"I am the best at what I do, and I'm fully aware of the reputation that precedes Mr. Locke. The whole world is, but trust me, if I can change Life of Debauchery's (LOD) rock star image to golden boys, then I can handle your CEO."

"I know." Claire beamed, sitting up in her chair. "It took me months to get a phone call with you. You're a very busy woman, and your resume speaks for itself."

"Thank you." I smiled, gazing around the table before I confidently added, "I've worked for High Society Public Relations for the last five years, and after my success with softening Life of Debauchery's image about two years ago, my phone hasn't stopped ringing with new clientele. LOD had endless stints in rehab and problems with authority, not to mention the law didn't hold well with their record label. When news got out that I was the woman responsible for their rebranding, things most certainly took a turn in my career. By the time I was through with them, they landed the cover of *The New York Times* and went from bad boy rockers to misunderstood musicians. I was in charge of their interviews, live appearances, and everything in between. Most importantly, I established and maintained cooperative relationships with industry representatives across a broad spectrum of media outlets which we're going to need now more than ever on our side."

I could tell by the expression on their faces they were eating up every word of what I was sharing. I wasn't exaggerating by any means. I'd graduated college early, top of my class in my master's program of Marketing and Public Relations. I wasn't just good at what I did—I was the best.

"Those are only a couple of things that I can personally handle," I continued on. "But rest assured that my entire team was handpicked by yours truly. Each person brings their own level of expertise, from writing press releases and any other media communications on promoting our clients, and in some cases, even monitoring their social media accounts. Their ideas are fresh, and they understand how this industry works. It can eat you up and spit you out in a matter of a few hours, and my job is to make sure our T's are crossed and our I's are dotted. We act as a safety net for our clients and the rest of the consumer world. We're a powerhouse and a force to be reckoned with. I am the best. Therefore, I only work with clients who are in desperate need of my services. The bigger the challenge, the more I accel." I paused to let my words sink in, loving the energy I was creating through the boardroom.

It was such a high.

Success was as addicting as any drug could be, and it was the only reason I agreed to this position in the first place. If I took Mr. Locke on as a client, I could make partner in my agency. My hands were tied, and I had no choice if I wanted to advance my career to the next level, Mr. Locke would be the man to make that possible. Everyone would want to work with me, and there would be no competition. I'd be at the top of my game, the peak of my career, and there was no turning that down.

Even if it meant I had to swallow my pride and work with the son of a bitch who deemed me nothing more than a fuck. I had to do what was in the best interest of my future.

I didn't tell them any of that. They didn't need to know my personal agenda for taking Mr. Locke on as a client.

It was no one's business.

Ignoring the thoughts in my mind, I proceeded with my pitch. "People love to feel like they're a part of something, and given the fact your CEO doesn't even participate in interviews makes it very hard for people to trust him with their hard-earned money. Especially when it comes to stock trade which is what you're transitioning from a private enterprise to a public one. No one is going to want to trade with someone who seems unstable. It's all about stability and image. Low risk, high reward. Mr. Locke may have a lot of money, but he needs to gain the notoriety and respect of his possible consumers. The media portrays him as a … well, please excuse my language, but he's nothing more than an arrogant, controlling, and demanding asshole. Although that may work in the boardroom, business deals, and running a multibillion-dollar corporation, it doesn't work for the average Joe Schmo."

"Yes," Claire agreed, smiling wide. "That's exactly it. You nailed it, Miss Troy. Mr. Locke has built this company from the ground up. He spent years overseas in Italy, France, and Japan. Truly learning his craft and the ins and outs of sports cars. He's always had a passion for cars being from Fort Worth, Texas, and he took that passion and built an empire. Being the first person to create an ultra-efficient motor with a high RPM without having to run down battery power has made him a very influential man. There was no electronic sports car before him, and it has most definitely piqued the world's interest in who he is and what he's capable of. It doesn't hurt that he's easy on the eyes and was voted most eligible bachelor by not only People magazine but Forbes three consecutive years in a row now."

"All that may look great on paper, Claire, but it doesn't mean a damn thing to him." It was obvious Carl spoke his mind, and I, for one, appreciated his honesty.

"He couldn't care less about the glorified titles from the media. He's a businessman through and through and has no interest in being Locke Enterprises' mascot. Regardless of the outcome."

Carl didn't know I was aware of what I was taking on, of *who* I was taking on.

He couldn't say anything I didn't already know just from personal experience and my history with him. I knew the son of a bitch better than anyone in this room did.

Or, at least, I used to.

With a curt nod, I countered, "You're going to have to give

him no other choice in the matter. If he refuses, then you need to make decisions based on what will benefit the company as a whole. Not Mr. Locke's ego. Going public is a whole different ballgame. One you need to be prepared for if you're going to dominate and succeed, and we have very little time."

Claire agreed. "Locke wouldn't have it any other way. When it comes to cars and business, Miss Troy, he's an expert. Now, when it comes to people… well, as you said, his bedside manner needs some work."

"Some work?" Carl chimed in again. "Jesus, Claire. The man never smiles. In the years I've known him, I've never once seen him smile. Not even when we grossed our first million within the first two weeks that Locke Enterprises was established."

"I'm hitting the ground running, and I already have an itinerary full of press for him in the next week. Beginning tomorrow, his days and nights will be jam-packed with editorial interviews, photoshoots, live interviews, dinners, luncheons, and those are just to name a few. I have one week to make the world fall in love with Mr. Locke."

"The media doesn't even address him by that name. They've branded him as the Alpha CEO. I don't know about you, but that doesn't sound like a family man to me."

I was about to open my mouth to respond to Carl when I felt *him…*

The double glass doors opened, and the atmosphere instantly changed. It didn't surprise me, he always had the ability to govern a room, even way before his net worth was 3.2 billion.

Without taking a look around, Mr. Locke merely announced, "I have no interest in becoming a family man, Carl."

The man walked into the boardroom exuding dominance, heading straight for his seat at the head of the table. Parallel to me. His confident stride was as demanding as his reputation. No longer the man I remembered, he'd come a long way from a

Texas junkyard, wearing grease-smeared jeans, to now dressed in custom three-piece suits that were worth thousands.

Once he was sitting down in his black leather chair, he leaned forward with his elbows on the table, and without so much as a "good morning" to his colleagues and staff, he simply got down to business, locking eyes with Claire then Carl.

Although, she was the first to speak to him. "We called this board meeting on your behalf."

"What exactly are we discussing on my behalf, Claire?"

"Before we get into that…" She smiled, nodding over to me. "I'd like to introduce you to the woman who is about to change your life."

Locke's inquisitive stare followed her gaze until his eyes landed right on me. For the first time in over ten years, I looked into his icy, bright, blue eyes.

And felt absolutely nothing.

two

I WAS A MAN WHO PRIDED HIMSELF ON CONTROL, AND FOR a brief moment, it felt like I didn't have any. My mind suddenly raged war with itself thinking about the last time I saw her bright green eyes connecting with mine. It didn't help that the aloof expression on her face was consuming and punishing me all at the same time.

It wasn't until she greeted, "Nice to meet you, Mr. Locke," that I mocked in a condescending tone, "Nice to meet me? It's Mr. Locke, is it?"

She nodded, her composure steady and unwavering, but it didn't matter how poised she appeared sitting there staring only at me, I knew what was beneath her designer dress and fuck-me heels.

Is she even wearing a bra?

As if reading my mind, she casually leaned forward emphasizing her chest to show me she was indeed not wearing a damn thing underneath her dress, and I couldn't tear my eyes away from her. She'd always been a beautiful girl, but now—as a woman—there was this alluring confidence and sexy demeanor that wasn't there when I'd left her.

She'd grown up and come into her own skin, only triggering the memory of her body naked beneath mine and making my cock twitch at the thought.

"Julian, Miss Troy is—"

"I know who Autumn is, Claire."

"Oh… I wasn't aware you knew who she was. Then you've heard of her?"

"You could say that."

Autumn didn't show any emotion over my presence or response. She was too busy portraying a woman I no longer recognized.

Coldly replying, "I would prefer you address me as Miss. Troy, Mr. Locke. You have to earn the right to call me by my first name."

I leaned back in my chair, narrowing my captivated stare at her. "Is that right?"

The sudden tension in the boardroom was so fucking thick you could choke on it.

"I'm not your friend, Mr. Locke, and if this relationship is going to work between us, then you're going to have to treat me like the professional I am."

She was right.

We weren't friends.

We were so much more than that.

She could pretend all she wanted, but I knew what she felt like riding me. The way she screamed my name when she wanted more, and the tiny purrs she'd make right before she'd come on my cock.

"Relationships aren't really my thing," I reminded her. Watching and gauging her reaction, I added, "But you already knew that."

Her eyes lit with anger.

Good. Two could play this game, sweetheart.

"Our *working* relationship, Mr. Locke."

"I wasn't aware we were in any type of relationship, *Miss Troy*, but by all means do enlighten me."

"Julian, she's here because you need her."

Claire brought my attention to her statement.

"We're going public."

"I'm fully aware, Claire."

"Of course you are. I didn't mean to imply—"

"Time is money, so stop wasting mine and get down to business. Why is she here?"

"Your team is concerned about your image, Mr. Locke."

My gaze shifted back to Autumn. "My image?"

"Yes. Your personality doesn't exactly speak highly for itself. Especially in the media's eyes."

"And why is this my problem? I've made everyone in this room a very rich individual, and that speaks for itself."

"It does for their bank accounts but not for the general public, which is who you are catering toward to invest in your company."

"My profits are public knowledge, Miss Troy. It's a Google search away. Knowing my favorite color isn't going to decipher if or how much money someone should invest in our shares."

"You'd be surprised how influential knowing someone's favorite color can be when it comes down to giving you their money."

"I have no interest in performing for the public like I'm some teenage boy who needs to have his dick stroked, Miss Troy."

Her cheeks slightly flushed, and I'd be lying if I said it didn't thoroughly please me that I still affected her, despite the game she was trying to play in front of everyone.

"I'm a businessman, Miss Troy. I make money, and that's all anyone needs to know."

"I'm not asking you to perform for anyone. It's actually quite the opposite, so check your ego at the door, Mr. Locke. I believe your best approach in this situation is to show the public how far you've come. Let them into your world. Show them there's more to you than just cars, business, and money. You came from nothing and made something of yourself. You're the American dream, and we need to capitalize on that."

"Julian, it's a necessary evil," Carl intervened. "It's what's best for the company."

"Carl, we both know how Wall Street works. I know people. The *right* people. I don't need to change my image any more than you need to kiss my ass."

"Julian—"

I interrupted him, "We need to clear the room, Claire. I'd like to talk to Miss Troy alone."

"I don't think that's the best idea."

I cocked my head to the side, stating the truth, "Whose name is on the building, Claire?"

She cleared her throat, nodding for everyone to leave.

After they were gone, I crossed my arms over my chest and focused solely on the woman who thought she could change me.

Again.

"Now that they're gone, let's cut the bullshit, Autumn."

"Mr. Locke, I won't remind you again to address me as Miss Troy."

"How long do you plan on playing this little game?"

"I don't know what you're referring to, but let me inform you that your team reached out to me. Not the other way around. I'm just here to do my job."

"Your job? Which is what? Wear a tight dress with no bra so your tits get you employed."

Her eyes widened. "That's not—"

I put my finger up in the air, silencing her. "That wasn't a question."

She glared at me. "I could report you to HR for that, Mr. Locke. Do you always sexually harass women in your office who are dressed professionally?

"I'm simply stating facts, and I never mix business with pleasure."

"I find that hard to believe considering you are referred to as Alpha CEO and the world's most eligible bachelor. What is it now? Three years in a row?"

I grinned. "Kept tabs on me, have you?"

"I researched you. It's what makes me damn good at my job."

"And what did this research inform you of, kid?"

She glared at me again, clenching out, "I won't be disrespected by you, Mr. Locke. You need to address me as Miss Troy—end of conversation."

"Sweetheart, we're just getting started."

"I'm not one of your employees you can treat like shit. Am I making myself clear?"

"You're on my payroll, are you not?"

"*You're* paying *me* to change your image—that makes me your boss."

I let out a throaty laugh, unable to remember the last time I'd done so. "The only thing you're the boss of, kid, is being a royal pain in my ass."

She abruptly stood, sliding documents across the table before strutting her way to the door. "Get used to it, Mr. Locke. Take a look at your itinerary for the next week because beginning tomorrow morning, I control you."

I resisted the urge to argue, realizing all too quickly that my sweet, innocent girl had changed, and in her place stood a confident and sophisticated woman dressed to impress. Her tight cream dress stopped just below her knees, accentuating every curve of her body.

Was she wearing a garter belt?

HR would have a fucking field day if they knew I was admiring her luscious ass that swayed with each step she walked. She knew exactly what she was doing and what I was thinking, only fueling the fire raging inside of me.

Her narrow hips.

Her ample breasts.

She was sporting diamond earrings, a gold bracelet, a

solitaire diamond necklace, and a gold watch with an oversized designer bag tucked in the nook of her arm. Topping her outfit off with red, sky-high fuck-me heels just as I presumed when she was sitting down. She had more makeup on than I'd ever seen on her before.

She was a goddess.

An angel.

Making me realize this was what Hell looked like.

Despite her temper tantrum, our connection was still alive and thriving all around us. It felt like forever had passed, waiting for her to walk by me. I contemplated if she must have felt the same way when it came to me all those years ago.

She was constantly waiting for me to admit I had feelings for her. Never understanding how it didn't matter if I had. We couldn't be together.

Not then.

Not now?

Too many emotions and questions tore through my mind in those brief seconds, one right after the other with no end in sight. I couldn't believe she was there with me, in my building, and with this unexpected ambush by my team of all places.

The clicking sound of her heels vibrated deep within my core with each step she took. One by one it added to all the chaos erupting in my mind. I had questions, and I wasn't going to stop until she answered each one of them to my satisfaction.

My head was already throbbing, a migraine was looming, and I was surprised I could still fucking see straight with the uncertainty racing through my body.

All I wanted to do was pull her into my arms and have her stop with the games she was trying to play. The wall she'd built against me was so thick, so high, so solid that for the first time in I didn't know how long, I feared I might lose this sudden battle between us.

I'd never lost at anything, except maybe her…

When she walked past me, I growled at my impulsive thought and grabbed her hand, tugging her back toward me. She instantly misplaced her footing and fell into my lap, catching herself on my chest.

As soon as she realized her lips were now inches away from mine, she gasped. The scent of her surrounded us, and for a moment, I almost lost control.

Almost.

Instead I rasped, "You can play this game all you want, but we both know it's only a matter of time until you're in my bed *again*, sweetheart."

She pushed off my chest, standing tall in front of me. "If you ever speak to me like that again, Mr. Locke, I won't just report you to Human Resources—I'll sue you for everything you're worth."

I smiled, unable to remember the last time I'd done that either. Eyeing her up and down, I didn't hesitate.

Speaking with conviction, I boldly stated, "As you know, kid, I never back down from a challenge." Before she could shove me away again, I leaned forward and gripped onto the back of her neck, roughly bringing her to me.

When our lips were centimeters apart, I declared, "Consider this war, Miss Troy."

Meaning every last word.

three

Then

"WHY IS THIS JUNKYARD SO FAR AWAY?" I asked, sitting in the backseat of Christian's truck while he drove.

Our parents had just bought it for his sixteenth birthday last week, saying he deserved it for being such a great son, friend, and big brother.

Christian wasn't like other brothers, not like most of my friends' siblings anyway. He was always nice to me and enjoyed having me around. Even though we were six years apart, he didn't make me feel like I was a little girl who couldn't hang around with him. He usually let me tag along with them wherever they went.

It was only the four of us, well, five of us because Julian never went home. He stayed at our house almost every night, and he even had his own room. Mom turned one of our guest bedrooms into his own space for his tenth birthday.

I didn't remember since I was only four years old at the time, but it was one of her favorite memories to share with us. Saying he never looked happier than he did the moment she'd surprised him with what she did for only him.

He was part of our family—always had been, always would be.

Julian didn't know his real parents. He was raised in the system, going from foster home to foster home. I didn't really understand what that meant, but I guessed the state-owned him until he was eighteen—a legal adult.

A man.

Julian always acted older than he actually was, though. Our parents said it was from him having to grow up fast.

Sitting in the passenger seat, he turned around to look at me. "When you see my new baby, you'll know why we drove so far away, kid."

I smiled.

I loved it when he called me kid. It was his nickname for me. No one else called me that, only him.

It was our thing.

"Is it like Christian's baby?"

I'd learned at an early age what cars and trucks meant to boys and how they called them their babies. Both of them loved vehicles since we lived in Fort Worth, Texas. Near NASCAR and street races, but Julian really loved them.

Cars were his everything.

He worked at a junkyard by our house, close enough he could ride his dirt bike through the woods before he got his driver's license a month ago. He'd been working there for the last four years helping Big Ben with all his classic cars.

Most of the time he wore a black cowboy hat or some sort of backward hat with a white t-shirt and jeans. His clothes were usually covered in oil or grease, and his hands and nails were normally stained with it too.

He smelled like gasoline and motor oil, and it was one of my favorite smells because it reminded me of him. I even stole one of his hoodies, and he never asked for it back.

Julian didn't like to feel like a burden on our parents, so he always tried to help out whenever he could. Buying random things at the grocery store or ordering food for us for lunch and dinner.

One time he tried to help out with the water bill, and it made our mom very sad. She started crying, telling him he didn't have to worry about adult responsibilities, and it was their job to provide for us.

A couple of years ago my parents wanted to adopt him, but Julian said no. Saying what they already did for him was enough. I still had nightmares about the time he'd shown up at our house with bruises on his face and body. I thought he'd been in a fight at school. Sometimes that happened. He had a short fuse and bad temper which got him into trouble a lot.

Especially with his foster parents.

In this situation, his foster dad beat him up pretty badly, and Daddy got really mad.

Since he was a super important and successful district attorney, he was able to pull strings and get him out of that placement. They put him in a home closer to ours, and that made us all very happy.

Christian met Julian in preschool, and from the moment they exchanged fist bumps they were best friends.

All my friends were in love with my brother *and* his best friend. But Julian was mine; he just didn't know it yet. The thought alone made my belly flutter and my face flush. I had to look out the window so Christian wouldn't see. He was very protective over me, even when it came down to his best friend.

Julian was the most handsome boy I'd ever seen. He had bright blue eyes that spoke for themselves. I could always tell his mood through his eyes. They would change to all different shades of blue depending on his feelings. His eyes were my mood ring.

He was tall, way taller than me. Big and with lots of muscles because he worked out a lot. His hair was dark, and he had the most perfect nose and teeth. They were straight and super white.

I thought he looked like Eric from the Little Mermaid—my favorite Disney movie. I wanted him to be my Prince Charming, and right now I was too little, but one day I wouldn't be little anymore, and we could be together forever and ever.

My brother's good looks had girls falling all over him since the day he was born too, but it didn't matter. He already had a girlfriend, Kinley. They'd officially been together since last year. Whatever that meant.

They'd known each other since middle school, though. She was pretty and nice to me, and I liked her; the whole family did.

"Julian, can I use your cell phone?"

He handed it over to me. I wasn't allowed to have one. Daddy said maybe next year when I was eleven.

Swiping over his locked screen, a text message appeared from Katie.

Who's Katie?

I can't wait to see your new car. Maybe you could take me for a drive… I mean, I'd love to ride you too.

"Julian, some girl named Katie wants you to take her for a ride in your new car and she said she'd love to ride you too."

He choked on his drink, and Christian's eyes widened. I could see the expression on his face through the rearview mirror.

"Are you okay?" I patted Julian's back to help.

He cleared his throat and coughed a few more times, snatching the phone out of my hands.

"Hey! I wasn't done."

"Yeah, you were up to no good."

"I was not! She texted you as I unlocked your phone."

He texted her back, and I glared.

What did he reply?

"Are you going to give her a piggyback ride?"

He chuckled, and Christian smacked him on the chest. I was the only girl he ever gave piggyback rides to, and I couldn't help but feel jealous.

"This conversation is over, Autumn. Hey, dickwad!" Christian smacked him on the chest again, harder that time. "Don't let her use your phone anymore."

"I didn't know she'd be texting me."

"Since when did you start talking to her?"

He grinned. "Talking isn't exactly what I'd say we were doing."

Before I could ask if she was his girlfriend, my brother pulled into a gas station and got out of his truck to fill his tank.

"Kid."

"What?"

Julian laughed. "What do you mean what?" He rustled up my hair with his fingers, making me giggle. "What's your problem?"

"Nothing."

"Then why aren't you looking at me?"

I shrugged. "I don't know."

"You mad?"

"No. Why would I be mad?"

"Do you want my phone?"

"No. Katie might text again, and Christian will be mad that I'm reading messages I don't understand."

"Autumn."

I deeply sighed, hating when he used that low tone with me.

"I'm not giving her any piggyback rides, okay? Those are only reserved for you."

I looked up at him. "Promise?"

He made a cross over his heart.

"Then what is she riding?"

"I'll tell you what…" He smiled. "One day you're going to know the answer to that question, but today isn't that day, kid."

"So then what? Is she your girlfriend now or something?"

"Or something."

"What does that mean?"

"Why does it matter?"

I shrugged again. "I'm just curious."

"You, curious? Never," he sarcastically joked.

This wasn't the time to make fun. This was serious. I needed to know about my competition.

What if he loves her?

Before I could ask, Julian added, winking, "You'll always be my number one girl, kid."

I smiled. He always knew what to say to make me feel better, but I wasn't naive, knowing he only saw me as a little girl.

Right now.

Christian jumped back into his seat, and for the rest of the drive, I didn't say anything while they talked about Julian's new baby.

I couldn't believe my eyes when I saw the car they were speaking about. It was…

Well, it was a piece of crap.

The outside looked like someone scratched off all the paint, the doors and windows were missing, the interior had been removed, the tires were flat, and the front windshield was cracked. You couldn't see through it. Those were just the obvious things. He hadn't popped open the hood yet.

I knew a lot about cars because Julian had taught me. Sometimes I'd go with him to the junkyard. I'd seen him work on lots of vehicles, but none of them looked this bad.

"Uh, Julian." My gaze found his. "I don't think this car is going to work. I think it died."

He smiled, I loved seeing him smile. It lit up his eyes.

"All the more reason to bring her back to life."

"Do you think you're going to be able to, though? I mean, she looks pretty dead to me."

"Kid." He tugged on the end of my pigtail, and for the next eight years, almost nine, he proved his next words to me on a daily basis.

Stating, "I never back down from a challenge."

four

Autumn

Now

T HE ABSOLUTE NERVE OF THAT MAN.
I couldn't believe the way he'd talked to me like he had a right to. If he thought I was going to forget everything he'd put me through, then he had another thing coming.

He was a job.

He was just another client.

Nothing more, nothing less.

I'd earned a shot at that partnership at High Society, I deserved it, and I'd be damned if he was going to mess it up for me.

By the time I stepped into my hotel room I was beyond exhausted, having back-to-back meetings here in Miami with other clients after what could only be identified as a power struggle between client and publicist.

It wasn't like I hadn't experienced this before. Sometimes influential men had to be knocked down a few notches. Their egos were as big as their bank accounts.

Mr. Locke wasn't any different.

I could handle him.

I was a professional.

I wouldn't let him get to me—not his words, not his devastatingly handsome good looks, not even the bullshit I was aware he was going to fight me on simply to stay in control. He'd always had an issue with authority, especially when it came down to telling him what he could and couldn't do. I definitely had my work cut out for me.

"Hmm…" I groaned, sinking into the hot bubble bath of my suite.

This was how I usually ended most of my days. It didn't matter where I was.

Part of my job required a ton of travel, particularly press tours. We were always flying from New York to LA, anywhere really. For the next week, my ass was stuck beside Locke's. Where he went, I went. Submerging myself into his life was the only way I was going to guarantee he didn't fuck this up.

For the both of us.

He was already proving to be everything the media had made him out to be. I had seven days to change him into the man I used to know.

Before he'd broken my heart.

I could do this.

"You can do anything," I reassured myself, sinking further into the jacuzzi tub made for several people while sipping the wine I had delivered from room service.

Out of nowhere, the hotel phone rang, and I answered from the tub. "This is Autumn."

"How did it go with our Alpha CEO?" my boss inquired, catching me off guard.

I replied, "It went great," with my voice steady and calm.

"Really?"

"Yes."

"He agreed to your week-long press tour?"

"Not in so many words, but we're getting there."

"You're getting there? His first editorial interview with *The New York Times* is tomorrow afternoon, Autumn."

"He will be there." *Even if I have to drag him by his balls.*

"Has he signed your contract?"

"Laurel, I know what I'm doing."

"I don't need to remind you what's at stake here."

She usually wasn't on my ass with any of my clients, but *he* wasn't just anyone. The notoriety we'd get from changing his image would take High Society to the ultimate level. We'd be number one, and that was a spot Laurel wanted more than anything.

We both did.

"You don't need to remind me. Once I'm made partner we'll be unstoppable."

I could tell by her silence she was smiling on the other end of the line.

"Keep me posted on how tomorrow goes."

"Will do."

"Try to get some sleep, alright? You have a busy and demanding schedule ahead of you."

Yeah, and that was only his press tour.

"Of course."

"Goodnight."

"Night."

I hung up, about to breathe a huge sigh of relief when the phone rang again.

I answered, "Laurel, I can deal with Julian, I promise."

"So when you're talking about me to other people I'm suddenly Julian?"

I jerked back, staring at the phone as if it had suddenly grown a head. "How did you get this number? Wait, how did you know where I was?"

"I asked you a question, and I expect an answer."

I rolled my eyes.

"Don't roll your eyes at me, Miss Troy."

"What the hell? How did you—" I looked around the bathroom. "Are there cameras in here? Are you watching me?"

"Would you like me to be watching you while you're naked in your bubble bath?"

"Juli—" I caught myself, fully aware he was grinning that I'd almost said his name to him. "Mr. Locke, how do you know what I'm doing?"

"Unlike you, I'm not pretending to not know everything about you."

"You don't know anything about me."

"I know your hair is held back by an ink pen right now, and you're drinking Merlot while you're soaking in a warm bath, contemplating how you're going to get me to agree to your little press tour."

My mouth dropped open. "How do you—" I sat up, peering around the bathroom again, covering my chest that time.

"You don't have to hide your breasts, Miss Troy. I've seen them."

Through a clenched jaw, I threatened, "If I find out you set up cameras in my suite, I swear to God, Mr. Locke, I will—"

"You'll what? Play with your perfect pink pussy so I can watch?"

"You're unbelievable!" I gasped. "How dare—"

"Relax, kid. My company set up your accommodations."

"Oh yeah … right. But how do you know—"

"I don't have to watch you through cameras if I want to see you naked. All I have to do is think about all the times—"

"Enough!" I roared, losing the last bit of patience I had with him. "You cannot talk to me like this. I won't stand for it."

"You used to love the way I talked to you. Especially when my face was buried in between your—"

I hung up on him. "The fucking nerve of that man!"

Of course, the phone immediately rang again, but I didn't answer.

Instead, I heard his rough, husky tone on the voicemail of the hotel suite as it echoed off the walls.

"If you don't pick up, I'll walk right into your suite. I don't even need to knock, Autumn. I have a key. You're staying in one of my hotels."

Tired of his bullshit, I picked up the phone and dialed his number. "Are you fucking insane?" I seethed into the phone as soon as he answered.

"No, but I won't go ignored either."

"You own hotels?" This was news to me. I had immersed myself into Julian's world without realizing just how deep I was in.

"I own a lot of things, kid. Locke Enterprises is just one of them."

"Oh my God." I rubbed my face. My head was suddenly pounding. "If you come here, I'll have you arrested for trespassing."

"Too late. Open your door." With that, he hung up.

And I lost my shit.

Julian

She answered the door like she was ready to beat my face in. Considering I was the one who taught her how to throw a mean right hook, I was prepared to block any advances.

Except for the one where she threw herself at me, but we weren't there *yet*.

"You cannot be here! This is not appropriate!"

"Since when have we ever been appropriate, kid?"

"You're not even listening to me! This is like ten years ago all over again!"

"But look what it's done for your perspective. At least you're recognizing our past."

"Oh. My. God."

While she threw yet another temper tantrum in the span

of a few hours, my eyes raked in her wet body. She was wearing a light blue silk robe that left very little to the imagination. Her nipples were hard, they were pointing right at me.

When she realized where my stare had drifted, she gazed down and instantly covered herself.

"You're violating so many HR rules, I don't even know where to begin to report you."

"You and I both know you're not going to report me, Miss Troy." I shoved open the door and walked inside. Heading straight toward the rectangular dining table.

She slammed the door shut behind me, turning around to lean against it. Her arms crossed over her chest. "You know most people wait until they're invited inside."

"I'm not most people."

"Right, you're Alpha CEO," she mocked in a condescending tone I wanted to spank right out of her. "You don't ask for anything."

"You're right, I don't." Sitting down at the head of the table, I met her pissed off stare. "I simply take, Miss Troy."

"Oh, trust me, Mr. Locke, I, understand better than anyone, how much you take from people."

"Are you referring to your virginity?"

Her eyes widened. "No! I'm referring to your asshole ways! How do you know I wasn't here with my husband tonight?"

"You're not married."

"How do you know I'm not married?"

"You're not wearing a ring and I know how much you love jewelry."

"That doesn't mean I don't have a boyfriend."

"I'm calling your bluff on the boyfriend," I confidently countered. "Given your reoccurring attitude, I'm going to bet you haven't been fucked in a very long time."

She connivingly smiled, cocking her head to the side. "Just

for that comment, Mr. Locke, I'm going to go down to the bar and find a real man who can satisfy my needs."

"Try to leave, sweetheart. You don't need a random fuck when I'm sitting right here."

"I said a real man who can satisfy my needs, not some pretentious, arrogant asshole who breaks into my hotel room."

"It's not breaking and entering when you own the whole damn building. As far as satisfying your needs, we both know how many times I can make you come without trying. This pretentious, arrogant asshole gave you your first orgasm, and that was just with my mouth sucking your greedy little clit. Would you like me to elaborate on how many times I made you come with my fingers, tongue, and cock, Miss Troy?"

"No! I don't need to be reminded about all the regrets and mistakes in my life."

"Great, because I'm not here for a trip down memory lane. I'm here to talk business." I nodded toward the chair next to me. "Sit down."

"I'm not a dog, Mr. Locke."

I resisted the urge to call her out on her bitch attitude, knowing it wouldn't get me anywhere other than proving my point and pissing her off further. Although the desire was there, I firmly nodded to the chair again instead.

Mumbling under her breath, she walked toward the table and sat in the seat parallel to me. "Why are you here? What do you want?"

"I'm here to make you an offer you can't refuse." I opened my suit jacket to grab my own contract before sliding it across the table.

"What is this?" she asked without looking at it.

"This … is *our* contract."

"Our contract? Our contract for what?"

"For your little press tour."

"Stop calling your itinerary a little press tour. You make it sound insignificant when it's far from that."

"Well, Miss Troy, I have yet to see anything worthwhile other than it bringing you back into my life."

"I'm immune to your bullshit charm. You said we were discussing business, and all you've done is piss me off."

"I'll do your press tour, but it's going to be on my terms."

"Your terms?" She jerked back. "Is that supposed to make me happy? I think you're sadly mistaken on who is in control, Mr. Locke."

"Quite the contrary, kid. I remain at the head of the table. Now turn to page two."

She did, reading out loud, "Publicist, Autumn Troy, agrees to spend personal time with the client, Julian Locke, that isn't considered working hours." Her eyes snapped to mine. "What the hell is this?"

"I'm a businessman, and these are my negotiations."

She slammed the contract shut, roughly sliding it toward me. "I don't need to read the rest to know I'm not signing that."

"You'll sign it, Miss Troy. If you refuse, I won't do the tour, and you won't make partner."

All the color drained from her face when she realized I knew more than she'd wanted me to.

"Let's face it, kid. You need me. I'm the key to your promotion."

She scoffed out in disgust, shaking her head, "You're unbelievable."

"So you've said."

"How did you find out?"

"You're not the only one who knows the right people."

"Get out! Now!"

I gave in to her demands. It was the least I could do. Before I left, I placed the contract on the table, where it would undoubtedly mock her, and then made my way to the door.

I'd won.

Game over.

She knew it too.

But I stopped dead in my tracks when I heard her exclaim, "I fucking hate you, Julian."

Without turning around, I simply stated the truth. "It's not the first or last time I'm going to hear those words out of your mouth, kid. You still haven't read the rest of my terms, and I'm certain it's only going to make you hate me that much more. Especially page three."

"Is that where it says I have to have sex with you?"

"This isn't about sex, Miss Troy. It's much deeper than that."

"Don't use words you don't understand, Mr. Locke. I was nothing more than a fuck, remember?"

Having her throw my own vicious statement back at me from all those years ago wasn't a surprise. I just didn't think it would happen this soon. Pretending as if it didn't kill me to hear her say those words, I regained my composure and opened the door.

"I'll be in my office by seven. Sleep well, kid."

Shutting the door behind me, I left, and as soon as I did, a loud banging shattered against it.

I grinned and walked away.

Autumn shouldn't have played with fire if she didn't want to get burned.

five

Day 1 of Press Tour

I WAS ALREADY SITTING IN FRONT OF HIS DESK IN HIS office when he walked in the next morning with the contract in my lap.

"Good morning, Mr. Locke."

"I see we're back to Mr. Locke." His dubious stare went from me to his assistant, Erin, who was sitting beside me, recording what we were saying by typing away on her laptop.

I smiled when I noticed the sudden smoldering expression on his face as he took in my dress. It wasn't what I would normally wear to a meeting, more like what I would wear for a night out on the town with my girlfriends if we were looking for men.

His gaze lingered on my cleavage. My nipples were hard from the cold air in his office, and I might have rubbed them a little bit before he walked in to ensure they were extra alert.

"We never left, sir."

"Sir?" He arched an eyebrow, sitting behind his desk. His eyes were firmly locked with mine. "Now that I could get used to you calling me."

Of course, you could, you cocky dick.

"I just want to start this meeting by saying thank you for the push I needed to finally get thoroughly satisfied last night. The random fuck I met in the bar that I brought back after you'd left excelled each and every one of my desires and fantasies. It truly was the attitude adjustment I needed. I'm bright-eyed and bushy-tailed for you this morning."

Despite him trying to remain calm and unfazed, I could still see the slight clench of his jaw and the vein on his neck protruding as his gaze shifted back to Erin.

I imagined her eyes were wide as saucers as she continued to type away.

"You can go to your office, Erin."

"No, no, no…" I intervened in a high-pitched tone. "I prefer she stay and cite our entire conversation. I would hate for anything to be taken out of context, especially when we're discussing the negotiations of your contract."

"There are no negotiations. You either take it or leave it."

"I think you should follow your own advice," I snidely baited. "I forgot how good it felt to have orgasms. I came over and over again. And trust me, Mr. Locke, there was no mistaking my orgasms this time. My soaking wet sheets speak for themselves. Please do apologize to your cleaning crew for me."

His jaw tightened again. "I'll relay the message, Miss Troy."

"Great."

"Well, given your night of satisfaction, did you have time to go over my contract?"

"Of course, Mr. Locke. Unlike you, I love mixing business with pleasure," I lied. I never did. I just wanted to get a rise out of him. "I guess you could say it's how I've gotten this far. Ask around since you know all the right people. Yet, you probably don't have to since you've had a taste of me yourself."

"I've had more than a taste, sweetheart."

"Did you get that, Erin?" I looked at her. "Make sure you accentuate 'more than a taste.' I believe it's against company policy to fuck an employee."

"Autumn, that's enough."

"But, Julian…" I leaned against his desk and pressed my

breasts together, giving him one hell of a view. I wasn't wearing a bra. "We're just getting started, *sweetheart*."

"Leave us," he demanded, his eyes now cold and calculated. "Now."

Erin didn't have to be told twice. She practically hauled ass toward the door and out of his office.

"Just out of curiosity, how many assistants do you go through in a month? I'm going to assume maybe one a week?"

"Erin has been with me for three years."

"She seems awfully shy and submissive. Huh, I guess that would work well for you, though. I imagine she's always ready on her knees for you."

"My assistant doesn't get on her knees for me, kid, but you sure as fuck can."

"I thought you don't mix business with pleasure, Mr. Locke?"

"For you…" He paused to let his words sink in. "I would."

"Is that supposed to make me swoon? I'm immune to your bullshit lines. I've heard them all before."

"Autumn—"

I threw the contract on his desk in front of him. "I highlighted what I agree to, scratched out what I don't, and added my own terms. If you don't like it, I'll walk right out of this office and never look back. I may need you, but you need me too. Unlike the eighteen-year-old girl you fucked over, I know my worth now. I won't let you use me again. I shouldn't have let it happen the first place, but I was young and stupid."

Every time I thought about how I'd let him use me the anger seared throughout my entire body. After years of trying to get over him, I finally did, and now all those painful emotions were tearing into me once again.

I hated that I was letting him get to me, but he knew how to push all of my buttons. Determined to not allow him to win,

I went in for the kill, knowing how to use his ambition to my advantage.

"You want to be number one on the market, and I'm the woman to get you there. Because mark my words, Julian, without me, you'll fail."

It was my turn to pause. I wanted him to really listen to what I was saying. He needed to understand this was a two-way street—we needed each other to advance in our careers.

I gave it a few more seconds before adding, "If we're going to make our working relationship succeed and flourish, then you're going to have to give me an inch."

"If I give you an inch, you'll take a mile."

"Everything I have planned for you in the next week is solely for the benefit of your company. I know you didn't come this far to stop now. You're going to have to trust me on this. This has to be a team effort if we're going to work together effectively."

For a moment he just sat there staring at me, and if I wasn't already sitting down, I probably would have fallen on my ass when he declared, "You want the man I was ten years ago, and he's not here anymore, Autumn. He died the day I left you."

"You're wrong," I countered, trying like hell not to let his words get to me. "He's just lying dormant inside of you. But this isn't about us. We were never an *us*, and it took me a long time to realize that. You were my brother's best friend, and I was just a stupid kid who thought her life began and ended with you. I don't hate you, Julian. At least not anymore. The truth is… I feel absolutely nothing for you."

He winced. It was quick, but I saw it.

"But from one successful person to another, I do respect the hell out of what you've built, and the world needs to know how far you've truly come. You know firsthand what it's like to grow up in the system, and there are still millions of kids who need to know that being dealt a shitty hand in life doesn't determine who they are and what they're capable of. It doesn't define them like it didn't define you. You had my father as a role model, and now here's your chance to pay it forward."

"How is your father?"

"I'm not here to discuss my family with you. If you want to know about them, their phone numbers haven't changed."

He didn't just leave me behind—he abandoned my entire family.

Including my brother.

The only difference between me and them was that he actually said goodbye to me. My family had spent years grieving the loss of a best friend and a son.

I could see the remorse on his face—he didn't try to hide it. He wanted me to see there was still a part of the man I used to know living inside of him.

For the first time since we saw one another again, I felt as if I was finally getting through to him. Making my emotions run wild with feelings I thought were gone when it came to him.

I shoved them aside, refusing to go down that road again.

"Did you practice that pitch, kid?"

"No," I simply stated. "I spoke from my heart."

Which scared me more than anything.

Julian

The times when I'd let my mind contemplate the past and what I must have put her family through were some of the darkest moments of my life. To hear her confirm how much I'd hurt her wasn't something I was prepared for, and I'd be full of shit if I said I didn't want to continue talking about us.

But this wasn't the time or place.

The new contract I had drawn up would allow me to have the time I wanted with her where we could do exactly that.

Instead of insisting that this conversation was far from over,

I peered down at the contract, looking through each page to see what she had in mind.

Publicist, Autumn Troy, agrees to spend personal time with Client, Julian Locke, which isn't considered working hours. No more than two hours a day.

There was a lot I could do with two hours…

For every interview that client, Julian Locke, has agreed to, Publicist, Autumn Troy, must have dinner with him. Only if I can choose the restaurant.

I guess she was still the picky eater she was as a child. She basically had an interview scheduled every day, which meant we'd be eating dinner together every night. On top of the two hours she was giving me. I could work with that.

My eyes shifted toward the next clause, and I couldn't help but chuckle at her response.

~~When the Publicist, Autumn Troy, is ready to throw herself at Client, Julian Locke, he will be willing and able to perform up to his full potential.~~ Keep fucking dreaming. It's never going to happen.

Publicist, Autumn Troy, is NOT ALLOWED to have contact and/or private encounters with other men for the duration of the client, Julian Locke's, press tour. That goes both ways with you and women, asshole.

I grinned. She felt nothing for my ass.

six

Julian

OVING ONTO THE NEXT CLAUSE, I READ...

~~During travel, Publicist, Autumn Troy, must sleep in the same suite as Client, Julian Locke.~~ ABSOLUTELY NOT.

I glanced up. "Are you worried you won't be able to keep yourself from crawling into my bed, Miss Troy?"

She glared at me. "Of course not."

"Then what's the problem with us sharing a suite? Unless you've forgotten, I was the first man to see you naked. I'd be happy to refresh your memory. I'm sure some things have changed since the last time you were in my bed, except for how many times I can make you come and scream my name."

Her eyes widened. "And that's exactly why! You think you're still allowed to see me naked, when you're not. You're never going to see me naked again, Mr. Locke. You don't have that effect on me anymore. I don't even find you attractive."

I deviously grinned, leaning back against my seat. I didn't say one word, allowing my predatory regard to do all the work for me. It went from her tantalizing green eyes to her pouty lips. Slowly, I sensually started rubbing my thumb over my mouth. Obviously, she was uncomfortable, squirming as my eyes wandered over her body.

I didn't give a fuck.

I wanted to look at her, so I did.

Reminding me of all the times she'd captivated my senses when she shouldn't have. I never stopped rubbing my callused fingers over my mouth, as her gaze followed the movement of my hand, causing her luscious lips to purse as she watched my every move. Only triggering the memories of how many times I'd bit her bottom lip.

She liked it.

A lot.

My heady gaze trailed down her neck toward her tits, which were on full display, just waiting to be freed from her tight fucking dress, right down to her narrow, tiny waist. I immediately envisioned all the times I'd gripped onto her hips, guiding her down my cock, or when I fucked her from behind.

She liked that even more.

Miss Autumn Troy was a dirty little girl.

Narrowing my eyes, I continued my visual assault down to her slender thighs, wanting to bury my face between them. My cock twitched at the thought of her riding my face, still remembering the first time I sat her on my mouth, on my bed. It was the second worst day of my life—the first was leaving her. However, she made that day better for me. The second I tasted of her, and fucked her virgin hole with my tongue, I knew there was no going back for me.

For us.

I seductively licked my lips, practically tasting her against my tongue.

Her skin flushed.

Her legs squirmed.

Her body completely reacted to my greedy perusal.

Autumn might claim she didn't feel anything for me, but her body and pussy were telling a different story.

"Stop looking at me like that."

"I thought I didn't affect you?"

"You don't."

"So if I slid my fingers into your panties, you wouldn't be wet for me right now?"

"Not that it's any of your business, but I'm not wearing any."

I laughed, throwing my head back.

The little fucking minx.

"And who's benefit was that for, Miss Troy?"

She ignored my question. "This isn't a slumber party, Mr. Locke. We don't need to share a suite."

"Well, I have no intention of sleeping."

"Which is exactly why we're not sharing a suite."

I smiled. "Don't trust yourself to be alone with me?"

"I'm alone with you right now."

"You had Erin sitting here when I walked in."

"That doesn't mean anything."

"You need to trust me when I say my intentions are pure."

"You literally just said you had no plans of sleeping."

"When you have hundreds of people relying on you to make a living, you don't sleep much. You took my words out of context. What I was insinuating was that we could go over our daily game plan for the tour. You know, get me ready for the world to fall in love with me."

She beamed. "We could absolutely do that."

"Great." I grabbed a highlighter to approve the same suite clause, and she yanked the contract from my hands.

"I can easily walk to my *own* suite from yours, Mr. Locke."

"I usually rent the penthouse floor when I'm traveling."

"Why? You're only one person."

"I enjoy my privacy, and if people see you leaving my suite at all hours of the late nights, they're going to assume we're doing much more than debriefing."

"Not happening."

"What about the paparazzi? You see how much they follow me around. You want to deal with the press?"

She thought about it for a minute before she reluctantly resigned. "Fine. But I want my own room and bathroom, and they need to be the furthest away from yours."

Pretending like I wasn't pleased I'd persuaded her to change her mind, I grabbed the highlighter out of her hand and added in her terms.

Reading on…

Publicist must be present during travel, car rides, and flights from one press juncture to the next. She also agrees to be present for all the itineraries she has scheduled for the client.

Do you honestly think I trust you to say the right things? I have to be there just to cover your ass and make sure I can do damage control when you fuck it up.

I smiled—she knew me well.

The next clauses weren't anything of importance, at least not to me. The ones I wanted her to approve, she did.

Closing the contract, I hit the intercom on my phone.

"Yes, Mr. Locke?"

"Erin, come to my office."

Moments later, she walked in, and I handed her the contract.

"Have HR re-draft this immediately and return it to me once it's finalized."

"Yes, Mr. Locke." She nodded and left.

It didn't take long for her to reappear with our new contract, and we both signed.

Except Autumn didn't realize she'd just signed…

Her future with me.

Autumn

WE WALKED INTO THE BUILDING WHERE *The New York Times* interview was being held.

Julian strode in like he owned the damn place, each stride more commanding than the last. With the confidence he exuded from head to toe, no one would assume this was his first official interview.

The man had a way about him. He never wore his emotions on his sleeve, and I wish I could tell you this was something he'd developed after he'd left me, but it wasn't.

He always had the ability to hold everything in. No one saw what he didn't want them to see, and the only times I ever did were the moments he'd let me in.

When I was a little girl, I thought I had the power to read him through his bright, blue eyes. But as I got older, he realized what I could see in his gaze, and that was when he stopped showing me his emotions. Somewhere along the way he deemed me unworthy to know what he was feeling, and it not only crushed my heart, but it destroyed my soul.

Keeping up with his stride, I matched his calm demeanor, fully aware of what we were about to encounter. I was beyond thankful I'd once dated the columnist who was conducting Julian's interview. I met him in graduate school. At the time, he was just starting at a lucrative magazine.

Now, he was what dreams were made of, being able to make

or break anyone's career with the influence he held as the top journalist in the industry.

"You ready?" I questioned, holding onto the door.

"I'm always ready." He walked inside, and to his back, I rolled my eyes.

"Don't roll your eyes at me, kid."

What the hell? How does he keep doing that?

"Cherry!" Charles greeted, bringing my attention over to him.

The last time I'd seen him was a little over a year ago. He'd interviewed one of my other clients.

"Charlie." I smiled, walking into his arms. "How are you?"

"I'm better now that I'm seeing your gorgeous face."

I giggled. "Always such a charmer."

"When are you going to let me take you out to dinner? I owe you a baseball game."

"You do. Maybe next time I'm in town."

My eyes connected with Julian who was standing behind me, staring at us like he recognized we'd once dated.

"This is Julian Locke. Julian, this is Charles Gordan."

"Do I get to call him Charlie too?"

I nervously chuckled. "That's just an old nickname I have for him."

"Cherry?"

"Another old nickname."

"I see."

"Nice to meet you, Julian." Charles extended his hand and Julian shook it.

"It's Mr. Locke, Charlie."

Jesus, we just got here, and he's already being an abrasive asshole.

I intervened, "Why don't you go get everything ready for Mr. Locke, and we'll be right over."

Charles nodded, feeling the sudden tension in the room.

Once he was gone, I turned to Julian. "Can you not be a snarky dick to the journalist who's about to run one of the most important interviews of your career?"

He tugged on the end of my hair. "He better be referring to the color of this, *Cherry*."

"Oh, don't worry. He totally is. I'm fully lasered. Brazilian to be exact."

Julian groaned, making me smile big and wide.

"Did he fuck you?"

"Uh, hello, none of your business."

"When was the last time he fucked you?"

"Again, none of your damn business. Now get your head in the game, Locke. You need to be nice."

"I'm not nice."

"I'm fully aware, but you need to try."

Charles announced, "I'm ready when you are."

We made our way over to him.

Julian, of course, sat at the head of the table, while I sat behind him, and Charlie was sitting in front of both of us with a recorder and notepad in his hands.

During the interview, I lost count of how many times I had to tell Charlie he couldn't use that.

"Tell me about your childhood, Mr. Locke."

"There's nothing to tell."

I kicked him under the table. "What he's trying to say is he doesn't know where to start."

"Would you like to do the interview for me, kid? Considering you haven't allowed me to answer one question."

"Kid?" Charlie chimed in. "What's that about?"

"It's nothing."

"Oh, so that's nothing?" Julian mocked. Using my own words against me, he added, "What she's trying to say is that Cherry and I go way back."

"Now this just got good. How far back?"

"The interview is about Julian, Charles. Not Julian and me."

"Julian? Are you usually on a first-name basis with your clients, Cherry? I don't think so. Besides, this is what people want to know. Trust me." He peered back at Locke. "You were saying?"

"I used to be her Prince Charming."

"This is not—"

Julian interrupted me, "I can handle it from here, Miss Troy. I'm sure your other clients need tending to."

"Lucky for you, I cleared my entire schedule this week, just for you."

"Now this is getting really good. She never clears her schedule for only one client."

"Charles!"

Locke grinned. "Is that right?"

I was about to explain myself, but my phone rang. "This is Autumn."

Laurel was on the other line, and I had to excuse myself from the table. By the time I was done with our conversation, Julian was walking out of the interview into the lobby where I was talking to my boss with the same confident stride he had going in.

"Should I ask how that went? Or should I assume?"

"You know what they say about people who assume, kid."

"Yeah, yeah, yeah."

I didn't give it too much thought. Charlie and I had an arrangement—nothing was published without my approval first. I'd go over his article once he emailed it to me. For the rest of the day, we went from one thing to the next until it was way past dinnertime, and I was starving. I wanted to try the restaurant at my hotel, well Julian's hotel.

He held the door open for me.

"Today started a little rough—"

"You used to love it rough."

"Oh my God," I exclaimed, stepping into the restaurant. "You cannot say stuff like that to me anymore."

"Try to stop me, sweetheart."

"Damn. I should have added a clause about your inappropriate behavior."

"It wouldn't have done you any good. I wouldn't have signed it."

"On that note…" I stopped at the bar, nodding to the bartender. "I'll take a martini with four stuffed olives, please."

"And you, Mr. Locke?"

"I'll just take a water, Sam."

"A water? What are you twelve? Order a drink."

"I don't drink."

"Since when?"

The stern expression on his face answered my question. "You really need to relax on the control. It's a drink, not heroin." I glanced at the bartender. "Do you have TX Straight Bourbon Whiskey?"

"Yes."

"Great, he'll take one of those, no ice."

The bartender turned, getting our drinks ready.

"What?" I asked, taking in the same stern expression. "You used to love that liquor."

"So we're back to you knowing who I am? How long is it going to last this time?"

"Why do you have to ruin every moment?"

He leaned in close to my face, and my stomach fluttered. The strong smell of his cologne assaulted my senses.

"I used to love a lot of this. Some I still do."

"What do you mean—"

"Oi!" a familiar voice hollered from across the room.

While another familiar voice called out, "There's our girl!"

Julian stared from them to me. "Their girl?"

"Look at you, Autumn Bum Bum." Jude, the bass guitarist from Life of Debauchery, looked me up and down.

It was his silly name for me, meaning my ass was nice.

"She's mine first," Beck, the rhythm guitarist from their band stated, standing in my face.

"Hey there," I greeted, amused.

They were by far my most entertaining clients.

Beck didn't hesitate, instantly picking me up off the ground in a warm, tight embrace.

"Mate, don't bloody hog her."

As soon as Beck put me down, Jude did the same. Except he twirled me around in a circle and then kissed both my cheeks.

"Fancy seeing you here in Miami."

He set me down. "Likewise."

"We're on tour, and I'm fucking knackered."

"You're always fucking knackered."

They went back and forth for a second, and out of the corner of my eye, I could see Julian's intense stare narrowed in on them before he leaned into my ear.

Murmuring, "Is that just an old nickname too?"

"And who's this?" Beck asked, bringing our attention back to him. "Are you fucking our girl?"

"Jude!" I shouted, glancing over at Julian. Knowing he wouldn't appreciate their crude personalities, but what did he expect?

They're rock stars.

"This is my client, Julian Locke." I swallowed hard, silently wishing I knew what he was thinking.

Feeling.

Wanting…

Truth was, the more I was around him, the more I realized how much I still couldn't read him. Before yesterday, the last time I'd seen him I was crying over him. Pouring my heart out and falling apart in his arms. Telling him I loved him.

Now, there he was, with me. And after all this time, all these years, he was still so damn hard to decipher. Giving me mixed signals left and right like he did when I was younger.

Our connection.

Our friendship.

His indifference when we were in public versus private.

It all came barreling down on me, and I wasn't anticipating it to.

eight

Autumn

I NEVER KNEW WHAT HE WAS THINKING, ESPECIALLY when he was around the guys I dated. He didn't stop denying his attraction to me until I was almost seventeen, and that was only because I'd made him. Thinking about that night made me pissed at him all over again.

The pushing me away, only to lead me on was definitely one of the worst games he'd played with me. Always blaming it on my brother.

Wait… Why am I thinking about this? Why do I care?

"Julian Locke." Jude looked at Beck, pulling me away from my reckless thoughts. "Where have we heard that name?"

"Fuck if I know."

"Oh! I know! Alpha CEO! You invented the eco-friendly sports car, right?"

"The engine."

"Yes! I fucking own three of those cars. Fucking spectacular, Mate! Let me buy you a drink."

"I don't need you to buy me anything."

"Julian…" I rasped under my breath, not used to this side of him.

Was he just being possessive and controlling, or was he jealous?

Jealousy wasn't something I was used to from him either. He was always so fucking confident and cocky when it came to me. It was such a turn-on and as much as I hated to admit it, it still was.

Goddamn it.

"Don't get your knickers in a bunch. We didn't fuck your girl, if that's what you're worried about."

"Not that we didn't try," Beck commented.

"Autumn Bum Bum is a fucking peach. She turned our entire lives around. Even partied with us. This girl can drink some fucking whiskey."

"I had to keep up with you."

"Yeah, babe, you did. But our singer has turned into a fucking pussy since he got married, and our drummer is sticking it to his assistant." Jude threw his arm around Beck. "It's just me and this fucking wanker now."

I giggled, missing these guys.

"Her girly squeal is absolutely delicious, isn't it? You sticking it to her? I give it a week before you're balls deep inside of her."

My face turned fifty shades of red—Jude had no filter.

Ever.

Beck joined in. "I want in on that bet."

"Five k on him sinking into her before the week is over."

"A week?" Jude scolded. "Her ass has gotten bigger. I give it two days. Max."

This was a reoccurring thing between them. They were always betting each other on stupid shit.

In less than two strides, Julian tugged me into his side.

My heart pounded so hard, I prayed he couldn't feel it against his abrupt, dominating hold. The simple touch of his arms around me had me weak in the knees and my body stiffening. I wasn't expecting him to do that in front of them.

What is he doing?

"If she'd give me half the chance, I'd make her mine tonight."

My breath hitched. Not only could he feel my hesitation, but he could also read my mind.

I tried to step away from him, but he wouldn't let me. Holding onto me tighter. Thinking quick on my feet, I turned around in his arms and set my hand on his chest, trying to make it look like there wasn't anything going on between us.

There wasn't.

Was there?

The last thing I wanted was for Jude and Beck to start rumors and people thinking we were anything besides professional with each other.

Using the best enthusiasm I could muster in the awkward situation, I announced, "Boys, get ready to invest in a sure thing. Someone is going to be making a huge announcement next week." I winked at them while Julian tensed, abruptly letting me go, and I instantly felt the loss of his touch.

Autumn, stop.

After I said goodbye to the guys, Julian wasn't happy.

When was he ever happy?

In a stern tone, he ordered everyone at the bar to leave us. Thank God it was only his employees and not his guests.

Why was he pissed? Was it because of how they'd treated me or—

"Why would you share that private information with them?"

I guess that answered my question. Why was I disappointed?

Before I could give it too much thought, he sneered, "I don't like to be kept waiting."

My eyes snapped to his. "Stop treating me like I'm an employee. I don't answer to you."

"Actually, you do."

"Listen, you condescending asshole. I didn't say anything. I hinted. So before you go crazy, I'm fully aware insider trading is illegal, but I'm simply doing my job, and they're going to be the best marketing you can get. Jude and Beck are going to tell people, those people are going to tell other people, and so on and so on. We want people talking, rumors like this are your best friend. By the time you actually announce, thousands of people are going to be chomping at the bit for you. What you should be saying is thank you."

Everything happened so fast. One second we were arguing, the next he roughly gripped onto the back of my neck and tugged me close to his mouth.

My breathing hitched.

"I don't like to be taken by surprise. Everything and anything gets approved by me first, understood?"

I tried to shove him away, but it was no use. He didn't budge.

In a dark, heady tone, he rasped, "Next time you're a bad girl, you'll give me your panties and face the wall with your legs spread, or I could throw you over my lap instead."

"Julian!"

"Yeah, sweetheart, you'll scream my name just like that, except it's going to be from me spanking your ass raw to teach you a lesson you won't soon forget."

I shoved him again. "Fuck you."

The next thing I knew, he spun my body and pinned my chest to the bar where I couldn't move. I huffed out a breath, instantly realizing I was at his mercy, and for a brief second, I thought there was no way he was going to do this. I was a grown-ass woman for fuck's sake.

"What the—"

He didn't hesitate.

SLAP.

Walloping my ass so hard, I instantaneously stood on the tips of my toes in my already six-inch stiletto heels.

"You rat bastard! Don't you fucking dar—"

"Talk back to me one more time, and I'll lift your dress, pull down your panties, and slap your bare ass instead."

My ass burned, and my pussy throbbed. I wanted to raise hell, although I wasn't an idiot. He'd follow through on his threat.

"Now," he bit. "Am I making myself clear?"

Going against all my instincts, I reluctantly agreed, "Yes."

"Great." He let me go, and there was no wavering on my part. I spun around with my hand shooting straight toward his face, but he caught it mid-air.

Holding onto my wrist, he yanked me toward him. "While we're on the topic of you being a very bad girl, I also highly suggest you make damn sure your future encounters with men don't provoke me again. You won't like me when I'm angry."

I jerked my hand away. "I don't like you right now."

"Prove it," he challenged all in one breath. "Spread your legs and show me you're not wet."

I glared at him. "You'd love that, wouldn't you? Tell me, Julian, what are you trying to accomplish here? What do you want from me?"

He stepped toward me, and I stepped back, putting my hand up.

"I thought you wanted to know what I wanted. I was just about to show you."

"I won't sleep with you. If this is about sex, I'm not fucking you."

"Don't worry, sweetheart, I have no problem doing all the fucking."

I pushed him as hard as I could, and he didn't move an inch. He was a cement block, fueling my fury like he was nothing more than the gasoline to my flames.

"So this is about sex? We're long past that. I'm here as your publicist—nothing more, nothing less. You need to get that through your thick, stubborn skull. I'll tell you this, though… I find it hilarious I spent most of my teenage years trying to get you to notice me, and I've gone from the girl you didn't want, to the one you can't have. How's that for irony?"

"I always wanted you, kid."

"You had a shitty way of showing it. But come on, you can't

be that hard up for someone to ride your cock, Julian. Just call Katie or whatever bimbo you have on speed dial. You never had a problem parading your hookups around me before, so why stop now?"

"If you're going to bring up the past, then I insist we talk about you and me and forget about the rest."

"How convenient. There is no you and me, and there never was."

"That's bullshit, and you know it. I'm not playing your little games, Autumn."

"You're not playing my little games?" I repeated, offended. "Holy shit! You're the king of playing games!"

"I'm not that man anymore."

"And I'm just supposed to believe you? After everything you did to me?"

"If I could go back, I wouldn't change a damn thing. I made something of myself. I wasn't the man you needed then, but I am now."

"Now? After all this time? Do you actually think I'm just going to jump into your arms like nothing ever happened? You have no idea what I went through after you left! It took me years to mend my broken heart and the damage you did to my brother and parents. My family and I were devastated, not to mention worried sick about you for years! We didn't know where you were or what you were doing. You didn't call, write, or text—fucking nothing! You didn't do anything but disappear on us! After everything they did for you, that's how you repaid them?! You're nothing but a selfish prick with control issues, Mr. Locke, so get off your high horse. You're not getting a damn thing from me!" I sidestepped him to leave. "We're done here!"

He grabbed my arm, making me face him again. "We're not done until I say we are." Looking deep into my eyes, he reminded, "You're my number one girl, remember?"

"How could I forget? It was just another lie you told me."

"No." He shook his head. "You know that's not true. I never lied to you. It's why I pushed you away to begin with. I couldn't lie to you."

"You could bold-face lie to me right now, and I wouldn't be able to tell the difference. You're a businessman. You have people believe what you want them to. It's why you're so successful. Trust me, you spent years practicing on me."

"You want a confession?" he challenged, getting close to my face. His eyes were in a craze. "I'll give you a fucking confession. The only times I ever lied to you was when I told you I fucked someone else."

I didn't just jerk back, I stumbled. "What?"

"You heard me. I didn't fuck anyone at Christian's bachelor party."

"But … Christian… No way. He said you did, and everyone that was there said you went into the bedroom with the stripper."

"I let them believe that."

"Why?"

"Your brother was getting suspicious of us, kid."

He was?

I opened my mouth to reply, but I couldn't get my lips to move.

"You were never just a fuck. I told you that to make you hate me."

"Well, mission accomplished. Why would you want me to hate you?"

"It was the only way I could leave you."

I promised myself I wouldn't go down this road with him. Bringing up the past wouldn't change what he did, what he put me through.

Our memories became nightmares.

My love that became hate.

It. Ruined. Me.

He ruined me.

That fateful day he shattered my heart and then walked away, leaving me to pick up the pieces of what was left in his wake. I desperately tried to focus on all the pain he'd caused, not wanting to care about his lies and truths. Yet there I was hanging on by a thread, anxiously awaiting his next words.

"And the only other time I've ever lied to you…"

I never expected what he admitted next, and it felt as though I was holding my breath.

With the utmost sincere expression on his face, he declared, "Was when I told you I didn't love you."

nine

Then

WE WALKED INTO THE HAND-IN-HAND WHILE I looked for my brother in the stands. Daniel and I had been hanging out for the last few weeks, and we were meeting him there. He was a senior, and I was a junior in high school. I was almost seventeen, and my parents had finally started allowing me to date.

But if it were up to Christian, I'd be a nun. He was more overbearing than our parents, saying guys only wanted one thing. Which didn't make any sense. He'd been with the same girl on and off for the last seven years. They were the perfect couple, and at times I envied what they had.

"I think I see him over there." I pointed to the far left side of the open arena, leading the way.

At least I had a bit more freedom now that Christian was in his senior year of college and wasn't around a lot. He was studying for his MCATs, deciding to be a doctor. Although he hadn't chosen which field yet. He was living in his own place with Julian. They were both almost done with college. Julian was majoring in finance with a minor in business.

He still loved cars, and since he'd turned sixteen, I swear I'd seen him with a new ride each year.

"Baby." Daniel pulled me against his chest while he walked behind me. "Have I told you how great your ass and legs look in that skirt?"

I beamed, listening to him.

We drove here after the football game tonight, and I was still in my cheerleading uniform. I was the only girl to make varsity my freshman year, but my excitement toward Daniel's words was cut shorter than my bloomers when I noticed Julian wasn't alone.

Shocker.

He was always with a girl. I couldn't remember the last time I'd seen him without a chick. Especially in the last four years. The man was never with the same woman. Julian didn't really have a type, he seemed to be an equal opportunist with all the different types of girls he'd bring around.

Julian made up for the fact that Christian only had Kinley, by pretty much sleeping with every hot girl from here to Dallas.

And I hated every single one of them.

Not that my brother couldn't have any woman he wanted, girls flocked to him like bees to honey. Often making his girlfriend jealous. Christian was covered in tattoos, inked sleeves down both arms, along with his chest and back. He was addicted to them.

To say I was head over heels in love with his best friend was an understatement. I think I was born loving him. My crush didn't ever go away, it didn't wear off, and I didn't grow out of it…

If anything, it became stronger.

My feelings for him became something I couldn't control or even begin to understand. I just knew I wanted him.

Then.

Now.

Forever.

I wanted him so bad it made my heart hurt and my chest ache.

Despite seeing him with several women throughout my life,

he'd never seen me with a guy before, and I secretly hoped this would be what he needed to get his head out of his ass.

I had absolutely no problem picking up guys, inheriting my mom's big boobs, slender waist, and curvy ass. I began developing at a younger age than most of my friends, and not one time did Julian recognize that.

My brother did.

My parents did.

Most guys in town and at my school did.

Julian, nope. Nothing. Not so much as a, "Hey, you're looking beautiful today."

I was at my wit's end. It wasn't fair that he looked at every single girl other than me. I even saw him checking out some of the girls on my varsity cheerleading squad during practice one day when he unexpectedly picked me up.

I didn't have a car. My parents wanted me to wait until I was seventeen, and I relied on my friends, Daniel, and my good ol' bicycle for transportation. Making me feel like I was still a little girl, when in fact, I wasn't.

I was a young woman, and I was determined to have Julian see me as something more than just his best friend's little sister. How he couldn't see I was madly in love with him only proved to me that men were stupid.

Or if he knew, he never showed it—always seeming unfazed by my presence.

The older he got, the more distant he became. Maybe it was because he was busy with school and other adult things, but the guy who used to take me to his shop didn't anymore.

Out of the blue one day, he started pushing me away. At least it felt like that to me, and I hated it more than anything.

"You'll always be my number one girl."

Those seven words haunted me, hanging over my head like a freaking avalanche. Ready to pile on top of me at a moment's notice.

Why did he say it if he didn't mean it?

Those were the types of questions I constantly asked myself.

Over and over again.

Pushing away those thoughts, I walked up the stairs and smiled at Julian. He smiled back, and my stomach catapulted into somersaults, waiting for him to say something about my uniform.

Please notice me.

"Autumn, what the hell are you wearing?" Christian asked, his tone clipped.

"Oh my God. Leave her alone," Kinley reprimanded him like she often did. "Babe, she'll be seventeen in two weeks. You've met Daniel, so have your parents. Let her be." She winked at me, and I smiled.

She was always on my side, knowing how overprotective my brother was. My gaze shifted toward Julian, praying he'd heard Christian commenting about my outfit.

He didn't.

He was too busy sucking face with the blonde he'd brought with him. I rolled my eyes again; he was the king of oblivion.

"Daniel, let's sit over here." I popped a squat near Julian, closest to him—not the girl he was with. Enough to where he could see me and Daniel.

For the next hour, I fawned over Daniel, desperately trying to make Julian jealous, and not once he did bat an eye.

Not one ounce of emotion.

Reaction.

What do I need to do to get his attention?

Nothing ever worked.

Not my cute outfits.

Not my makeup.

Not my bikinis.

Not even the guy I'd brought around him for the first time.

It was as if he was immune to anything related to me and the more I thought about it, the further it pissed me off.

"There's Rob and Dave," Daniel murmured in my ear, bringing my attention back to him. "They have booze. Let's go over there with them."

"My brother… You know what? Fuck it. Let's go." I called out Christian's name. "We're going to hang out with some friends who just got here, okay?"

"No—"

Kinley covered his mouth. "Okay. Have fun."

I mouthed, "Thank you," to her.

"Don't go too far," Christian called out behind us as we walked away.

"Babe! Just leave her alone. She's a big girl."

My eyes wandered toward Julian's direction.

Did you hear what Kinley said? I'm a big girl!

Nope. He was still sucking face with the blonde.

Why even come to the rodeo if you're not going to watch the show?

We made our way to Daniel's friends, and I didn't think twice about it, when he handed me the bottle of Jack, taking it down like a fucking champ. It burned all the way down my chest, warming my body in the process.

I wasn't much of a drinker, but tonight would fix that.

One chug, three chugs, five chugs … shit, I'd lost count.

Giggling up a storm, I swayed my hips to the music Daniel was playing off his cell phone. Bringing the bottle up to my lips, I drank way more than I should have. Wanting to numb my thoughts of Julian and his indifference was the only remedy that seemed worthwhile.

I saw Daniel eyeing me over the rim of his bottle, staring at me with nothing but mischief in his eyes.

I wanted to forget.

And he was the perfect guy I could do that with. He was trouble in the best possible way.

My lips tingled, my face was on fire, and my body was numb. *Good.*

It was the first time in forever I'd felt so carefree, throwing my head back and laughing, enjoying the way he made me feel. We exchanged flirty banter, dancing close together to the music. My head was spinning with thoughts of Julian, and I stumbled a little, catching myself in Daniel's arms.

He caressed the side of my cheek, rubbing his thumb over my lips in a back and forth motion. "You're beautiful, Autumn."

Why can't Julian think I'm beautiful?

I pushed off of him, dancing all around while he leaned against a tree.

Were we in the woods? I guess we went for a walk.

Seductively, I worked my hands up the sides of my body, bringing my skirt up with it. Peeking over at him, I moved my hips to the beat of the music, provocatively looking into his eyes as the song continued to blare into the night. I spun around with my back now facing him, closing my eyes. Wanting to get lost in the moment, I lifted my hair off the nook of my neck.

I was sweating.

It was scorching outside.

Texas heat was no joke, and tonight was proving to be one of the hottest nights of the summer.

Slowly, I continued to move my hips in a slow, steady rhythm until I felt a strong arm grab around my waist, tugging me back against his hard chest.

It was super aggressive.

"Daniel?" I was about to spin around when I heard the voice of the man I least expected.

Angrily spewing, "You wanted my attention. Now what are you going to do with it, kid?"

ten

M Y WIDE EYES SNAPPED OPEN, AND I SWEAR MY heart stopped beating.

Was I hallucinating? Was this actually happening? How drunk am I?

Question after question tore through my mind. I couldn't move, I was frozen to the spot. I was standing with Julian's steady arm wrapped around my stomach, holding me firm against his torso. My body aligned perfectly with his like it was made for only him.

I opened my mouth to say something, anything, but Daniel beat me to it.

"Who the fuck are you?" he roared, stepping toward us.

I was shocked when Julian snarled, "I'm the reason she's dressed in that uniform, grinding her ass against your cock. I'm the reason she's drinking and acting out right now. I'm the fucking reason she's even with you. You should be thanking me, you little shit. She's only with you to get my attention."

My mouth dropped open, realizing he knew all along how I felt about him.

Julian didn't stop there, possessively adding, "I'm the man she's trying to make jealous, that's who the fuck I am. You're lucky it was me who found her out here with you drinking, dancing like a slut, and not her brother, or you wouldn't be standing. Now tuck your dick in between your legs and walk the fuck away, or else you're going to have a problem *with me.*"

I couldn't form words. The only thing I could do was feel intense anger. From head to toe, I was ready to explode.

"Daniel, leave."

"You sure?"

"You heard her, run along before I change my mind and show you what happens to little shits like you who try to take advantage of drunk, naive girls who have no fucking business being alone in the woods with you."

"Julian—"

"Don't fucking try me, Autumn. Not. Right. Now. Not with how I'm feeling."

I felt each word beating into my back. He still hadn't let go of me.

"Listen, I don't want any trouble."

"Then go!" I shouted to Daniel.

Finally, he nodded and left.

Julian didn't waste any time, spinning me around to face him. "What the hell do you think you're doing alone out here with that boy? What did you think was going to happen if I didn't show up when I did?"

"We were just hanging out."

"Kid, he was seconds away from lifting your skirt, pulling down your panties, and finger fucking you against the tree. Is that what you want for yourself? A meaningless fuck in the woods? You're better than that."

"You don't even know me anymore."

"Bullshit. I know you're not the girl you mess around with in the woods."

"You would know since you fuck anything that walks."

He jerked back, stunned.

"Well, actually, you fuck anything that walks other than me. Me, you push away. Me, you forget. Me, you don't even acknowledge. Newsflash, I'm not a little girl anymore."

"Really? Then stop acting like one."

"That's your reply?! Are you for real?!"

"What do you want me to say, Autumn? I'm your brother's best friend, and I'm saving your ass. If Christian had seen what I just did, if he knew you had been drinking, trust me, your ass would never be allowed to leave your house again." He eyed me up and down with only craze in his gaze. "And trust me, sweetheart, I'm tempted to tell him, if this is how you're going to be acting. Because of me, nonetheless."

Each word that erupted from his mouth was another knife in my chest.

"And what about you?"

"What about me?"

"You heard me. What did you feel when you saw me? You still want my boyfriend standing?"

"Kid…"

"What? I want an answer! What did you feel? Do you ever feel anything when you're with me? Do you ever think about me? Dream about me?" I knew I sounded like a child, but I couldn't help it. Those questions constantly plagued me. I needed to know his feelings.

Right now.

"I'm not having this conversation with you."

"Why? Because maybe, just maybe, you feel the same things I feel for you?"

"Quit fucking baiting me."

"No!" The liquor coursing through my veins made it easier to ask him all the questions I wanted to know. "Tell me!"

"Autumn, stop! Don't do this to yourself."

"But you said I would always be your number one girl."

"You are. But I can't tell you what you want to hear. I'll never be able to tell you what you need to hear."

"Why? I don't understand! Why do you look at every girl other than me? Why can't you see me? Why can't you look at me? Please, I just want you to look at me! Really fucking look at me! I'm standing right here! Telling you I'm in lov—"

"Don't you fucking dare." He put his finger out in front of him, silencing me. "What do you want me to say, Autumn? You want me to tell you that I wanted to rip him apart the second I saw him pull you into his arms as you made your way over to your brother? You want me to tell you that every time you wear that little uniform, I think about all the ways I could take you in it? Is that what you want to hear? What else do you want me to tell you?"

His expression turned heady, matching my own. Our stares tethered, and for a moment, I saw a certain vulnerability and uncertainty pass through him I could feel deep within my bones. However, just as quickly as it appeared, it was gone. His primal gaze disappeared, shutting off our connection and truths we briefly shared for just a few moments in time.

There he was, balancing on the thin line which had suddenly become us.

Me.

With a hard edge in his voice, he asked, "What do you think would happen if your brother knew what I just said to you?'

"I don't care."

"Well, I do. Your family has done more for me than anyone in all my life. I won't fuck that up. Not even … for you."

I jerked back, feeling the weight of his statement.

"I'm sorry, kid. I never wanted to hurt you. It's easier like this. Me staying away from you."

"Easier for who?"

"I'm not that guy. I won't fight for you. I won't choose you over them. I can't. Please try to understand and stop trying to force my hand."

I didn't know which was worse—thinking he didn't care about me or knowing he did but wouldn't do anything about it.

"Do you think it's been easy for me to push you away? Do

you think it's been easy on me to see you go from a little girl who used to follow me around and look at me like I was the answer to her little fairy tale? Do you think it's been easy on me to know that I'm not? You're not mine, Autumn, and you never will be. Stop trying to make me claim you because I won't."

I didn't want to cry. I wouldn't be able to stop.

It would consume me.

And it did.

I blinked, and tears fell down the sides of my face. I had never felt worse. Only adding to my tears and the hurt of his replies I so wanted to forget.

I wouldn't.

I couldn't.

Getting your heart broken for the first time was like having the wind knocked out of you by the force of a level five hurricane.

I wanted to die.

I felt like I was.

With the back of his fingers, he wiped away my tears. His flesh burned my skin, making me feel like maybe this was hell. The one I'd created for myself.

He held his head up higher, maintaining his strong composure. Every devastated bone in my body wanted to beg him to give me a chance.

To give us a chance.

Knowing it was no use. His loyalty didn't stand with me—it stood with my family, and that was the hardest pill to swallow.

Wasn't I his family too?

"You need to forget about me."

"You say that like it's so easy."

"It should be."

"But all I've ever wanted is you."

"You don't even know what that means, kid."

"That's not fair."

"Life's not fair."

Neither one of us said anything for I don't know how long until he tugged on the end of my hair.

"Let's go get you some food, and then I'll take you home."

"Where's Christian?"

"He left with Kinley. I told him I'd find you and make sure you got home safely."

"Did you know what I was doing?"

"Something like that."

"So now what? We go back to pretending you don't notice me?"

He didn't say anything, but he didn't have to. The expression on his face spoke for itself. It spoke volumes.

"Awesome. Thanks for nothing."

I turned and left him there, ready to go break down in the bathroom at the arena of the rodeo. I didn't realize we'd walked so far out to the woods. My heart hurt so profoundly I was surprised I was still breathing.

Head bowed.

My world tumbling around me.

Tears continued to cascade down my cheeks, and I bet I looked like a mess. Dark black mascara leaving lines on my face.

When it felt as if I couldn't walk any longer, my legs giving out on me, I heard Julian loudly exclaim, "For fuck's sake!"

I stopped and turned around at the same time he gripped onto the nook of my neck and slammed his mouth against mine.

He. Kissed. Me.

Julian kissed me.

I was shocked, confused, and overwhelmed. My eyes shut tightly, my breathing hitched, and my arms fell to my sides in defeat. All the sadness in me was gone. Feeling what I had wanted for so damn long. His lips were rough but smooth against mine. My heart drummed so fast, I swear he could hear it. My knees went weak the longer his lips stayed on mine. It was the most overpowering, mind-blowing, consuming emotion I'd ever felt in my entire life.

There would be no coming back from this. Ruining me for every other boy who might come along.

Reading my mind, he slowly parted his lips and pull me closer. Molding us into one person. I melted against him as I parted my lips, following his lead. Matching the same rhythm he'd set for me.

The second his tongue touched mine, I thought I was going to die. Right then and there, in his arms, with our mouths fused. I pulled back my tongue, and he took it as an open invitation to slide his into my awaiting mouth. Our tongues whirled in their own game of push and pull, turning this kiss into something more than I'd ever expected.

I wasn't the only one losing my mind—Julian was getting lost in me too.

No words could come close to describing what was happening at that moment between us. The feelings he stirred deep within my heart matched my emotions with each stroke of his tongue. Feelings I didn't think were possible to experience. Emotions I didn't even think existed.

I never wanted him to stop kissing me.

When a soft moan escaped my mouth, he pecked my lips one last time before gradually pulling away from me. Leaving me breathless and wanting more.

Wanting him.

Incoherent thoughts ran rapidly in my mind while my eyes fluttered open. Leaning his forehead against mine, he gazed profoundly into my eyes.

"This was your first kiss, wasn't it?"

I swallowed hard.

Eyes wide.

Heart open.

Love pouring out of me.

"Yes."

"*Fuck me.*" I could hear the regret in his tone.

"Please … please don't ruin this for me. Not now. Not after that."

"Let's go," he growled, stepping away from me. "I need to get you home. Now!"

He was mad.

Pissed.

Fuming.

Except for this time, I didn't care…

He loved me.

And with that first kiss, he declared war.

eleven

Day Two of Press Tour

I WOKE UP TO MY CELL PHONE RINGING BRIGHT AND EARLY after tossing and turning most of the night. I ended up leaving Julian at the bar with his confessions unsure of how to proceed with it. My mind was spinning, and it didn't stop for the rest of the evening.

For the first time in I don't know how long, I dreamt about the first time he kissed me. The dream played endlessly throughout the night, annoying the hell out of me.

I didn't open my eyes to see who was calling, groaning, "Hello," into the phone.

"Autumn! How could you not tell me you leaked your own story?" Laurel questioned, and I yawned.

"What are you talking about? What story?"

"You didn't tell me you had plans to do this. I mean, don't get me wrong, I think it's brilliant, but why didn't you tell me?"

"Laurel, you're speaking in circles. I don't understand what you're talking about. What story?"

"Your history with Julian. The world loves a second chance romance—they're going to eat this shit right up."

I shot up, sitting in bed. "Second chance romance, what the hell are you talking about?"

She knew Julian's and my history. Of course, I told her. It was why she knew I could handle him, topping it off with the promotion to make partner once I had.

"Autumn, it's all over the internet. Charles' interview set the stage on fire."

"Charles' interview?" My heart dropped. "Oh my god." Quickly, I grabbed my laptop off the nightstand, hitting the Safari button.

In less than a second, my whole world and life as I knew it was the headline of every news media outlet. Reading…

High Society Publicist, Autumn Troy, has not only taken Alpha CEO, Julian Locke, on as a client, but she has also claimed his cold, brutal heart. The two go way back—he was her first love. She was his. Can we say second chance romance?

All the blood drained from my face.

"That motherfucker! No, he did not tell Charles we have history! I'm going to fucking murder him! Do you hear me, Laurel? I'm going to jail because I'm going to fucking kill him!"

"Autumn, calm down. Is this not true? Have you guys not rekindled?"

"No! We haven't rekindled shit. The only thing I feel like rekindling is my knee in his balls."

"Oh, honey, this can work to our advantage, though. You need to calm down."

"Laurel, I can't—"

Beep.

I looked at my screen, Mom calling.

Deny.

Dad calling.

Deny.

Christian calling.

"Fuck!"

Definitely deny.

"I gotta go." I hung up, searching Yahoo News and getting smacked in the face with a picture of Julian and me kissing on his bed. It was one of the last pictures he took of us.

"Oh. My. God. He even leaked a personal fucking photo!" Grabbing my phone again, I called Charles.

"Hey, Cherry. You're welcome."

"How could you do this to me? How could you publish an article without my approval? We had an agreement!"

"What are you talking about? I just made your client the most adored man in the world. Did you read the article? Did you see how he spoke about you and your relationship?"

"No! I didn't read the article! I didn't get past the fucking title, Charles! You blindsided me! And we're not in a relationship—other than I'm his publicist, and he's my client!"

"Umm… That's not what he said."

"He was lying! How you, of all people, couldn't tell he was full of shit is beyond me."

"So you guys don't have a history? He wasn't your first love?"

"It's not as black and white as you're laying it out to be."

"Did you or did you not have a relationship?"

I wasn't expecting his interrogation, feeling like I was suddenly on the stand at my own trial.

"If you could call it that."

"So he wasn't your first kiss? Your first sexual experience?"

My eyes bulged out of my head. "He told you that?!"

"I think you need to read the article."

"I think you need to pray that I don't find you and kick your ass!"

"Cherry—"

"Don't you Cherry me! I'm so pissed at you I can barely see straight!"

"I didn't mean to upset you, but he said you guys were back together."

I rubbed my face. "I can't believe you printed a bullshit article. If you would have sent it to me, I would have—"

"He said he wanted to surprise you."

"Oh." I paused, nodding. "He surprised me alright."

"The good news is you're trending across all social media platforms."

"I'm done talking to you now."

"Aut—"

I hung up on him, throwing the sheets off my body. I jumped in the shower and then got dressed, before I ran out of the hotel to meet Julian at his photoshoot with Vanity Fair, but the maid stopped me in the hall.

"Miss Troy."

"Yes."

"I'm so sorry to bother you."

"I'm kind of in a hurry. Could we talk later?"

"This will only take a second. Mr. Locke insisted that I check your bed sheets yesterday morning. He said something about them being wet, and I told him they weren't. They were perfectly dry. Was there a problem I need to know about?"

I scowled, the fury coursing through my veins making my face hot. The son of a bitch had the balls to confirm if I did or didn't have sex.

The nerve of that man!

I bit my tongue. "There's no problem. Thank you." I rushed into the elevator, fuming on my way down.

My blood was boiling, and it didn't simmer down the entire drive to the shoot. I walked into the building ready to spit fire, finding Julian in his dressing room.

Looking up from his phone, he smiled. "Good morning, Miss Troy."

"Good morning my ass!" I slammed the door shut behind me.

"Is there a problem?"

"You bet your ass there's a problem!"

"You need to watch your damn tone when you speak to me. You don't have to yell. I'm sitting right here."

"Julian, you're lucky the only thing I'm doing is yelling at you and not punching you in the face!"

"Oh, so now I'm suddenly Julian again?"

"I'm going to fucking murder you." I threw the article at him. "What the fuck is that?"

"It's *The New York Times* interview I did *for you*," he emphasized the last two words with a conniving grin. "You said you wanted me to be honest with the public. Share my past, my history, show them the man I used to be."

"That is not what I meant, and you know it! You sharing your past has nothing to do with me."

"But you're such a big part of it."

Ignoring his statement, I argued, "We're not a couple, Mr. Locke. Why on earth would you lie about us?"

"Do I need a reason?" He nonchalantly placed his cell phone inside his suit jacket before leaning forward, setting his elbows on his knees. "I thought you wanted people talking? Rumors are the best publicity. Your words, kid."

I glared at him. "Rumors for your announcement, not rumors for our relationship!"

"You didn't specify, Miss Troy. But since you need a reason, how about this one? After your encounters with men yesterday, I decided to take matters into my own hands to prevent any future indiscretions playing out in front of me."

My mouth dropped open. "You lied to the world because you were jealous? What kind of fucked up excuse is that?"

"The only one I have."

"You can't do this!"

"I already did."

"Fine. I'll just deny your allegations."

"Making me look like a liar when I need people to trust me isn't going to sit well with your promotion."

He was right, and I wanted to claw his eyes out. "So what's your plan now, huh? We pretend like we're in love?"

"I'm not pretending."

My stomach dropped, and my heart skipped a beat. Stupid fucking heart. *Did he just tell me he loved me?*

Shaking away the thought, I responded, "I don't love you. In fact, right now it's the complete opposite."

He fell back against the couch, placing one arm over the back. How I could be furious with him, but still find him incredibly sexy and attractive only further incited my rage.

It wasn't until he simply stated, "Well then, fuck me like you hate me, Miss Troy."

That I truly lost my patience with him.

Julian

She grabbed the first thing in her sight and chucked it in my direction. "I wish I'd never met you!"

The vase crashed against the wall, shattering on the floor beside me.

"If you're going to throw shit at me," I snapped, further wanting to piss her off, "then I insist you start with your pussy."

She gasped, and in three strides I was in her face, backing her into the wall. "Are you mad, Autumn? Angry? Seething from the inside out?"

"Yes! Yes! And Yes!"

"Welcome to my fucking life every time I had to push you away."

"Get out of my face!" She shoved me, but I didn't move an inch.

"Be careful what you wish for. For years you wanted my attention—well, now you have it. You're my sole focus, sweetheart. Is it everything you ever wanted?"

"You're ten years too late."

"I gave you my attention back then in my own way."

"Yeah, which usually involved your dick inside of me."

I growled, "Don't degrade what we have."

"What we *had*."

"What we have going on right now is fucking foreplay."

"I didn't know foreplay involved my knee to your balls." She lifted her knee, but I blocked her advance.

"I'm not into that. How about we begin with your mouth instead?"

"Only if you intend on me biting it off."

"The only thing you'll be biting is your lip when I make you come." I narrowed my eyes at her, arching an eyebrow and trying to keep my temper at bay.

"I didn't know you were going to lie to the world."

"That's pretty damn clear."

"You're being unreasonable."

"Which part of me is unreasonable, Autumn? What's unreasonable about me saying something that I should have been saying a long time ago? What's unreasonable about me claiming what has been, and always will be, mine?"

"You can't do this to me. Ten years, Julian! Ten! I waited for you to come back and apologize. What do you want from me? I can't forget about what you did to me. I can't just let it go like you expect me to. It's so fucking easy for you. I didn't leave you. I didn't fuck you over. I did nothing but love you. I'm trying to remain calm and be professional with you, but you're making it really damn hard to not hate you."

"I can't apologize any more than I already have."

"You haven't apologized at all."

I stepped back. "I see you didn't read the article."

"You apologized to me in an article?" She pushed me again. "What the hell kind of apology is that?"

"Autumn, I know I fucked up, and I have to live with the repercussions, but I lost you too. You weren't the only one grieving the loss of our love. I lost everything that ever mattered to me. Including the only family I've ever known. Do you not realize that?"

Bing.

Her cell phone dinged with a text message.

"Oh, don't mind that. It's more than likely another text from my brother. You wanted the whole world to know about our history, and not for one fucking second did you think about the consequences. You're so selfish you didn't think about my brother or my parents and what they would think and say about your interview. We spent years denying and hiding our relationship, or whatever the fuck you want to call it, and you just openly confess it to the entire world without even running it by me first. Now, once again, I have to deal with the fallout. How the hell am I supposed to explain to them when I barely understand it myself?"

"Do you honestly think I'm that much of a heartless bastard? You don't think it killed me to leave you? To leave all of you? Kid, I lost my best friend because of us—the only family I ever knew, ever had."

"As a matter a fact, I do!"

"I've never stopped being yours!"

"You were never mine!"

I needed to catch my bearings and compose my thoughts, having to step away from the situation before it escalated to the point of no return. I couldn't control my temper when it came to her, and it was why she loved to provoke me in the first place. I didn't know what else I could do to make this right.

I was out of answers.

Out of options.

I couldn't fucking think straight when she was glaring at me with so much hatred. I despised not being in control, so I did the only thing I could in this situation.

I unbuckled my belt.

Preparing for more of her bullshit.

twelve

"**W**HAT ARE YOU DOING?" I questioned, caught off guard.

He unbuttoned his pants. "I'm getting ready for you."

"Excuse me?" I jerked back. "Have you lost your mind? Do you actually think I'm going to have sex with you right now?"

There was a knock on the door.

"Come in," he called out.

"Mr. Locke," Erin greeted, walking in with a garment bag in her arms. "Here is the suit you requested."

He nodded, unbuttoning his shirt.

I was grateful she'd interrupted us when she did, giving me a chance to calm down and see some sort of reason. What I didn't expect was Julian's tense body catching my attention. From his chiseled physique to every sleek muscle on his chest, arms, and back. His abs contracted, highlighting his six-pack and the V right above his happy trail.

The man was almost thirty-five-years-old and looked better than he did when he was twenty-four. His back muscles flexed as he removed the dress shirt he was wearing to the black one Erin was taking out of the garment bag.

In the matter of a few seconds, I went from wanting to rip him to shreds, to watching him undress like he was my very own private peep show.

Erin just stood there, unmoving, and I couldn't help but feel bothered that she didn't leave the room. Simply waiting for him to take off his suit to hand him the one he was going to wear.

How often did she see him naked?

When he started taking off his slacks, my body moved in autopilot, snatching the garment bag from her hands.

"I got it from here, Erin. You can go."

She nodded and left, and as soon as I turned around, Julian was grinning at me like a fucking fool. I never wanted to slap the smirk off his face more than I did at that moment.

"I don't like green on women, but jealousy suits you, kid."

"I'm not jealous."

"No?"

"Not at all."

"Care to elaborate on what that was then?"

"It's unprofessional for you to change in front of her."

"But not unprofessional for me to change in front of you?"

"No. I've already seen you naked." My reply didn't make any sense, but it was the only one I had.

"So has Erin."

My jaw clenched, and he chuckled noticing it.

"Professionally, of course." With that, he grabbed the garment bag out of my hand, beginning to undress again.

Since he was busy, I regarded him with fascination, trying to pretend like I wasn't. Mentally chastising myself that I was falling for his antics. It wasn't until he dropped his pants that my gaze flew to where I had no business looking.

Jesus.

It looked better than I remembered. His briefs perfectly hugged the curves of his cock, and my mind reminisced on what it felt like in my mouth and inside of me. My legs swayed, trembling a little. Thinking about all the times he'd stroked it in front of me while he was going down on me.

Wetness pooled in between my legs.

"Sweetheart, why don't you just bend over since you're star-ing right at him?"

I. Stopped. Breathing.

My lust-filled gaze shot to his amused expression, immedi-ately washing away all the desire I was feeling for him. However, his dick decided to make an appearance, jutting up and standing at attention. Once again inciting the lust to course through my core at a speed I could no longer control or deny.

"What did you think was going to happen when you're staring at my cock like you want to be fucked?"

I ripped the garment bag from his grasp and presented my back to him. I ignored his question and perfect dick as I walked to the corner of the room where there was a rack of clothing, and discarded his suit on the couch.

"I need to get dressed if I'm going to make your photoshoot. They're waiting on me, and I don't make a habit of being late to anything I commit to."

"Oh. You commit to things? I wasn't aware that you were capable of committing. Anyway…" I continued as if he hadn't said a word. "Your photoshoot isn't in a suit, Mr. Locke. You've been on hundreds of magazine covers wearing a suit. My stylist personally coordinated your outfits. I'm just getting it for you."

After I faced him, he took one look at the Levi's jeans, white t-shirt, black cowboy hat, and boots in my hands and argued, "I'm not wearing that."

"Yes, you are." Making my way back to him, I set his clothes on the couch, ordering, "Now get dressed."

"Autumn, I won't repeat myself."

"Great." I nodded. "Because I don't want to hear your mouth anymore."

There was another knock at the door. "Mr. Locke, are you ready?" a voice asked through the door.

I answered, "He'll be out in five minutes."

We were having a power struggle of who would win.

Me or him?
I should have known better…
He always won everything.
Especially when it concerned me.

Julian

Further drilling her point, she added, "This is what I meant by the world seeing the real you. This is what you used to wear, so this is what you'll wear today." She smiled, playing coy. "Okay?"

I took a deep breath, silently counting to three. "What did I tell you last night, kid? I don't like to be taken by surprise, so the real question is, do I punish you now or later?"

She grabbed another vase, aiming it at me, and I cocked my head to the side, daring her to do it. She thought about it for a second before biting her lip and setting the vase back on the table.

"Good girl."

"Touch me, and I'll scream."

"You already did that." Using the situation to my advantage, I bartered, "If I wear that outfit for you, then you have to be in some of the photos with me."

"Fuck. No."

I walked toward my garment bag.

"Ugh!" She stomped her heel. "Why are you always this much of an asshole? Why can't you just do what you're told? You're worse than a child."

I stared at her, waiting.

"Fine. Alright? I'll take some stupid pictures."

"Great." I got dressed while she called her stylist, telling her she needed a few pieces for the shoot.

I couldn't believe I was doing this for her. I hadn't dressed like this since I'd left Texas. I didn't even own a pair of jeans, let alone a fucking t-shirt. Once I was ready, I stared at the man in the full-length mirror, not recognizing who was staring back at me. It was as if there was a stranger in my reflection, one I hadn't seen in over a decade.

The knock on the door yanked my mind back to the present, and for the next two hours, I shot photo after photo after photo.

Saving the best for last.

Gesturing toward Autumn, I ordered, "Come here."

She'd changed into a soft yellow floor-length dress, reminding me of all the times she'd dressed like that for me. The annoyed expression on her face didn't bother me in the least as I pulled her in between my legs since I was sitting on a stool. Her hair was in a low bun with a clip, and I reached up and freed her long red locks. Grateful she still wore it long, it was one of my favorite features about her appearance.

"I always loved your hair down."

When my thumb began wiping the makeup off her cheek, she jerked back. "What are you doing?"

"Your freckles, I want to see them. Do you remember how much I used to love them?"

"Julian—"

"If you want the world to see me as who I used to be, then I get to show them what my favorite trait about you is."

She narrowed her eyes, taking in what I disclosed. I could see the hesitation in her gaze, knowing I was the reason it was there to begin with. She used to look at me with nothing but love, but now it was somewhere between hate and lust.

"This was always my favorite color on you. Remember all the times you wore yellow for me?"

"No."

If it were even possible, she was more stubborn than she used to be. I didn't expect her to welcome me with open arms, I had my work cut out for me, and I was alright with that. If she thought she could get rid of me that easily, then she was in for one hell of a rude awakening.

I wasn't going anywhere but back into her life where I belonged. At least we were headed in the right direction. The photographer snapped away, and Autumn was so entranced by the way I was looking at her, she didn't notice. She was lost in my truths which were on full display for her.

When she was a child, she could always see right through me. As she got older, I had to hide myself from her, or she would have known how I felt before I was ready to tell her.

The truth was, I was never ready to tell her.

The longer I hid my emotions, the harder it was to push her away. I hated seeing her cry, it was one of the hardest things I had to endure, and I'd been through a lot of bullshit in my life. Her tears were my undoing—they were always my defeat.

With my thumb, I rubbed her lips in a back and forth motion, and her breathing hitched.

I wanted to kiss her.

Claim her.

Though not like this, in a fucking photoshoot of all places. I had to wait—it wasn't the right time.

Would there ever be one?

"You've always been such a beautiful girl, Autumn, but now as a woman, you're truly stunning."

She swallowed hard, hearing the sincerity in my tone. She was captivated by my honest expression and the feel of my hands on her.

"What are you doing to me, Julian?"

"I'm loving you, kid."

My statement broke the spell I had her in, and she shook her head. Glancing back at the photographer who was still snapping photos, she said, "You can't use any of those pictures."

"Autumn," I coaxed in a stern voice when all of a sudden, a woman appeared out of nowhere, walking into the shoot.

"Julian, I saw your name on today's itinerary. Of course, I had to come say hello."

Our attention drifted to the woman in question, realizing all too quickly, who she was.

And when I used her…

To push Autumn away.

thirteen

Then

THIS WAS THE FIRST TIME I WAS GOING TO SEE Julian since he'd kissed me two weeks ago. I still felt his mouth on my lips, and sometimes I'd catch myself touching them to feel him all over again. I couldn't wait to see him. I was wearing a yellow maxi dress, anxiously waiting for his arrival.

It was my seventeenth birthday, and my parents were throwing me a huge party. I knew he'd be here. He wouldn't miss it.

"Honey, you look amazing," Mom announced, coming into my bedroom. "Where did my little girl go?"

I smiled. I did look older, and I felt older too.

Would Julian notice?

"Your brother was looking for you."

"What did he want?"

"He said something about Julian's date."

It was as if a pile of bricks fell right on my head. "Julian's date?"

"I know." She chuckled. "Maybe he will actually settle down with this one for a little while. Who knows. I stopped trying to keep track of all his dates when he turned sixteen, but I swear he's been a heartbreaker since he was a little boy."

I wanted to cry.

"Are you okay?"

Our eyes connected. "Yeah."

"Honey, you look like you've seen a ghost. You're so pale. What happened?"

"Nothing." I turned around, trying to hide my pain.

"Was it something I said? Are you upset with your brother? Is it Julian?"

"It's nothing, Mom."

"Sweetie, it doesn't look like nothing to me. Talk to me. What's going on?"

"I just think Julian hasn't met the right girl yet. That's all. I think you need to give him more credit than his bedhopping ways."

"Autumn," Christian announced, and our stares snapped in his direction. He was leaning against the doorframe of my bedroom. He looked so handsome, wearing a gray button-down and black slacks.

"You clean up nice," I remarked, smiling.

"Don't try to change the subject. Do you really think Julian is ever going to settle down?"

I shrugged. "Maybe."

"Oh, come on!" He laughed. "You can't be serious! Julian Locke? My best friend? The biggest womanizer from here to Dallas? He's going to die an eternal bachelor. Trust me. I live with him, and he brings home different women all the time. Just last weekend, he brought home two."

Last weekend?

I wanted to ask Christian so many things. The pain of hearing Julian had been with not one, but two women since he'd kissed me was an agony I wasn't expecting. And now, he was bringing a date to my birthday party.

My heart clenched, making it almost hard to breathe as I tried not to fall apart in front of my mother and brother.

"Christian!" Mom exclaimed. "I don't want to know that. I just hope he's being safe. With all the diseases and pregnancy, you need to make sure he's wrapping it up."

"Mom, he's been wrapping it up since Dad gave him condoms when he was thirteen after he found a girl in Julian's room."

"A girl here?" I asked, taken back.

"Yeah." He nodded, chuckling. "Just ask Mom how many times they found a girl in his room."

"Too many to count and remember."

It was blow after blow, and I didn't have a clue as to how I was still standing.

"Autumn, why do you look so upset?"

"It's nothing, Christian."

"It's not nothing. Do you have a crush on him or something?"

I knew he wouldn't let this go—his overprotectiveness wouldn't allow it.

"Of course not." *I wish it was only a crush.* "I'm just shocked you're talking about him like this. He's your best friend."

"I'm not saying anything to you I haven't already said to him. Julian is well aware of what I think about him and women. He treats them like shit. You're too good for him, Autumn. Besides, he'd never do that to me. He knows that you're off-limits."

"Now you're telling guys I'm off-limits?"

"No, just him."

Those three littles words made my head spin.

Is that why he abruptly stopped hanging out with me?

"Oh, honey." Mom smiled. "Julian is like another son to us, and she's like his little sister. He would never…" She giggled, eyeing Christian. "You're being ridiculous. Protect your sister from everything, but you don't need to worry yourself over Julian and Autumn. She's family to him."

I couldn't listen to this anymore. "Guests are starting to arrive, Mom."

She stood, kissed my cheek and left, but to my disappointment, my brother didn't follow.

Hoping he'd catch a clue, I remarked, "I need to finish getting ready."

"I'm being serious, Autumn. If you do have a crush on Julian, you need to forget about him. When it comes to women, he couldn't care less about them. The last thing I want is for you to be another notch on his belt. I'll tell you right now, if he broke your heart, I'd fucking kill him."

"Christian!"

"What? Why does that surprise you? It's my job to protect you."

"I know, but you don't have to be so scary about it."

Pushing off the doorframe, he warned, "Don't give me a reason to."

I should have stopped him.

I should have told him.

It could have changed our future, but I didn't. Instead, I watched him leave. My pain overruling our reality. In fact, it won in the end. I did the only thing that made sense to me in a moment purely driven by my chaotic emotions.

I went to look for Julian, finding him downstairs by the bar. A date by his side. I couldn't believe he had the balls to bring someone with him. Of course, she was gorgeous.

Long blonde hair.

Legs for days.

A rack the size of my head.

She was dressed in a tight skirt and bodysuit, emphasizing her perfect figure. I'd never felt more like a child than I did when he reached around her waist and kissed her. The truth of who he was staring me right in the face. With his lips still on her mouth, he locked eyes with me for a minute as though he felt my presence from across the crowded room.

Maybe he felt my pain.

I didn't look at her at all, not for one second. However, I was the first to break our connection. If I didn't, I would have blown up on him in front of everyone.

Our family.

My parents.

Christian.

The party went off without a hitch. Well into the night, there were still hundreds of people dancing, drinking, socializing. I tried to have fun, but my eyes kept wandering toward Julian and his date.

He was caressing her face.

Whispering things in her ear.

Kissing her lips.

Holding her close to him.

He was trying to prove a point, and I couldn't fathom the reason for his actions, so I left. I went out into the woods behind our house, needing air, needing space, needing to break the fuck down.

"What an asshole!" I shouted into the forest, kicking a rock, except it wasn't a rock. It was a stone rooted into the ground. "Ow!" My foot instantly started aching, and I fell to the dirt. "Great, now my dress is ruined too." I took off my heel—the nail of my big toe had sliced in half, and blood was oozing off my skin.

"Shit, kid."

His voice caught in the wind, and my furious glare met his concerned expression. "Get away from me."

He stopped dead in his tracks.

"Go back inside to whatever girl you're sleeping with tonight."

"Do you think if she mattered to me, I'd be out here for you?"

Unable to resist, I sassed, "Two girls at once last week, huh? Must have been quite a night for you."

He gripped onto the back of his neck, bowing his head.

"I can't believe you brought a date to my birthday party after you stole my first kiss! Well, guess what? I want it back!"

"If I could, I would."

Talk about a dagger to my heart.

"I had no business stealing that from you."

His expression quickly turned desolate, and I lashed out, "I thought you said I was your number one girl? If you treat me like this, I can't imagine how you treat all the other women you sleep with."

With a neutral expression, he informed, "I don't cuddle. They never spend the night. I fuck them, Autumn. It's that plain and simple."

I grabbed a rock and chucked it at his head, but he ducked. "You shameless bastard!"

"Keep your voice down."

"Why? No one can hear me! Is the truth too hard for you to hear, Julian?"

He disregarded my outburst, crouching in front of me. "Let me help you. You're bleeding."

I pushed him, and since he wasn't expecting it, he fell back onto the grass. Powerless to control my anger, I lunged at him. "You fucking asshole!" Hitting his chest with all the strength I could muster, I yelled out my frustration, "I hate you! I hate you!" I repeated, wanting it to become part of him as I slammed my fists into his torso.

"You're right! I am a fucking asshole, and you need to stay away from me."

"You're the one who followed me out here! Just like you followed me out into the woods with Daniel! You're the one who kissed me, remember?"

He knocked me senseless, professing, "How could I forget? It was the only kiss that has ever mattered to me."

fourteen

Autumn

Then

I HIT HIM HARDER. "STOP PLAYING GAMES WITH ME!"
All my sadness.
My anguish.
My love for him that wouldn't go away.
My hate for him for pushing me away.
I saw all the girls he'd bring around. All the times he'd ignored me. Every time he didn't look my way. I saw it all. With each blow, I felt a little more of myself die inside.
I went to hit him again, but he caught my wrist, so I tried with my other fist, and he caught that one too.
"Enough!"
"Fuck you!" I flung my body, whipping all around, desperately trying to break free from his strong hold.
On my wrists.
On my heart.
On my soul.
"How could you use me like that? I thought you cared about me! I thought I was different! Why would you kiss me if you were just going to screw me over like you do every girl you sleep with? Why?"
"For fuck's sake!" He immediately flipped me over, getting on top of me, and holding my wrists above my head while the weight of his body held down my legs. "What do you want me

to say? You want me to tell you I'm sorry, kid? Is that what you want?"

"No! I don't want your bullshit apologies you'd only be saying for Christian!"

"Did I kiss you for Christian too?"

"Just tell me how many more times you're planning on breaking my heart, you dickwad!"

He jolted back for the first time like I had hit him again, but this time it wasn't by my actions—it was the reality of my words instead.

Julian

Tears slid down the sides of her face, cascading onto the dirt behind her. The guilt was eating me alive.

"I'm no good for you."

"Oh yeah, Christian made that really fucking clear."

"No shit, I heard him."

Her eyes widened.

"And he's right. I'm no fucking good for you. I'm hurting you when I'm with you. I'm hurting you when I'm not. I can't win either way, and I hate seeing you cry over me. I should be the last man you're crying over. Do you understand me?"

"What am I supposed to do, huh? I can't be with you, and I can't be without you. I'm in lov—"

"Don't you fucking dare."

"What? Can't hear the truth? Well too bad! I'm in lov—"

Helpless to hear Autumn say those words, I crashed my mouth against hers. My lips immediately betraying me, I kissed her as if I had a right to, as if she was mine, as if I was hers—as if this kiss would change the course of our lives.

It was uncontrollable.

The urge.

The rage.

The desire to claim not only her lips, but her heart, her soul, her goddamn body were driving me to the brink of insanity. I loved and hated it. The emotions she stirred were ones I'd never experienced before. It was overwhelming, the thrill of her, the thought of her, the feel of her.

My tongue slid into her mouth, and she tasted like everything I ever wanted and didn't think I deserved. Kissing me back like she was trying to prove she was indeed all the things that wreaked havoc in my mind.

She glided her tongue into my eager mouth, moaning, panting, clawing at my senses. My dick throbbed, aching as she writhed beneath me and enticed my cock to rock against her virgin pussy.

The mere thought of knowing she'd never been touched was fucking agonizing to every part of my body. I needed to stop, but I couldn't help myself. The truth was, I did want her.

I wanted her innocence.

Her happiness.

Her love for me.

I didn't deserve it, yet it still felt like it all belonged to me. Where things took a turn in our dynamic was beyond me. It seemed as though it was out of nowhere, hitting me like a fucking freight train. One day she was my best friend's little sister, and the next she was this forbidden fruit I wanted to taste.

It was wrong.

We were all wrong for each other.

I'd spent the last two weeks trying to fuck her out of my mind. From one random girl to the next. It was no use. I couldn't stop thinking about the way her mouth moved with mine. I was well aware of the crush she had on me—it was easy to see. At times it felt like Christian knew it as well. Which was probably why he'd threatened to slice my dick off if I so much as looked her way. I was laying our friendship on the line for his little sister.

What the fuck kind of best friend was I?

Everything with Autumn felt like it was new. It didn't matter how many girls I had been with, no one came close to her. The emotions she incited in me were feelings I'd never expected. Never thought possible.

I didn't believe in love.

But I believed in her.

Our movements became headier and more urgent since we were both searching for something. My hand started roaming, beginning at her hair, then traveled down to her face and breasts. Her nipple hardened against the palm of my hand. She pushed her chest further into my grasp, and I gripped it harder, earning me another moan.

The friction between us was intense, consuming, dry fucking the shit out of one another. Her hips moved faster against my cock, and it was only then that I noticed how frenzied her movements became, how precise her hips rocked, how warm her skin felt.

I opened my eyes.

Her face was flushed.

Her forehead perspiring.

Her hands fisting the grass.

"Fuck!" I stopped and pushed myself off her.

"No!" she shouted, instantly feeling the loss of another thing I refused to steal from her. "I was so close!"

"No shit!" I yelled out, pushing my hair out of my face and holding it back with my hands. Wanting to wring my own fucking neck.

She inhaled deeply and rapidly, trying to steady her aroused body.

"Fuck!" I shouted out again, only pissed at myself. "I shouldn't have done that."

"You did it because you want me as much as I want you."

"Wanting you isn't the problem, kid."

She smiled, sitting up. Her toe was still bleeding, and I needed something else to focus my attention on. Taking off my tie, I wrapped it around her foot before looking up at her through the slits of my eyes.

"What am I going to do with you?"

"I have some ideas."

"I bet you do."

I just couldn't believe…

I'd almost made her come.

fifteen

Autumn

WE WERE SITTING IN LOCKE'S PRIVATE JET, AND I was in the seat furthest away from him. Between everything that had happened at the photoshoot three days ago and then ending it with us running into the woman he'd brought to my seventeenth birthday party, I needed some serious space. The last two days were jam-packed with press interviews, and there was no time left over to discuss us.

Thank God.

Today was going to be hard enough. It was probably the hardest day we'd confronted on this tour so far. The timing was shit, seeing as I didn't want to talk about the past, and there we were, going to face it head-on.

Fort Worth, Texas.

Julian Locke was coming home for the first time in over a decade.

A production crew was meeting us there to get footage of him in his old stomping grounds. Beginning with the group home he'd lived at in between his foster placements. I didn't think it would affect me as much as it was, but something inside of me shifted at that damn shoot.

The outfit he was wearing.

The words he was confessing.

The way he was looking at me.

It was all too much to take in at once. Now, we were flying

back home, where our tumultuous past existed, and it was breathing fire down my back. By the way Julian was acting in the last forty-eight hours, I imagined he was feeling the weight of our history on his shoulders like I was. Other than when he was answering questions from the press, he was quiet and distant.

We both knew how heavy the load of Texas would be, and the silence was deafening on his private jet. I swear I could hear his thoughts, and every single one included me and my family.

Particularly my brother.

I still hadn't explained anything to them. I'd been dodging their calls and texts, trying to figure out what I would say. The flight was only two hours, and it felt as if an eternity was slowly passing us by. Although the anxiousness I was feeling wasn't only about Texas—we'd be sharing the penthouse floor of the hotel we were staying at while we were in our hometown.

Why did I agree to share a suite with him?

Taking in a deep breath, I counted to three before exhaling on four breath counts. If Locke noticed my unease, he didn't show it. He wasn't talking, and he didn't move from where he was sitting. Aimlessly, he just stared out the window like it had the answers to all the questions that were obviously plaguing him.

I breathed in and out a few more times until I couldn't take his silence anymore and had to ask, "You really haven't been back since you left?"

Without looking at me, he simply stated, "There was nothing there for me anymore."

I winced, narrowing my eyes at him. "You really think that, don't you?"

"I don't think, I know."

"I was there," I reminded, standing my ground on the truth. "So were my parents and my brother. Despite what you said to me the night of his wedding, I was still waiting for you to come back home, Julian. You wanted to cut ties with me, then you didn't need to do that with my entire family. They had nothing to do with us."

"They had everything to do with us."

"Bullshit. That's just an excuse you've convinced yourself of to excuse your shitty behavior. They didn't deserve what you did to them."

"Neither did you."

"I don't want to talk about us."

"Then don't ask questions you don't want answers to."

"I'm talking about my family. They mourned the loss of you as if you died. You didn't even say goodbye to them."

"How many times do I have to tell you it was the only way I could leave you?"

"Oh," I snapped, feeling his response in the pit of my stomach. "So saying goodbye to me made it easy for you to leave?" I nodded. "Good to know."

"I thought you didn't want to talk about us?"

"Ugh! You're the most stubborn man I have ever met! Do you know that?"

"I've been called worse, sweetheart."

"Stop staring out the window and fucking look at me, Julian!"

Reluctantly, he did.

"You could have left town and still had a relationship with them."

"In one way or another, it still would have included you in it."

"Who cares?! We were friends once, and after some time, we could have been friends again."

His expression quickly turned heated. "I've tasted you, kid. From your mouth, to your pussy, to every inch of your body. I stole your first kiss, your first orgasm, your first fuck—there's no coming back from that, Autumn."

"You also stole my heart. Let's not forget that."

"Yes," he agreed. "I stole that too."

"Not only did you steal it, but you also broke it, and don't you ever forget that."

"You have all the answers to your questions built-in, kid."

"Again, that has nothing to do with my family."

"Knowing you were always mine, do you honestly think I would have been able to see you move on from me? Come on, Autumn. You know me better than that."

"If I was able to see you sleep with half of Texas, I'm sure you would have lived, Julian."

"Up until four days ago, my life has been completely private. All it took was seeing you with good ol' fucking Charlie, and I didn't hesitate to tell the world who you belong to." He cocked his head to the side. "How's that for living?"

"You make it sound like moving on from you was easy."

"It would have been worse had I stayed for your parents and your brother."

"I didn't say you had to stay, but you still could have kept in touch with them."

"And the second someone would have told me about a new man in your life, I would have flown back and done something incredibly stupid, landing him in the ICU and me in jail. Is that what you would have wanted?"

"Of course not."

"I couldn't bear to tell your family goodbye. I couldn't explain to them why I was leaving—see the devastation on their faces when I told them. It would have been too hard—too painful. It would've felt like a betrayal." He paused for a moment. "You wanted the truth, kid, and I'm giving you the fucking truth. These are just a few things you need to consider before you start attacking me about what I should and shouldn't have done."

"But lying about our current relationship seems reasonable to you?"

"I didn't lie." He shook his head. "I want you back in my bed."

"The same bed you've probably shared with thousands of women? No thanks, I'll pass."

"No woman has ever been in my bed."

I rolled my eyes. "Is this where you tell me you haven't had sex since me?"

"No. I'm a man, Autumn, I fuck."

Hearing him say those words didn't surprise me, but the next ones he openly shared were staggering, nearly stopping my heart, leaving me awestruck and blindsided when he confessed…

"I've never made love to anyone but you."

Julian

"Has anyone ever told you that you come on a little strong?"

I was prepared for the animosity she'd have toward me, but it still hurt like a son of a bitch that she kept blowing off my sincerity.

Instead of losing my temper yet again, I changed the subject. "How about you tell me how your family is doing?"

She shrugged, not giving me an inch. "Call them and ask them yourself."

"Or you could save them from telling me to go to Hell, and just answer my question."

"Fine." She caved. "My parents are doing great. My dad is still working at his firm, and my mom is impatiently waiting on grandkids from Christian and Kinley."

"Not from you?"

She shook her head. "Not from me."

"What field did your brother end up in?"

"Believe it or not, he's a gynecologist."

Despite feeling out of control, which was never a good thing, I chuckled. "That doesn't surprise me."

"Really?"

"No. Your brother has always loved pussy."

"Ew." She flinched. "Gross. Don't ever say that to me again."

"How are he and Kinley?"

"Good, I guess. I don't see them very often."

"Why is that?"

"I don't live in Texas."

I arched an eyebrow, surprised at her response. "Where are you living?"

"None of your business, Mr. Locke."

"So we're back to that now?"

"We never left."

"You're worse than whiplash, kid. How about you save me the trouble of pulling your records from HR and tell me yourself?"

"That's illegal."

"It would only be illegal if I wasn't your boss."

"How many times do I have to tell you I'm not your employee? I'm not beneath you—I'm your equal."

"But you used to love being beneath me."

"I think that's always been our problem. The love I felt for you."

"Autumn… I've always lov—"

She abruptly stood, cutting me off on purpose. "We landed." She hurried toward the exit, and as soon as she walked past me, I stood and grabbed her arm to urge her to look at me again.

"Mr. Locke."

"I've had enough of your Mr. Locke bullshit, kid. I'm done playing your little games."

"Wow," she rasped. "I played your games for years, and you can barely stand it for six days. How's it feel?"

"Whether you want to face it or not I do lov—"

"No!" She yanked her arm out of my grasp. "I don't want to hear it."

"It doesn't matter if I say it to you now or later, it's going to be said, and the sooner you realize that, the faster we can move forward with it."

"What exactly are we moving forward with?"

"Us."

"There is no us."

"There will always be an us, and you know it."

"Listen." She stepped back, making her way to the exit. "If you want me to forgive you, how about you start with reaching out to my family and we go from there, alright?"

"Will it get you back in my bed?"

"No. But maybe we can be friends."

"We've never just been friends, Autumn."

Before I could stop her, she turned and stepped off my jet.

Bottom line, when push came to shove, she chose to confront our past in Texas rather than dealing with me and my confessions.

sixteen

Julian

I FOLLOWED AUTUMN INTO THE GROUP HOME I HADN'T seen since my eighteenth birthday. The day I became a legal adult I was out of there and never looked back.

She must have sensed my hesitation. "You okay?"

Eyeing the production crew in front of my face, I warned, "You'll be lucky if I don't break that camera by the end of the day."

"Julian," she coaxed. "We need footage for your social media."

"Excuse me?"

"You heard me."

"I never agreed to that."

"I know. I did it for you."

"It's going to cost you, kid."

"I imagined it would." She smiled at the camera. "Can we talk about it later?"

"You mean after I'm done taking you over my knee?"

She glared at me. "I'm not a child, Mr. Locke."

"No, but you're in definite need of some discipline."

"Julian," the director of the facility greeted, bringing our attention over to her. "It's so good to finally see you after all these years."

I nodded, extending my hand, but she smiled, pulling me into her embrace instead.

"I can't tell you how proud we are of you. These kids idolize you. You have no idea how big of a role model you've been to them."

I was never any good at receiving compliments, so I nodded again, pulling away with Autumn hugging her next.

"Good to see you, Miss Jones."

"Please call me Anne." She stepped back, holding Autumn's hands. "Look at you! Oh my God! The last time I saw you, you were what? Ten? Eleven?"

"Twelve."

"Right! Well, you look amazing." She glanced back and forth between us. "I read *The New York Times* article. I can't say I was too shocked over the news of you two falling in love with each other. You've always had such a special friendship, and those always turn into the best relationships. I bet your parents are ecstatic. Do I hear wedding bells in your future?"

Autumn nervously giggled. "I wouldn't go that far."

"I would."

Both their stares snapped toward my direction.

"Julian…" Autumn zeroed in on me, not appreciating my answer.

"What, baby?" I reached around her waist, caging her in with my arms as I held her against my chest to run my nose along the nape of her neck. I inhaled her comforting scent, leaving a trail of longing in my wake. She tensed in my arms, but I didn't give a shit. If she was insistent on taking a trip down memory lane, then I was using it to my advantage as much as I could.

Whispering into her ear, "Smile for the camera, kid."

"Oh, my goodness!" Anne exclaimed. "You two are absolutely perfect! The gorgeous babies you will have!"

"Who knows, Anne." I winked at her while kissing Autumn's neck. "There may already be one in there."

She squealed, and Autumn glanced at the camera. "You can't use that."

"Baby, now's not the time to be shy." For only her to hear,

I murmured in her ear, "You want the world to know me, and I'm just showing the best part of me."

Without taking in what I'd addressed, she elbowed my ribs, making me groan and let her go.

"Let's go see the kids." She grabbed Anne's arm, rushing to get away, but before she could take a step, I grabbed her hand.

Determined to remind her who was still in control.

Autumn

For the next few hours I watched in fascination how Julian was interacting with the kids. I had no clue he liked children—we'd never been around any before. This whole time I thought I was going to have to threaten him to play with the kids, but he genuinely seemed happy and not showing off for the cameras who were filming his every move.

Anne wasn't exaggerating—the kids were ecstatic over having him there with them. They adored him, and the feeling was very much mutual. Half the time I couldn't believe what was in front of my eyes. Julian was laughing, joking, bonding with each of them. From playing basketball to soccer, to throwing around a football. At one point, he was carrying around two toddlers in his arms, showering them with affection.

"I'm not surprised," Anne observed, sitting beside me at one of the picnic tables while we watched Julian throw a kid on his shoulders, in order for him to dunk the basketball into the hoop. "Julian has always had a big heart, especially when it came to children."

"Really?" I peered at her.

"Oh yes. He's always known how to calm the little ones down even as a teenager. I think it was because he lived their lives himself. He knew what they needed to hear to feel safe in a new environment. This place can be rough on a child who just lost their parent or parents. Did you know he donates millions of dollars every year?"

I jerked back. "What?"

"Yeah, he not only donates to the group home, but he also helps the kids get into colleges, paying for their books and sometimes their tuition and dorms."

"I had no idea."

"This surprises you?"

"Yeah, it does."

I fed into the gossip from the press. They labeled him as a cold, heartless bastard, and I figured he was like that in every aspect of his life. Especially after being with him the last few days and witnessing it for myself. Never in a million years did I imagine he'd cared about this place, let alone these children living there.

"He's a good man. You're lucky to have him."

My heart fluttered, hearing her say those words to me.

Was I lucky?

The time flew by, and I'd be lying if I'd said I didn't love every second of seeing him with his guard down. His suit jacket was in my lap, his tie was hanging from his neck with the first few buttons undone. He was relaxed, comfortable, and in his element.

My heart wasn't just beating fast, it was hammering against my chest when Julian took off his collared shirt. Sweat glistening off every inch of his muscular, defined chest as he made his way toward us.

I could see it in his eyes—he was coming for me.

"Julian, don't you dar—"

I didn't have a chance to finish my sentence, as he flung his sweaty body on me, wrapping me in his manly scent.

"Julian!"

"What? You used to love it when I made you wet."

"You're all sweaty, and you're ruining my dress!"

"Can't have that now, can we?"

"What's that supp—"

Clutching onto my waist, he sat on the bench, sitting me on his lap. My back to his front, his lips nuzzled my neck.

"Feels damn good to finally hold you in my arms, Autumn."

I smiled. I had to, all eyes were on us. Including the camera.

Julian wasn't deterred, muttering into my ear, "Do you have any idea how much I missed you?"

He was acutely aware of what I was experiencing with his whole body engulfing mine. Completely in tune with my emotions.

We were an illusion.

An act.

A charade.

Nothing about our relationship was real. We were living a lie in front of all these people, and the millions who'd eventually watch this intimate footage the videographer was capturing. Only suffocating me further into the reckless thoughts of what my family and brother would think when they saw us like this.

"Julian, please…"

"You know I love it when you beg."

"You can't do this."

"I already am."

"You need to let me go."

"No, I have waited too long for you."

The space began closing in on me, holding me hostage against my will. Sweat formed at my temples, my hands began to shake, and my heart started beating profusely through my chest.

I couldn't breathe.

All I wanted was to breathe. Just for one second, one moment, one hour in time.

Tick…

"You'll always be my number one girl."

Tick…

"I lov—"

Boom.

I forcefully escaped, ignoring the disappointed expression taking hold of his face.

What did he expect?

"Kid—"

I didn't allow him to finish, quickly walking away. I thought facing our past would be too much to bear, never thinking our future would be harder to endure.

Future? Where did that come from?

He was messing with my head. I took a walk while he showered, and once he was fully dressed in his suit, appearing like the Alpha CEO, it was much easier to be around him. His guard was back up, and I couldn't help but remember that for most of my life, I'd prayed for him to bring it down, and now I wished for the opposite to happen.

We said our goodbyes, and I didn't speak to him the entire drive back to the hotel. Except we didn't go to the suite. When the driver pulled into my favorite restaurant, I was well aware Julian had told him to.

"I'm not going in there with you."

"Autumn, one way or another, you're going to have dinner with me. The choice is yours on how you'd like to enter that facility."

Flinging my door open, I stepped out. Pretty much stomping my feet the entire way in. With one foot in front of the other, I walked inside with Julian behind me at the same exact time my life came tumbling down on me. Right there in front of our faces was our past beating me senseless.

My stare locked with the person I'd least expected, but he was focused on the man behind me.

Both men ready for a battle.

Over me.

seventeen

"Christian," I breathed out, overwhelmed by the turn of events.

His eyes flew from Julian to me. "What the fuck is this?"

"It's not what you think."

"Actually, it's exactly what you're thinking."

I glared at Julian. "Stop it."

"Stop what, kid? He knows the truth. There's no need to hide it from him anymore."

"Is this why you texted me to meet you here? For this, Autumn?"

"I didn't text you to meet me here. What are you talking about?"

"It wasn't her," Julian declared in a steady, calm tone. "It was me from her phone."

"Are you fucking kidding me?" I bit. "Why would you do that?" I couldn't believe he'd undermined me again, going behind my back to confront the one person I didn't want to deal with right now. Like dealing with us wasn't already enough for me to handle.

"Because there was no better time than the present. You said you wanted me to reach out, make things right, and that's exactly what I'm doing. I'm done hiding our relationship from him."

"We're not in a relationship!"

My brother chimed in, "So who's lying, Autumn? You or him?"

"Christian, just let me think for a second."

"You haven't answered your phone or replied to one fucking text I sent you in the last three days, and you're telling me to let you have another minute?"

"Jesus! Can you relax? I'm as shocked as you are right now. I wasn't expecting this! He blindsided me too."

In one sudden movement, Julian shifted me aside and stood up to my brother. This was the first time in all our lives I was truly worried about what was going to go down between them. From best friends to enemies in a matter of seconds, at least it was with Christian's perception of the man standing in front of him. I'd never seen him glare at Julian with such disgust and hatred. The tension, thick and palpable swarmed through the restaurant as if bees were suddenly set free, protecting their queen.

Me.

The expression on Kinley's face mirrored my own, her concern evident through her dark brown eyes as she grabbed onto Christian's arm, like she knew he was ready to strike and attack. Taking no prisoners.

"Let's go outside, okay? This is a family establishment, and there's no need to make a scene. I don't want someone calling the cops."

Christian considered his wife's apprehension before his anger quickly turned to rage, and all the color drained from his face as he shoulder checked Julian on his way out of the restaurant. I couldn't take the strain between the two of them. The years of waiting for this to happen was finally here, in a moment I'd least expected.

I hastily followed him out, not knowing what to say or do to make this okay. Once Christian rounded the corner of the building, he snapped back around and got in Julian's face.

Spewing, "Is it fucking true?"

"Christian, please," I begged for I don't know what. I still hadn't read the damn article, but I could only imagine the details Julian revealed just from briefly speaking to Charlie about it.

Julian didn't hesitate, simply stating, "Yes."

Everything happened so fast, yet it still felt like it played out in slow motion.

"Christian, no!" I shouted as his fist slammed into Julian's jaw, causing his body to whoosh back from the impact of Christian's forceful blow.

Julian tried to catch his balance, stumbling around for a second, while I stared with a wide, petrified gaze back and forth between them. Not knowing who to focus on more. Julian caught his bearings, massaging his jaw and moving it around.

Kinley lunged into action, gripping onto her husband's arm. Her attempt at holding him back pitiful. She was no match against my brother's strength. "Babe, come on," she begged. "This isn't the right way. He's your best friend, and that's your sister."

"He was my best friend!" Christian growled, roughly yanking his arm away from her. In one stride he was in Julian's face again, shoving him back with so much force. "Is she the reason you left without so much as a fucking text?!"

I'd never seen my brother so mad before, scaring the absolute shit out of me.

But it wasn't until Julian responded, "Christian, I have loved your sister ever since I can remember."

That I truly almost fell to the ground.

He didn't stop there, speaking with conviction, "I've wasted over ten years being away from her, and I can't do it anymore. I pushed her away so many fucking times—letting our friendship and my gratitude toward your parents get in the way of my decisions and the future I wanted with her.

How I left was fucked up, and I'm the first to admit that. I'll apologize as many times as I need to in order to make things right between us, but don't think for one second that I'll ever apologize for loving her. Do you understand me?"

My head wasn't just spiraling, it was tossing and turning, barely keeping up with what was happening and what he was declaring. I desperately wanted to stop Julian, but I couldn't get my lips to move, to speak, to do anything other than watch with an open mouth because of what he was admitting.

I didn't know what to think, let alone how to feel. He was sharing all this information with both of us for the first time, and he didn't stop there…

Professing, "Up until last week, I hadn't seen her since I'd left. Over ten fucking years I stayed away from her for you and your parents and I won't do that again. *I can't.*"

Breaking my heart all over again.

Julian

This was the only way to finally get over our past and move into our future. I was tired of all the games she was playing, so I once again took matters into my own hands. She'd left her purse on the table while she used the bathroom at the group home, and I didn't think twice about it—I found her phone and texted her brother. Telling him to meet us at her favorite restaurant nonetheless.

I was back in control, and it was the only reason I wasn't losing my temper with the man who used to be my best friend. He had every right to be furious, what I did was truly fucked up, but I was there now…

Ready to fight for her.

For us.

No matter what, she was mine. Even if I had to prove it to *her* and her brother. Man to man, we would have it out. Regardless of the outcome.

"Don't fucking try me, Julian! Not right now!" he spit out with a menacing tone, drawing my attention back to the present, where I was willingly putting myself on the line.

For her.

"Or what?" I countered, cocking my head to the side. "You're going to hit me again? Then just fucking do it! Hit me! Hit me as many goddamn times as you want! If that's what it's going to take to make you realize I'm not going away. I'm not leaving her. I'm right fucking here, waiting!"

He shoved me, and since I was expecting it, I didn't waver. Further inciting the fury to course through his veins. "I thought you were my best friend!" He pushed me again. "I thought you were my brother!"

"I know, but it's been over ten years, ten fucking years for us to get to this point. She's not a little girl anymore. She's a grown ass woman, and I fucking love her."

"You think that matters to me? I don't give a shit if you waited for the rest of your life after what you fucking did!"

"Christian, please," Autumn coaxed.

"Kid, stay out of it. This is between me and your brother."

"Actually, this completely involves me! So just shut your mouth and walk away. He's not going to listen to you, and I don't want to either!"

My eyes snapped to her. "Too fucking bad! I'm done playing your little games."

"Julian—"

Christian cut her off, seething, "I had to find out about you guys from a picture of you kissing on your fucking bed, Julian! I had to find out you were her first love, her first kiss, her first fuck in a *New York Times* article I had no intention of reading! I had to find out that not only did you betray my trust, you're also back together—"

"We're not back together," Autumn interrupted. "We were never even together! This is ridiculous. You both need to calm the hell down. Nothing is going to get worked out. I don't want Julian. I haven't in years!"

Just to prove my fucking point, I gripped onto the back of her neck and crashed my lips against hers. Kissing her as if my life depended on it, and in the most significant way, it did. I tugged her closer to me as if she wasn't already close enough, devouring her mouth in the same way I always did her pussy. I softly pecked her lips one last time before I pulled away to look into her eyes.

They were shut tight like she was trying to hide the truth I frantically wanted to see for myself.

"Now," I coaxed, fully aware of the truth behind her closed lids. "Tell me you didn't feel that?"

She didn't reply, not that I'd expected her to.

"You shameless fuck!" Christian roared, shifting my gaze back to him.

"She's my sister, you piece of shit! I loved you, and I fucking trusted you, man! I didn't know you at all, did I? Because the man I thought I knew would've never betrayed me with my own family!"

"Fuck, Christian! What do you want from me? I'm telling you the truth!"

"How am I supposed to get past this?"

"I tried not to love her. I've tried for years… I can't. I never wanted to do this to your family, especially after everything you guys did for me, and you know that."

He shook his head, disappointed. "How long were you lying to me? Huh? How long were you fucking my little sister?"

"It wasn't like that, man. She was never just a fuck to me."

"Every woman you ever came across was just another fuck to you, and you expect me to believe that she was any different?"

"She was. She meant … she means everything to me."

"Is it you?"

I jerked back, confused. "Is it me, what?"

"Christian! Enough! Now!" Autumn pleaded, standing in front of him with her back to me.

"How can you even be with him after what he did to our family?"

"It's not like that," she explained. "Please just calm down and let me explain. I'm just his publicist."

"So what's the difference now? Huh? You don't suck his dick for free anymore? Now he just pays for your pussy instead?"

My fist connected with his jaw, sending him flying back against a car.

Autumn's stare went wide. "Oh my god!"

Kinley darted to her husband's side while Autumn snapped around, getting right in my face. "Are you fucking insane?!"

I sternly pointed to him. "He cannot talk to you like that."

"Why not? You do!"

Unable to control my temper, I roared, "What did he mean by is it me, Autumn?"

"Nothing."

Christian shoved his sister out of the way, standing in front of me again.

"Christian, please!" she pleaded in a desperate tone that shook my body to the core.

"What's going on?" I asked, torn and baffled by what was happening between them.

"How the fuck can you defend him, Autumn?!" His glare

flew in my direction. "Is that why you left, Julian?! Huh? Couldn't deal—"

"Christian, stop! Please!"

"It is you, isn't it?! That's why she's defending you! Well, I won't let her take the fall for you again, motherfucker!"

"For fuck's sake! Just out with it, Christian! What the hell are you talking about?"

"It's you!" he raged, knocking me on my ass, and my world as I knew it came plummeting down on my head.

When he added…

"You're the fucking father to her daughter!"

eighteen

Julian

"DAUGHTER?" I BREATHED OUT, ALL THE AIR FROM my lungs vanishing while I stood there unable to move, but for a much different reason this time. My eyes shot to Autumn. "What is he talking about?"

She stared at me with wide eyes and a terrified expression. The blood had drained from her face, and her chest rose and fell while she was frozen in place.

"Autumn." I stepped toward her. "I won't ask you again."

She placed her hand over her heart like she was trying to hold it together, and in two strides I was in her face.

"Julian, please…"

"Please what, Autumn? I want you to look me in the eyes and tell me what the fuck Christian is talking about." When she didn't respond fast enough, I ordered, "Now!"

She jolted out of her skin, shuddering. "I don't know what you want me to say."

"I want the truth."

"Holy shit." Kinley jumped in, standing in between all of us. "Everyone needs to take a second and calm down, okay? This isn't helping anyone."

I didn't pay her any mind—my focus was still on the liar in front of me. "Either you answer my question, or you'll be answering my lawyer, kid."

"Your lawyer?" she exclaimed, appearing every bit the

damsel in distress she was trying to portray. "What do you need to call your lawyer for?"

"For a daughter I didn't know I fucking had!"

"Stop yelling at me!"

"In a second I'm going to be doing a lot more than yelling at you."

Christian shoved me back, placing his sister behind him. "You're going to have to go through me, motherfucker."

I growled from deep within my chest, not backing down. His threat meant shit to me. "I'm only going to say this once, so you better fucking listen. If you think I won't go through you or anyone else who is trying to stand in between me and my child, then you have no idea who you're dealing with."

"You can't take her away from me!" Autumn shouted, shaking her head. "I swear to God, Julian, I'll—"

"You'll what? Keep more secrets? Play more games? Lie to me some more? Tell me, sweatheart, what will you do?"

"You have no right to be angry with me! You left me, remember?"

"Did you know you were pregnant at your brother's wedding?"

She winced.

"Answer me. Did. You. Know?"

Taking a deep breath, she hesitantly nodded.

"I want to hear you say the words."

"Julian," her brother stated. "This isn't helping—"

"Fuck you, Christian!" I pushed him, needing to take out my frustration. "You have the audacity to stand there and come for me, when you knew I had a daughter, and you couldn't bother to pick up the damn phone and tell me?"

He jerked back. "I didn't know she was your daughter—none of us did. She looks nothing like you. She's Autumn to a T. Besides, Autumn told us it was a one-night stand, and no one knew you guys were fucking around up until a few days ago."

"Your parents may have not known, I'll give you that one, but you sure as shit were getting suspicious, so try again."

Autumn stepped aside him to stand in front of me. "I've been telling you this since day one, and I'll say it again. This is between you and me, it has nothing to do with my brother and family."

"Is that right?"

"Yes."

"So you kept the truth from all of us then?"

"What was I supposed to do, Julian? Tell them we were sneaking around and you got me pregnant and then took off like a bat out of Hell?"

"If you would have told me you were pregnant, I never would have left you, and you know it."

"When was I supposed to tell you?" she scoffed out in disgust. "Before or after you told me you screwed someone else at Christian's bachelor party? Or would you have rather I waited until after you told me I was nothing more than a fuck to you? Please tell me when I should have told you I was expecting your baby? Because I just don't know."

"You should have told me the second you found out."

"I was going to tell you the night of the wedding. It's why I went outside by myself. I knew you'd follow me. But you didn't give me a chance before breaking my heart and then stomping all over it."

"How long did you know?"

"I really don't want to talk about this in front of my brother and his wife. Can you at least give me that?"

"I don't have to give you shit."

"I know, okay? I'm asking for mercy."

Before I went off again, I abruptly walked away.

"Can you guys go please? I need to handle him alone."

"Fuck no," I heard Christian retort. "I'm not leaving you alone—"

"We're a phone call away," Kinley interrupted him. "Okay?"

My glare shot to Christian when he warned, "We're not done here, Julian. It's far from over." He turned and left with his wife following close behind him.

Once they were gone, I got right down to the point. "Where's my daughter?"

"None of your business."

"Oh, trust me, kid. It's going to be my business when I'm serving you with custody papers."

"Are you insane? She doesn't even know you!"

"Whose fucking fault is that?"

"Yours! You left me, asshole! What did you expect me to do? Grovel and beg you to stay for me and a baby you didn't want?"

"I wanted you, Autumn. I've always wanted you."

"Well, you had a shitty way of showing it. I've been trying to tell you—"

"You haven't been trying shit. You want to know how I know? Because I still don't know the fucking truth!"

"Oh my God! Will you ever stop?!"

"Do I look like I want to be yelled at?! Do I seem like I want to be fucked with?! Now tell me where my daughter is before I lose the last bit of patience I have with you."

She pushed me. "Get out of my face! You have no right to make these demands! You told me you'd never love me!"

I stood closer to her. "How could you keep this from me? Christ, kid. After everything, how could you not tell me we made a baby?"

"I thought you would come back, alright? I waited for you. I didn't think you wouldn't come back for me and after time went on, I realized you weren't ever coming home again. By that time it didn't matter anymore."

"Oh, it mattered, Autumn. How the fuck could you keep this from me? Were you ever going to tell me?"

"Yes. I was trying to figure out the right time."

"You expect me to believe your bullshit lies?"

"I'm not lying."

"Well, I don't trust you."

"Great. Don't trust me. If you want to stand there and pretend like I'm the villain, then go right ahead. I'll be the bad guy, if that's what it's going to take for you to not involve your lawyers in this. Please, Julian…"

I shook my head, eyeing her up and down as I backed away. I had to remove myself from this conversation before I said something she could use against me if we needed to settle this in court.

Unable to hold back, I threatened, "This whole time you've been saying I'm an asshole. Well, sweetheart, you haven't seen anything yet."

Fear replaced the anger in her expression, and for some reason, my mind kicked to another place and time.

Where looking at her didn't make me hate her.

nineteen

Then

I SAT IN MY CAR WITH A BOTTLE OF TX STRAIGHT Bourbon Whiskey in my grasp, staring at a house that held one big, happy family. For the last three hours, my car was parked behind a huge oak tree. No one could see me, not that anyone was looking. I chugged my bottle, drinking away the uncertainty of what I was going through. I didn't think I had it in me, but there I was…

Sitting.

Waiting.

Fucking numb.

I'd only just searched for her in the last month, never imagining I'd actually find her.

Them.

Their toys were scattered all through the yard, there was even a fucking basketball hoop in the driveway. A white picket fence circled their home with a bright red door. This house was straight out of a *Home and Gardens* magazine. The grass was perfectly cut, flowers and plants accentuated the property flawlessly. There was a white swing on the porch with pillows and a blanket. This house was everything you would want to raise a family in.

When an Audi SUV pulled into the driveway, the next thing I knew, I was getting out of my car, watching as they exited their vehicle too. The woman stepped out last, heading straight toward the back-passenger seats where she opened the door to reveal a car seat. She unstrapped a baby and pulled it into her arms as two other kids flew out and hauled ass toward their father, who was walking out the front door.

A boy.

Two girls.

Three children.

Happy.

Laughing.

Loved.

I was powerless, unable to stop myself from witnessing the reality of a family I wasn't good enough for. I couldn't help but notice that the man was an older version of me. He was sporting a beard with gray hair intermixed, and it was also around the temples of his head. Though, it was his piercing blue eyes that caught my attention the most—they mirrored my own. It was almost like I was looking into a mirror of what my appearance would be in thirty years.

I didn't expect to see him or meet him. I was only prepared for her. After all these years, I always assumed she was the one who gave me up. Now to learn that it was both of them triggered feelings I didn't know I felt until that very moment.

Sadness.

Confusion.

Abandonment.

The emotions were endless, piling up one right after the other.

Taking a deep, reassuring breath, I inhaled through my nose and exhaled out of my mouth, trying to shake off the bullshit they evoked. From then on everything sort of played out in slow motion.

The man greeted, "Hey, honey," kissing her on the lips.

She responded, "Hey," smiling lovingly at him. "Can you help me with this little guy?"

He smiled and grabbed their son from her arms, throwing him up in the air, making the baby squeal in delight. I felt as if my body was giving out on me—the emotions were ruthlessly taking ahold of me.

Why didn't they want me? What was wrong with me? Why was I so easy to give up? Why not them?

Maybe they were too young and thought I'd ruin their future. We might have looked the same, but I would never abandon my kid to the fucking system of all places.

One thought led to the next, making me sick to my stomach. I never considered them still being together and having a family. I wanted to give them the benefit of the doubt. But the longer I stood there, the further my resentment and anger grew.

It wasn't until the woman's gaze found mine through the yard that I truly wanted to scream, "*Why didn't you want me?*"

She didn't move.

She didn't speak.

She didn't show me anything.

Nothing of what I'd hoped I'd see.

Seconds, minutes, hours could have flown by, and not once did I look away, openly showing her my agony and dismay. She knew who I was, that much I could see. Except, she didn't give a flying fuck. She was the woman who'd brought me into this world, and at that moment, it was obvious that it was all she'd ever be. I wasn't her son. I was just an accident and mistake she gotten rid of. She must have read my mind, because she simply turned and left. Everyone followed her into their home, and I continued to stand there and consider my options. I could knock on their door, make a big, ugly scene. Confront them, ask them everything, but in the end it wouldn't matter.

It wouldn't change one damn thing.

Instead of getting answers, I locked up my emotions like they never existed to begin with. Getting in my car, I left. Wanting to get lost and not be found. My mind was a jumbled mess of what the fucks. My head was pounding so hard I could barely see straight. It felt like a hammer was beating in my skull.

I drove around aimlessly, drinking away my sorrows before I snapped out of whatever stupor I was in. The last thing I needed was to get a DUI. By the time I'd made it back to my house, it was well into the night. Past midnight. The whiskey was long gone, and all I had left was my misery.

Christian wasn't home, which meant he was at his girlfriend's, or should I say fiancée now. Seeing as he'd asked her to marry him a couple months ago, spending more time at her place ever since. I was glad he'd found someone to spend the rest of his life with. That future wasn't in the cards for me, not when I couldn't be with the one I wanted the most.

"Get your shit together," I uttered to myself, wanting to wash away the day and the booze. I walked into my bathroom to take a quick shower, and after I pulled my shirt off, I remembered I'd left my toiletries in Christian's bathroom. The drain in my shower was clogged, and I'd forgot to pick up Drano to fix it.

Grabbing a beer out of the fridge first, I made my way into his bedroom and stopped dead in my tracks when I saw her.

Sleeping.

Peaceful.

Fucking beautiful.

Christian gave her a key to our place in case we lost ours, and I was beyond grateful for it. Especially then. Her head was on a pillow, wrapped in a throw blanket she'd bought me for my twenty-fourth birthday last month. She must have gone into my bedroom and grabbed it before she'd fallen asleep in her brother's bed.

Over the last year, since she'd turned seventeen, I'd kept her at arm's length. Pushing her away was the only way I knew how to live. She wasn't mine and never would be, yet I couldn't stop myself from picking her up and carrying her into my bed with me. Softly, I laid her on my pillow, watching her for a minute.

Fuck, she was gorgeous.

There was no resisting the urge to feel her beneath my body. Careful not to wake her, I laid on top of her and caged her in with my arms around her face. She fit seamlessly against my chest.

"Kid," I whispered, faintly rubbing my lips on her mouth.

"Mmm…" she groaned, stirring awake.

"Wake up, Sleeping Beauty."

Her eyes fluttered, but sleep won out.

"Autumn, if you wake up, I'll give you anything you want."

"Mmm-hmm," she hummed as I kissed my way down her neck.

Once I reached the top of her breasts, I lightly bit her hard nipple through her dress. Her breathing hitched, and her eyes snapped open, big and wide. Coming face-to-face with the last person she expected to see hovering above her.

The world seemed to stop spinning, stop moving, and time just sort of stood still for us. In the last year there were times I couldn't help myself and gave into the temptation that was her mouth.

We'd kissed.

Made out.

Nothing went further than dry fucking. Anytime we got close, my reaction was to push her further away the next time I saw her. She hated me for it but loved me way more. I was toxic for her—she was poison for me. With the way I was feeling that night, I needed her in a way I'd never needed any-one in all my life.

Her warmth.

Her comfort.

Her love.

Home.

Despite the dim lighting in my room, I could still see her bright green eyes grasping the compromising position we were currently in.

"How did I get in here?"

"I carried you."

"Oh." Her eyebrows pinched together. My demons might have been silenced by her presence, but Autumn's was lying right on top of her. "Why?"

"Because I wanted you in my bed."

She searched for something in my gaze, narrowing her eyes. "I must have fallen asleep."

"Why were you waiting for Christian?"

"I wasn't. I was waiting for you."

"For me?"

"Yeah."

"Why?"

"I don't know. I was heading home from a study group, and out of nowhere it felt like you needed me. By the expres-sion on your face, Julian, I was right. Are you okay?"

"I am now."

"What's wrong?"

"I don't want to talk about it."

"You never want to talk about anything." She placed her hand over my heart. "Please don't push me away. Just let me in."

"Kid, I've let you in so much I don't know how to kick you out."

"I'm not a little girl anymore."

"I can see that."

"I'm eighteen now."

"I know how old you are, Autumn."

Almost immediately my mind battled my heart, raging a war I never had a chance to survive. It was her innocence and vulnerability that were eating me alive, swallowing me whole. There was no denying our connection, and for the first time in our relationship, I sought refuge within her.

"Will you tell me later?"

"There's nothing to tell."

"Julian…"

"Don't whine, kid. I don't like it."

"I'm not whining. I'm just trying to be here for you."

"You are. You're lying beneath me. It's all I need right now."

"Have you been drinking? You smell like whiskey."

I smiled, rubbing my lips against her mouth.

"Have you eaten?"

"No." I grinned. "Are you offering?"

She giggled. "You're drunk."

"And you're breathtaking. Do you know that? Do you have any idea how fucking beautiful you are?"

She blushed, making her freckles much more enticing.

"Those freckles of yours are going to be the end of me."

She rolled her eyes. "I hate them. I can't wait to get them lasered off."

"Your long red hair and the scattered freckles on your nose and cheeks are two of my favorite traits about you. Don't ever change, Autumn. You're perfect just the way you are."

She blushed again, biting her bottom lip.

"Your pouty mouth is another one of my favorites."

"Oh, yeah? What else?"

"Your green eyes. They show me everything I need to know."

"So you love my face the most?"

"No. Your perky tits, your slender waist, your luscious ass, I like those too."

She chuckled, stirring my cock to twitch.

"But it's your laugh, your smile, your heart, the way you can see through my bullshit—it's what really takes ahold of me."

She mischievously smirked. "See through it or put up with it?"

"Either or."

I knew one thing for sure, tonight I wouldn't be pushing her away. Giving into temptation, I claimed her lips.

With no intention ... of just stopping there.

twenty

Julian

I KISSED HER UNTIL NOTHING ELSE MATTERED, knowing deep down in the pit of my stomach this wouldn't change anything between us. She was chasing away my demons while I was merely becoming one of hers.

Our mouths were starving for affection.

Aching for relief.

I desperately wanted to lose myself inside of her.

"You want me, Autumn?"

"Always."

It was all I needed to hear before I reached for the hem of her dress and slid it off her body, leaving her in nothing but her panties. With a predatory regard, I devoured every inch of her bare skin. From her rose-colored nipples to her perky, supple tits, down to her narrow, slender waist, and her luscious ass and thighs.

"Fuck," I groaned, slipping off her panties, I crawled my way up her body, kissing, licking, caressing.

The addictive sounds she was making.

The way her body kept shuddering beneath mine.

The smell of her fucking arousal.

It all had me losing my goddamn mind.

"Autumn," I rasped. "I want to fuck you with my tongue."

She swallowed hard, her chest rising and falling, waiting, eager, ready… This was definitely a bad idea, but I was going to make her feel so fucking good, and it was the only thing that mattered at that moment.

"You going to come for me, baby?"

She moaned in response and there was no hesitation on my part when I took in her pink flesh for the first time.

"Autumn." I blew on her clit. "You have the prettiest pussy. All this under your yellow dress."

She moaned again, and her thighs clenched.

Grinning, I nudged my nose along her folds, faintly blowing against her heated flesh. Lightly running the tip of my tongue over her clit, her breathing instantly became heavy and intoxicating. I knew her heart was beating rapidly out of her chest, making it difficult to catch her next breath. With each stroke of my tongue, I showed her how fucking weak I was when it came to her.

"Tell me, kid. Have you ever touched yourself?"

She thought about it for a second, blushing profusely. "No."

"Are you being shy? There's no need for it—my face is already buried in between your legs."

"Julian..."

"You are being shy." I smiled, peering up at her through the slits of my eyes. "Sweetheart, you have nothing to be shy about. You have the prettiest pussy I've ever seen. It's the perfect shade of pink."

She covered her face, and I licked from her opening to her clit.

"Are you going to be a good girl for me, Autumn?"

"Please," she begged in a breathless tone.

"Please what? All I keep thinking about is how good you're going to taste when I make you come in my mouth."

Her eyes widened.

"How fast do you think I can make you come?"

"Oh, so you're being cocky now?"

"Not cocky when I'm about to make you sit on my face."

"Wha—"

I flipped us over, placing her pussy where I wanted it. Our eyes locked, and all I could see was lust.

"Tonight, you're mine, and you're going to give me what I want. Fuck my face, Autumn."

She purred.

"You like that, do you? The wetter you are, the harder I'm going to tongue fuck you."

And the little minx replied, "Prove it, Julian."

I didn't have to be told twice. I sucked her clit into my mouth, and she loudly moaned, melting against my lips. There was no stopping there—I was just getting started.

Savoring the taste of her.

The feel of her.

Her hips rocked against my face as I pushed my tongue into her cunt before sucking her clit into my mouth. Up and down, side to side, I took what I wanted. What she was giving. Knowing I was the first man to have her this way did something primitive to me. I turned into a fucking caveman.

She was so wet.

Tasted so good.

Her pussy throbbed.

Her body shook.

It didn't take long to have her come undone.

"Julian," she panted, climaxing in my mouth. "Julian, please..." she begged for mercy, but still—I didn't stop. I couldn't.

She consumed me.

From my mind to my soul, to my goddamn cock.

A heady growl vibrated from deep within my chest, conscious of the fact that she was trying to save me from myself while I was destroying her in the process. Ruining her for every other man. The mere thought pissed me off, and I took my frustration out on her cunt.

"Julian!" she exclaimed, coming down my neck. Her body fell forward, and she held herself up on the headboard.

"Are you a squirter, baby? We're about to find out. Give me what I want, Autumn."

She did, proving that she was indeed a dirty little girl. Squirting down my face and chest, but it wasn't enough for me. I was a man possessed, licking her fucking clean, from her opening to her clit. I wanted every last drop of her come. Not allowing her any time to recover, I flipped us over and crawled my way up to her mouth, kissing her and making her taste herself.

She moaned, sucking on my tongue.

"So fucking good." I sat up on my knees, never once breaking our heated stares as I unbuckled my jeans to kick them off with my boxer briefs.

Through dark, dilated, hooded eyes, she took in the size of my hard cock for the first time. I fisted my shaft, jerking myself off in front of her. She watched with an expression full of desire and nothing else. I smiled, appreciating the look in her eyes.

I was a fucking goner. There wasn't a chance in hell I wouldn't have stolen her virginity.

It was mine.

It belonged to me.

I'd stolen everything else, and this would be mine as well.

Still fucking my hand, I made my way back up her body. "I can go as slow as you need."

It was her turn to smile as she sat up, kissing me. Silently demanding I keep going. When I didn't move fast enough, she reached for my dick and wrapped her hand around my shaft, causing my breath to hitch against her lips and my dick to jerk in her grasp.

"Yeah, baby, just like that," I scoffed out, biting her bottom lip. "Stroke my cock. Harder. Faster."

She was a very good listener. Driving me to the brink of insanity. I'd never been with a virgin before. It was too personal, and I was the fuck 'em and leave 'em kind of man.

With Autumn, it was different, and there was no denying that.

"After I'm done with you, I'm going to fuck you again. Just so you remember, only I belong inside of you."

She slid her tongue into my mouth, and I let her take the lead.

"Julian, I want you." She positioned my dick at her entrance.

I groaned, "I want you more than I've ever wanted anything. Are you ready for me?"

"Yes, I've always been ready for you."

"Once I thrust my cock inside of you, there's no going back, kid. You know that, right?"

She beamed. "Promise?"

"I don't deserve you. Not your heart or your pussy, but I'm a selfish bastard, and I want both regardless."

"I'm yours forever."

"Don't say things you don't understand."

"I love—"

"Don't say things I don't understand."

"Julian—"

I kissed her, mostly to shut her up. I didn't want her to have expectations after this, and I was beginning to realize she would. And still, I couldn't stop myself.

Slowly, inch by inch, little by little, I thrust inside of her. She felt incredible, like nothing I'd ever felt before. The sensation of her walls tightening around me was indescribable.

My balls ached.

Her barrier pushed against the head of my cock. "I'm right there, baby. About to steal another part of you."

"I know. Just do it already."

I chuckled, and in one deep thrust I tore through her virginity. She gasped, clinging onto my back.

"I know it hurts, but I'll make it better." Reaching below, I rubbed her clit, trying to make this better for her.

"Yes…"

"Yeah? You okay?"

"Yes, I like that. Keep going."

"I'm going to start fucking you now."

She moaned, fisting the sheets as her head fell back against the bed. Preparing for the pain and pleasure my cock would bring.

Thrusting in and out, I played with her nub. Her pussy constricted every single time I massaged her clit up and down. The faster my fingers moved, the harder and deeper my thrusts became. It wasn't just her blood on my dick that made her soaking wet and drip down my balls.

Her cunt loved my cock.

Spasming.

Squirming.

Falling apart.

"Your pussy was made for me. How are you this fucking delicious?"

"I was made for you."

Hearing her affirm what I'd spent years disregarding was another emotion I wasn't expecting. Unable to confront the truth, I hid my face in the crook of her neck. Aware it wouldn't matter in the end—she owned my heart and soul.

Always had.

Always would.

Our mouths parted, both of us panting profusely, helpless against our bodies coming together as one. She gasped the second she felt my cock hit her g-spot, and I picked up the pace of my assault.

"Julian ... right there..."

"Here, baby? You want my cock, here?" My dick throbbed to come balls deep inside of her now.

"Oh, God ... yes ... right there..." Her moans got louder and louder, squeezing the hell out of my cock.

"Yeah, baby, just like that. Come hard for me."

"Yes... Don't stop ... please don't stop."

"I won't. I can't. You own me."

She pulsated, and her sweet pussy sucked my cock dry. I came so hard, my vision blurred, and my body trembled right along with hers. Both of us going over the edge together, where I could barely see straight. We stayed like that for I don't know how long, in our safe haven that would eventually turn into our hell. It felt as if an eternity had passed between us, and it still wasn't enough time with her.

It was never enough time with her.

Kissing all over her face again, I slowly, unwillingly, pulled out of her, causing her to wince from the sting of my dick.

"I'll be right back." I kissed the tip of her nose and got up, going straight into the bathroom. Needing a minute to myself for what I wasn't prepared to face. "Fuck." I looked in the mirror. "We didn't use a condom."

My emotions held me hostage while I cleaned myself up. Taking a solid breath, I dampened a washcloth and made my way back into my bedroom.

"Autumn—"

"Don't say it. Please don't ruin this for me." She was staring up at the ceiling. Lost in her own thoughts with my white sheet wrapped around her naked body.

"What exactly do you think I'm going to say?"

"That you regret it."

"Kid, look at me."

She did, her eyes already welling up with tears.

"Awe, baby." I went to her and kissed her lips.

"Every time something intimate happens between us, you always push me away after. Please, just give me this. I can't hear you say that you regr—"

"I don't."

"Really?"

I shook my head.

She sighed, fresh tears falling down the sides of her face.

"Don't cry for me, Autumn."

"They're happy tears."

I didn't want to ruin the moment, but I had to ask, "Are you on the pill?"

"Ummm … no."

"Fuck!" I sat up, and she went with me, grimacing when the bed hit her core. "You're going to be sore."

"It's fine. Don't freak out, okay? I'll get on the pill."

"A little late, kid."

"I mean for next time."

I arched an eyebrow. "Next time?"

"Yeah, there's going to be a next time, right?"

I opened my mouth to reply, but nothing came out.

"Julian, this isn't a one-time thing, right?"

"I need to clean you up."

The next thing I knew she was kissing all over my face, wrapping her arms and legs around me, seeking the comfort she needed in my embrace. I kissed her, softly pecking her lips, taking my time with each stroke of my tongue as it tangled with hers.

I tasted her tears.

Her hope.

Her love.

When I opened my eyes, I saw every sentiment I felt through her gaze. We locked eyes.

I surrendered.

To her.

To us.

Because for the first time, I didn't stop when she wholeheartedly expressed, "I love you," all in one breath.

twenty-one

Day Six of Press tour

H E COULDN'T EVEN GIVE ME A DAY TO FIGURE SHIT out.

Not. One. Fucking. Day.

We were supposed to be getting footage of him at the old junkyard he used to work at, not sitting at a rectangular mahogany table in the building he owned in Texas which was another extension of his office in Miami.

Of course, Julian Locke was sitting at the head of the table, and I was parallel to him with our lawyers by our sides. They were both personally flown in on Julian's private jet—God forbid he give me any time to think things over. I didn't want to involve lawyers. We could have worked this out on our own, but now I had no choice in the matter.

Like with everything, he'd stolen that away from me too.

For the last twenty minutes, all we did was fight back and forth over his ridiculous demands. He wanted joint custody, one week off, one week on, when we didn't live in the same state. Along with exchanging of holidays, switching each year on who would get Thanksgiving and Christmas. The last demand he had was a real kicker—Julian wanted our daughter to carry his last name.

I'm sorry, what?!

The desire to punch him and his stuffy lawyer, Anderson, in the face was palpable.

Especially when Anderson stated, "May I remind you, Miss Troy, that Mr. Locke has been more than flexible with the terms of his agreement."

"Flexible?" I choked out. "You call this flexible? He just found out about our daughter yesterday, and he hasn't even given me any time to explain anything to her. This is the complete opposite of flexible! This is entirely selfish on your part and utter bullshit, Julian! She doesn't even know who you are!"

"Whose fault is that, Autumn? It sure as hell isn't mine."

I glared at my lawyer. "He doesn't even know her name! Greg, do something!"

He nodded, looking over at them. "Miss Troy has been the sole parent for the last nine years—"

"I don't need to hear your bedtime story. She either agrees, or I'll take her to court for sole custody."

"Julian! Do you hear yourself? What the fuck? You can't do this to her!"

"I'm doing it *for* her. Big difference, kid."

"I'm trying to keep my calm, alright? Do you know how hard that is for me right now? Please." I paused to let my words sink in. "Just think about it for a second. She doesn't know you, and I know deep down you understand how hard it will be to uproot her from everything she's known for the last nine years. I promise I won't keep her from you. I want her to get to know you, but we can't do it the way you want."

"You've left me no choice."

"We don't even live in the same states. How is joint custody going to work?"

"I have three private planes, Autumn. Pick one."

"So you're just going to completely turn her life upside down? What about school? And her friends?"

"I can get her a private teacher, and she's a kid—she will make friends in no time."

"Do you hear how insane you sound? You! The man who

grew up from foster home to foster home. Why would you want her to go through that?"

"She's not being tossed away like I was. I'm her father, and I have just as many rights to her as you do, sweetheart."

"You're being unfair."

"I don't give a shit what you think I'm being. I stand by my demands. If you don't like it, I'll see you in court."

I wanted to bash his face in. "I've raised her for the last nine years, and no judge in their right mind would give you sole custody of a child who doesn't even know you."

"It's a risk I'm willing to take, but as you know, I never lose, kid."

"What is that?" I jerked back. "Is that a threat? You have judges in your back pocket, Julian?"

"What you're doing is called entrapment, Autumn. And I'm not stupid enough to fall for your desperate antics."

"I'm not trying to trap you. I'm just trying to make you see reason."

"What do you suggest we do?" He leaned back against his leather chair. "What's reasonable for you?"

I sighed in relief, feeling like I was starting to get somewhere with him. "I don't think joint custody is the right answer, and I'm not saying it's not something we can't discuss later, but for right now, it's too much for her. She needs to get to know you first."

"And what exactly does she know? Have you told her anything about me?"

"For the last year or so," I reluctantly gave in, but he'd left me no choice. "She's been asking who her father is."

"And?"

"And since she's so incredibly stubborn like you, I had to tell her, but I didn't give her your name. The last thing I wanted was for her to Google you and find out that you're Alpha CEO."

He narrowed his eyes at me, unaware of what I meant by that.

"You're an asshole. That's no surprise to you. The last thing I wanted was for her to find out the man you've become." I took a deep breath, already dreading the fact that I was going to admit this. "To say I was shocked when Claire called me to help you would be an understatement. It was like fate or something. I guess, I mean … I know. It's one of the reasons I agreed to take you on as a client. I thought … I hoped … I could change you back. Okay? I wanted to help you become the man I used to know, not for me, but for Capri."

"You named her Capri?"

"Yeah. I wanted her to have a part of you, and you always liked the name. I know it's silly, but it was something I could use without my family getting suspicious of who her father was. I couldn't give her your last name, Julian, so I worked with what I had."

"After knowing I was raised without a father, how could you do that to me? How could you betray me like this?"

"What was I supposed to do? You left me."

"I would have taken the first flight back if you'd told me, Autumn."

"And then what? Huh? What would have happened next?"

"It's really quite simple, kid."

Never did I expect him to declare, "I would have asked you to marry me, and we could have been a family."

Julian

"You don't mean that."

"I never say anything I don't mean."

"Other than when you're lying to me."

"If you're going to bring up our past every time you don't get your way, we're in for a rough road ahead."

"We're in one nonetheless." She abruptly stood. "You can't say shit like you would have asked me to marry you!"

"Whether you want to hear it or not, it's the truth."

"It's so easy for you to say that now, in retrospect, but back then … it wasn't like this. *You* weren't like this. You spent years pushing me away. Years, Julian!"

"I know, and you don't have to remind me every chance you get. I was there, Autumn."

"You're so fucking arrogant. How can you sit there and make all these demands when the only reason we're in this situation is because of you and your choices in the first place? You're the reason things went down this way."

I slammed my fist on the table, making her jump. "Don't you think I know that? I'm trying to make it right. I've been trying to make it right all week."

"It's going to take longer than a week to make things right between us, and now you're throwing our daughter in the mix, and it's not fair!"

"You want to know what's not fair? I'll tell you what's not fucking fair! First and foremost, missing out on your pregnancy, watching your stomach grow with our baby. Feeling her kick, seeing you pregnant with my child, glowing, radiant, and fucking breathtaking. The first ultrasound, finding out we're having a baby girl, and then preparing for it. Her birth, cutting the cord, seeing you hold her for the first time, me holding her for the first time, taking her home from the hospital, her first bath, her first steps, her first word, her first birthday! All the firsts I missed! Every. Single. One. Now that's not fucking fair! You took everything away from me, and you're damn lucky I'm not demanding to knock you up, so I don't miss out on those first again!"

She didn't just fall back—she stumbled from the truth of my words. With wide eyes, she replied, "Knock me up again? Are you hearing yourself? We're not together, Julian!"

"Again, not by my choice, sweetheart. If I thought for a

second there was a possibility of you saying yes, I'd get down on one knee and ask you to marry me, right here and now."

"I'm not eighteen anymore. You don't need to marry me because you got me pregnant."

"That's not the only reason I'd ask you to marry me, kid."

"I don't want to talk about this anymore."

"Great. Sign the papers then."

"Julian, please… I don't want to keep her from you. She deserves to know who you are and to have a father. I promise I'll do whatever I can to make this easy on all of us."

"If I agree to wait this out, what do I get out of this new arrangement?"

"You'll get to know your daughter."

"I'll get that regardless."

"I don't know. What do you want?"

I folded my arms over my chest. "I want a month."

"What?"

"You heard me."

"What does that mean? A month of what?"

"A month of getting to know our daughter."

"Julian, I don't understand—"

"For the next month, I want you and Capri to move in with me."

She jerked back. "Move in with you?"

"Take it or leave it."

"I can't move to Miami for a month."

"Not Miami. Here. In Texas."

"You want us to move into a penthouse suite?"

"No. I own a ranch about an hour out of Fort Worth. We can live there. It's close enough to your parents where we can see them, and I can try to fix what I broke with your parents and your brother."

"I have to work."

"No, you don't."

"Yes, I do."

"I'll handle Laurel."

"Laurel? What, you're on a first-name basis with my boss now?"

"She's going to make you partner, and that means you're in control. You can start your new position next month."

"I can't work, but you can?"

"I haven't taken a day off since I started Locke Enterprises. I'm more than due."

"What about the rest of your tour? Your announcement is in four days."

"My tour is over tomorrow, and I can make my announcement anywhere. Including the ranch."

"People are going to think we're a couple."

"They already do."

"Ugh! You have an answer for everything!"

"It's what makes me Alpha CEO."

She shook her head. "You're delusional if you think I'm going to agree to this."

"From where I'm sitting, you don't have much of a choice. Either you agree to my new terms, or you deal with settling this in court, where I go after full custody of Capri."

"Wow. Now you're bribing me?"

"Again, you've left me no choice."

Her stare shifted to her attorney. "Greg."

"Autumn, I think this is the best it's going to get. If he does take this to court, there's a huge chance he will win."

"How? He doesn't even know her."

"I know, but you're leaving it up to the judge and they could rule in his favor. He has money, and you lied to him about having a daughter—that'll hold up in court. I've seen it happen before."

Anderson added, "Mr. Locke is being more than fair, Miss Troy."

"Unbelievable. Now it's three against one?"

"Believe it, kid. This is your best option. You'll be there, and you can help me get to know our daughter and her to get to know me."

"I don't even know you."

"Then we can all get to know each other. After we finish the tour tomorrow in LA, we can fly straight from there to pick up Capri. You guys can pack, or I can buy you all new things. We can head back to Texas in the morning."

"Oh my God, Julian. This is too fast."

"On the contrary I'm being very lenient with you."

"You're being an asshole is what you are!"

"At this point, it's your term of endearment for me."

"I hope you can get our daughter to like you, because I sure as hell don't."

"I'll take that as a yes."

She threw the contract across the table. "I want my own room. Furthest away from yours."

I grinned, looking at Anderson. "Write it up."

For the next month, she would be mine. They both were.

And I was going to make damn sure it stayed that way.

twenty-two

Autumn

Once again, we were sitting in Julian's private jet. Except this time, we were flying from LA to San Diego, where I lived with our daughter. I couldn't believe this was happening. One minute we were fighting about his demand's, and the next he was hitting me with a whole new one, which might as well have been worse than his first ones.

I was stuck by his side for the next month, as if the last week wasn't hard enough. Now, we were also involving Capri, and I was sick to my stomach. I told her I was coming home, but I didn't tell her with who. I honestly didn't know what to say or where to start, and I knew Julian wasn't going to allow me to go by myself to get her. This was my only choice. He was going to meet her for the first time, and my nerves were on edge.

I swear I could strangle him for putting us through this. I never imagined he'd take it this far, and that was my first mistake.

Julian always got what he wanted. Especially when it came to me.

I anxiously waited in my seat, trying to play it off like I wasn't losing my shit.

"You need to relax."

"You need to go to Hell."

He chuckled. "You're going to have to reel in that feisty attitude once we're around Capri. You don't want her to think her mommy hates her daddy, do you?"

I glared at him. "I swear you're enjoying this."

"I'd be lying if I said I wasn't."

"You actually think this is going to go over well, don't you?"

"I'm going to try like hell to make sure it does. There's nothing I can't give her. *Either* of you."

"That's your answer to everything. Money can't buy love, Julian."

"You're right, but you loved me when I had nothing. Now I can offer you the world if you want it."

"I don't need the world."

"Then what do you need, Autumn?"

"I don't need anything. Especially from you."

"At some point you're going to have to forgive me, kid."

"I was starting to, but you fucked it all up again by making us move in with you. But it's what you do best. You always fuck things up in my life."

"I don't regret getting you pregnant, and if you'd let me, I'd do it again."

"Stop! Stop saying shit like that to me. If you say stuff like that in front of Capri she's going to—"

"Get the happy family I'm sure she's dreamed about with two parents who love each other and want the best for her?"

"I don't love you, Julian. How many more times do I have to say it for you to believe me?"

"I'm not the one who needs to believe it."

"Oh, that's rich."

"You might hate me, kid, but you also still love me. It's a very thin line, you and I."

"If you break Capri's heart like you broke mine, I'll take you for everything you're worth."

"You don't have to worry about me breaking anyone's heart, Autumn. It's you who holds that power now."

"You know what?"

"What, baby?"

"I fucking hate you."

"Great." He deviously smiled. "Now say it again until you believe it."

"We're done talking now." With that, I stood and walked into the back. Trying to find the bathroom, instead I found a bedroom. "Awesome, I wonder how many times he's joined the mile-high club?"

"I haven't."

He was standing behind me, and I could feel his heat searing into my body.

"Want to make me a member?"

I couldn't take it anymore—it was all too much to take. I felt as if I was that eighteen-year-old girl all over again, completely at his mercy. I snapped. Spinning around, I went for him. Hitting him on his chest. "I can't believe you're doing this to me! I hate you! Do you hear me, Julian? I fucking hate you!"

"That's enough!"

"Fuck you!"

He gripped onto my wrist, and in three strides I was on my back with him hovering above me on the bed.

"Get off of me!"

"Not until you calm the fuck down!"

"How do you expect me to when you're forcing your hand on everything?!" I thrashed my body around, trying to get free, but it was pointless. He was much stronger than me.

With one hand he held my wrists above my head, hooking them, while the other began skimming the inside of my thigh and I froze, locking eyes with him.

I cleared my throat, trying to steady my voice. "You're obviously ignoring what's in front of your face."

He looked me up and down. "Sweetheart, you're the only one that's in my face." Slowly, he slid his fingers higher. "What do you want to do about that?"

I had nowhere to go.

I could barely move.

"Because I can think of plenty of things to do with that sweet little mouth of yours that loves to push all of my buttons."

"I—"

"Did I say you could talk?"

My eyes widened, and mouth dropped. "Who the hell do you think you are? This is not how it's going to go, Mr. Locke."

"So, I'm Mr. Locke when my hand is near your pussy?" His eyes dilated, dark and daunting. "Or what, kid? What are you going to do? I'm not the one under you, now am I?"

I jerked my body around, trying to break out of his hold, but the second I felt his fingers get closer to my core I froze again.

"Miss Troy, you're not going anywhere unless I want you to."

"You can't keep doing this to me."

"And what's that? Making you wet?"

"Julian—"

"Oh, now I'm Julian again?"

I changed the subject. "I'm over your cockiness. It doesn't work on me."

He arrogantly smiled, calling my bluff and my body's response to him. Back and forth, he caressed the soft skin of my bare thighs. My breathing elevated, proving to him I was lying.

"I am doing what's in the best interest of our daughter, Autumn. You can think I'm asshole for it, but I honestly don't give a fuck. I've lost nine years of her life and I plan to make up for it. With or without your consent."

"You could still do that, and we don't have to move in with you for the next month. What the hell are you doing with a ranch in Texas anyway? You don't even live there anymore."

"If I tell you, what do I get?"

"What do you want?"

"*You.*"

My thighs clenched, hearing his response. Seconds later, his fingers glided closer to my core, and I resisted the urge to moan.

"What's wrong, sweetheart? Where's your smartass mouth? My tough girls gone? I guess she's not so tough when I'm lying on top of her."

I sucked in air, alarmed by his reply. He continued his gentle torture, loving the feel of my skin against his calloused fingers. As if reading my mind, he tilted his head to the side, enticing me with whatever he wanted to do. I could see, feel his internal struggle. Julian was fighting something deeper than what I imagined.

"You can't have me," I found myself saying, though I was torn. I may hate him, but my body seemed to love him.

"Fine," he stated. "I'll take your pussy in the meantime."

"You know what?" I challenged, my pussy challenging him for me. "I should just let you to make you back off."

"Kid, if you think that than you're surely mistaken."

"I'm serious."

"As am I."

"No, not about that… I mean about the ranch. Why do you own one?"

"If you must know, I've owned it for a while."

"Wait, what?"

"You heard me."

"I don't understand."

"You don't seem to these days. I'll make it very simple, I bought it for you. It even comes with farm animals like you've always wanted."

The memory of the day I told him my dream of owning a ranch and a farm played out in front of me like I was saying it to him right then and there.

"You gotta be kidding me?" You bought a ranch for me? Julian, we're not even together, that makes no sense."

"I have no intention of letting you leave."

"I don't care what your intensions are. I'm leaving when our contract is up."

"We'll see." He grinned. "Not that I need a reason for purchasing your fairytale, but Capri needs a steady home and she'll get that in Texas. We're near you family and that's important to me."

"What about Miami?"

"What about it?"

"You live there."

"I may live there, kid, but it's never been my home. Texas is where my heart is." The tips of his fingers lightly touched the edge of my panties. With a wicked expression, he taunted, "Should I keep going?"

"What does it matter what I say? You're going to do what you want anyway."

He grinned again, and instead of pushing my panties aside, he simply grazed my folds through the silk fabric. "I know you want me to touch you, and all you have to do is say the magic word."

I cunningly smiled. "Fuck off."

"I'd much rather fuck you."

When his finger slid over my clit, I released a heady moan, my body once again betraying my mind.

Causing me to counter the same words he bribed me with at my hotel suite, "I'll make you an offer you can't refuse."

twenty-three

He arched an eyebrow. "We're making sex deals now?"

"Why not? You've been making them for everything else. My offer is I'll have sex with you right now."

"If?"

"If you'll let me tell Capri about you alone."

He opened his mouth to reply.

"No," I sternly interrupted. "Hear me out. I want to tell her who you are and that you're with me, by myself. I don't care where you are, you can wait in the car if you want. But please… let me talk to her first. I need to try to explain things to her before she meets you. I haven't seen my girl since I've been with you and I'd like to tell her what's going on, on my own. Can you give me this? Please, Julian."

His gaze zeroed in on me, thinking about it for a second. There was so much emotion behind his stare, and I knew it mirrored mine. There was no need for words. Our eyes spoke for themselves as his fingers began to really caress me. My mouth parted, and he laid his forehead on top of mine, his lips inches away from my mouth.

I could feel his erection.

Inhale his musky scent.

I felt him everywhere and all he was doing was rubbing my clit. His fingers were soft yet demanding, controlling yet eager, and fucking intense as all hell. I couldn't remember the last time I had a man's hands on me in this way, between being a full-time mom and having a full-time job, both of them occupied most of my time.

On top of that, I never found another man who caught my attention quite like Julian. Through the years, I often wondered if I'd ever find someone and be able to move on from him. He may have broken my heart, but a huge part of me felt like it didn't matter—he owned my soul. I had no interest in dating or to give my heart to someone else.

Maybe you were only allowed a love like ours once in a lifetime and I guess I'd become complacent with that.

Peering into his eyes, I erratically breathed out, "Julian." Trying to catch my next breath, I added, "Do we have a deal?"

My thoughts.

My words.

They all seemed to be intertwined with one another.

Especially when he slipped my panties to the side, touching my pussy for the first time in over a decade. I shuddered against him, melting into his caress, wanting to kiss him.

Why wasn't he kissing me? I refused to demand it.

His rough fingers moved to my opening, soaking up my wetness before he glided them back and forth on my clit. "Fuck, you're so wet," he growled. "Your pussy has always been so responsive to me, it's one of the many things I love about you."

Did he just say he loved me? I refused to ask that too.

He slid his fingers into my core, ordering, "Fuck my hand, Autumn." Curving his fingers toward my g-spot, he rhythmically stimulated it in a come-hither motion. I began to rock against him as he increased his speed, harder and faster he manipulated me. No one knew my body quite like Julian, he was the first and last man to give me an orgasm.

"Please," I shamelessly begged. "Make me come…"

He released another growl from deep within his chest,

vibrating against my breasts. I opened my eyes needing to look at him. He was staring at my face through a hooded gaze, completely taking me in. Showing everything I always wanted to see.

His love.

His devotion.

His regret.

It poured out of him, and I had to close my eyes again.

Don't fall for his trap. You're just doing this for Capri. It's a deal. Nothing more. You don't love him anymore.

Softly, he rubbed his lips against my mouth. "When's the last time someone touched your pussy, kid?"

"Really?" I panted. "You want to talk about this right now?"

"I can't think of a better time than now." He fucked me faster with his fingers, and I rode him harder.

"I don't know… it's been… a while."

I didn't have to open my eyes to know that he was smiling wide.

"How many men have you been with since me?"

"I'm… not…" He worked me over fervently. "Jesus… that feels amazing…"

"I'm waiting, kid."

"What?" I shook my head, overwhelmed by his touch and questions.

"Men, Autumn. How many?"

"Oh… god…" My eyes rolled to the back of my head. "None of… oh fuck… business…" I bit my bottom lip, feeling my legs quiver and my pussy pulsate. "Don't ask questions… you don't want… answers to."

"Is that right?" he asked in a devilish tone, breathing into the side of my neck, making shivers crawl up my skin and throughout my entire body. "You're not being a good girl." Before I could retort, he slapped my pussy, catching me off guard and my body jolted forward. "You want me to finish you off?"

"If you don't, I'll kill you."

He smiled with nothing but mischief in his eyes. "Then answer my question."

"Ugh!" I fell back against the bed. "Four."

His eyes glazed over with a predatory regard that made my stomach flutter.

"Including me," he stated as a question.

"Yes."

He leaned forward, close to my mouth. "Was one of them good ol' fucking Charlie, Cherry?"

"I'm not answering that."

"Oh, you'll answer it."

"I don't want you to get him fired."

"You just did."

"Julian! You better leave him alone."

His fingers slid back inside me, causing my back to arch. "Did any of them make you come?"

Giving him what he sought, I admitted, "No."

"I'll tell you why," he adamantly affirmed. "It's because I'm the only man who knows where and how to touch you, I know how to lick you and how hard to fuck you." His voice was laced with possession. "You're mine, Autumn. I'm yours. Always and forever, kid."

I whimpered into his mouth, but he quickly repositioned his face in between my legs and I just about came undone when I felt his tongue on my clit—licking, sucking, tasting. Devouring me as if he had something to prove.

"Say it," he insisted, eating and finger fucking me still. "Who do you belong to?"

"Not a chance."

Deeply, he growled, for a much different reason that time.

"You don't have to say it. Your squirting pussy will do it for you."

"Julian…" I let go, coming all over his face and fingers.

After I was done riding the high that was Julian Locke, he looked profoundly into my eyes as he got up off the bed. Slipping his fingers into his mouth, he licked them clean.

Simply stating, "Your pussy doesn't hate me, Autumn. You still taste as sweet as ever."

twenty-four

W E DIDN'T TALK FOR THE REST OF THE FLIGHT. *What could we say after that?* It was a clusterfuck. Now we were sitting in the backseat of an SUV, Julian was on the phone yelling at someone while I looked out the window, lost in my own thoughts as the driver drove us to my home. I was a wrecking ball of emotions, good and bad. I couldn't believe I allowed him to touch me. I didn't think it through. All I did was evoke more feelings I thought were long gone.

They weren't.

They were staring me in the face, like a fucking beacon of bright lights. Blinding my sight with nothing but conflicting emotions about him, us, our family.

Shit. Did I just say our family? You're not a family, Autumn. He's the father of your child. You're moving in with him for Capri to get to know him with you being there to make the transition easier for her. This is for your daughter.

Not. For. You.

Not. For. Him.

I repeated the words, desperately trying to believe them. I should have never let him touch me. It just added more fire to our already blazing inferno.

"Robert," Julian bit. "You either make it happen or I'll find someone who will." With that, he abruptly hung up his call.

"Wow, you're just peachy keen to everyone today."

Smirking, he placed his cellphone back into his suit jacket. "You of all people should know my patience wears thin."

"You are aware our daughter is going to test all your limits, right?"

"She's different."

"How? Patience is not your virtue. You just admitted it yourself."

"I have over nine years to make up for, Autumn. My patience is going to be endless when it comes to her."

"We'll see." I looked at the driver. "You can pull up to my window and I'll punch in my code into the security box."

"Or you could just give it to him."

My gaze shifted to Julian's statement. "I don't want you to have access to my neighborhood."

"We're back to this?"

I ignored him, dialing the code.

"Let me guess, it's either your birthday or Capri's?"

"Nope."

"Would you tell me if it was?"

"Nope." I looked at the driver. "It's the house at the end of the road, 2473."

He nodded through the mirror and moments later we were pulling into my driveway. My home was beautiful, it was three stories, coastal living kind of vibes since we were on the water. It was perfect for Capri, Emily, and me. Emily was our nanny, she'd been with us since Capri was three. I actually met her through one of my mom's friends, she was around her age, and had moved with us through a couple of cities and states. She was the best and we were lucky to have her.

"You did good for yourself, kid. Your home is beautiful. I'm sure Capri has fond memories here."

The satisfaction I felt by hearing him say those words was a feeling I didn't think I'd have.

"Thanks."

"When you're ready for me to come inside, you know where to find me."

I nodded, instantly feeling relieved he was following through on our deal. Although, I knew he meant his statement as a double innuendo. "Okay." I opened the door, but at the last second, I turned around. "Oh, and umm… thank you for allowing me to talk to Capri alone. I appreciate it and I know she will too."

"I would have allowed it regardless of you coming in my mouth."

My gaze snapped to the driver. "I'm sorry you had to hear that."

He chuckled. "I've driven for Mr. Locke for a long time. There's nothing I haven't heard."

I shot Julian a questionable expression, wondering how many women he might have entertained in the back of his car.

"I have an extended office in San Diego as well."

"Great, is there any state you don't have an office in?"

"I own the world."

"I see that."

"And now I have a family to enjoy it with."

"Julian, I'm not your family."

"You've always been my home."

I knew I wouldn't win this argument with him, so I shut the door and made my way toward the entrance of my house. My heart was beating out of my chest, I had no idea what I was going to say or how I was going to say it to her. I figured it would be easier and smoother if I spoke from my heart and not a speech I had prepared.

Capri could always see through me, she had the same power as her dad. It was one of the reasons I moved from Texas to begin with. The older she got, the more she started to possess a lot of his traits or maybe it was obvious to me since I knew the truth.

His stubbornness.

His perceptiveness.

Having no filter.

She was wicked smart like him too. She even had some of his mannerisms, holding her fork in the same way he did, she was left-handed like him. Loved old classic cars like Julian.

It was surreal.

Capri had my appearance, but she was her father's daughter in every other way. Pushing away those thoughts, I inhaled a solid breath as I unlocked the door and walked inside.

"Capri?" I called out, laying my purse on the entryway table.

"I'm in the kitchen with Emily, Momma!"

Quickly, I rushed into the kitchen. Excited to see my girl.

"Momma!" She jumped into my arms. "I missed you so much! I'm so happy you're home early! I thought you weren't coming back until tomorrow?"

I tightly squeezed her against my chest. My girl was getting so big. She'd be ten in a couple of months.

"I missed you, baby." I kissed the top of her head.

"Momma, are you okay?" See, perceptive as all hell.

I nodded, glancing at Emily. "Thank you for everything."

"Of course. I'll let you two get reacquainted. I'm going to get the groceries for the week."

"Oh, yeah… umm… you can just buy groceries for yourself. Capri and I won't need anything."

"We won't?" Capri asked, looking up at me. "Are we going somewhere?"

I nervously laughed. "Something like that."

"Sounds great," Emily replied. "You can tell me all about when I get back."

I smiled, and she left.

Giving my girl another big hug, I coaxed, "Baby, we need to talk." Julian was waiting in the SUV, I didn't have a lot of time to tell her what was going on, needing to get right to the point sooner rather than later.

"Am I in trouble?"

"No, you're not in trouble, but what we need to talk about is serious, so let's go in the living room and sit down."

"Okay."

Once we were sitting on the couch, I grabbed her hands in my lap.

"Momma, you look really pale. Are you sure you're alright?"

"Mmm-hmm… I'm just having a little trouble finding the right words to say."

The concern was evident on her beautiful face. "What's this about?"

"You know how I told you that I was taking on a client that I used to know?"

"Yeah, you spent the last week with him, right?"

"Yes, I did."

"Is this about him?"

"Yes, baby, it is."

"What is it? Do you like him or something? Because it wouldn't bother me, Momma. I'd love to have a daddy. All my friends have daddies."

"Honey." I paused, needing a second. It absolutely killed me she missed out on having a father and was starting to feel his absence so profoundly. I tried my best, always playing both roles, but in the end… she longed for her dad. Making me feel intensely guilty I waited this long to tell him.

Maybe I was wrong?

Resisting the urge to cry, I pushed through. "On the topic of that, do you remember when you asked me about your dad?"

"Yeah. Why? Is this about him?"

"Yes, baby, it is."

Her eyes lit up like a Christmas tree. "Momma! Tell me! Please!"

"I'm getting there. There's just no easy way to say this to you."

"Just say it, Momma. I'm a big girl, I can handle it."

"You are a big girl, but you'll always be my baby."

She smiled. "I know. Now tell me! What is it?"

"Okay, here goes nothing. So, the client I've been with this last week, well… he's… I mean… it's your dad."

She jerked back. "I don't get it. Your client is my daddy?"

"Mmm-hmm. It's one of the reasons I took him on as a client."

"You've been with my daddy this whole last week?"

"I have."

"Why didn't you tell me?"

My heart dropped, the last thing I wanted was for her to be upset with me. I couldn't take it. Not after everything Julian has put me through.

"I hadn't seen him in a very long time, sweetie."

"How long?"

"Since before you were born."

"Why?"

"He moved away."

"Oh…" She considered it for a minute. "Did he know about me?"

I shook my head. "No, baby, he didn't."

"Why didn't you tell him?"

"Listen, it's a long story, and it really doesn't matter."

"But does he know about me now?"

"Yes." I nodded. "And he's very excited to meet you and get to know you too."

She beamed. "Really? My daddy wants to be my daddy?"

My heart was breaking into a million pieces. "Yes, honey, he would love that."

"Really, Momma? You swear? You promise?"

"Cross my heart."

"Then when can I get to meet him? Today? Tomorrow? Oh,

please, Momma! Please! Can I meet him soon? I'll be a good girl! I'll be the best girl!"

Talk about a kick to my stomach. "You're always my best girl."

"Yay! When can I meet him? Please say soon!"

"Well, babe, you can actually meet him right now."

She jumped up off the couch. "What?! He's here? Where?"

"He's outside in the SU—"

She took off.

"Capri! Wait!"

She didn't listen, not that I expected her to. This wasn't going how I imagined. If I thought my heart was beating fast when I walked through the front door, there was no comparison to how it was pounding now. I hurried behind her, trying to catch up with her pace, but she was too fast. Too excited. Too eager. Nothing was going to hold her back, not even me.

The door swung open and I knew my whole life would never be the same. It wasn't just Capri and me anymore. Now our lives were about to...

Forever intertwined with Julian's.

Julian

When the front door opened, I never expected to see our daughter hauling ass out of it. From that point forward, I moved in autopilot. Swinging open the door, I stepped out of the SUV and rounded the back. Coming face to face with a mini Autumn. I gasped at the sight of her. She was breathtakingly beautiful, exactly like her mother. She had freckles on her nose and cheeks, green eyes and bright red hair.

She halted in front of me, smiling wide. "Hi, I'm Capri."

I tugged on the end of her hair. "I know who you are, sweetheart."

She giggled, sounding so much like her mother at that age. "Momma says she's been with you all week! She said you wanted to meet me, and I've always wanted to meet you too. But Momma says you didn't know about me, and I don't know why she didn't tell you, but she says it doesn't matter. Will you tell me? You don't have to tell me now! I'm so happy to finally meet you! My name is Capri Marie Troy and I'm a super cool girl. I have a lot of friends at school and I'm really smart. All my classes are advanced. My best subject is math! I love numbers. Did you know that?"

I shook my head, trying to keep up with everything she was sharing. Hearing and seeing her for the first time was almost just crippling as not knowing anything about her.

"I'm sorry. I talk really fast when I'm excited and I'm just so excited to meet you! But I can tell you everything and all about me! Is that okay? Do you want to know?"

Choked up from all the emotions, I expressed, "I'd love that more than anything."

"Okay, good! I love to talk. It's one of my favorite things. Momma says I can talk her ear off and my teachers nicknamed Chatty Capri, but you can call me anything you want. Momma usually calls me baby even though I'm a big girl. I'll be ten in five months! Momma says I still can't have a cellphone." She rolled her eyes. "Maybe when I'm eleven."

I swear I was thrown back to another place and time, sitting in Christian's truck with Autumn in the backseat, asking for my cellphone.

"Do you live here? Are you close? Can I come to your house?"

"Your mom didn't tell you?"

Autumn walked up to us, mirroring the expression on my face. "She didn't give me a chance."

"Tell me what?" Capri enthusiastically asked.

"You're going to move in with me."

She gasped. "We are?"

"Yes, but only for a—"

I cut Autumn off, "You're moving into my ranch in Texas."

"Texas?!" she squealed. "Oh my God! I love it there! Are we close to Grammy and Grampy? I miss them so much."

"Yes," I replied. "You can see them as much as you want."

Before I could get another word in, she threw her arms around my waist, hugging me as hard as she could. "I'm so happy! Thank you! Thank you!"

I blinked away my tears and cleared my throat. "I'm happy too." I closed my eyes and held her as tight as I could against me too, trying my best to keep it together.

Capri was the first to pull away, and I resisted the urge to pull her back toward me and never let her go. I locked stares with Autumn when I opened my eyes. She was hugging herself in a comforting gesture, with tears in her eyes.

"Momma!" Capri hugged her next, looking back at me.

Although, my stare never wavered from her mothers.

"Daddy," Capri said for the first time, instantly tearing my attention to her. "When do we leave?" She must have misinterpreted the expression on my face. "Oh, I mean… is that okay? Can I call you my daddy?" Looking up at me, she waited for an answer with nothing but love in her eyes.

Her mom used to look at me in the same way. I'd give anything for her mom to look at me like that again.

"Capri, baby girl, I'd…" I couldn't form words. Never did I imagine I'd be a father. I didn't date or do relationships, my life consisted of work and casual sex. Right then, in that moment, I'd give my soul to the devil to have the last nine years with my daughter. From the second Autumn told me she was pregnant. "I would be honored if you called me daddy."

"Yay!" she exclaimed, jumping into my arms again. "We're going to finally be a family!"

"Capri," Autumn cautioned, and I recognized that tone.

There was no hesitation on my part, I tugged her into the side of my body. Holding my entire world in my arms in what seemed like a lifetime.

I gazed down at our daughter, simply stating the truth, "Yes, baby girl. We're going to be a family."

twenty-five

Packing was taking longer than expected and we decided to leave tomorrow morning instead. Julian invited himself to spend in the night in my house. He was going to sleep in the guest bedroom. Yesterday didn't turn out as planned, and although we did share his penthouse suite, we steered clear of each other, both of us lost in our own thoughts.

The anxiety I felt having him in my home wasn't as emotion I'd expected. This was my safe haven, the place I'd go to escape the stressors of life. He was invading my personal space in a way I wasn't prepared for or anticipated. It didn't help that he was bonding with Capri right off the bat. He was in her room, helping her pack while I cooked dinner.

It felt like we were playing house, and it was too close for comfort.

Capri walked into the kitchen alone.

"Where's your dad?"

"He's taking a shower and asked me to tell you he needed a towel."

Julian clean.

Wet.

Naked.

It sounded like a bad idea to me, but I couldn't exactly say that to Capri. I nodded, grabbing a few from the linen closet before walking across the house toward the guest bedroom.

I knocked on the door. "Julian?"

He didn't answer, so I opened the door to find the bedroom and bathroom empty. I realized all too quickly the son of a bitch probably had the balls to use my shower. Stomping one foot in front of the other, I marched into my bedroom, and the first thing I heard was the sound of the shower in my sanctuary.

I shook my head, the audacity of that man. As soon as I opened the door, I shrieked and instantly placed my hand over my heart while my other hand was firmly placed on the doorknob. There was Julian, in all his naked glory, water glistening off his chiseled physique. He was freshly showered and stepping out onto the tile.

My gaze shifted from his face, to his chest, to the place I had no business looking.

His cock.

Jesus.

I. Stopped. Breathing.

Licking my lips, I actually envisioned myself licking from the V in between his hips and tracing my tongue down to his dick. The memories of us showering together and having sex under the showerhead immediately assaulted my mind.

When my lustful glare finally met his, I noticed the cockiest fucking grin plastered on his handsome face, and it instantly washed away all the desire I was feeling for him. It didn't matter he was fully aware of the effect he still had on me which was more than likely the reason he decided to use my shower instead of the one in the guest bedroom. Knowing I'd walk in here with a towel in my hands to drool over his perfect dick.

"What are you doing in here?" I asked, throwing the towel at him, and he caught it mid-air.

"What does it look like I'm doing, kid? I'm showering," he simply stated, drying off and not bothering to cover his cock.

"No shit, smart ass. But why are you showering in my room?"

"I wasn't aware you assigned showers for your guests."

I rolled my eyes. "Don't play that game with me. You know exactly what you're doing. Down to telling Capri to ask me to bring you a towel."

"I don't know what you're implying. All I wanted was to shower. It isn't my fault you don't know how to control yourself, and you're still staring at my cock."

"Oh my God! Then fucking cover it!"

He laughed, wrapping the towel around his waist. "Seeing as I have no clothes, I might have to wear just this towel for the rest of the night."

"I'm sure I can find something of Christian's for you. He's always leaving his clothes behind when he comes to visit."

"Or I can use the clothes you've stolen from me over the years."

"Like I still have them."

"I saw my black hoodie in your closet, kid."

My mouth dropped open. "You snooped through my things?"

"No, but it got you to admit you still have my shit."

I glared at him.

"You shouldn't poke the bear."

"Oh, so you're the bear now? Here I thought you were the asshole."

He winked. "Sweetheart, I can be both."

"You're just a shameless bastard at this point."

"At least I'm not asking you to call me daddy."

"Ewww ... don't ever say that again."

He chuckled, tugging on the ends of my hair. "Have I told you how beautiful you look today?"

I smirked. "Just today?"

"You know you're drop-dead gorgeous, kid."

"What's with the flattery? What do you want?"

"For you to tuck me in."

"It's too early for your bedtime, Mr. Locke."

"We're back to Mr. Locke, are we?"

Backing away from the bathroom, I informed, "Dinner's almost ready. I don't think your hoodie is going to fit you anymore. You're bigger than you were back then."

He arched an eyebrow. "How about my cock? Is that bigger too?"

"No." I shrugged. "It wasn't ever that big to begin with."

He growled as he reached for me, but I was quicker and jumped out of his grasp.

"I'll get you some of Christian's clothes. Don't come out of my room. I don't want to scar our daughter with her thinking men are all this small."

This time I wasn't fast enough, and he threw me over his shoulder and smacked my ass so fucking hard.

"Julian!"

"I'll show you fucking small, kid."

"Put me down!"

"Keep your voice down, or our daughter is going to think I'm torturing you."

"Umm … you're spanking me! Same difference!"

"If you'd be a good girl, you wouldn't need any discipline."

"Julian, put me down!"

He did, tossing my ass on my bed. Except, he hovered over my body and caged me in with his arms around my face. My heart beat rapidly against his chest, feeling his dick against my core.

To prove his point, he thrust against my pussy. "How's that for small?"

I smiled. "Didn't feel a thing."

With that, he flipped me over and pinned my hands above my head, locking my wrists together.

Rasping, "I used to love you in this position."

I inadvertently moaned.

"There's my good girl."

When his hand slipped in between my legs, Capri called out, "Momma, Daddy? Where did you guys go?"

"I guess it's true what they say about kids being little cock blockers." He let me go, and I got up, slapping him on the chest.

"Don't look so disappointed," he teased. "You could always play with your pussy later with the arsenal of toys you have in your drawer."

My face paled. "You *did* snoop through my thi—"

Capri walked in. "There you are." She peered back and forth between us, smiling. "What are you guys doing?"

"I was just about to get your dad some clothes. Do you know where Uncle Christian left his sweats and sweater the last time he was here?"

"I think they're in the laundry room cabinet. I'll get it for you, Daddy." She excitingly ran out of the room.

"Payback's a bitch," I threatened in a lighthearted tone. "Just wait until I snoop through your things."

"What's mine is yours—you can look through anything."

I tried to hide the smile on my face as I walked out the room to go finish dinner, playing it off like his words didn't affect me.

Julian

Autumn cooked my favorite dish, and we ate together as a family. It was crazy how effortless this was. How natural it felt being here in her home, watching as she finished up dinner while Capri set the table. I enjoyed watching their routine, thankful to be a part of it. How Autumn was able to balance being a successful publicist, and a loving and attentive mother was not lost on me.

It was sexy as fuck.

She was amazing with our daughter, and I could tell that

she and Capri were very close. Seeing their special relationship warmed my heart. Making me realize how much I'd truly missed out on.

After Autumn introduced Emily to me, she told her to stay and eat with us, but Emily didn't want to intrude, saying she wanted us to eat together alone.

During dinner, Capri asked, "Daddy, what was your high and low today?"

I cocked my head to the side. "High and low?"

"Yes. My high was meeting you, my low was eating this broccoli."

I chuckled.

"It's just this thing we do during dinner."

Capri nodded. "Momma, what was yours?"

"Well, my high was coming home to you. My low was… I don't think I had a low today."

"That was your high, kid?"

Her eyes burned, understanding my subtle reference to what had happened on my plane earlier today."

"Kid?" Capri noted. "Why do you call Momma kid? She's not a kid. She's big."

"She wasn't always."

"You knew Momma when she was a kid?"

"I've known her since she was born."

She beamed. "Really?"

I nodded.

"What was she like? When she was my age?"

"A lot like you."

"That's what everyone says."

"She was always up to no good."

"Not true," Autumn disagreed. "I was always a good girl."

"And look how much that's changed."

"How did you know Momma?"

"Well, I was her b—"

"I think that's enough questions for tonight."

"Oh, come on, Momma…"

I grinned, loving the fact I had another teammate now. Two against one were always the best odds. After Autumn finished clearing the table, she told Capri to go get ready for bed while loading the dishwasher.

I grabbed the glass out of her hand. "You cooked—I got this."

"You're going to clean up?"

"I do know how to load a dishwasher."

She smiled. "You're Alpha CEO now. I assumed you had maids who do everything for you."

"I do, but you're not my maid, kid."

Taking the glass out of my grasp, she suggested, "Why don't you go tuck Capri in. I'm sure she'd love that. She picks out a book, and I read it to her, but she's usually passed out before I get to the third page."

I didn't want to intrude on their time. "Are you sure?"

"I've read her a bedtime story for the last nine years. I think I can give you one night."

"You know I'm going to want a lot more than one night."

"I know, but let's begin with one."

"Fair. I'd like for Capri's life to stay as normal as possible, and also for Emily to live at the ranch with us."

"I'd love that."

"Great. Let her know I'll be responsible for her salary now."

She shook her head. "You don't need to pay her. I've been pay—"

"You have me now."

"You're not going to let me win this, are you?"

"I don't lose, kid."

"Fine."

I left before she could change her mind, walking up the stairs to Capri's room. She was already laying in her bed with a book in her hands. Her bright green eyes lit up when she realized I'd be tucking her in.

I didn't have to look up to know Autumn was watching us from the doorway, listening to every word I was reading. I could feel her presence anywhere, and for years I felt it from states away. Although, Capri fell asleep in the crook of my arm, I continued until I was done with the story. I didn't want to let her go. I was going to capture every moment for as long as I could. Once I was done, I kissed her forehead.

"Hmm… I love you, Daddy."

I froze hearing her say those words to me for the first time. Letting my lips linger, I replied, "I love you too, baby."

By the time I actually left Capri's room, it was well into midnight. On my way to the guest bedroom, I walked by Autumn's door. It was closed, and I resisted the urge to open it and demand to sleep in her bed. I'd been demanding everything else, and this shouldn't be any different.

When my hand was on the doorknob, I heard her exclaim, "That son of a bitch!"

I smiled, I couldn't help it. Deciding I didn't need to sleep in her bed for her to know I was near. She was about to play with herself, thinking about me.

Too bad for her…
I stole all her toys.

twenty-six

Julian

"Wow," Capri breathed out, looking all around. We'd just taken off. "You have your own plane?"

"I have three."

"My daddy has three planes! That's so cool! Momma, did you hear?"

"I heard." Autumn was sitting the furthest away from me, staring out the window.

She was quiet which was never a good thing. It usually meant she was overthinking. It didn't matter that she was no longer the eighteen-year-old girl I'd left, her personality hadn't changed. I could still read her like the back of my hand. She might have thought she wasn't the same young girl, but in reality, she absolutely was.

"Daddy, what do you do that you have so much money?"

I chuckled, and Autumn scolded, "Capri! You can't ask—"

"I'm an entrepreneur, and you can ask me anything."

Autumn groaned, snapping her attention out the window.

"What does entrepreneur mean?"

"It means I made something from nothing."

"Oh, that's so cool. How do I do that? I want to make a lot of money too."

"Capri!"

I laughed. She had no filter, exactly like me. "I'll tell you what, baby girl. You can take over my empire one day."

"Really?" Her gaze went wide. "I can be an entrepreneur too! Momma, did you hear? I'm going to be just like Daddy!"

Autumn pinched the bridge of her nose. "Julian, do you have any pain meds? I have a pounding headache."

I pressed the button by my chair.

"Yes, Mr. Locke," Katie, the stewardess, announced through the speakers.

"I'd like some ibuprofen."

"Yes, sir. I'll be right out."

"Daddy, do you always order people around?"

I grinned.

"Momma says I'm bossy." She shrugged, giggling. "I guess I get it from you."

"You're too smart for your own good." In my eyes, she was perfect.

"Daddy, do you think we can get a puppy?"

"Capri," Autumn chimed in. "I already told you. I don't have time to take care of a puppy."

"I know, Momma, but it'd be *my* puppy, so I would take care of it."

"I can barely get you to clean your room."

"Why do I have to clean my room when we have a cleaning lady?"

I nodded. "Valid point."

Autumn rolled her eyes. "Why do you think we have a cleaning lady?"

"But, Momma, a puppy would give me responsibilities. Don't you want me to be a responsible child?"

This kid.

"No puppy, Capri."

"I didn't ask you—I asked my daddy."

"Sweetheart, don't speak to your mother like that." I winked at her. "Even though you have a solid argument."

She smirked, reminding me so much of her mother. Christian was right—I swear, Capri could be Autumn's twin.

"Daddy, can I tell you about all my favorite things?"

"I'd love that."

She unbuckled her seatbelt and walked across the aisle to sit next to me. For the next hour, she did all the talking. Catching me up on her favorite colors, shows, books, clothes, numbers, food, ice cream, and everything else in between. I loved every single second of it.

When she grabbed my hand, laying her head on my arm, I was a fucking goner. She had me wrapped around her little finger, and I'd only met her a few hours ago. Kissing the top of her head, I allowed my lips to linger for a moment before I leaned my chair back and laid against the headrest. I never slept much, but having my baby girl holding me close made it easy to pass out.

I woke up to the airplane landing, and Capri was now in my arms, her head on my chest with half her body over mine. There was a blanket covering us, and I didn't have to wonder who did that, knowing it was Autumn. Our stares connected. Her eyes were red, and her face was flushed. She'd been crying.

I cocked my head to the side, silently asking.

She replied, "I just have a migraine."

I opened my mouth to respond, but the pilot announced through the speakers we were home. Unaware of how true his words were, Capri grabbed my hand, holding the stuffed animal I'd bought for her, not wanting to meet her for the first time emptyhanded.

My driver was waiting for us on the tarmac. I opened the door for Capri and Autumn. After they were inside the SUV, I sat down, and Capri slid closer to my side again. I could sense Autumn was getting jealous of the attention she was giving me. She was used to having her all to herself. Instead of allowing it to become an issue, I moved a seat over from her, leaving the empty one in the middle for Capri.

Autumn hid back a smile when she realized I'd done that for her.

Autumn

In less than an hour, we were driving past the gold security gates of Julian's estate. To say this ranch was massive would be a definite understatement. I'd seen some huge properties with my clients, but this one might take the cake. We drove down a long, circular driveway which was surrounded by beautiful land-scaping and a fence that looked like it was made out of high-end wood. No one could see onto the land unless they had access to enter though the security box.

A ranch-style home was in the center of the open field, sur-rounded by stone pathways in between the tall columns that split up the different wings of the house. There was a big garage port on the side of the main home, where I imagined several of Julian's vehicles were housed. The smell of the farmhouse from the back of the estate made me smile wide.

"Wow, Daddy." Capri took the words right out of my mouth. "Is this where we're going to live?"

He simply nodded as if this place wasn't incredible. His driver parked in front of the courtyard doors, revealing four older women dressed in maid uniforms. They greeted us as we exited the SUV. Of course, Julian instantly dismissed them with a wave of his hand.

"You don't have to be an asshole to everyone, you know?" I whispered in his ear.

"But it's one of my best qualities, kid."

I rolled my eyes, walking into the house where angled grand

stairs were the first thing you see. It opened to a wide foyer with shiny marble floors. Walls as far as I could see. I let go of Capri's hand, knowing she wanted to look around and wander.

"Daddy! Can I go see my room?"

He gestured to one of the maids, who quickly took over and led her up the stairs, away from us.

My jaw dropped as I turned in a full circle, taking in my surroundings. I only stopped to look at him. He nodded again with a small smile playing on his lips, giving me the okay to go explore. I made my way into the stunning main sitting area. The sun was shining bright through every window in the wide-open space, illuminating the furniture and décor.

I heard his footsteps coming in my direction, abruptly stopping when they were close. I turned around, peering at him as he leaned against the archway, his strong arms crossed over his chest.

"This house is exactly what I described to you, Julian."

"I'm fully aware."

"How did you find this?"

"I had it built like this for you."

"What?" My voice echoed through the mansion.

His intense gaze never left mine. "I bought the land and had it built several years ago. It was initially supposed to be an investment property that I would eventually sell off, but I could never bring myself to actually do it. Up until yesterday, I had every intention of following through, but when the terms of our agreement changed, I figured the time had finally come to put your ranch to good use."

"Julian … several years? We only just saw each other a week ago. Why did you build my dream home when we weren't in each other's lives?"

"It's really quite simple, kid. I was going to come back for you."

My eyes widened. "What? When?"

"After I bought the land."

"Then why didn't you?"

"Because old habits die hard. I broke your heart and didn't know where to begin to piece it back together. Each year, I told myself this would be the year I'd come for you. Then the following would come around, and history repeated itself. I just didn't know where to start with you anymore."

"Oh my God."

He stepped toward me, and I stepped back, holding my hand up to stop him. He raised his hands in a surrendering gesture, meaning me no harm. However, it wasn't his caress I was afraid of this time. His words were affecting me far more than his touch.

"All I want is to make a life with you here, Autumn."

"Julian, my mind is spinning."

"For the first time in my life, mine isn't. I'm standing in front of you, hoping that you'll stand with me."

"Jesus," I breathed out. "And I thought you were coming on strong before."

"I go after what I want. It's who I am, it's how I'm made. I don't ask for anything, kid. Yet, here I am, asking you to be with me. Truly be with me. Out in the open—no secrets, no hiding. Where we're together and nothing else matters. I know you still love me, and I'm not asking for this to happen overnight. But I have a month, and I need you to seriously consider what I'm saying. You can't push me away forever. You have to give me a chance. Not just for us, but for our daughter too. She deserves to have what you had growing up, Autumn. Two loving parents under the same roof, a family." He grinned. "And several siblings."

"Siblings?"

"Yes, I plan to knock you up. A lot."

"Do you hear yourself right now?"

"I'm not the one who needs to hear me, kid, it's you."

"I don't know what to say. I barely know what to think when it comes to you."

"I'm coming for you. And it's going to make this last week look like child's play compared to what I have planned for us this month."

My heart beat rapidly against my chest, waiting for I don't know what. At this point, I wouldn't be surprised if he got down on one knee and professed his undying love. The irony was not lost one me. For years I waited for this exact moment, even after he'd left. Now, here it was, and I didn't know how to handle it.

Without wavering, he finally uttered the three little words I'd been waiting for all my life…

"I love you," he expressed all in one breath. "I've always fucking loved you, Autumn."

Although my mind was a jumbled mess, I knew without a shadow of a doubt that this was the first time he'd ever professed those words to anyone before.

And the fact that it was me resonated deeply.

twenty-seven

Then

It had been over two months since I'd lost my virginity, and Julian and I were spending a lot of time together behind everyone's backs. We were lucky that Christian was engaged to Kinley, spending most of his time at her place, letting their apartment become our little oasis.

We spent a great deal of time at their place, pretty much christening every surface we could. From his bedroom, to the couch, to the kitchen counter, against the wall, in the shower, in the tub, on the floor, on his dining table, and even on his bedroom furniture. There wasn't an inch of my body he hadn't explored. Even down to my back door.

Yeah … he'd stolen that from me too.

"What are you thinking about over there, kid?"

I smiled. We'd just eaten dinner. He'd cooked me spaghetti and meatballs.

"Of all the spots we've had sex here."

He grinned. "I think we've covered every crevice by now."

I was on the pill, and Julian definitely took advantage of that. Saying I was the first girl he'd ever gone bareback with.

"What would you do if Christian came home right now?"

He lifted his phone in the air, showing me the text from him, confirming he was indeed staying the night at Kinley's.

"What do you think about them getting married in a few months?"

He shrugged. "I don't think anything. It isn't my life."

"I know, but he's still your best friend. Are you scared you're going to lose him to married life?"

"That isn't what I'm scared of losing him to." With that, he got off the couch and walked into the kitchen. I knew what he meant by his not so subtle response.

"Is that the end of our conversation?"

Opening the fridge, he grabbed a beer. "I wasn't aware we began one."

"You can't fool me. I know everything about you. Especially when you're blowing me off."

He twisted the cap from the bottle and threw it in the trash before making his way over to me. "It's why I fuck you so much. I need you to keep me around despite my shitty personality."

"Your personality is not shitty, Julian. I'd say you were more of an alpha asshole than shitty."

His hand went under the blanket, tickling my inner thigh. I laughed, thrashing around.

"You need to go put some clothes on."

"I thought you preferred me naked."

"I do, but I want to take you somewhere."

"Where?"

He smiled, big and bold. "For a joyride."

I arched an eyebrow, confused where he was going with this.

"You better hurry before I change my mind and eat you out instead."

"Well…" I giggled. "That isn't going to get me to move any quicker. If anything, I think I'll lay here and make you follow through with your threat."

He laughed, pulling off his hoodie to throw it over my body. Grabbing my panties off the floor next, he stated, "You won't be needing these anytime soon."

For a moment, I took in his chest and arms. Making my mouth water. Julian was a work of art. Chiseled muscles, broad shoulders and back, a six-pack showcasing a V—he was completely breathtaking.

"If you keep looking at me like that, we're not going to be leaving this couch, and I really want to take you for a ride."

"All the more reason to keep looking at you then."

Grabbing my hand, he pulled me up and put his hoodie on me instead. "I like seeing you in my clothes, kid."

"Good, because I love wearing them."

Holding my hand, he dragged me off the couch and led the way into his garage. When he opened the door, I gasped. There in front of my eyes, was a bright green Audi R8.

My eyes shifted to him. "Did you rob a car dealership today?"

He chuckled. "No, not today."

Julian always had different cars every month. They were usually classic cars he'd fix up. This was new.

"Who's is this?"

He winked. "If I told you, I'd have to kill you."

I laughed. "You're wicked."

Rounding the front of the car, he opened the driver's side door. "Want to go for a ride?"

"You're serious?"

"I mean, I'd much rather you ride my cock, but it'll happen soon enough. Especially if you go for a ride with me right now."

"I can't think of a better way to end my day."

He stepped inside the car, and I followed suit, sitting on the passenger side. He started the car, and the engine purred to life, vibrating my entire body.

Particularly my pussy.

"You feel that, kid?"

"I do."

"Good. I'm only getting started."

It all happened in a flash, although it felt like it played out in slow motion. The adrenaline pumping wildly through my veins was a feeling I'd never forget. I felt every roar of the car as his foot eased down on the clutch. Popping the shifter into reverse, he backed out of the garage.

"Holy shit!" I exclaimed. "This is amazing!"

Quickly shifting into second, then third, he tore down the street. Fifty, sixty, seventy miles per hour, he gunned it onto the highway. I watched in astonishment as he downshifted to first, fishtailing out onto an old, abandoned road. The only sounds that could be heard were the squealing tires while he did a burnout.

It was such a thrill.

I was hot, burning up. Part of it was from the engine, and the other was from Julian. The rush surging through his veins controlled his actions, and I was damn lucky it did.

The next thing I knew, he ordered, "Spread your legs for me, Autumn."

"What?"

When I didn't move fast enough, he did it for me. Reaching over, his hand slid in between my thighs. "I'm going to do two of my favorite things at once, driving this sports car and making you come."

Halting all the air in my lungs, I sucked in a breath as soon as he started rubbing my clit. He downshifted into second, jerking the wheel to make a sharp right turn. The car slid, and my head fell back from his skilled fingers working me over.

The engine revved as he shifted into fourth gear, sliding his finger inside me at the same exact time. The adrenaline coursing through me was releasing endorphins I didn't know I had, sky-rocketing my entire body and bringing me to a new high. It took over all my senses, my entire being. My chest heaved, trying to catch my breath.

"Oh God…" I panted, as he hit my g-spot over and over again.

Shifting from gear to gear, he floored it down the street, the speedometer indicating we were hitting ninety.

"Let's see what this baby can do."

"Julian…"

Going faster and faster, he ripped through the secluded back alley. Harder and harder he fucked me with his hand. Waves of ecstasy barricaded my mind as wetness rolled out of my core. Our heated emotions were running wild, fueling my need to come.

One hundred miles an hour.

One fifteen.

One twenty-five.

I was a ticking time bomb, counting down until I exploded.

The engine was loud, rumbling, coming to life the faster he drove. Taking everything along with it, like a tornado spinning around in circles. It elicited feelings I never thought possible.

I felt every loss of breath.

Every curve of his finger.

It cluttered my mind, and I couldn't keep up with his skilled assault.

"Come for me, Autumn."

That was all it took for me to fucking ignite. I shattered, coming apart at the seams. I came so hard that my vision blurred, and my body shook uncontrollably. Julian didn't miss a beat, slamming his foot on the brake, and causing the car to do a complete three-sixty. Around in a circle we went. My body flew to the side from the impact until we came to a stop.

Before I could say a word, he threw his seat back and gripped onto my waist and carried me onto his lap. His cock was out and inside me before I even blinked.

"Ride my cock, baby."

I didn't have to be told twice, I did as I was told—riding his dick as if I was in a rodeo. He gripped onto my hips and moved me harder against him. It was something I'd learned about him early on—Julian liked it rough.

"Come on my cock, Autumn, like you just came down my hand."

Once again, I exploded. Seeing fucking stars.

Galaxies.

A lunar eclipse.

I didn't hold back, repeating, "I love you, I love you, I love you."

Which was also new between us, I told him I loved him all the time. Every chance I could get. And since the first time I expressed those three words the night he stole my virginity…

He never stopped me anymore.

However, he never said it back either.

twenty-eight

Julian

Day of Locke Enterprises Announcement

MSNBC, Fox Business, and Yahoo Finance were all setting up their camera equipment in my office on the ranch. Autumn wanted the world to know the man behind the expensive suits, and this was the perfect place for them to learn who I was.

Over the last three days, Autumn had kept her distance, and after what I shared, I knew that she would. I'd spent most of my time with Capri—my daughter was the light of my life. She was catching me up on the last nine years of hers, from all her favorite memories to her interests. I was surprised when I learned of her love for classic cars, considering I owned several. I had them imported from Miami, and now they were stored in the garage at our home.

We'd spent most of our time hanging out in the garage, her helping me fix up a few car projects that had kept my mind occupied when I needed to think of something other than work. Capri could barely hold in her excitement the day they'd arrived.

"Daddy!" She walked around the front of my 1967 Chevy Truck. "Are these all your cars?"

"Mmm-hmm."

"How do you have all these classic cars?"

"I've collected them over the years."

"That's so cool!"

"I'm glad you think so. Your mom wasn't much of a fan of your old man's addiction."

"Oh my God!" Autumn chimed in, walking up behind me. "That is not true—don't believe your father. I used to love all his cars. If you think these are something, he had an arsenal of them back in the day too."

"Really?" Capri exclaimed. "How many cars do you think you've owned in all your life?"

I thought about it for a moment. "At least fifty, sixty maybe."

Her eyes went wide. "Daddy, that's a lot."

"All those cars helped me figure out how to make an eco-friendly sports car."

Capri nodded. "That makes sense. Can I help you in the garage with these that still need to be finished?"

"I'd love your help." I gazed at Autumn. "Maybe your mom can help too?"

"Yesssss, Momma!"

"I think you guys can handle it on your own."

She walked inside, and I turned my attention to our baby girl, trying to play it off like I wasn't disappointed that Autumn didn't want to help us.

The best part of my day was when I'd walk in the house, wearing jeans and a shirt covered in grease and motor oil, my hands covered in it too, and I swear the look in Autumn's eyes had the power to bring me to my knees.

With a grin, I called her out, "Like what you see, kid?"

She instantly looked away, and I wasn't going to let this one go. I came up behind her, wrapping my arms around her waist.

"Julian! You're all messy."

"You used to love me all messy."

She turned around, placing her hands on my chest. "That was when I wasn't wearing a thousand-dollar dress."

I smiled. "I'll buy you a new one."

"I don't need you to buy me anything."

"I know you don't, but it doesn't mean I won't."

"You need to take a shower."

I grinned again. "You should join me. You know, to make sure I get everything off."

"I have a feeling that isn't the only thing you'd be getting off."

I laughed and backed away, leaving her with the residual effect of my touch.

My appearance brought me back to another place and time when she undeniably loved me, immediately making me regret the choices I'd made when it came to us. I tried not to let my mind wander to any of that. She knew where I stood, and all I could do was wait for her to come to me. After today, I hoped it'd lead her in the right direction.

Into my arms.

My life.

Our future as a family.

Capri walked into my office, where I'd be making the announcement of Locke Enterprises going public.

"Daddy, what does going public mean?"

I smiled. My daughter's thirst for knowledge resembled mine. "It means my company is going from a private entity to a public one where people can buy shares to make money."

"Oh…" She scratched her head. "I don't understand."

"It's a bit confusing. You'd have to learn about the stock market."

"Daddy, will you teach me?"

"Of course, baby."

"Good." She nodded. "Because I want to be just like you."

I beamed, hearing her say that made my heart soar every time.

"So you're going to tell the cameras, and then what?"

"They're going to ask questions."

"What kinds of questions?"

"Number, stats, reports—boring stuff like that."

"Are they going to ask you about us?"

"More than likely."

She cocked her head to the side. "What are you going to tell them?"

"What would you like me to tell them?"

"Hmm…" She thought about it for a second. "I think you should tell them all about us."

"I think you're right."

"Daddy." She sat on my lap, playing with my tie. "Can I be in the announcement with you?"

"If you'd like." At least one of my girls wanted to be seen with me.

Her eyes lit up. "Really?"

"Of course."

"Yay! I'm going to go change into my pretty yellow dress!" She jumped off my lap and ran out of my office, almost running into Autumn on her way out.

"Why is she in such a hurry?"

"She's—"

"Mr. Locke," the reporter interrupted. "We'll be ready to go soon."

I nodded.

"You clean up nice," Autumn coaxed, bringing my attention to her. "I've gotten used to you looking like you used to."

"Do you still like me all messy, kid?"

She blushed, bowing her head. "Should we go over what you need to say?"

"No," I replied, disappointed by her changing the subject yet again. "I can handle it."

"Okay. I'm going to go answer a couple of emails. I'll be back toward the end of the interview."

"Or you could stay, be in the announcement with me."

"I don't think that's a good idea."

"You're right—it's a great idea."

"Julian…"

"What more of a family man can I portray with you sitting beside me? It's what we're aiming for, right?"

"Yes, but this is your business, and I don't need to be involved in that."

"I'd love to have you involved in everything. Including my company. All I have is for us."

"Okay, Casanova, I'm going to get some work in. I'll be back in a bit to check on how things are proceeding."

Reluctantly, I let her go. What other choice did I have in the matter? At least our daughter would be present on one of the biggest days for my business. Capri hurried into my office, wearing a yellow sundress. Her hair was in pigtails, and she was holding the stuffed animal I'd bought her.

"I'm ready, Daddy." She posed for me. "How do I look?"

"Beautiful, exactly like you're mother."

She smiled, sitting on my lap. "Okay, let's do this."

I chuckled, I couldn't help myself. She was fucking adorable.

Lights.

Camera.

Action.

The reporters sat in their chairs while we were behind my desk. For the next ten minutes, I made my announcement with Capri never moving from my lap. She was smiling the entire time, nodding when she thought I'd said something important, really trying to understand what I was informing the world of.

She was a CEO in the making.

"Mr. Locke, how about we address the elephant in the room?" the MSNBC reporter stated. "Who is this gorgeous little girl who has taken over your announcement?"

They didn't know how to mind their own business on a normal day, let alone on an occasion like today. Question after question about my personal life was about to be thrown in my face. This was what Autumn wanted, and it was the least I could do after what I'd been putting her through.

"This is my baby girl, Capri," I hugged her close to my chest.

"Hi. I'm Capri, and I'm ten years old, but one day, when I'm bigger, I'm going to be just like my daddy."

I grinned, honored I'd become her hero.

"Your baby girl?" the Yahoo journalist chimed in. "Oh wow, so not only are we learning about Locke Enterprises officially going public, but you're also telling us you're a father?"

I nodded. "No better time than the present."

"And who is the mother of this lovely girl?" the same journalist questioned. "Although, I don't think you need to tell us. She looks identical to Miss Troy."

"Then I don't need to tell you."

"Tell us anyway," he added.

"Yes," Capri replied, handling them like a pro. She must get it from her mother. "My Momma is Autumn Troy, and she's the best publicist in all the world. My daddy is her client, and now we're a family."

Bringing her little hand up to my mouth, I kissed it. "I worship the ground her Momma walks on. Have for as long as I can remember."

"That's right!" another *Fox* interviewer exclaimed. "We all read *The New York Times* article—you two have known each other all your lives. Your relationship started when she was young, correct?"

"Something like that."

"We know you're a very private man, Mr. Locke, but I think we can all say we're loving this new you. Can you tell us about your first kiss?"

"Not with my daughter present."

Everyone laughed.

Even the loud eruption of chatter in the room didn't steal the memory of the first time I stole her mouth.

"To follow up on that question," *Yahoo* added. "In the article you said you've always loved Miss Troy. When did you know it was true love and she was the one?"

"I gravitated toward her without even realizing it was happening. She consumed me, I've always been held captive by the beauty that is Autumn Troy."

Autumn

I watched from the television in the other room with tears falling out of my eyes.

"As you read in the article, I was a foster kid. Her family is all I've ever known. If it weren't for them, especially her brother who used to be my best friend, she'd already be carrying my last name. I was a different man back then. If could I go back and make things right, I would."

My heart skipped a beat the second he went on with, "She's always been my whole world."

"Mr. Locke," *Fox Business* addressed. "Can we expect to see more children in your guys' future?"

"If it was my choice, she'd already be pregnant."

I can't believe he's sharing this. I wiped away the tears.

"How do you feel about that, Capri?"

"I'm not sure." She shrugged. "As long as I can still have my own pony."

Julian scoffed out a chuckle.

After all these years, all the bullshit we'd been through together, the ups and the downs. This moment seemed surreal.

Our spark.

Connection.

Love.

It was all wrapped into one.

The interview continued, and I prepared for the aftermath that was Julian Locke. Once everyone left, I walked into his office. Capri was in the farmhouse, feeding the baby chickens.

"I can't believe you blindsided me. You couldn't have told me that our daughter was going to be in the announcement with you?"

"She requested it. And as you know, I can't say no to her."

"I've spent years making sure the press didn't find out I had a daughter, Julian. And you just throw her to the wolves without even discussing it with me first."

"We both know why you didn't want the press to know about Capri, and it has nothing to do with you protecting her from the world. You were hiding her from me."

"It doesn't matter. I still have the right to know what you're planning on doing when it concerns her."

"What do you want from me, sweetheart? You wanted the world to know the man behind the expensive suits, and I gave you exactly what you asked for. Now, you're giving me shit for it? You need to learn how to pick and choose your battles. This is a war in which you fucking started."

"Julian—"

"I'm not going to sit here and have you come for my balls. I did nothing wrong. You got what you asked for—end of story."

"Listen, you stubborn asshole—"

He slammed his fist on his desk before he was in my face, backing me up against the wall. Caging me in with his arms on either side of my face, he leaned forward close to my lips. "Why can't you just admit the real reason you're giving me shit, kid?"

His scent was making me dizzy, the smell of his cologne driving me insane.

"What's worse, Autumn? The fact that I told the world how much you own every last part of me, or the fact that you want me to kiss you right now?"

My eyes followed the movement of his mouth, and I

swallowed hard, unable to wait any longer. In less than a second, I kissed him for the first time in what felt like a lifetime. He didn't hesitate, gripping onto my ass and wrapping my legs around his waist. Pinning my back against the wall, he devoured my mouth.

Our battle was far from over. We'd fight again, but for a moment, his words had me surrendering.

To him.

To us.

To our family.

Our kiss took on a life of its own. Something neither one of us could understand or deny. Something neither one of us could control. It seemed like all we had to do was look at each other and sparks flew from here to kingdom come. My lips parted as he slipped his tongue into my mouth, demanding a response that only he stirred within me.

He kissed me deeper.

Harder.

Slower.

My breathing picked up, engulfing him in nothing but my need to keep going and have him claim my body the way he used to.

But…

This time it wasn't me who stopped.

It was him.

He pulled away, dropping me on the ground to my feet. I lost my footing, trying to catch my balance. My legs were unsteady, wobbling from his embrace.

"Fuck," he rasped, backing away. "I won't play this game of cat and mouse with you anymore."

"Julian—"

"There's more at stake now, Autumn. You either want me, or you don't. I won't mess with Capri's emotions because you can't make up your mind."

I bowed my head. "I just… I don't want you to hurt me again. I won't survive it."

He tugged on the ends of my hair. "I love you, Autumn. I loved you then, I love you now, I'll love you always."

"Do you have any idea how long I waited for you to say that to me?"

"I know. I couldn't say it back then, but I can say it now. And I'll say it to you every single day for the rest of my life to make up for the years I didn't."

"Momma!" Capri ran into his office, breaking our intense conversation. "Did you see? I did the announcement with Daddy!"

"I did, baby. You were perfect."

She ran into her father's arms. "Thank you, Daddy. I'm so happy to have you in our lives. Promise me you won't leave this time?"

The pained expression on Julian's face rendered me speechless as he crouched to the floor, getting eye level with her.

Capri caressed his face. "I'm sorry. I didn't want to make you sad. I just don't want you to leave Momma again. Cause then you're leaving me too this time."

He kissed her hand. "You're stuck with me, baby girl. I love you more than anything."

She smiled while tears rimmed my eyes. "I love you too, Daddy." Throwing her arms around his neck, she hugged him tight.

He embraced her, except his gaze was locked with mine when he mouthed…

"I love you," to me.

twenty-nine

Then

"Are we almost there?" I questioned. My ass was numb from sitting in his car for the last three hours.

"How many times are you going to ask that question?"

"Depends on how much longer we have to drive to get there."

He glanced at me. "We're almost there, Miss Impatient."

"This better be the best classic car show ever."

"Would I lie to you?"

"So I would join you on this long-ass journey, maybe."

"One day I'll own every car we're about to see today, and then you're going to thank me for taking you to this."

"Cars are your thing, not mine."

"What's your thing, kid?"

"Mmm… I'm not telling, or you'll make fun of me."

"Do I ever tease you?"

"Every chance you get."

He grinned. "Tell me anyway."

"Nah."

"Come on, kid. Tell me your dreams. I want to hear them."

"Fine, but you can't make fun of me."

He did a cross over his heart.

"I want to own a ranch."

"A ranch?"

"Yes, with a farmhouse and animals."

"I can't see you shoveling shit, Autumn."

"I won't. I'll have a crew who will do that for me. My job is to feed them and give them all the love."

"And what kinds of animals live in your farmhouse?"

"Goats, chickens, pigs, horses, maybe a pony, cows—you know, the usual."

"I see. That's quite an interesting fairy tale."

"My house will be the best part, Julian."

Now that piqued his attention. "Your house?"

"Mmm-hmm…"

"You've thought about your house?"

"Of course. I'm a girl—I think about everything."

"Fair." He nodded. "Tell me about this house?"

"Well, it will have a huge iron gate that no one can get through unless they have the code. The estate will be private, surrounded by tall trees and beautiful landscaping. My house will be in the middle of the property, and it will be breath-taking. There will be marble floors, huge bay windows where the sun can come through in every square inch of the place. I want a grand angled staircase right when you walk in. A massive foyer. It will have the works."

"That's quite a floor plan. You've given this a lot of thought. Where did this dream come from?"

"We live in Texas. I think that answers for itself."

He laughed. "I like your dream."

"I didn't get to the best part yet?"

"You'll have a sex room?"

"Only if you want one." I giggled. "But I was talking about a massive carport where you store all your classic cars."

"Oh, I'm in your dream too?"

"Of course."

The expression on his face turned serious, and I quickly

played it off like it wasn't a big deal when it was. I didn't want to scare him off, and Julian scared easily with anything that involved me.

"It's just a silly dream, Julian. You don't have to read that much into it."

He didn't say anything for what felt like forever, until he finally revealed, "I think we should just stay in the here and now and not think too far ahead, Autumn. Especially when it comes to me in your future."

I flinched, quickly looking out the window. It was pointless to hide my emotions from him because he could sense my disappointment.

"Yeah, whatever you want."

"You know what I want?"

"Hmm…"

He gripped onto my inner thigh. "To hear that contagious laugh."

"Don't you dare—"

He squeezed, sending me reeling into a fit of laughter. Almost making me pee my pants.

"Please!"

"Begging me isn't going to help your disposition, kid. You know how much I love it when you beg me."

"Oh my God! Stop!"

He squeezed harder.

"You're going to crash the car!"

"If I can finger fuck you while I'm driving a sports car, I can certainly tickle you."

"Julian!"

"I love it when you scream my name." Finally, he stopped and pulled his hand away. "Now, be a good girl and tell me more about your dreams."

"I thought you didn't want to hear about my future?"

"I never said I didn't want to hear about it. I just don't want you to include me in them."

"You're my brother's best friend, and my parents consider you a second son—you're going to be in my future whether you want to or not."

"Is that all I am?"

I shrugged again, and neither one of us spoke for the rest of the drive. Once we parked in the open field, I opened the door, but he grabbed my hand and held me in place, and I looked over at him.

"I don't like it when you get quiet on me, kid."

"You weren't talking either."

I could see it in his eyes, he wanted to say something, and I eagerly waited for his response. Julian never gave me hope for the future. He knew I was head over heels in love with him. However, he never expressed his feelings for me, through actions or words. He never gave me an inch, and I stupidly waited for a centimeter.

Gripping onto the back of my neck, he kissed my lips. "I know your dreams will come true."

"Really?"

He nodded.

"How?"

Silence.

He simply pecked my mouth and exited the car. I was shocked as shit when he reached for my hand as we were walking toward the entrance of the car show. Julian never gave me any public affection, and I didn't know if he'd noticed that he was. Instead of making a big deal out of it, I internally squealed.

Maybe it was because we were hours away from home, and no one would know us here, but either way, it didn't matter. I cherished this moment and lived in the present with him.

Silently praying, my future consisted of only him.

Julian

Hearing her say she envisioned me in her dreams wasn't a surprise. It was the fact that I wanted what she was saying more than anything, but I refused to give her false hope. All we had were these stolen moments where no one could see us, and I didn't fear losing the only family I'd ever known.

Being thrown around like I was nothing more than garbage for all my adolescence made it hard to live in anything other than the present. Despite being on my own and that life far behind me, it was difficult to think of a future other than financial stability. Coming from nothing gave you another perspective on life. I valued each day for what it was, and not knowing what tomorrow would bring was the only way I'd survived for so long.

Autumn was the light in my life.

Her smile.

Her laugh.

Her love.

It was everything I'd ever wanted and didn't think I was worthy of. Without her being aware of it, for the next few hours I showed her my world. I was determined to make something of myself and never again be that little boy always looking in at someone else's life. I wouldn't allow my mind to wander to a future that included Autumn.

All we had was the now, and I took full advantage of that.

"Which is your favorite car?"

I led her toward the black Lincoln Continental with the suicide doors, nodding to it.

"This is one sick ride, Julian."

"She is a beauty." And I wasn't referring to the car.

"Too bad we can't christen this one, huh?"

I pulled her into my side. "Never say never, Autumn."

If I had one life goal, it was to make love to her in that

vehicle. At the end of the day, I couldn't tell her I loved her, even though…

I did.

By the time we got back to my apartment it was dinner time, and I ordered us a pizza and chicken wings. We were sitting on my bed when we heard the front door open. Our eyes went wide.

"Fuck," I breathed out.

Her car was in the driveway, there was no hiding she was there with me.

"Autumn?" Christian called out, and her eyes went wide.

Neither one of us moved, but the second we heard his footsteps coming toward my room we both stood up. Once he stopped in front of my door, his stare shifted back and forth between us until he focused on me.

"What is my little sister doing in your room?"

"Christian, I was looking for you," she replied, bringing his gaze to her.

"In Julian's room?"

"No." She smiled. "He was just showing me his new TV."

His eyebrows pinched together. "Mom says you've been hanging out here a lot, and I haven't been here much, so explain that one to me?"

"Christian, just ask what you want to know," I snapped, unable to bite my tongue.

"I just did. What's my little sister doing here all the time if I'm not here, Julian?"

"Stop calling me your little sister, I'm not a child."

"That doesn't answer my question, Autumn. What are you doing with Julian?"

"We're just hanging out. He's my friend too."

"Since when?"

"What are you insinuating?" Autumn asked, not backing down. "I've known him all of my life, Christian. It's no different than coming here to hang out with you."

"I'm your brother."

"Most of the time I'm looking for you."

"You can text me, and I can tell you if I'm here or at Kinley's."

"I will next time."

That response seemed to appease him, and I could see it in his eyes—

he definitely suspected what was going on.

"Anyway, it's getting late. I'm going to head home." Autumn glanced back at me as she was leaving. "Good choice on the new TV. It's awesome." She hugged her brother. "I'll see you at dinner tomorrow."

Once we heard the front door close, Christian didn't waver. Not that I expected him to. "What the fuck was that?"

"I don't know what—"

"Don't give me that shit. You know exactly what I'm talking about. Why are you hanging out with my little sister?"

"You don't have to keep calling her that. I know what she is to you."

"Doesn't look like that to me."

"You need to relax. I was just showing her my new TV."

"What about all the other times she's been here? What were you doing then?"

"What are you insinuating, Christian?"

"You fuck anything that walks, Julian. I don't need to remind you Autumn's off limits, do I?"

I shook my head. There was no need for the reminder. I thought about it every time we were together, and when I was inside of her.

He nodded, slowly backing away, never taking his intense stare off of me. I knew what he wanted to ask…

Are you fucking my little sister?

He just couldn't bring himself to say it, and to be completely honest, I wasn't sure if I'd be able to look him in the face and lie to him. He was my best friend, my brother, and I was fucking it all up by betraying his trust.

"Great, keep it that way." He turned and left.

For the rest of the night, I thought about what I was putting on the line for Autumn. His bachelor party was coming up, and I was going to have to prove to him one way or another that there was nothing going on behind his back.

My phone dinged with a text message, and I didn't have to wonder who it was. Grabbing my phone from the nightstand, I read it.

Please don't push me away again.

I didn't reply. I couldn't. Unable to lie to her.

Although, her text didn't matter. I knew deep down in every fiber of my being…

This was the beginning of the end for Autumn and me.

thirty

Now

JULIAN WASN'T WORKING, AND NEITHER WAS I. AFTER the afternoon in his office last week, things had taken a turn for us. We started doing things as a family. Eating all our meals together, taking Capri to all of Julian's favorite places, and showing her a bit of our history. My favorite day was today—we took her to her first rodeo.

"Capri, your momma had a first here too."

"Julian…"

He leaned into her ear. "You want to know what it was?"

"Yesssss!"

Julian didn't heed my warning, simply stating, "She got her first kiss here."

I groaned, leaning against my seat.

"What?! Momma, who was your first kiss?"

"You're looking at him," he casually replied.

"Oh my God! Daddy was your first kiss? That's so romantic."

"Romantic isn't the word I'd use for it."

"Kid, I almost beat up your date for you. I think that classifies as romantic."

"You did?" Capri asked, completely enthralled and amazed that her father was suddenly Prince Charming.

"Your mom tried to make me jealous with a boy who was half my size."

"He was not half your size."

"The boy was a wimp. I would have swept the floor with him. It's the only reason I didn't. He would have wound up in the hospital, and everyone would have learned about us."

"What do you mean 'learn about you,' Daddy?"

"Your mom and I were secretly seeing each other without your grandparents and uncle knowing."

"Julian!" I scolded. "You did not just tell her that!"

"You want me to lie to our daughter?"

"Yeah, Momma, you want him to lie to your daughter?"

I laughed, it had become two against one.

"Tell me more, Daddy. Why did you have to hide?"

"Well, your uncle was very protective of your mom."

"Oh yeah," Capri agreed, nodding. "He's like that with me too."

Julian smiled. It was obvious he appreciated Christian looking out for our baby girl."

"So what happened?"

"It's a long story," I stated, not wanting to talk about this anymore.

"It's okay. We're in the intermission. Tell me, Daddy. I want to know."

Of course, he gave her what she wanted. "Your uncle used to be my best friend."

"Oh," Capri breathed out. "I didn't know that. He's never talked about you before. Is that why you left, Momma?"

"Something like that."

She scratched her head. "Do Grammy and Grampy know who you are?"

"They do. Your grandparents did a lot for me back then. I didn't have a family."

"What do you mean you didn't have a family?"

"My parents gave me up when I was born, and I was raised in foster homes."

Her mouth parted. "They gave you up? Daddy, I'm so sorry."

"There's nothing to be sorry about. I'm a better man for it."

She grabbed his hand and then mine, linking ours together. "It's okay. Because now you have us. We're your family. Right, Momma?"

Julian and I locked eyes.

"Yeah." I nodded. "Now you have us."

He beamed, not trying to hide it.

"Can you tell me more?"

"I'll tell you everything you want to know."

And he wasn't lying. Capri didn't stop until she knew everything about us. She'd spent most of the rodeo asking Julian our history versus watching the bull riders. As much as I loved watching the show, I couldn't help but pay attention to his every word.

Later that night, when we got back to the house, I went up to my bedroom and grabbed the photo albums I'd brought with me before I went back downstairs to find them on the couch, watching a movie. Capri was tucked into the crook of his arm, and I sat down beside her.

"Momma!" She recognized her baby album. "I didn't know you brought these."

"I did," I replied to her, only looking at her father. "I brought them for you too, Julian."

Julian

Capri grabbed her baby book, placing it on her lap. "Daddy, do you want to see?"

Unable to find the words of what I was feeling, I simply nodded. Her little hands opened the photo album, and right there in front of my eyes was a picture of her birth.

"She was six pounds, five ounces, and I was in labor for thirty-six hours."

It was like I was there, but I wasn't. It was the first time in I don't know how long that I felt so unbelievably helpless. I thrived on being in control, and in that moment, I had none. The more photos Capri showed me, the further my heart fucking broke. I'd never felt pain like this before. Not even when I'd left Autumn.

To see the last nine years of her life playing out before my eyes was a kick to my fucking stomach.

Autumn continued narrating all the pictures. From the first time she'd crawled, walked, ate solid food, to her first birthday, her first bike, her first everything. I'd missed it all. The longer I sat there hearing Autumn's voice and seeing all those memories I'd missed because she didn't tell me we had a daughter, the further the pain inside of me grew, and it quickly turned into anger.

Fury blazed through me like a fucking tornado, taking down everything in its path.

"Daddy, are you okay?"

I abruptly stood, needing a second to compose myself before I lost my shit on Autumn in front of Capri.

"Capri," Autumn coaxed, taking the album off her lap. "Honey, I think this is a lot for your daddy to take in. Let's show him the rest later, alright?"

"Yeah, okay. Daddy, can you tuck me into bed?"

I nodded again. I was so pissed I could barely see straight, but I kept it together for Capri. Holding her hand, I led her out of the living room and into her bedroom. She went to her bookshelf and grabbed a story. I couldn't tell you what it was. I moved in autopilot, reading it to her. She passed out cold before I finished, and I kissed the top of her head. Capri was a solid sleeper, and nothing could wake her up.

"I'm so sorry," I found myself whispering to her, needing to get it out. I had to say it to her. Although she couldn't hear me, it felt like I owed it to our daughter. "I missed so much of your life, and I'm trying so hard to let it go. But… I can't get those years back. With you or your mother. I feel like I failed both of you, and I'd give everything I have to get back that time with you." A tear slid down my face, and my chest heaved.

I was a grown-ass man. However, in that moment, I felt like nothing more than a father who'd wished he could have been there to watch his baby girl grow up. I missed out on so much, and I didn't have anyone but myself to blame. I wanted to take my anger out on Autumn, and a part of me felt some resentment brewing.

She could have told me.

I would have been there.

God, I would have fucking been there.

"My life hasn't been easy. My parents didn't want me, and I always promised myself I would never be like them. I would never abandon my children, and yet here I am, hoping that one day you won't hate me for missing so much of your little life. The things I've seen, the stuff I've endured, I wouldn't wish that on anyone. I can't help thinking that maybe I'm being punished for something because why would your mother not tell me about you? Why would she do this to me? Knowing how I grew up?"

More tears slid down the sides of my face, and I felt as if I was breaking down, shattering in my baby girl's bed with her in my arms and her mother in my heart.

"Seeing those pictures of you tonight… I don't think I've ever felt pain quite like this before. I thought I could get past it. I thought I could push through. But seeing you, so little, so innocent, looking so much like your mother, it's just… I'm finding it hard to breathe. I can't tell you how profoundly sorry I am for not being your daddy. When all I've ever wanted was to have one of my own. I swear to you. I promise you I will be there for you for the rest of your life. I won't miss another milestone, another moment, another birthday. It's me and you, Capri."

The sound of a shudder brought my attention to the door. Autumn was standing there. Fucking wrecked. Her face was flushed with tears streaming down her face.

"I'm so sorry, Julian. Please… I'm just so fucking sorry. I never meant to hurt you. I never met for Capri to not have a father. I was young and stupid, and if I could go back, I swear I'd change everything. I would have told you. I would have begged you to stay for us, but you broke my heart. You killed me inside, and for years it felt as if I was only surviving for our daughter. I thought about you every day. There were so many times I wanted to call you and tell you, but I couldn't find the words to say that I'd fucked up. When I finally did find the nerve to call you, your number was disconnected, so was your email. I couldn't reach you. What else was I supposed to do? I hate myself for hurting you. I hate myself for hurting her. I just… Fuck…" She sucked in a breath, her body shaking, her heart breaking. "I never stopped loving you. Not for a second, a minute, an hour. I've loved you all my life. All I ever wanted was you, and I know the only reason I was able to go on was because you'd left me with a huge part of you."

"Autumn." I sighed, getting off the bed, careful not to wake Capri. "I don't want to resent you, but I'm not going to lie to you. I'm trying to forgive you for keeping her from me for nine years when you know without a shadow of a doubt I would have been there. By your side, through it all."

"You said it yourself, Julian. Old habits die hard, and it was the same for me. I didn't know where to reach you, and when you became this big shot and were all over the news and tabloids, it was hard to see you for the man you once were. You know what everyone said about you, and I couldn't bring myself to tell you about Capri because I was terrified you were that man everyone said you were. And I wasn't going to let you break her heart too."

"I became that man because I'd left my heart and soul with you."

Her hands flew to her face as she openly began to bawl. "I don't know how to fix this. Maybe we're just too broken beyond repair. We've both hurt each other so much, and I can't keep doing this. It hurts too fucking much."

"Kid—"

"I love you, okay? I fucking love you."

She turned to leave, and I chased her down the hall. Grabbing her arm, I turned her to face me, but I couldn't get a word in. She started hitting my chest, her fists pounding into my pecs.

"Why?! Why did you have to lie to me? Why couldn't you just have faced them with me? We could have told them! They would have accepted it! My parents loved you, and so did Christian! Why did you have to break us?"

I let her hit me.

Over and over again.

I wanted her agony. I deserved it.

"I'm sorry, kid. I'm so fucking sorry."

"You ruined us! We could have been a family!"

"Don't you think I know that? Don't you think I fucking hate myself for it? I can't change the past, and looking at that photo album proved it. I want so desperately to make things right with you. I can't live without you anymore. Not after being with you these last few weeks. My life belongs to you, Autumn. Always has, and it always will."

She sobbed, falling to the floor, and I went with her. I held her in my arms.

Until there were no more tears.

No more hurt.

No more mistakes.

Until there was nothing but the future for ours to take.

I carried her into my bedroom and stripped off all our clothes. Leaving us bare where only our skin touched. I didn't kiss her, I didn't make love to her, I didn't do any of the things I truly longed for.

Instead, I held her close to my heart. Where she could feel it only beating for her. She cried most of the night, and I kissed away every last tear. Breaking down with her.

Knowing we both needed this … to heal.

thirty-one

Autumn

THE DAY HAD FINALLY COME, AND MY FAMILY, including my brother and Kinley, were coming over for the day. Julian had invited everyone. This was the first time I was going to see my brother since our altercation over two weeks ago. We'd been living here for seventeen days, and the truth was—it was starting to feel like home. Capri was loving every second of it, and I'd be lying if I said I wasn't also.

I was beyond nervous of what today would bring. Fully aware of Julian's intentions, they were pure. He wanted my family in his life. I knew he'd missed them, probably in the same way I'd missed him. Christian didn't want to attend our gathering at first, but our mom was able to change his mind.

Julian spared no expense, having it fully catered with some of my family's favorite food. The liquor bar was stocked, our home was ready, and the atmosphere was perfect. The minute my parents' SUV pulled up, Capri hauled ass outside to greet them. We hadn't seen my parents in a couple of months, the same with Christian other than the day at the restaurant.

"Grampy!" Capri jumped into my dad's arms.

"Sweet pea, look how big you've gotten!"

"I know! Momma says I've grown an inch since you last saw me. What do you think, Grammy? Do I look bigger?"

My mom hugged her tight. "You sure do. You have to stop growing, or who's going to be my baby girl?"

"I'd love to give you another grandchild, several actually."

I glared at Julian.

He hasn't seen my parents in over a decade, and that's the first thing he says to them?

"Julian," Mom announced, looking at him with so much affection in her stare. "You always did speak your mind. It was one of the things I loved the most about you."

He smiled, and she didn't hesitate, opening her arms to give him a hug. They embraced, and my father hugged him too, all of them peering at each other with warmth and love.

"Look how handsome you are." Mom beamed. "I always knew you'd accomplish big things. We can't tell you how proud we are of you."

"Thank you," he replied. "You have no idea how much that means to me, and I just want to start off by saying I'm so sorry about—"

She waved him off. "It's in the past. You're here now, and that's all that matters."

"The way I left after everything you guys did for me. It's in-excusable, and I'll spend the rest of my life trying to make things right with the both of you."

"We just want you to be happy. It's all we've ever wanted."

"I know." He looked over at me. "Autumn has always been the woman to do that for me."

I hadn't spoken to my parents about anything pertaining to Julian since *The New York Times* article hit the stands. I didn't know what to say, and I figured it was better to discuss it in person than over the phone or through text. The expression on Mom's face was enough—she had questions. Lots of them.

We showed them around the estate, and I could tell my parents were enamored with the property. It was as if no time had passed between Julian and my parents. Despite them being hurt by his actions, I always knew they wouldn't hold a grudge. Now, my brother was a much different story. Christian and Julian had been best friends, and Christian had missed Julian like I did when he'd left. At least I got a goodbye—not a very good one but one, nonetheless.

Julian went out to the farmhouse with my dad and Capri, while my mom and I stayed behind in the kitchen.

Which was made for a queen.

Me.

"Okay, spill, Autumn. I can't hold it in anymore. You've been ignoring my calls and texts."

"I wasn't ignoring you."

"Then how do you explain every miscall and text?"

"I just didn't know what to say. When I first learned about the article, I was so mad at Julian."

"First learned? You didn't know about it either?"

"Absolutely not! I would never want any of you to find out that way, but Julian … he's Julian Locke, Alpha CEO, and he does what he wants."

"He's always done what he's wanted, Autumn. You were too young to realize that before."

"I've always known. I just ignored it back then."

"And now?"

"He drives me absolutely insane."

"What's going on between you two? Is it true? Are you guys together because of the way that man looks at you, I can't imagine this is just a publicity stunt."

"I don't know what we are, and that's the honest truth."

"Alright… And the article? What happened back then?"

I deeply sighed. "We lied to everyone."

"So he was your first love? You were his?"

"Yeah, well, I mean he was mine, but I didn't know I was his until the article hit the stands."

"Oh wow." She shook her head, dumbfounded. "How did we not see any of this?"

"We were really good at hiding."

"I guess I don't understand why you guys were hiding in the first place."

"We didn't think you guys would approve, and we knew Christian definitely didn't."

"Oh, honey … all we've ever wanted is for you to be happy. Both of you. And if you found that with one another, who are we to say anything about it? Your brother has always been so overprotective of you, but he would have eventually come around. His little sister, his best friend, he couldn't ask for a better outcome."

"You would think, but you should have seen him a few weeks ago when Julian told him to meet us at a restaurant."

"I saw your brother's busted lip. I can imagine what happened."

"Did he tell you?"

"He told us he saw you guys, and Julian and he exchanged words. Christian is hurt, but he'll come around."

"I can't believe you guys are so forgiving. I know how sad you were with the way he left."

She lovingly smiled. "Honey, it was a long time ago. Julian has always been a very complex man, even as a child. At first, of course, his abrupt departure was painful, but I know he didn't mean to hurt us. Now, finding out about you guys, I understand why he thought leaving the way he did was the best idea."

"Really? Because I barely understand it."

"You were raised in a loving home. Julian may have stayed at our house a lot, but he's always been thrown away like he was nothing more than yesterday's garbage. Kids that are abandoned like he was and thrown into the system usually tend to mess everything up before someone they love can do it for them. It's sad, and I'm not making excuses for him. I know he believed he was doing what was in everyone's best interest."

I nodded. "I know. I'm glad you guys are so forgiving. You mean a lot to him. He loves you, both of you."

"And we love him. He's always been a special boy, and we knew he'd amount to great things. I had a suspicion it would be something to do with cars. He's always had a passion for them. How are he and Capri? From the looks of it, they've already taken to each other."

"They're two peas in a pod. I'm the odd man out these days."

"Give it time. It will all work itself out."

"I'm trying."

She pulled me into a firm embrace, murmuring, "All the pieces will fall together."

"I love you, Mom."

"I love you more."

The front door opened, and Christian called out, "Autumn?"

I pulled away and swallowed hard, making my way toward the front door to greet him. "Hey."

He smiled, pulling me into a tight hug, and I was relieved. My brother was very important to me, and I didn't want us to have any issues. Especially when it came to Julian and me.

"Hey, Kinley." I hugged her next, whispering into her ear, "Thank you for making him come."

"Believe it or not," she replied. "He came willingly."

Which surprised me more than anything.

Julian

"Daddy! Do you see? Look! I'm riding Buttercup all by myself!"

"I see, Capri!"

She was riding her pony with one of the ranch employees, while Autumn's father and I were talking.

"I want to thank you for coming today."

He put his hand on my shoulder, reminding me of all the

times he did. "You look good, Julian. Happy, content, relaxed. Fatherhood suits you, son."

I nodded, feeling his encouragement in the same way I did as a boy. With just a couple of words, he always had the ability to make me feel like I was wanted, cared for, loved…

"I don't think I've ever felt this happy about anything in all my life."

"Not even when you grossed your first million?"

"Money has never made me happy. I don't think I've ever taken a moment to realize how far I've come. I'm always contemplating what's next, what happens now. It was so hard for me to be present until Autumn came back into my life. All I was doing was moving from one day to the next, but for the first time in over a decade, I'm actually standing still and enjoying every second of life. I haven't worked since I made Locke Enterprises announcement, and it's been some of the best days of my life."

"Glad to hear it. You deserve it."

I looked into his eyes. "I've always admired the man that you are. Always strived to be like you. I can't tell you how relieved I am to know you don't hold any grudges. What I did was truly fucked up."

He chuckled. "It was very fucked up."

I chuckled back.

"We spent a lot of years wondering if we did something wrong."

I rubbed the back of my neck. The weight of his words was unsettling.

"My intention isn't to make you feel bad, Julian. It's to make you aware."

"Either way it's hard to hear."

"You've always been like another son to us. When we read the article the other day, it all made sense, and we understood why you handled things the way you did."

"I never meant to betray your trust with Autumn. I spent

years pushing her away, but you know your daughter—she's hard to resist."

"The apple doesn't fall far from the tree. Her mother is the same. If you would have told us back then what was going on between the two of you, we would have understood. You grew up together, so it was only natural if things took a turn in your relationship."

"I know that now, but I didn't back then. I was so grateful for everything you guys did for me, and I couldn't bring myself to disappoint either of you. I didn't want to make problems in a home where there weren't any. Toward the end, Christian was getting suspicious, and I didn't know what else to do. I knew if I'd stayed in Texas, I wouldn't have been able to stay away from her. I loved her, I still do. She's the only woman I've ever loved, and all I can do is make amends with everyone."

"We don't have to forgive you, Julian, we already do. It's you who has to forgive yourself."

"You may not have to excuse my behavior and betrayal, but I know I have my work cut out for me with Christian. He's far more stubborn than your daughter."

"You bet your ass I am."

Our stares shifted toward Christian, who was walking up behind us.

I nodded. "Glad to see you could make it."

"I came to see my niece and sister."

"Christian—"

I stepped out in front their old man, interrupting him. This wasn't his argument to fight—it was mine.

"I fucked up."

He got in my face. "I fucking loved you, man. How could you betray me like that?"

"Don't you think I know that? I missed nine years of my daughter's life because I fucked up so bad. I'm the reason she's spent all her life without a father." I pointed to myself. "Me. The man who grew up in foster care, going from piece of shit parent to piece of shit parent, and you think I wanted this for her? You don't think I've been punished enough for my poor choices?"

"I knew." He sternly nodded. "I fucking knew you were messing around with Autumn. That's what hurts the most! You blatantly looked me straight in the face, making me feel like I was crazy for even implying you two were hooking up behind closed doors."

"You're the last person I would ever want to betray, Christian, and you know that. It's why I left the way I did."

"You're nothing but a coward."

"I know, and I have to live with that. I lost everything that ever mattered to me. You were the only family I ever had. I fucking loved you too. It's why I had to leave. I couldn't tell you that I was in love with your sister, but I can now. And it's the truth. I've loved her for as long as I can remember. I can't lose her again—I won't. I'll spend the rest of my life trying to be the man she deserves and the father Capri needs." I paused to let my words sink in. "I'll prove to you how much I've always loved Autumn, but I need you to forgive me. I'm sorry, Christian. I'll apologize to you until I'm blue in the face. Anytime I think about how I handled things it makes me sick to my stomach. You're one of the most important men in her life, and she wants your approval. It would help me tremendously if you gave it to us."

"I don't know if I can do that. At least not right now. I just… I'm here for my sister and my niece. It's all I can offer you, Julian." With that, he turned around and left.

And my mind was thrown into the past.

thirty-two

Then

I KNEW HE WAS GOING TO DO THIS SHIT TO ME AGAIN. I was expecting it. For the last two weeks, Julian had been blowing me off and pushing me away. How he could go from one extreme to the next was not lost on me. I couldn't believe he had the audacity to think I'd sit back and take his cruelty. I thought we were past the back and forth mess, but then Christian had to unexpectedly show up and ruin everything we were building.

He was beginning to let his guard down, and it was such a beautiful sight to witness, and knowing I was the reason made everything he'd put me through worth it. I wanted to go off on him. I was a ticking time bomb, and he wasn't going to be able to manipulate his way out of this one.

I wasn't a little girl anymore. He couldn't treat me like I was his everything one day, and then the next I was suddenly just his best friend's little sister he needed to stay away from. Christian was not responsible for the decisions I made in my life. He was just my older brother, and they both needed to understand I could make my own choices.

My happiness was mine, and they were ripping it away from me as if they had a right to.

Grabbing my phone from my back pocket, I texted Julian.

Answer your door. I'm outside.

Seconds later, the door flung open, and there was Julian dressed to the nines. The smell of his cologne immediately assaulted my senses. Tonight, was Christian's bachelor party, and Julian looked like he was made exclusively for sex. He was wearing a light blue collared button-down shirt with black slacks. His bright blue eyes were mesmerizing, and I found myself enraptured in his gaze before he ruined it.

Angrily spewing, "What the hell are you doing here? Christian was just here, Autumn."

"I know." I nodded. "I saw him leave."

He shook his head. "You shouldn't be here."

"That's all you have to say for yourself? This is bullshit, Julian! We've gotten so close these last few months, and now you're back to treating me like I'm just some girl you were fucking! I thought I meant more to you than that?"

"Keep your voice down. Our neighbors—"

"I don't give a fuck about your neighbors!"

He grabbed my arm, dragging me inside his apartment before shutting the door behind me. "You will when they're telling Christian his little sister was standing outside screaming at me."

"What the hell do you expect? I haven't seen you since Christian caught us in your room, and you haven't answered any of my calls or texts! You've completely dropped off the face of the earth, and it's complete and utter bullshit!"

"Kid, I'm not going to stand here and have you yell at me like I'm a fucking child."

"Well, you're acting like one!"

He inhaled a deep breath. "What the fuck do you want me to do?"

"I want you to treat me like I'm more than just a random fuck to you!"

"Autumn," he calmly stated, placing his hands out in front of him. "I'm trying to do the right thing."

"The right thing? Isn't it a little late for that? You already stuck your dick in my ass, Julian!"

He didn't hesitate, viciously countering, "It was a mistake! From the very start it's all we've been! One big fucking mistake!"

"Which part?" I stumbled back from the harshness of his response. "Taking my virginity or leading me on?"

"All of it. I had no right to steal any of that from you. I'm a selfish bastard, and for that I'm very sorry, kid. You don't deserve a man like me."

"That's not your choice to make! It's mine!"

"This never should have started between us."

It was blow after blow, after blow. It felt like he didn't care about how much his brutal honesty was affecting me, how much it was destroying me inside. Julian had the ability to shift from hot too cold at the drop of a dime. Showing me this Jekyll and Hyde side to him too many times to keep track of.

Words failed me, and all I could do was fight for us. He was worth the hurt and devastation along with my tears and sorrow, my love, my devotion, the uncertainty of a future that felt destined from day one.

Trying to hold my heart together, I placed my hand over my chest. Arguing, "You don't mean that."

"You have no idea how much I do."

Tears welled up in my eyes. "You can't do this to me again."

Sweeping the hair away from my face, he tucked it behind my ear. "I don't have a choice, kid."

"Yes, you do. Choose *me*, Julian. I love you. I'm in love with you."

He didn't answer, barely demonstrating any emotion. I did the only thing I could. I bared my heart and soul to him, only to have him crush it into a million tiny pieces.

"What do you want from me, Autumn?"

"I want you to fight for me! Who cares about my parents

and Christian? This is our lives, and if we want to spend it to-gether, then it's no one's business but our own."

"I don't see it that way."

I started to sob, feeling like a little girl when I should have been stronger.

Harder.

However, I always wore my emotions on my sleeve. It was who I was—it was how I was made. I didn't want to shatter in front of him, breaking like a cheap piece of glass.

At this point, I'd come this far, and I couldn't hold back. Openly bawling, I asked, "Why don't you want me? Why don't you love me like I love you?"

"Oh, kid…" He tugged me into his arms, holding me close to his heart while I broke down. Proving to him I was just a child, begging the man I was hopelessly in love with to love me back.

I cried in a way I never had, sobbing until I felt as though I had no more tears to shed.

Words to say.

Pain to feel.

It was all a clusterfuck of emotions and memories. Good times that were some of the best days of my entire life. Where nothing else mattered but being with him.

In his presence.

His bed.

His heart.

Home.

He was always my home, and for the life of me I didn't un-derstand why I couldn't be his.

"Autumn, I'm barely hanging on by a thread here. Please don't cry over me."

"Then stop making me."

"Baby…" He picked me up and carried me to his bed. Laying me down, he hovered above my body, and I desperately wanted to remember the feel of him on top of me.

Using this position to my advantage, I expressed, "Why am I not good enough for you?"

"It's the other way around."

"Why won't you be brave like me?"

"It has nothing to do with being brave, Autumn, and I wish you could understand that. I'm so deeply sorry for fucking with your heart, but I can't lose your family. They mean everything to me."

"But you're willing to lose me? Do I mean that little to you?"

"Kid, I can't answer that. I'm sorry."

I lost my shit, heaving, hyperventilating, wailing. I was a blubbering mess, and there would be nothing left of me after this. He was stealing it all. Every last part of me now belonged to him.

"Is this what dying feels like? Because you're killing me, Julian."

He kissed away my tears, and what once gave me peace, now gave me war. It created havoc in my body, not refuge anymore.

I was desperate.

Aching inside.

Instead of leaving with a bit of my pride, I did the only thing I could in a moment where I felt lost.

I kissed him.

Praying I could use my body to change his mind.

Julian

I could physically feel her agonizing emotions radiating off her in waves as she kissed me like her life depended on it. I wish I could tell you I didn't expect what happened next, but I'd be lying.

I should have stopped her.

I should have told her no.

I should have done something, anything…

Except allow her to slide her dress off her body, leaving her in nothing but panties. When my stare didn't leave her face, it wasn't long until I lost this sudden power struggle we were in. Her delicate hands moved down my chest in a gradual, struggling motion, causing my breath to hitch. Her touch was different.

It was afflicting.

Torturous.

And so damn loving.

When her hands started moving lower toward my belt, I roughly shoved them away. It didn't stop her assault—if anything it only provoked her.

But then…

She bit her lip, fucking baiting me.

"What do you think is going to go down here, kid?" My hands craved to grip onto her waist and show her who was in control which was exactly what she sought. My fingers pleaded with me to touch her, feel her, aching for something I shouldn't, completely aware it would only lead to more trouble.

Chaos.

Conflict.

"Please," she interrupted my thoughts with the sincerest expression I'd ever seen. "Don't push me away." Grabbing my hand, she placed it over her racing heart.

Revealing, "Feel my heart—it's breaking for you."

thirty-three

Julian

I GROANED. "WHAT DO YOU WANT FROM ME, AUTUMN?" I could see all the buildup in her eyes, days of anticipation, longing, and desire in her gaze as she hesitantly leaned forward, placing her hands on my chest. Slowly, she brought her lips to meet mine. It started off with just a peck until she opened her mouth, seeking out my tongue.

This was all her now, showing me everything *I'd* taught her. I let it go on. Carelessly letting my walls and reserve come crumbling down. I'd spent the last two weeks feeling like a dick, but I couldn't continue with her. Not after Christian warned me she was off limits again. I remembered the first time he'd threatened me. She had just turned fifteen. Even back then he'd suspected something might eventually occur between Autumn and me.

Her kiss had me on the verge of fucking losing myself, getting lost in the moment. Becoming lost in her. A man could only take so much, and I was at my breaking point.

I wanted her.

In every way possible.

And more…

I never stopped kissing her, hovering above her heady frame, causing her breathing to escalate when she realized she was getting to me.

"For fuck's sake, what are you doing to me, Autumn?" I rested my forehead on hers, looking down at her swollen lips.

She was so beautiful.

So loving.

So fucking mine.

The way she was looking at me as if I was everything she'd ever wanted simply encouraged me to keep going. I couldn't help myself. I never could with her. I kissed her more aggressively than before, crashing our lips together. Chastising myself mentally the entire time as I continued to consume her mouth.

Her hands went to the back of my neck, pulling me closer, but not nearly close enough. The kiss turned urgent and demanding, as she met each and every pull I was delivering. It was full of emotion, mixed with pure lust and something else I'd never felt before.

My hands continued to roam over her body. Knowing I was the only man to have ever touched her this way was doing all sorts of things to my cock, like it always did. She tilted her head back, giving my lips more access to her flushed skin. My mouth moved, kissing from her neck down to her collarbone, stopping just above her breasts that were rising and falling with every movement of my lips.

I ran my tongue along her nipple, leaving goose bumps in its wake. Looking up at her through hooded eyes, I lightly blew her aroused flesh, watching her come undone in the way she always did. My mouth kissed down her stomach, savoring the elevated heat of her body pressed against mine, getting hotter with each caress of my lips, touching her skin as I made my way to where I wanted to kiss her the most.

A moan escaped her lips.

And that was my undoing. Like a fucking atomic bomb dropping on my head, my mind took the control back from my cock, realizing what I was just about to do. Having sex with her wasn't going to do anything other than lead us back to square one.

I jumped off the bed, leaving her there panting and exposed. Breathless and stirred. I tried to shake off all the emotions she'd triggered inside of me. Holding my head between my hands, I paced around the room. Knowing I'd just royally fucked up.

AGAIN.

I took a deep breath while grabbing my hoodie off the chair and tossed it at her. "Put some clothes on," I snapped, mostly pissed at myself for letting it go this far.

The last thing I wanted to do was to lead her on more than I already had, and it was all I had done since day one. I walked out onto our patio, leaving the slider open behind me. Leaning over the railing, I needed to calm down. She stepped out shortly after, closing the slider behind her.

"Hey…" She grabbed my arm, turning me to face her. "What happened back there?"

"I can't do this with you anymore. This is my fault. I never should have kissed you, or crossed the line with you. But throwing yourself at me isn't the right answer either. I stole all your firsts—it's why you think you're in love with me. It's an illusion. You're young, and I should have known better. I'm the adult here, and I took advantage of you. I fuck, Autumn. I'm not your boyfriend—you're just my best friend's little sister." I regretted the words as soon as they came out of my mouth, and she jerked back like I had slapped her in the face, and I guess in a way I had.

"Kid…" I reached for her, but she stepped back.

"Just your best friend's little sister?" she repeated, hurt and dismayed. She stood taller, eyeing me up and down. "You're not fooling anyone but yourself, Julian. You're a coward, a fucking pussy, who's pushing me away because I'm getting too close to you. You're in love with me too! You can pretend and deny it all you want, but I know you. I feel you. You can fight it all you want, but we're connected in a way that even you can't destroy. We're soulmates whether you want to be or not." She stepped toward me, getting right up in my face. "If you didn't love me, then you wouldn't have chased away Daniel—you wouldn't have been jealous! You wouldn't have dry fucked me on my birthday.

You claimed me. Making sure your lips, your hands, your fingers, your tongue and cock were all my firsts. You made damn sure it was only your touch, your scent, your body that I'd remember."

"Autumn—"

"You want me to be yours, and that fucking scares you more than anything, because you've never wanted that from anyone else. Not any of the women you've slept with. My brother will understand, and if he doesn't, then I don't fucking care! This is my life, and I want you in it in every possible way."

I arched an eyebrow and cocked my head to the side. "You think you got me all figured out? Well, here's the truth, sweetheart. I don't love you. I'm not in love with you. You're not my girlfriend and I don't want you to be. I'm sorry I risked my friendship for you, but you're not worth the sacrifice.

She shook her head, her eyes immediately watering with tears.

I spoke with conviction, even though it killed me inside. "The truth hurts, Autumn. You deserve better than me. Now take your ass back inside and leave my house. You don't belong to me."

Tears streamed down her beautiful face. I watched them pour out for a minute, unable to witness it any longer. "If you won't leave, then I'll do it for us." I sidestepped her and left her there.

Her heart broken on my floor.

It wasn't the last time I'd walk away from her, but it was the first time I wanted to stay. That realization alone sent me spiraling down a bottle of fucking whiskey. Losing the only family I ever had wasn't an option, but staying in Autumn's life wasn't one either.

There was no one I could vent to, so I had to go through this alone. Which shouldn't have been a shock to me, I had been abandoned from the moment I was born.

Before I knew it, I was sitting on a black leather couch, in a house we ended up at for Christian's bachelor party. I was exhausted from the day and the never-ending plaguing emotions torturing me day in and out.

Christian had been watching me like a fucking hawk for most of the night. I had to prove to him I wasn't fucking around with his little sister behind his back. There was no way out of it, and I needed to do what I had to.

End of story.

"What's your name?" the luscious brunette enticed with her red, pouty dick-sucking lips. Wearing nothing but a tiny G-string and a bra that barely covered her tits.

"Don't worry about it."

The stripper laughed, swinging her long hair over her shoulder. I didn't have to look over to know that Christian was staring at us. Waiting to see how I'd react and what I'd do. She took it upon herself to straddle my lap, grinding her pussy on my cock to the beat of the music.

"I want you," she breathed out, leaning in to kiss me, but I turned, and she got the corner of my mouth.

From where Christian was sitting, it appeared like we were making out. I gripped onto her hair at the crook of her neck, tugging her head back, hard and making her whimper. Getting pussy had never been an issue for me, and she wasn't any different.

I let go of her hair and slowly moved my hands from her neck to her ample tits, down to her narrow waist. She licked her lips, sucking in another breath when I suddenly gripped onto her hips. I placed her on the table in front of me so Christian could get the show of a lifetime, feeling sick to my fucking stomach the entire time.

Autumn and I weren't together. I wasn't cheating on her, yet it still felt like I was betraying her in every way that mattered.

I stood, spreading her legs to stand in between them.

Getting close to her face, I rasped, "If you go into the bedroom with me, I'll pay you whatever you want to say I fucked you."

She inhaled, holding her breath as my hand continued its descent, running along her smooth, heated skin and down to the seam of her panties.

"Say that you did?"

"Yes, I don't need you to ride my dick."

"What about suck it?"

"I don't need you for anything other than a lie. Do you understand me?"

She nodded. Money was money, and it didn't matter what she had to do for it. Carrying her up my torso, I wrapped her legs around my waist and walked us to one of the bedrooms. Kicking open the door, I shut it behind me.

Everyone at the party saw what had just gone down.

Especially Christian.

After all this time…

The ups and downs.

The heartache.

The betrayal.

It felt like I'd finally done something right.

thirty-four

Autumn

O NE DAY.

Twenty-four hours.

Our month was almost up, where we'd lived and breathed our family. We were playing house, doing everything together, and our time was coming to an end soon. I didn't know what to do, and I barely knew how to feel. Still, I kept Julian at arm's length.

We flirted.

Teased each other.

Kissed a few more times.

However, that was it. When things started to get too heated, he'd stop, and despite being frustrated and wanting him to keep going, I was relieved. If we made love, it'd only fuck things up further than they already had been. We never touched each other in front of Capri, but kids had a way of picking up on anything. She could feel our love in the same way my family could.

Christian had stopped by a few more times to see us. We were still close, especially now that I had Capri. In a way, he'd stepped up and helped be a male role model in her life, and he wasn't going to stop just because Julian was back. The last two times he was here, Julian and he exchanged more words than they had before.

"Where's Kinley?" I questioned while finishing up dinner.

Julian was grabbing a beer from the fridge, handing one to Christian who was sitting at the kitchen island.

He nodded, silently thanking him.

See … progress.

"She's out with her girlfriends for the day."

Julian nonchalantly asked, "How are you and Kinley?"

"We're good."

"You guys have been together what? Twenty years now?"

"Coming up on it, but as you probably remember the first couple of years we were on and off."

Julian chuckled. "I was a bad influence."

"You sure as shit were. Who would have thought you were fucking my little sister the entire time?"

"Christian!" I exclaimed. "We didn't even kiss until I was sixteen, and we didn't have sex until I was eighteen, so no … we were not hooking up the entire time. Your best friend was still screwing any girl in a skirt."

"Hey!" Julian scoffed out. "She didn't have to be wearing a skirt."

I chuckled, but it was the truth.

Putting his hands up in the air, my brother mischievously smiled. "Relax, I was kidding." His eyes shifted to Julian. "You actually waited until she was eighteen?"

"First girl I ever waited for anything." He winked at me. "She was worth it, though."

"Alright, alright," Christian chimed in. "Let's lock that shit up."

Julian smiled. "Any kids in your future? Capri needs a cousin, don't you think?"

The expression on Christian's face quickly turned somber, and before either of us could call him out on it, Capri walked into the kitchen. The rest of the night, we all hung out as if it were old times.

Now don't get me wrong, they weren't friends by any means, but at least they were talking and on friendlier terms with one another.

Christian said he was doing it for Capri and me, but I knew better. He was full of shit. He missed his best friend, and the more he was around him, the further his guard came down. It helped that Julian was determined to have Christian back in his life the way he used to be.

Julian didn't lose.

Ever.

I shook off the constant thoughts, making my way into the garage to tell Julian and Capri dinner was almost ready.

I stopped dead in my tracks when I heard Capri ask, "Daddy, what's going on with you and Momma?"

My heart dropped to the floor as did my jaw. I'd been waiting for her to start questioning things between us. I just never imagined she'd ask him over me. My heart began pounding against my chest, and I placed my hand on top of it, willing it to slow down for a second. I hid behind a wall, able to hear but not see them. They couldn't see me either which only aided my current situation.

"Sweetheart, that's a difficult question to answer."

"Why? Don't you still love her?"

"I'll always love her, baby."

"Then why don't you tell her?"

"I have. Many times."

"Then I don't understand? I know Momma loves you too. She looks at you like Ariel looks at Eric from *The Little Mermaid.* Besides, she's never had a boyfriend or even been on a date, so I think that means something because Momma is super romantic. But since we've been here, she's smiled and laughed more than I've ever seen. You make her happy, like really, really happy, so I don't understand. Can you explain it to me?"

He sighed. "You're too smart for your own good."

She giggled. "I'm a genius like you."

Julian didn't say anything for what felt like forever, and

when he finally did, he admitted, "Capri, I've messed up so many times when it comes to your momma."

"What do you mean? Like from before you left her?"

"Yes."

"Why?"

He inhaled another deep breath. "I let everyone influence what I wanted. I didn't want to ruin my friendship with Christian or my relationship with your grandparents."

"Oh … so you broke Momma's heart instead?"

"I did, baby. I'm not proud of it, but I broke your momma's heart so many times I've lost count."

"Then just say you're sorry. When I'm a bad girl, I tell momma I'm sorry, and she always forgives me."

He teased, "When are you ever a bad girl, Capri?"

Not backing down, she added, "Daddy, just tell how sorry you are. I know she will forgive you if you do. Momma is a super forgiving person."

He laughed. "Sweetheart, sometimes people can forgive, but they don't ever forget. I've hurt your mother deeply, and I don't know how long it's going to take for her to forget about the damage I've caused."

"But I don't want to leave. I want to live here forever with you. Can I stay, Daddy?"

Hearing Capri say those words to him was like taking a fucking bullet to my heart.

Did she want to stay with him over me? Would I lose our daughter to him if we left?

I shuddered, causing an eerie feeling to course down my spine.

"Capri, you'll have both of us. I promise. You don't need to worry about any of that."

"Then we're living here forever?"

"Baby girl, I pray that you are."

"Daddy, this is so confusing."

"I know, and I'm sorry. If I could go back and change things I would, but all I can do is keep trying to make things right with your mom. I don't want to lose her again."

"I don't want to lose you."

I rubbed my face, feeling the weight of her statement.

How can I do this to our daughter? How can I rip us apart when we only just found each other again?

The truth was I wanted to stay for Capri.

My parents.

Christian.

Me.

The sound of his footsteps crept close to where I was hiding, and I swear I stopped breathing until I realized he'd moved closer to Capri, probably crouching to her eye level.

The tone of his voice was laced with sincerity. "You won't lose me, sweetheart. No matter what happens with your momma and me, I'll always be your daddy, you'll always be my baby girl, and nothing can ever come between that. It's me and you forever, baby."

She sniffled, "You promise, Daddy?"

He didn't hesitate in replying, "Cross my heart."

"Okay. Do you want me to talk to her? Maybe I can tell her you're super sad and how much you want us to stay. I can help, I know I can. Momma listens to me."

Wiping away a tear that escaped my eye, I waited on bated breath for his response.

Disappointed when he said, "You need to let the grown-ups handle their business, Capri."

"But I want to help you. I don't want to leave. I want to live here forever with you."

"I'd love that more than anything."

"Then make her stay, Daddy. Please…"

Several tears slid down the sides of my face, and I never wanted the ground to swallow me whole more than I did in that second. I wasn't only hurting Julian, I was also hurting our daughter, and that pained me deeply.

I couldn't listen anymore. Hurrying back inside, I busied myself with finishing up dinner and tried to keep my emotions in check in case either of them walked in. I didn't want Capri to see me upset, or for them to know I was eavesdropping on their private conversation.

Through my haze of what-ifs, I opened the wrong drawer and came face to face with *The New York Times* article. Like a fucking beacon shining bright, it was staring right at me. From then on, I moved in autopilot. Opening the magazine, I found his interview and read it from his first words to his last. He opened up about everything. There wasn't one thing he didn't tell the public, especially his feelings and love for me.

Our history.

His remorse.

It was all there in black ink on white paper.

"Autumn was born to be mine."

"She was made for me."

"I fought to not love her, realizing early on how much she completed me."

"She's the only woman I've ever loved."

"She's my soulmate."

My head was spinning.

"I don't know how I've lived over a decade without her."

"She's my beginning and end."

"The first time we made love I knew I was done for."

"I'll spend the rest of my life proving to her how much she consumes me."

"I want to marry her. Make her my wife and the mother of my children."

Faster and faster it spun with no end in sight.

"She's my everything—she's always been my everything."

"I didn't know what love was until I left myself truly have her."

"There's nothing I wouldn't do to keep her by my side."

I slammed the magazine shut. The emotions were one right after the other as I stood there frozen, unable to move, to think, to do anything other than feel like the floor was caving in on me.

I wanted to run to him.

To tell him I loved him.

To forgive him.

But I couldn't get my feet to move or my guard to come down. Something was holding me back, and I couldn't ignore that. Instead, after we eaten dinner and Capri went to bed, I found him in his office. Lost in his own thoughts, staring blankly out the window.

"I read the article," I shared with him.

He turned around and locked eyes with me.

Without reservation, I coaxed, "I forgive you, Julian."

His bright blue eyes flashed with a blaze of happiness as he stepped toward me, but I lifted my hand, halting his descent. Peering around the room for a few seconds, I battled a visible internal struggle in my mind.

It didn't take long for him to address the obvious. "You're here to say goodbye, aren't you?"

thirty-five

"Julian." I paused, wavering for a moment. "I can't do this with you again. It almost killed me the last time. I'm here to say my piece because we leave tomorrow."

He narrowed his eyes at me. "Do you honestly think I'm going to just let you leave?"

Taking a deep, solid breath, I willed myself to tell him the truth.

The one I'd been holding in for so damn long.

Opening my mouth, I confessed, "I wanted to get pregnant with your baby, Julian. It wasn't an accident. I purposely stopped taking my birth control."

His face paled, and it felt so fucking good to finally admit that out loud.

"You lied to me?"

"Yes."

"Why?"

"Because I knew you. I knew how you were, and it was only a matter of time before you pushed me away again. It was the only way I could ensure you wouldn't anymore. You always wanted a family, so I gave you one."

He immediately closed his eyes, the hurt evident all around him. It burned deep into my core. I hated knowing I was hurting him, but I needed to tell him the truth. He had to know.

As much as it killed me inside.

"How the fuck could you do this to me, Autumn?"

"I didn't do it to you, I did it for you."

"You did it for me? Are you fucking kidding me? What exactly did you do *for me*, kid? Get knocked up on purpose and then not tell me about it? What the hell kind of plan was that?"

"I didn't know you were going to tell me you were leaving. I had no clue you were going to take it that far."

"That's your fucking excuse? How could you do this to me?"

"I thought we were going to be a family."

"We still could have been! All you had to do was open your mouth and tell me you were pregnant!"

"I know. I'm sorry."

"You're sorry? For fuck's sake! I can't even look at you right now!"

"I swear the last thing I want is for us to leave and for you to hate me." Fresh tears streamed down my face, the ones I had been trying to keep at bay. "We've both hurt one another so much, Julian! How could we possibly come back from this? I don't trust you with my heart, and you resent me for not telling you the truth! That's our reality, not this made up happily ever after you've created in your head!"

In three strides he was in my face, backing me into the wall. "You fucking betrayed me, and still—I want you!"

I couldn't fucking breathe.

I hated myself for destroying him.

"We have to let each other go. It's what's best for our family."

"You leaving is not what's best for our family, and you know it!"

"Stop screaming at me! I'm hurting too! You broke me! Can't you see that?"

"So this last month was what, Autumn? Fucking payback?"

"Of course not."

"Bullshit!"

"You left me! After you fucked me over!"

Julian

My resolve broke like a chain that had been stretched to the max. I heard it snap, loud and clear. With wide eyes, I ran my hands through my hair, wanting to tear it out. Trying to remain calm but becoming defeated with each passing second.

I couldn't keep up with the torment—it clasped onto me like a vice as I stormed around my office, my feet stomping everywhere I stepped, leaving a path of destruction in its wake. Throwing anything and everything I could find, I unleashed my fury on my office instead of her.

"Julian, stop!"

Hearing the desperation in Autumn's voice halted the chaos coursing through my veins. Neither one of us said a word for I don't know how long, facing each other, panting profusely. We didn't need to, though. Our eyes spoke for themselves.

Our connection was present, and she wanted me to see it, giving me the hope I needed to go on. I growled out my frustration, releasing the craze, the wrath I no longer had any control over. It pounded into me as furiously as what she'd just admitted.

"I'm hanging on by a thread here. So unless you want to see a side of me you haven't seen in years, I suggest you weigh your words before you come at me with more bullshit. We're far from fucking over. Nothing will ever be done between us!"

"Just let me go!"

"I can't! You belong to me! You always have, and you always will!"

My mind was spiraling with more thoughts and questions, trying to find some clarity. Some truth within the haze. I shut my eyes and bowed my head in between my hands. Needing a minute to process what the hell she'd just said.

She could see it.

Feel it.

She could feel me.

I never wanted to shake her and hold her as much as I did in that moment. Showing my weaknesses wasn't something I ever did, but it had always been different with Autumn, and she knew it too. I couldn't think about the future without contemplating the past, and for the first time it had me questioning how we would make it through this.

I stared up at her through the slits of my eyes, longing to feel some sort of connection through what I was about to say to her. "I fucked up! How many more times do I have to say it to you?"

"But that's always been the problem between us, Julian. You fuck up, and I forgive you. It's an endless cycle I want to put an end to. I don't know what you expect from me because the woman you see standing in front of you—you made her this way."

I jerked back. With each blow she delivered, I felt a little more of myself die inside. I didn't know which one was worse— her lies or her truths.

"You're so full of shit," I confidently countered. The thread I was hanging on to snapped. "You've loved me your entire life. I'm embedded in your skin. I'm flowing in your blood. I'm beating in your heart." Before she knew it, I was standing directly in front of her, pulling her hair away from her face and grazing my knuckles against her rosy cheek. "I'm a part of you, sweetheart, and you're not going anywhere." I moved away, even though it was the last thing I wanted to do. I wanted her to miss my touch before my resolve exploded.

With the way I was feeling right now, I was damn ready to throw her over my shoulder, kicking, screaming, putting up one hell of a fight, and lock her the fuck away until I proved my point and made her mine again.

"I can't talk to you when you're like this."

She turned around to leave, but I gripped onto her arm. "Don't you walk away from me." Stepping right into her personal space, I backed her against the nearest wall. My six-foot-two muscular build loomed over her petite frame as I tugged her hard against my chest.

She didn't cower—if anything she stood taller. I cocked my head to the side, sweeping her hair away from her eyes to stare deep into them as I locked her in place in front of me. Her chest rose and fell with each brush of my hand.

I held her tighter.

To look at me.

See me.

Feel me...

I switched my grip to the back of her neck in a possessive act, running my thumb up and down her windpipe. Her breathing hitched, and her lips parted when my other hand lightly grazed her inner thigh.

"Julian, stop," she weakly let out as my fingers inched higher and higher up her leg.

"Stop what? I would've been there for you, taken care of both of you, like I still fucking ache to do. Please," I begged. "Just give me a chance to make it right. I can't live without you."

Before I even realized what was happening, she was crying against my chest, and I wept with her.

"I'm sorry, baby. I'm so fucking sorry for everything I put you through. I put us through. I ruined us when all you did was try to save us. Losing you will be the biggest regret of my life. I love you so much, and I need you to please never forget that," I pleaded in a tone I'd never heard out of my own mouth.

"I love you too, Julian."

She stayed there in my arms, both of us knowing this was our end.

This was goodbye.

I kissed her, she kissed me back, and for a moment we lost ourselves in each other. She pulled away first, and I wiped away all my tears, kissing along her face for the last time. She sucked in air that wasn't available for the taking as my arms fell to my sides.

Empty.

Alone.

Broken.

She took one last look at me and left.

For the first time in our love story, I watched her walk away from me instead.

thirty-six

WE'D BEEN HOME FOR TWO WEEKS.

Home.

It didn't feel like that anymore.

Capri and I were miserable.

Why was I doing this to us again?

She was mad at me, devastated I'd actually made us leave. My mind kept thinking about that morning, and it killed me every single time.

"Momma!" she pleaded with tears streaming down her precious face. Please don't make us a leave! Please, Momma! I want us to stay with Daddy!"

"Capri, please don't do this to me right now."

"I love you, Daddy!" She ran into his arms. "Please don't forget about me!"

He picked her up off the ground, and she clung to him like she'd never wanted to let him go for anything.

"You have to be my big, brave girl, okay?"

"But I don't wanna go!"

"I know, baby." He kissed the top of her head, looking at me with so much hurt it crippled my stance.

He held her in his arms until she cried herself to sleep before he gently laid her down in the SUV. Kissing her head one last time, he quietly shut the door.

Shaking his head, he bit, "I hope you're happy with yourself. You didn't just break my heart. You broke our daughter's too."

Her words played in my mind as if they were a broken record on endless repeat. My head was pounding, overly thinking about what I'd done to us when my phone suddenly rang.

"Christian," I answered it. "I can't talk right now."

"Good, because I'm the one who needs to do all the talking now."

"What are you—"

"Are you happy?" he questioned out of nowhere.

It was all it took for me to breakdown. "No…"

"Don't cry in front of Capri, Autumn."

"I'm not. She's out with Emily. What did I do, Christian? What did I do to my family?"

"Autumn, stop crying."

"I can't. I feel like I've been crying since I left him. When all I want to do is go back, but I can't."

"Why can't you?"

"I don't know. I just can't."

He deeply sighed, breathing out, "It's because of me, isn't it?"

"What?"

"You heard me."

"I don't understand."

"Yes, you do."

"This has nothing to do with you."

"Bullshit, Autumn. This has always been about me. Mom and Dad would have accepted you guys—fuck, they probably would have been thrilled about it. The only thing holding him back was me, and we both know it."

"Christian—"

"No, it's my turn to talk, and you need to listen. I fucked up. My job was to protective you, and I protected you from the man you needed most. He's always loved you. I saw it clear as day. The way he'd look at you when you were speaking, when he'd never give any girl his sole focus. The way he'd smile when you were around, when he was usually a broody bastard. How he'd think of you even when we were at the fucking grocery store, buying you your favorite candy or magazine. He was completely devoted to you."

"What are you saying?"

"I'm saying that I was wrong. I never should have kept you two apart, and for that I'm truly sorry, Autumn. It's your life. He makes you happy, and for years I saw you suffer with Capri alone. Knowing deep down in my heart that he was more than likely the father."

I gasped. "You knew?"

"I wasn't a hundred percent positive, but he started changing. He wasn't bringing girls home anymore. He was always busy, and when I saw you in his room that night, I knew he was busy with you. He didn't hit on girls when we'd go out. My best friend became a man I didn't recognize because of you. I saw through the bullshit charade he did during my bachelor party. Julian would have fucked her on that chair, not giving a shit anyone was in the room. He wouldn't have taken her to another room. He was trying to prove something to me, and I saw it for what it was."

"Oh my God."

"When you told us you were pregnant, I tried to reach him. I called around to all our friends, everyone who knew him, the places we used to hang out, trying to see if I could find him, but I never could. For months I tried, only to come up empty."

"I didn't know that."

"I wanted to fucking kill him, but I couldn't prove he was the father. All I had was my intuition. Than Capri started growing up, and I could see so much of him in her. Her mannerisms, her confidence, the way she holds her fucking fork, it's all Julian."

"Why didn't you ever say anything to me?"

"What could I say? I couldn't offer you anything, give you any information on his whereabouts. The only thing I could do was be there for you and her. I felt so fucking guilty she didn't have a father because of me. It was the least I could do. Again, I'm so sorry, Autumn. I never meant to hurt you. I fucking love you."

It all made sense, and I had no idea how I couldn't see it until now.

"It was never him, Christian. It was always me." I paused to let my words sink in. "I pursued him. For years it was all me. He never wanted to disrespect you, our parents, or me. For the longest time I didn't understand his reasoning. A little part of me resented him for it. I felt bad I didn't feel that way and he did. Even up until his article, I was terrified of you finding out. Not Mom and Dad. I didn't want to lose you like I'd lost him."

"You're not going to lose me. I promise. All I've ever wanted is for you to be happy. You're always going to be my little sister. Do you love him?"

"More than anything in this world."

"If he hurts you again, I'll fucking kill him. You've been warned. I'll always be here. I'm your big brother, and you're stuck with me for life."

"I know. You've been the best big brother a girl could ever have."

"He's a mess, Autumn. You need to come home."

"Wait? You've seen him?"

"Yeah, the owner of the bar we used to hang out at called me at three in the morning a couple nights ago to come pick his ass up. He was fucking hammered. I could barely get him in the car. He passed out in our guest bedroom, and we talked the next morning."

"Wow. Julian losing control. That's never a good thing."

"No shit. We're fine. I'll get over it. I want you happy. I want my niece to have a family. The same one we have with two loving parents who want what's best for her."

"Do you mean that?"

"Of course I do."

"Where is he now?"

He chuckled, and the doorbell rang before he added, "At your front door."

Julian

There she was, finally standing in front of me. Before she could say a word to me, I bent forward and threw her over my shoulder.

"Julian! What the hell?"

I walked into her house, looking around for Capri. Ready to throw her over my other shoulder and leave with what belonged to me.

"Where's our daughter?"

"She's out with Emily. Put me down!"

"Not a fucking chance. You're coming home with me. Now!"

"Julian—"

"Where are they? I'll go get her."

"They'll be home any minute. Will you please calm down?"

"This is me calm."

"Really? You're literally carrying me on your shoulder like a freaking cave man. What's next? Going to hit me over the head with a club and drag me out of my home?"

"This isn't your home. Your home is at the ranch with me."

"You're right. It is."

Now that got my attention, and I set her down on the entry table, caging her in with my arms.

"Are you fucking with me?"

She smiled, shaking her head. "I never should have left, and I'm so sorry I did. I'm also sorry about the birth control and Capri. I was young, but I don't regret it. I couldn't imagine my life without her in it."

"How could I be upset with you? You gave us our baby girl."

"I love you, Julian. I've always loved you, and I always will."

I laid my forehead on hers, rasping, "You mean I don't have to spank you into submission?"

"No, I'm not really into that."

"Unlucky for you, I am."

Grabbing my face, she looked deep into my eyes. "Take me home. Please. I want to go home."

I didn't have to be told twice, claiming her lips like she did my heart.

"I love you, Autumn. I want to forget about the past and just focus on the future. Can you give me that?"

She nodded. "Yes, I can now."

"You're not going to run away from me anymore?"

"No. My life belongs to you. It always has. I love you, Mr. Locke."

"Say it again."

"I love you, I love you, I love you!"

Kissing her passionately, I almost made love to her right then and there, but Capri walked in with Emily beside her. Through my craze, I didn't close the door.

"Daddy!" The expression on my baby girl's face almost brought me to my knees.

I let go of Autumn, and Capri jumped into my arms.

"You're here!" Capri celebrated. "You came for us! I knew you would! I just knew it!"

Holding her close, I pulled Autumn into the side of my chest. Embracing both my girls after what felt like forever of missing them.

My world.

My heart.

My soul.

Was finally with me, and I was never going to let them go again.

thirty-seven

"**M**OMMA!" CAPRI EXCLAIMED, RUNNING INTO the kitchen with a little ball of fur in her arms. "Look what Daddy brought me home!"

"Oh my God, no he did not."

Julian walked in after her. "Capri! I told you to let me talk to your momma first. Now I'm in trouble."

"Oh, yes you are, Mr. Locke."

"We just flew back this morning, and I'm already Mr. Locke?"

"You bought her a puppy? Without even discussing it with me first?"

"I was planning to, but Capri beat me to it."

"You're supposed to discuss it with me before you buy the puppy, Julian."

He grinned. "Is that the way it works? I got it confused, but thanks for clearing that up for next time."

"Next time?"

"But, Momma, look how cute he is!"

I rolled my eyes, shaking my head.

"Kid, it's just a puppy."

"A puppy I'm going to have to take care of."

"Not true, he's my puppy. I will be responsible for him. I promise."

I shook my head again. "I'm not going to win this one, am I?"

"I think you already lost, Momma. The puppy is here."

"You're not winning me any points with your mother, Capri."

She giggled. "Sorry, Daddy."

For the rest of the afternoon, we played with Capri's new Miniature Cockapoo. He was adorable, weighing only five pounds.

Later that night while Julian was putting Capri to bed, I listened at the door without them knowing.

"Daddy, I knew you'd come and get us. I just knew it."

"And now I'm going to make sure you stay forever."

What did he mean by that?

"That's a good idea, just in case Momma gets mad at you again."

"Baby, Momma is definitely going to get mad at me again."

"Facts."

I scoffed out a chuckle. She truly was too smart for her own good.

"Would you like me to make sure you guys are here forever, baby?"

"I would love that, Daddy. I think it's a very good idea."

"Good. You can cuddle your puppy for a little while longer, but he needs to sleep in his crate, okay?"

"Okay, I promise. I'll be a good girl and put him in there before I fall asleep."

Yeah, that wasn't going to happen.

I made a mental note to circle back before I went to bed, knowing she was going to sleep with that puppy if I didn't. To say I wasn't nervous to be sharing a bed with Julian would be a complete lie. I was so freaking anxious I couldn't control the emotions.

Making my way back to our bedroom, I jumped in the shower to wash away the unease I was experiencing. After I was done, I slipped on my cream silk robe, and when I walked back into the room Julian was sitting on the edge of the bed, waiting for me.

"You're nervous," he stated, fully aware he was the reason.

"Maybe."

He grabbed my hand, tugging me forward to stand in between his legs. "Why the anxiety, kid?"

I shrugged.

"Don't give me that."

"Well, we haven't had sex in over a decade, so I think that's reason enough."

He smiled. "Oh, we're having sex tonight?"

"Julian … don't tease me."

"But you used to love it when I teased you, especially when you were sitting on my face."

Arousal crept through every inch of my body, and my skin heated immediately.

However, it quickly decreased the second he informed, "Your house in San Diego went on the market the moment your feet touched my plane, Autumn."

My mouth dropped open. "Julian! I didn't say I was selling my home."

"It isn't your home anymore. This is our home."

"What if I wanted to use it for investment purposes, like renting it out?"

"I'm worth 3.2 billion. You don't need the money."

"Exactly, you're worth that. Not me."

"How many times do I have to tell you that what's mine is yours?"

"We're not married—"

I almost fell to my ass when he simply stated, "Marry me."

Julian

There was no hesitation on my part. I reached into my pocket and pulled out a Cartier ring box.

Her eyes went wide as I opened the box, showing her a five-karat princess cut diamond ring.

"That ring probably costs as much as my house, Julian."

I nodded. "Give or take."

I pulled it out of the box and slid it down her ring finger. "Perfect fit."

With a mischievous smile, she exclaimed, "I didn't say yes, Mr. Locke."

"I didn't ask, *Mrs. Locke.*"

"Mrs. Locke does have a nice ring to it."

"I've had that ring since I bought this ranch."

Her face paled. "You're lying."

"I always intended on coming back for you."

"I don't know what to say."

"How about we start with how much I want to make love to you for the first time in over a decade with you only wearing that ring?" I opened her robe, gliding it off her shoulders, and it pooled at her feet.

My breath actually hitched as my eyes devoured her bare flesh. She was fucking sexy as sin, looking better than I'd remembered.

"Do you have any idea how many times I've fucked my fist to the image of you like this? And it wasn't even close to how you look right now. Christ, Autumn. You're stunning." Cupping onto her tits, I grinned. "These are bigger."

Shyly, she smirked. "Motherhood, I guess."

My hands skimmed her skin down to her stomach. "I can't wait to see you pregnant."

"Pregnant? Jesus, Julian. You're not wasting any time."

"I've wasted over ten years." Shifting my fingers to her pussy, I rubbed her clit back and forth with the palm of my hand, and she melted into my touch. "Your body has always been so fucking responsive to me. It's one of the many things I love about making you come."

"Okay, cocky sir…" Her knees buckled as I thrust two fingers into her warm, welcoming heat.

There wasn't a place on Autumn's body I hadn't explored, and tonight I'd planned to revisit each one several times.

Finally, I had everything I ever wanted.

Hoped for.

Loved.

I didn't care how long it took us to get to this place, all that mattered was we were there, and we weren't ever going back. She was lucky I didn't have a wedding officiant at the house, wanting to marry us this instant, but I knew she'd want a wedding with her family and friends, and it was my job to make all her dreams come true.

"Mmm…" she moaned, her eyes closing as she leaned her hands on my shoulders, trying to hold herself up.

It didn't take long to have her coming down my arm. Gripping onto her waist, I laid her on the bed and kissed her pussy with my mouth. She still tasted the same, and I couldn't hold back, going to town on her cunt.

"Ahhhh…"

"You think you can do something for me?"

"You're asking me now? When your face is buried in between my legs?"

"Less chance of you saying no."

I sucked her clit into my mouth, moving my head side to side and up and down.

"I'm going to come…"

I stopped, and she jolted forward glaring at me. "Julian! Why did you stop?"

I licked her nub before speaking with conviction, "Give me a baby."

She smiled, big and wide. "I'm not the one who determines that—it's your seed."

"Do you know when we made Capri?"

She nodded.

"Care to share?"

All she replied was, "The Audi R8 drive."

"I always did love that sports car."

"And now you own three."

"Five actually." I began fingering her, and her head fell back. "How long were you off the pill?"

"Oh… I see where you're … going with this."

I finger fucked her g-spot, and she was having a hard time answering my questions. "I'm waiting."

"Your balls are on point … Oh God … at least they were … back then."

"That doesn't answer my question."

"I got pregnant…" Her eyes rolled to the back of her head. "The first month."

It was all I needed to hear. "Good to know. I plan on knocking up right now."

"You're such … a cave man…"

I growled, hitting her sweet spot while I fucked her with my mouth. "That feel good?"

She panted.

Legs trembling.

Body shaking.

She exploded in my mouth, soaking the seam of my shirt in the process. Her legs tightened so hard around my head as she came all the way down my face. I savored the taste of her against my tongue, swallowing all her come before I kissed her clit one last time and crawled my way off her body.

"I'm not even going to get undressed. I'm going to fuck you just like this, and then I'll make love to you when I'm done."

I could never get enough of her sweet, sweet pussy.

Not then.

Not now.

Not ever.

Mine.

In one swift motion I pulled out my cock and thrust inside of her so damn hard that her body flew back toward the headboard. Never letting up, I angled my leg and took her like a madman.

"You going to give me a baby?"

"Yes..."

"I want at least five more."

We locked eyes.

"Five?" she countered as I pounded into her, wanting my seed to go as deep as possible.

"At least."

"Julian! I'm not a cow."

I slammed into her, relentless to get her pregnant while shoving my tongue in her mouth. "Fuck, I missed you. You've always had such a tight pussy." I angled my leg higher, making her leg incline. Our mouths parted as I roughly took what had always been mine.

Feeling myself start to come apart, I fucked her like a man who was starved.

"I love you," she moaned.

"Say it again."

"I love you, I love you, I love you..."

Her cunt squeezed the shit out of my cock and after I made her come a few more times I finally let myself go. Spreading my seed so far inside her core, there was no way I didn't get one in there. I kissed her one last time, peering deep into her eyes.

My world was staring back at me, and it was hard to breathe.

I was home.

Where I belonged.

Without any uncertainty, I told her the truth of how much she always owned my heart and soul...

"I love you, Autumn. Now, then, always.

epilogue

Julian

"Daddy, how do I look?"

"Like the most beautiful flower girl in all the world."

Capri beamed, grabbing onto her uncle's hand. "I'm ready now."

"Are you?" Christian questioned, nodding at me.

"Never been so ready for anything in all my life."

"Good to hear." My best man patted me on the back.

The last three months sped by, and I'd wasted no time in demanding Autumn to begin planning our wedding. We were exchanging our vows on the ranch, and she was adamant on it being in our home. Saying it was part of her dream from when she was a little girl.

It was small and intimate. I was still very much a private man, and I didn't want to share our day with anyone other than family and close friends. The press was having a fucking field day with our wedding, and I had to hire security and built tents because reporters were flying over our estate, trying to get the first picture of us as man and wife.

Although, I didn't let any of that get to me. There wasn't anything I wanted more in this world than to have Autumn take my last name. Capri's last name was also changed to Locke.

By law, my family was mine now.

As soon as I witnessed my girl coming down the aisle to

become Mrs. Locke, all I could think about was how lucky I truly was. My gaze never left hers the entire time.

She was breathtaking.

Her hair flowed loosely down her face, wearing very minimal makeup, fully aware I wanted to see those freckles. She wore a fitted white gown that accentuated all the curves of her body, but I was the only one who knew what was really beneath her wedding gown, triggering my cock twitch at the mere thought.

I smiled a reassuring smile as her old man placed her hand in mine. "I couldn't be happier for you."

"Thank you, Dad."

He nodded, loving the fact that I'd called him that. Even when I was younger, they always insisted I address them as Mom and Dad, but I couldn't bring myself to do it. I no longer had that issue. Winking at her mom, who was sitting in the front row, I turned my attention back to the woman who was moments away from becoming my wife.

The minister proceeded, until he finally arrived to the part I craved the most…

Our vows.

"Autumn, if it weren't for you, I'd be living a lonely life. I found my soulmate through my best friend, and I will forever be grateful for the gift that is you, kid. You make me a better man, father, and human being. I'd be lost without you, and I was for over ten years. Everything I've made for myself is because of the love and faith you had in me. Words can't express how much I love you, how much I need you, how much you mean to me. Capri and you are my entire world, and your parents and brother make it better."

Tears slid down her face, and I wiped them away.

"You were made for me. I knew that then, and I know that now. I can't wait to spend the rest of my life with you. I love you."

Although she was still crying, she'd never looked more beautiful in my eyes.

Autumn

"Julian," she breathed out. "You're everything I ever wanted. From the first piggy back ride I was yours."

He scoffed out a chuckle.

"I fought for you and lost, but a part of me thinks we had to go through that to appreciate and value what we really do share. Our love has always been all consuming, and I wouldn't have it any other way. You're the best thing that's ever happened to me, and I can't ever thank you for giving me Capri. The way you love her…" I sucked in a breath. "It's just … everything I knew it would be. You're everything I knew you would be. I love you so much. I never stopped, and I never will. You're the best part of me. I love you, Julian Locke."

The minister proceeded. "By the power vested in me by the state of Texas, I now pronounce you husband and wife. Julian, you may kiss your bride."

He gripped onto the sides of my face and brought me over to him. I went effortlessly, and we claimed one another's lips for the first time as husband and wife. We spent most of the evening dancing in each other's arms, enjoying all the wedding traditions. Wanting to savor every second of our day. Until he grabbed my hand, leading me to the barn where we could be alone for a couple of minutes.

"I can't believe no one suspects."

"Julian… stop it."

He kissed my lips. "Kid, you're six weeks pregnant."

"I know! I didn't want the press to find out and say you're only marrying me because I'm pregnant."

He laughed, kissing me again. "I don't give a fuck what the press thinks and says."

"I know. It's one of the things I love the most about you. It's why you have me as your publicist. I put out the fires you love to start. Well, that and your huge cock."

He laughed so hard his head fell back. "God, I fucking love you, Mrs. Locke."

"I love you, Mr. Locke."

Crouching, he kissed my belly. "I can't wait to meet you."

I rubbed his head, and when it disappeared under my dress, I exclaimed, "Julian!" before I could stop him—who was I kidding. Before I could come in his mouth, we were interrupted by Kinley's voice.

"Christian! I can't be here! I need to leave!"

"For fuck's sake, Kinley! You can't leave my little sister's wedding!"

"I don't care! It's your fault that no one knows the truth, and the longer I'm there, the harder it is to not tell everyone."

Julian popped back up, staring straight at me. The concern evident all over his handsome face. We were both rendered speechless when Christian announced…

"We're not ruining their wedding because you want to tell everyone right now that we're getting a divorce!"

The end.

For Julian and Autumn.

It's only the beginning or is it *the end* for…
Christian and Kinley.

I met my soulmate when I was thirteen years old, never imaging our love wouldn't be enough to save us from circumstances beyond our control.
Dr. Alpha (Standalone/Second Chance Romance)

meet
M. ROBINSON

Wall Street Journal & *USA Today* Bestselling Author M. Robinson loves her readers more than anything! They have given her the title of the 'Queen of Angst.' With several bestselling novels under her belt, she loves to write and couldn't imagine doing anything else with her life.

Her readers are everything to her and she loves to connect with her following through all her social media platforms, also through email! Please keep in touch in her reader group VIP on Facebook, if she's not in there than she is on Instagram or her author Facebook page.

She lives in Brandon FL with the love of her life, her lobster, and husband Bossman. They have one Wheaten Terrier, a Miniature Cockapoo, and a user Tabby cat. She is extremely close to her family, and when she isn't living the cave life writing her epic love stories, she is spending money shopping or living boat life. Anywhere and everywhere. She loves reading and spending time with her family and friends whenever she can.

She truly appreciates her readers being on this writing journey with her. She thanks God every day that this is her life of telling stories to make people feel and disappear to another world.

Being an author is her first passion in life. It was what she was meant to do on this earth. Be a portal for characters who want their stories told.

acknowledgments

Executive assistants & all around the reason I can write: Silla
Webb & Heather Moss
Editor: Silla Webb
Publicist: Danielle Sanchez
Agent: Stephanie DeLamater Phillips

Bloggers/Bookstagrammers: Without you I'd be nothing. Thank
you for all your support always.

My VIPS/Readers

Street Team Leaders: Leeann Van Rensburg & Jamie Guellar
Teasers & Promo: Heather Moss & Silla Webb

My VIP Reader Group Admins:
Lily Garcia, Leeann Van Rensburg, Jennifer Pon, Jessica Laws,
Louisa Brandenburger

Street Team & Hype Girls: You're the best.

My alphas & betas:
Thank you for helping me bring this book to life.

tell me you want me

WILLOW WINTERS

From *USA Today* best-selling author, Willow Winters, comes a sexy office romance with a brooding hero you can't help but fall head over heels for … in and out of the boardroom.

I didn't get to where I am by being nice.

I'm the boss, the CEO, the owner of whatever I want. Right now, that includes every person in this building of the company I just bought.

I stop at nothing once I've decided I'm taking something.

And then she showed up … full of spitfire just for me, the man she's decided is her worst enemy.

Like I said, I stop at nothing once I've decided I'm taking something. This pretty little thing just moved to the top of my "must acquire" list.

prologue

Adrian

"C AN YOU BELIEVE HOW WE STARTED?" Suzette questions, her voice barely above a murmur. I've gotten used to her whispers this late at night. It's nearly midnight now. I've gotten used to far too much because of her. This room, on the top floor of the most coveted skyscraper facing Bryant Park, has been hell every morning when the partners arrive. When they leave, and most of the lights turn off, and Suzette hesitantly knocks on the large walnut door to my office … it's been nothing but heaven.

As if I would ever turn her away. As if I could possibly deny myself, let alone her.

"Can I believe how we started?" The low timbre of my voice carries an echo of her question, a chill flowing along my shoulders as the air conditioner switches on. My gaze slips to the dark wood flooring barely lit by a single lamp in the corner of the office. Then it falls to my silk tie atop the puddle of Sue's cashmere blouse, both items thrown carelessly on the floor. She's still naked, completely bared to me, although I've pulled up my slacks. I relax into the high-back chair, my bare skin against the leather, and watch Sue reach for the bottle of scotch. The glasses clink together when she grabs them next. Her pale rose nipples are soft now that she's sated and the sight of them persuades me to run my thumb along the pad of my pointer, desperate to toy with her and bring them back to hardened peaks for me to suck and pluck, forcing more of those delightful sounds from her cherry-red lips.

As she turns slightly from where she's lying across my desk, the dim lights of the city shine through the large paned glass windows and cast shadows along her tempting curves. She is my safety, my temple of solitude, my everything. At this moment, I'm far too aware of what she means to me.

"Yes," she speaks confidently, raising her voice as the amber liquid is poured into the first glass. "I was just thinking that I never would have imagined we'd have …" she pauses, her chest rising and falling with a single breath before carefully placing herself in front of me. The bottle sits to the left of her, and both glasses are to the right. "This," she finishes. With Suzette seated on my desk, her bare feet planted on my chair between my spread legs, her ass balanced on the edge and her breasts directly at my eye level, I have to tilt my chin up to meet her gaze.

The little vixen smirks. She knows what she does to me. I didn't even realize I'd fallen for her until it was too late.

It was nothing more than a game at first. I don't know when it all changed and turned into "this," as she put it. I don't know when it became what it is, but now that I have it, I don't want to lose it.

Can I believe how we started? Did I know it would turn into this?

"No," I say, giving her the answer I know she wants to hear. Her simper and huff of a laugh warm the coldest depths of me, but they're quick to freeze the moment she hands me the cut crystal tumbler of whisky.

I sip it regardless, because she wants me to and because as I do she indulges herself, relaxing and confiding in me. It's all I want, for as long as I can have it.

She has no idea that everything is going to change only hours from now. I'm the only one suffering of the two of us.

I can only imagine the betrayal she'll feel tomorrow when the headlines reveal the truth in black and white.

With the soft hum of a satisfied woman, Suzette leans forward, lowering her lips and positioning them right there for the taking. The glass landing with a hollow *thunk* on the maple desk is the only sound in the room besides the raging of my blood pounding in my veins. A moment passes, the heat blistering in her gorgeous gaze as if she can see through me. My stomach sinks and a sick feeling takes over in only a split second as her head tilts and an unasked question seems to linger at her lips.

I act before I let on that anything is wrong. My kiss is nothing shy of ruthless. I don't hold back a damn thing. I take exactly what I want from her because I know, in the depths of my soul, it will be our last time together. Tomorrow, she'll want nothing to do with me. Nipping her bottom lip, I take advantage of that sweet mouth of hers when her lips part with a provocative moan.

"I want you again," I confess to her in a low groan that rumbles up my chest. Both her hands have gripped my shoulders so it's no surprise when her nails dig into my skin and she calls out in surprise as I grab her ass off the edge, pushing her back flat against the desk so I can take her again as I have a dozen times or more.

I have to have her at least once more. One more time where she's mine. Where we have *this* ... before I lose it all when the sun rises.

one

Adrian

Several weeks earlier

My polished Oxfords smack on the sleek marble tile. The floors are the only thing that look expensive in the foyer of this building. It's old and dated just like their business practices. But that's all about to change now that I'm in charge.

Although I keep my expression neutral, maybe cold, as I make my way to the elevator and then to the top floor where the conference room is located, I smirk to myself as I hear the soft whispers and see the secretaries huddling together.

They know who I am. Everyone who's *anyone* does.

Asshole. Prick. Hell, I've even been called a villain. And I couldn't care less.

I pull at the sleeves to my suit and fix my cufflinks before opening the glass door. A dozen people instantly still as I walk into the room, one swivel chair squeaking as everyone goes silent. The conference room smells like the lemon polish the cleaners use on the large oval mahogany table.

That'll be the first thing to replace. The table needs to be glass so I can monitor their body language with every meeting. My father says I was blessed with two gifts: reading people and placing bets. As a gambling man with a head for stocks and companies, I know damn well he was right. And I've left a sea of people who hate me for it in my wake.

I didn't get to where I am by being nice.

I'm the boss, the CEO, the owner of whatever I want. And right now, that includes every person in this building. Straightening my tie, I remind myself I'll have to cull the herd sooner, rather than later. For the sake of both profits and efficiency. The numbers never lie; people always do, though.

"Good afternoon," I say, greeting them as Mr. Holt stands from his spot just to the right of the head of the table, which is empty. No one's seated there because it's reserved for me.

"Mr. Bradford, it's nice to see you again," Jonathan Holt says as he shakes my hand. He's the former owner and now a wealthy man.

A nondisclosure agreement was signed. No one knew I've been the acting CEO for the last quarter. Every email, every camera feed, every contract and meeting was passed through my team. They had a quarter to prove to me this company is worth salvaging.

Not that Holt gave a fuck. He was getting paid regardless. With a tailored gray suit and fresh shave, he's already a lighter, wealthier man than he was when I first met him six months ago to negotiate this deal.

As my eyes skim across each of the members I've invited for this meeting, half likely to stay, half likely to leave, a gorgeous woman catches my interest. She's in a skintight, bloodred dress that matches her perfectly manicured nails. I've seen her wear it before, if I'm not mistaken. Twice, and this makes the third. The third time is the charm.

I already know who she is before she dares to stare back at me with an openly hateful look.

Suzette Parks. Passionate. Dedicated. And hot as hell. I can't help the smirk that slips into place when she meets my gaze directly, daring me to call her out. I've witnessed her lose her patience, all alone in her office, on the brink of losing it. Entertaining isn't enough of a description. I wanted nothing more than to push her against the wall and fuck the frustration out of her. My cock stirs just thinking about how her nails would dig into my back. She's wound tight but not easily shaken. No matter what happens to this company, I'll be damn sure to keep stock of my little vixen.

She's the first to back down and break eye contact. At the same time, the door closes behind me thanks to Mr. Holt, and it signals the beginning of the meeting.

My smile widens and I cover it with my fist, clearing my throat and getting a grip. I knew she'd distract me, I knew she'd get under my skin but I wasn't prepared to be this ... off-balance.

I begin, still standing, and Mr. Holt follows suit. He nearly takes his seat but stands upright when I speak. "I'll make this short. Last quarter was unimpressive and changes will be drastic. That will include layoffs and budget cuts, but is not limited to other necessities. I will rely on each of you selected from your teams for this advertising management firm." I meet all eleven of them eye to eye as I speak. Noting which ones nod, and which ones tense up. I'm not surprised in the least until I get to Ms. Parks, who doesn't bother to peer up. As I speak, her attention is on the pen in her hand. It's an ink pen with a sleek silver body and it silently taps against her leatherbound book. No notes are being taken.

My voice is harder when I state, "I don't believe in failure. Even mistakes are lessons." The quote I've heard her say a dozen times in the last month rewards me with her icy blue gaze. That's better.

I hold her there, pinning her down as I let a second pass and then another. I can practically feel the temperature rise in the room as she struggles not to squirm. The fucking table should have been replaced already.

"Unless you have anything you'd like to say, Mr. Holt," I say and gesture toward the man. He shakes his head, his thin lips pressed in a straight line. "I don't have anything to add," he states and glances across the room.

I don't miss Ms. Parks's hardened expression toward him as well. Good. I'm not the only one she blames.

"Meeting adjourned." I remain where I am, standing tall and watching them disperse while what I was supposed to say comes back to me. I have every name memorized and anger rises inside of me that I didn't make it clear to them I know every detail and statistic that matters. My jaw clenches and with that, they move faster, nodding and giving short waves as they leave.

The annoyance morphs into something else as I peer back at Ms. Parks, the pen tapping harder. She hasn't budged.

"Did you want to say something?" I question her lowly. The last two men in the room pause where they are beside Mr. Holt. Jeffries and Woods. Both were seated farthest away, both paused to my left. Woods knows what he's doing but he's far too casual with clients. I'll be surprised if the threat of a severance package turns his performance around.

In her silence, I add, "You look like you have something to say."

"Adrian Bradford," she states, looking me in the eyes and giving me a tight smile, "we all know why you're here."

For the first time today, I let my emotion come through, simply raising a brow in curiosity. "Is that so?" I ask her.

"You want the company," she says matter-of-factly and then sits back. It's a confident move on her part as if she knows my cards.

"You're very astute," I say clearly condescendingly, and I love how she raises a brow back.

"To rip apart," she adds and then pushes her chair back, standing up and letting me finally see her curves in person. The short red dress rides up just a bit too high on her left thigh, exposing more of her skin and teasing me. I'm usually able to keep my focus, but for her, I let my gaze slip.

She yanks it down.

"Leave my department alone. I won't let anyone ruin it,"

she warns. Warns me. Like this is a tit for tat. Like she has any authority at all in this game we're playing.

"If I want to ruin something …" I pause to adjust my stance slightly as I take another long look at this woman.

"You can try all you'd like, Adrian." The faint smile on her face when my expression hardens upon hearing her use my first name only adds to the insult.

"Suzette Parks, correct?"

Suzette. I taste her name on my tongue. I love everything about it, from the way it rolls off my lips to the manner in which it lingers there, tempting and taunting me.

She offers a nod and that's all, swallowing down her spite and leaving the room.

"Is she typically so … combative?" I ask Mr. Holt as the glass door slams shut so hard that I wouldn't have been surprised if it had shattered. I haven't been on the receiving end of her wrath, but damn if it doesn't make me harder than steel for her.

Jonathan clears his throat, obviously uncomfortable as he shifts his weight where he stands, gripping the back of the chair. "I apologize, sir," he tells me, but that's not the answer to the question I asked.

"Not a worry at all," I comment, not bothering to look back at him as he rambles on. Instead I watch her go, loving that she can't get away from me. Loving that I'll be seeing more of her any damn time I please.

two

HOW FUCKING DARE HE.

How dare this man who doesn't know a single thing about me get to me the way he did? The way his piercing gaze seemed to see through me made my entire body heat. He pinned me where I stood. I felt the intensity of his hunger ignite through every nerve ending in my body, rendering me paralyzed.

I couldn't even speak, let alone look at him. It was embarrassing. Every little thing I did in that room was horribly embarrassing. I'll apologize, only because it's the professional thing to do, but I'm not backing down. My team is worth saving, worth keeping. *If he dares to fuck with me …* I swallow thickly, knowing there's not much I can do to stop him, but he's going to hear every reason why he needs to back down before he ruins what I've spent a decade building.

I've heard rumors about him. All he does is rip apart things that aren't profitable, selling them off or merging what's worth salvaging with other companies. Adrian Bradford is a death sentence. He's my worst enemy come to life and I despise Holt for leaving me in this man's hands.

Steadying my breath, I raise my hand and form a fist at his door. One breath in, and I can't even knock. My knuckles graze the wood and I can't bring myself to do it. "Fucking hell," I mutter beneath my breath.

How has he gotten under my skin the way he has? I'm a

strong woman. I pride myself on it. And yet here I am, cowering in front of a closed door.

It makes me hate him all the more.

It's not just the way he looks at me. Shaking off the anxiousness, the pent-up anger, and the desperate need to get out the rage boiling inside of me, I try yet again.

I'll blame the hell I went through last night for being so shaken.

If I wasn't so shocked, if I wasn't so sleep deprived, if I wasn't so passionate about everything that has to do with this job, storming into his office would be easy.

I know every nook and cranny of this business. When I got here, I knew nothing and quickly discovered the upper-level executives knew even less. Holt was a trust fund baby in over his head. I climbed a steep learning curve and brought my team with me.

How dare he come in here and think that he can take everything away from me? Everything that I've worked for. Everything that *we've* earned.

With an audible exhale, I nod. That's right; that's what I need to be focused on.

With another deep breath, I straighten my spine.

The image of him standing at the head of the conference table is burned into my memory. The hint of a five-o'clock shadow showing already. His dark gray, perfectly tailored suit and sharp jaw. He's like the devil—charming and wicked; threatening yet thrilling. There's a power beneath him that's undeniable. A thought creeps into my mind. Even if he was stripped bare of every expensive fabric that graced his lean but muscular frame, even then, I imagine that man would look expensive as hell. It's not wealth, it's something else. Something entirely different than what I'm used to.

All of these men can walk around in whatever designer suit they'd like but they'd still look cheap. They wouldn't know their dicks from the pens they use to sign away their inheritances. And yet here's a man, the first one I've seen in a long damn time since my divorce has been settled, who makes all of those bastards who have hit on me, who have expected things from me simply because of their bank accounts, look like the arrogant pricks they are.

Every man I've ever laid eyes on in all of New York City pales in comparison to Adrian Bradford. And I was safely surrounded by others, in the light of day, for a total of less than ten minutes.

Here I stand, outside his door, daring to get closer to him and all alone, after hours … this door will remain wide open so long as I'm here. That's for damn sure. There's not a soul on this level and truth be told, I'm not even sure he's in this room. It's Holt's former office and the top floor was reserved for him and meetings only. So … even if this door was open, we'd still be alone.

With my blood heating and my nerves running high, no matter how much I'd like them not to, I imagine what he'll do. I imagine Adrian saying the kind of things that have been said to me in the past by men who have held power over me, like my husband used to, and it has a completely different effect on me today than it ever has before. The very idea of it turns workplace harassment from a lawsuit waiting to happen, into late-night thoughts in bed I share with my vibrator.

Knock, knock, knock.

My hand trembles at my side, but I hold my ground.

Raising my voice, I call out, "Adrian, I'd like—" The door opens far too quickly. I'm left with my mouth hanging open, my words spoken far too loudly and the rest of whatever I was going to say jumbled at the back of my throat.

My heart races as I realize just how close to this man I am. It's no longer a thought, it's reality. He's a man who intimidates me. Not only because of his power, of him merely being in this building and what that means. But also because of what he does to me simply by existing. It's sinful, it's wrong. I fucking hate it.

"Ms. Parks."

Fuck.

My name sounds positively sinful in the rumble of his baritone voice. His steely gaze never leaves mine as I stand there, once again paralyzed. Taking one step back, barely giving me enough room to come in, he motions with his right hand, his left hand holding the doorframe. I break the hold he has me under, shifting my attention to the wall of windows behind his desk.

They're paned windows running from floor to ceiling, and the city is vibrant behind them. I know from experience it's loud as hell far down from this high-rise. But right now, this sight could be a painting, a beautiful masterpiece of a deep blue sky turning a dusky gray with silver buildings that creep into the clouds, the yellow squares of illuminated office windows slowly bringing light to the incoming night.

I've never stepped foot in this office before. I've never been invited here by Holt, I only knew it was his office. From here on out he'll be known as the asshole who took a hefty paycheck instead of giving this company what it truly needed. Essentially, he got a get-out-of-jail-free card and we got … Adrian Bradford.

The room is sparsely furnished. A hardwood maple desk carved with intricate detail catches my eye first. From the smell of lemon in the air, it's been freshly polished. A dark auburn leather wingback chair sits at its head, with two high-back lounge chairs across from it.

Other than that, the vast room is empty, with blank walls that have been freshly painted as if it were brand new. In other words, on the market for the new buyer.

Anger simmers inside of me.

It's only when the door shuts behind me that I remember exactly what I'm doing here. Although the city will never cease to amaze me. I shudder at the click behind me, turning quickly to find Adrian between myself and the door. Tapping the face of his watch, Adrian tells me, "It's nearly six, Suzette."

"Suzette?" is all I can manage. There's tension between us, thick and hot.

His full lips slip into a smirk. "That's what I said." He's calm and so damn sure of himself. Everything I normally am.

"Oh, I'm Suzette now?" Even to my own ears the indignation sounds feigned. My voice quavers as I add, "Only a moment ago I was Ms. Parks."

With a single step forward, Adrian adjusts the expensive silk tie around his neck and his expansive, barren office ignites in an instant.

For a moment, a very quick moment, his icy blue gaze drops to my lips but then they reach my eyes again before I can object to wherever his thoughts have gone. "I said it's nearly six," he murmurs. "Well, after five."

My fingers busy themselves with the hems of my sleeves. I haven't felt so nervous in ages, not since I first stepped foot in this city. All of the anxiousness that comes with starting over, starting something new that pushes you out of your comfort zone is not unfamiliar to me, although it's been a long damn time since I last felt this way. Not since my divorce was finalized.

"Is that a way to tell me to hurry up, Mr. Bradford?"

"No. Not at all. After six I have other business to discuss with you."

"After six?"

"Once work is over." He swallows and my treacherous mind focuses on the cords of his neck. The curves of it, the strength there and that masculine scent, fresh and clean with a hint of sandalwood.

"I beg your pardon, but I'm here on business."

"Yes … other business than what we discussed this afternoon." My pulse races as he locks his gaze with mine. I can't help but to feel like the prey, already caught by a much too powerful hunter. One who wants to play with his dinner before devouring it whole.

"Other business?" Again my voice falters. I make the next statement firm. "What could I possibly want to discuss with you? Other than the threat of you simply stepping into this building." I add with indignation, "My building."

With the little courage I can muster, I lift up my chin. Feeling what I felt hours ago in that boardroom creep back into the forefront of my mind, I try to shove it down. He's no longer a sex god reducing me to a puddle of want. He's the man who threatens my very career. And for what? For statistics on the balance sheet? For the likelihood of an easy payout rather than doing the hard work?

Just as the thought hits me, Adrian checks his watch again. "It's six now, Ms. Parks."

His domineering stature abates as if he's slightly more relaxed. He reaches up to loosen his tie. The act does horrible things to my conviction.

"You're in need," he states beneath his breath. I can barely focus on his lips as his deft fingers work to undo the top button of his shirt. In one step, he's far too close and the smell of his cologne turns heavenly.

"Excuse me?" I whisper, not as confidently as I'd intended. It's darker than it was, as if the night fell around us, granting much-needed privacy.

Leaning down so his lips grace the shell of my ear, he whispers, "All you have to say is that you left something outside of this office." Shivers run down my shoulder, then lower. My nipples are already hard and I curse the fact that I haven't been touched in months for how much I want this man to do horrible things to me right now.

With my lips parted I can barely comprehend what he said. As he takes a single step back, giving me more room to think, he removes his tie completely. The silk whispers in the air as it slides against his collar. It's the only sound I can hear other than the beating of my heart. He doesn't turn around fully and he doesn't take his eyes from mine. He locks the door with one hand and tosses the tie on the floor.

"You very much have the wrong impression of me," he says and I breathe out although I don't know how. My chest rises and falls with every heavy breath I take.

"I was praying you would walk through that door," he tells me. Adrian takes a step forward with his right hand undoing the buttons of his white dress shirt one by one, starting at the top. My gaze slips down his torso, following the line of buttons to the bulge in his pants.

My God. The temperature in the room erupts.

"I was hoping you'd come see me to work out our … differences. I was prepared to spend all fucking day listening to you rant, taking every insult with stride. I was ready to let you get it all out." For every step forward he takes, I take one step back until my ass hits the edge of the desk.

"I would be very surprised if I had the wrong impression, Ms. Parks. But I'd like to get one thing clear." With both of my hands gripping the edge of the desk, I peer up at him, bracing myself. He reaches out and brushes against my jaw with his thumb.

His touch is as commanding as his tone, his stare, every detail about him. I'm left paralyzed. Caught in a trance.

"After six o'clock, all of that shit ends and what's between us is between us." I stare into his eyes, barely breathing as he continues. "I'll say it again; all you have to do is say you've left something outside of this office." His eyes search mine and I believe him. If I were to say it, he'd back away. He'd let me leave. And then what? Would this tension be gone? Would he pretend it didn't exist?

The reality of what's happening and the consequences of the decision I'm about to make are far too real in these few seconds.

With his eyes on my lips, his thumb moves there, parting them slowly so that just the tip of his thumb presses down, enticing me to suck it. He's far too close, far too intoxicating, far too tempting.

"Have you left something outside?" he questions. That deep voice rolls through me again. I know what's appropriate in this situation. I should jerk my head back from his touch and tell him that I did leave something outside. Mention the HR complaint I'm filing against him. That's what you're supposed to do when an asshole like Adrian backs you up against his desk.

It's what I should do. I know it. And yet … I know damn well that I want him. I want this.

The aching need between my thighs reassures me that I fucking *need* this.

Instead of answering, I move my mouth just enough to bite down on his thumb, my teeth sinking into the tip of it. The deep groan at the back of his throat is stifled and with that little movement, I force this rather dominating man to shift in front of me. "I'll need you to answer me, Ms. Parks. Because if you haven't left anything outside, I'm going to fuck you against this desk like I wanted to the second I laid eyes on you."

It's a heady feeling to bring a man like him to the point of desperation. The desire ignites in his eyes and I push him just a little further, flicking my tongue against his thumb.

His eyes close and he speaks without opening them. "Have you left something outside?"

It seems simple, in a way. He was right when he said I was in need. And letting this man do whatever he wants to me would soothe an ache I've had for days. A pent-up need that's been dying to be sated. It would be everything I've needed since I gave my ex the finger and fell down the black hole of an endless to-do list.

Of course it would. Look at him, in his expensive suit with his thumb still tracing a path on my lip and his eyes shut. He's hot. He's more than hot. He's everything I could possibly want in a man. Physically, at least. It doesn't matter that he's an arrogant asshole. I can still hate him as much as I did when I first stormed in here, but right now ... I'm worked up and hot for him.

When his eyes finally open and he stares back at me with an intensity that burns inside of me just the same, I barely speak, "I didn't leave anything outside."

Before the last word is spoken, his lips are on mine, devouring them. Both hands cup my face, pulling me in and my hands splay against his broad chest. He's all man beneath the suit. Strong muscles bulge and tense.

The layers of fabric between us are in the way and I do my part to help strip them off. Adrian isn't hesitant about a damn thing. His hands roam, his lips mold against mine and with every small movement I make, he meets it tenfold. I don't think a man like him is capable of being timid about anything. He puts his tongue in my mouth, glides it against mine, and seems to taste me more deeply than any man ever has before. Wanting more and forcing small sounds from me as his hands roam and the zipper is pulled down my back. The chill of the air greets my bare skin and I have to break the kiss, breathing in the cool air as I arch my neck and throw my head back. Adrian doesn't stop, doesn't pause for anything. His nimble fingers work my dress, sending goosebumps down my skin where his fingertips leave traces of his heated touch.

As I stare up at the ceiling, he leaves a trail of openmouthed kisses down my neck. Hot and greedy, it's enough to pull me back to him.

To rid myself of any thoughts other than those drenched in lust.

Scorching desire prickles over my skin and I find myself kissing him back, maybe a little desperately. Shamefully so. I've always wanted to be kissed like this. It's every girl's dream to be kissed like the other person can't get enough of you. It's only fair if I kiss him back just as hard and make him think I want this. Adrian can think whatever he wants about me. He can think I hate him. He can think I'm melting for him.

If I'm going to do this, I'm going to take as much as I give.

All I care about is the way it's going to feel when he takes control of all the heat between my legs. Will he kiss me there too? Will he be just as ravenous as he is now?

He kisses me harder, demanding more with a rumble from deep in his chest when he puts his hand on one of my legs and slides it slowly up under my dress. There's no hesitation at all with this movement. He got all he wanted from me when I told him I wasn't leaving. Now I'm his to take.

He pauses there before breaking our kiss and letting me breathe, his hand gripping my upper thigh. It's only then that I feel his cock pressed against my leg. He's hard and I wasn't mistaken earlier … no wonder he's so fucking arrogant.

I shiver when he reaches my panties. They're not full coverage ones, because those don't sit well underneath my work clothes, but they're not a thong, either. His fingertips play at the band. Then he cups me through the cotton fabric and I moan into the kiss.

"You're hot for me," he says into my mouth. "I knew you would be the second you started to mouth off to me." Adrian strokes against the fabric and when his knuckles brush against my clit I'm all too aware of how sensitive I am for him. My head lolls to the side and I sink my teeth into the fabric of his shirt. My hands fist his dress shirt, pulling it from his suit pants with a desperate need for it to be ripped from him so we can get on with it.

"Good girl. Such a good little slut for me." My back arches

and I rock myself into his hand. "Fuck you," I mutter but even as I do, the pleasure builds and Adrian chuckles. He's playing me like a toy.

The words make me hot even though I know they shouldn't. I roll my hips against his hand and he groans a deep rough sound, wrapping his other hand around the nape of my neck to pull me in close.

"Do you want to be my whore or my good girl?" he asks me.

I can only gasp as his fingers slip past the band and his thumb rubs ruthless circles against my clit. Moaning, I don't answer him.

"Degradation or praise?" he presses further.

I have both hands on his chest, slid under the expensive fabric of his shirt. "Whatever you want. I just need you inside of me." The plea is desperate, and I don't give a fuck.

He doesn't say a word as he smiles down at me like he's won. For a half second, I worry he'll leave me like this, wanting and admitting it so boldly. The fear is gone just as quickly as it came. His hands go under my ass and he roughly lifts me onto the surface of his desk. Adrian uses one hand to push my legs apart and I balance myself on the desk while he shoves the hem of my dress up to my hips. The fabric rolls up in an awkward bunch and remains there. This dress isn't meant to be treated like that, but he doesn't care. He's busy pulling my panties off and down over my shoes, which fall to the floor with dull thuds. Finally, his fingertips meet my bare, wet center.

It turns me into a woman I don't know. A woman who five minutes ago was coming in here to tell him to keep his hands off my department. Now I'm so hungry for his touch that I practically throw myself into it. Adrian doesn't allow it. He takes what he wants, and he pushes me away from him, one hand splayed across my chest while reaching for his belt buckle with the other. His cock springs out with a flash of lust in his eyes. "Spread wide, Suzette."

I obey and he pulls my hips closer to the edge.

His eyes sweep down to my spread legs and he groans, his hand working at his cock. He wants the same thing from me that I want from him. He wants to work off some of the tension from endless meetings and boardrooms and constantly working, constantly holding everything in.

With a hand on the back of my head, he bends low to kiss me as he nudges the tip right where I need him. Adrian isn't taking time to make sure I'm ready and he doesn't have to. I'm more than ready for him. He pumps his hips and I hang on to the desk to stay on it.

Fuck! He fills me with a single hard thrust, his hand coming down to brace my ass so he can fuck me deeper. My hands fly to his shoulders, needing to hold on to something more solid. My body's hot all at once and tense. My heels dig into his ass.

"Fuck," I moan. Not slowing down in the least, Adrian's lips find mine again. "Fucking perfect," he groans. I bury my head into his chest, my eyes closing and my teeth biting down on my lip as he fucks me like he owns me. He whispers, "Take it like a good girl."

A cold sweat covers my forehead as I pull away, stifling my moans as best I can.

It's dirty to do this and so wrong. It's against every rule of office life to spread your legs on a man's desk … especially when he's your boss. And certainly when he's your boss's boss. My body doesn't care. It clenches around him, making him grunt, and his lips capture my screams of pleasure. My release builds and rises like the tides on the shore until it's crashing down on me. The only option I'm left with is to hang on for dear life.

three

Adrian

NO MATTER HOW MUCH SHE TRIES TO HIDE IT, I CAN still hear her catching her breath.

Fuck, it's hard enough to keep steady myself. My muscles are still coiled with adrenaline rushing through my veins. That was exactly what I needed.

With a hushed moan slipping through her lips as I button up my shirt, I amend the thought: *She* is exactly what I needed.

With my back turned to her, a satisfied smile creeps to my lips and I bend down to pick up my tie. "Do you have plans for dinner?" I ask, balling up the silk and pocketing it rather than attempting a professional appearance in the least.

The unmistakable sound of a zipper replaces the silence in the room, as do the muffled sounds of her attempting to slip her heels back on. I turn to see her peering up at me.

Fuck.

There are so many questions that dance in her gorgeous light blue eyes. The vulnerability is unexpected. Her red dress is still open in the back; her attempt to zip it up only moved it partway.

Distrust riddles itself in every small movement she makes. It's so damn obvious as she stares back at me like she's afraid to even breathe.

"Turn around," I command her, not liking wherever her pretty little head has taken her. "Let me help you with that."

She only hesitates a moment, still not having answered my

question. I take my time, using the backs of my fingers to brush her brunette locks to the side. My hand brushes against her bare back before I zip up her dress to the top. I don't miss that she uses her right hand to brace herself on the desk and she stares down at it rather than looking back at me. The obvious insecurity has my dick hardening already. If she thinks I only wanted her once or that this was some kind of manipulation tactic, my little vixen is dead wrong.

"I have reservations for dinner. Come with me."

She's silent still as she comes back to reality. Her cheeks are still flushed, her lips still swollen from my bruising kiss. With her hair disheveled, she looks well and thoroughly fucked.

Stepping to her right so as not to be trapped between myself and the desk I've just fucked her on, she leaves me wanting.

"I should go," is all she says.

Panic is something I didn't expect to feel. Certainly not with a woman like her, confident and transparent. If she leaves right now, I'm fucked. We barely spoke. There's no chance in hell she'll let me near her again.

This is not at all the way it was supposed to go.

"We have reservations and we're going to be late."

"We? *We* have reservations?" she says and finally looks me in the eye. That's better. Wherever her head is, whoever screwed her over to the point of not trusting another man, it's in the past.

"I don't want to go alone. So yes. We have reservations at the Waldorf."

"I'm not dressed for that," she responds far too quickly.

I make a point of letting my eyes undress her from head to toe. "The hell you aren't. You look utterly delectable."

"I would never wear something like this to the Waldorf."

Watching as she smooths her hair, her gaze dancing between me and the door, I offer her a simple solution. "We can stop on the way."

She rolls her eyes and my cock answers in response,

hardening and wanting so desperately to punish her. "I have plenty of money if I—"

"I could buy you a thousand times over." My voice is harder than I'd like but I'm through with this little back-and-forth. "If I say we can stop to buy you whatever the hell I want, it's not because I wish to spoil you or show off. It's to save time and for your comfort."

My statement must have come off harsh, because her jaw clenches. I add, "I couldn't care less what you wear."

"I wouldn't want to be seen with someone like you, showing off your recent conquest." The bitterness to her tone might as well slap me across my face.

Is that what she thinks this is? Is that who she thinks I am?

Invading her space, I tower over her and say, "When did I give you the impression you were something to conquer? I want you because I want you, and I couldn't care less what anyone else thinks of that."

All that anger, all that resentment—it all vanishes the second I exert any dominance over her. It's addictive. It's heaven and hell, a concoction I'd gladly get drunk on every second for the rest of my life.

"I am one thing in the boardroom. I'm another outside of that. If you can't compartmentalize, tell me now."

"I'm sorry," she says and her doe eyes fall to my chest. She's on the verge of running and that's the last thing I want.

"I don't want you to apologize," I say, gentling my voice, tipping up her chin so she'll finally look at me. See me. "I want you to come to dinner with me."

WHAT THE FUCK JUST HAPPENED? I'm not certain how I made it downstairs from his office with his hand splayed across my lower back, in front of anyone who dared to look. My legs are weak and there's an odd mix of satisfaction and nervousness that has my head clouded.

Adrian Bradford just fucked me across his desk like I was his personal toy. The feel of him between my legs is all I can focus on. How effortlessly he destroyed every wall I've built and fucked me like he had every right in the world to ruin me.

I'm barely with it as he helps me to his car until he speaks to his driver, who politely greets me before opening the back door. Adrian says something to him that I don't quite make out because I'm still catching my breath from the sex.

The cool spring air brings me back to the present as I thank his driver. He's an older gentleman with a lean frame and silver hair. His wire-rimmed glasses and black suit complete his polished look.

"Thank you," I say, barely getting out the words before I'm left alone in the back of the car, until Adrian climbs in on his side.

It's a Mercedes, one of the new ones from this year, and it smells like he just drove it off the lot. Adrian's driver rolls up the divider that separates the spacious back seat from the front the moment he gets in.

Adrian sprawls out on the seat next to me as the driver navigates the city streets. He's on his phone like nothing happened and I try to act like nothing happened too. I'm having a bit of trouble with that. He seems casual, swiping at the screen and no doubt answering emails, but there's tension crackling between us. No matter how hard he tries to make this into nothing, it's anything but.

Gaining a semblance of balance and sanity, I peer up at him and say, as clearly as I can, "I'm not a toy to be played with."

He glances at me, then slips his phone into his back pocket. "You seemed to enjoy it quite a bit."

My face reddens. "I did. But that doesn't mean it can continue or that my job ..." my voice trails off and I can barely swallow. *What the fuck did I just do?*

He studies me with his pale blue gaze. "Would you like it, though?" There's far too much space between us in the back seat of his car. Adrian's taking care not to touch me. It feels deliberate. He doesn't move his body toward me or reach for me, but I can still feel his hands on me from just a moment ago. I can feel where he gripped my ass and held me close for a kiss by my neck, and where he stroked between my legs. "Would you like it if I toyed with you again?" he asks, his voice low and his words sinful.

The rest of my body feels as hot as my face. Now that we're out of the office and away from the moment, I can't believe it happened. What was I thinking? I can't answer him, because I'm not sure of myself enough to speak. It's all too much and far too fast. Suffocating.

"I'd like an answer, Suzette," he says and his murmur is laced with something different. Concern.

Swallowing thickly, I admit, "I enjoyed it very much, but now—"

"I enjoyed it immensely and I intend to toy with you, to

fuck you until you're as limp as a little ragdoll, and to walk back into the office tomorrow knowing full damn well you may give me hell."

The leather groans in protest as he leans back, moving farther away as he studies me. "Nothing that just happened will interfere with our work," he reassures me.

With a jostle of the vehicle, the driver pulls the car to the curb, and I blink at the scenery outside my window. The Waldorf, another public arena for his games ... and a far too expensive one at that. I murmur, "You should take me home."

He's silent for a moment, just watching me. "If that's what you'd like. I believe I owe you more than just a drink, though, Suzette."

Hearing my name from his lips like that ... like every syllable rolls off his tongue as if he was the first to utter them, turns me even hotter. It also makes me speechless, which isn't like me at all. None of this is like me at all. I don't get swept up into anything.

Adrian holds me in place with his piercing gaze. "I'd very much like to play with you, Suzette. I'd like to kiss you. I'd like to fuck you. And not just because you're a pretty little thing who stormed into my office making demands you have no authority to make."

With every word, he inches closer to me until he's close enough to kiss me. The proximity is comforting in a way I don't care to admit. Adrian actually leans down and does it. He kisses me full on the mouth, his lips steady and confident. When he pulls back I have to keep my hands in my lap from grabbing his shirt.

"It was a brutal day, and the only thing that kept me grounded and kept me looking forward to tonight was the very idea that you were coming to my office to do exactly what you did." His admission shocks me.

"Adrian ..."

"You may see me as ruthless and heartless, and you may not like what I do, but I'd like to see you again. In and out of the office."

It's strange for him to admit this to me. Most men won't ever acknowledge they're aware of other people's feelings. Men like Adrian aren't supposed to care what anyone else thinks. It's possible he doesn't care, but at least he's aware of it. It causes a shift in the way I see him. The hatred softens and becomes something else.

"When the workday is over, there are other things we must do. And then there are things that we *want* to do." He leans in closer, whispering at the shell of my ear, "I want you."

His hand comes down on my knee and without hesitation he pushes it up between my legs, forcing my skirt up as his fingers brush against my slit. It's the softest of touches and my eyes close, my lips parted and my head falling back. Adrian lets out a groan, the tip of his nose running along my neck, teasing me. "You didn't put your panties back on."

I shake my head, unable to speak. I didn't. I tucked them into my purse, not liking their condition after … well, after what he did to me. Adrian dips his head again, close enough to kiss, and I want it so much that tears come to my eyes. I'm not even sure what they mean. Adrian seems to know.

"You," he says, "are exactly what I want."

He takes a deep breath and then exhales, the warmth of it lingering as he pulls away slightly. Trapped in his car, every sensation feels heightened, knowing how easy it is for him to admit his desire. I become aware of his hands. One holds the seat behind me, just above my head, and the one that was between my legs is now braced against the door, like he must hold on to something to keep him from touching me. From doing whatever it is he so desperately craves to do. Adrian's eyes close for a moment and when he opens them, he seems steadier than before. "If you'd like to go home, I'll take you home. I'll have my driver take you wherever you need. Though I'd very much like to take you to dinner."

"I'm not dressed for this place."

"We could go somewhere else."

"You have reservations," I say and my pulse races, not wanting me to deny him … or myself.

"That's a weak excuse, Suzette." Disappointment flashes across his face, and surprise grips my heart. I'm surprised I care about his disappointment and I'm even more shocked that I *want* to go to dinner with him. He feels dangerous, like he could crush me if he wanted. Yet I find myself wanting to be under his thumb, wondering what he'll do to me.

I don't know where I'm supposed to draw the line, though. This is … this is something that could certainly destroy me, and then what would I have left?

I imagine how it will feel to have the car pull away from the curb and drop me at my place. And then I imagine what it would be like to let him help me out of the car and take me inside this restaurant. Both options leave me wanting, but only one feels safe.

"Is it a business dinner?" I ask, keeping my voice low and even.

A grin tugs the corners of his mouth upward. "No. It's after six."

"If someone asks?" A bit of desperation creeps into my tone, and I can't stop it. "Could it be a business dinner if someone were to see us?"

"You'd like to be discreet?"

I have to be discreet. I don't even know what this is. A hate fuck turned into a dinner date? There's no telling what I might want to keep hidden later.

"Yes," I answer. "Please. It would make me feel better."

He seems to consider it, searching my expression as we sit

in the back of the parked car. "Would you like to see me again after tonight?"

There's a pressure in my chest, like a balloon getting filled up with helium. It reminds me of the excitement I felt when I was young and dumb and dating. Before I got married and everything went to shit. There was a period in my life when it seemed like anything could happen. That woman would revel in this moment. But that woman got her heart ripped out long ago. She's long dead and buried.

"It depends," I finally make myself say. "On how our discreet dinner goes."

Adrian smirks, charming and seductive, making him all the more handsome. It sends a shiver of desire down my spine. I already want him again. Even at this point there's so much heat between us and it seems impossible to turn it down. Above all, I want to see him smile at me with approval. I've never been a people pleaser. I've always been about making change, and change is often uncomfortable for others. Part of me still wants to *please* him. *I want to hear him call me his good girl again.*

"So you'll come to dinner with me and then decide? That's a fair deal."

Adrian stares at me across the table of our rather private curved booth. His gaze is fire; everything about him is possessive, but in a manner that's effortless. Every little thing, including the way his touch never left me when he escorted me into the Waldorf, is dominating yet in a way that's gentle. I could have walked faster or simply pulled away from him, but there was never a moment where I considered such a betrayal. Both to what he obviously desires, as well as my own.

Tucked away in the corner of the restaurant, with fine leather upholstery covering the padded wooden frame, it's easy enough to peek out at the other guests, although they feel miles away. It feels like they're all staring at us, though they're not. I shift in my seat. If they're looking over here, they'll notice I'm underdressed.

"I love seeing you squirm," says Adrian in a low voice.

"About the meeting today …" I begin.

"We're off the clock," he says simply, ending the conversation without breaking my gaze.

I bite my lip and try to keep from bringing up work again. It would be so easy to fall into that.

The tension is still there, and I do my best to not so nervously lay the napkin across my lap as the waiter presents the menu to us.

I let the menu fall as Adrian orders for me. He's quick and confident, as if we already know each other.

"Would that be all right?" he asks and inclines his head toward me before the waiter can leave. Nodding, I give my seal of approval.

I wait until the waiter has stepped out of earshot before I speak to him. "You're lucky you chose what you did."

"I guessed right? Or are you just saying that?" His eyes on mine seem to see right through my dress, as if he's remembering earlier at the office.

"You did guess right." My fingers slip along the stem of my water goblet.

"If it's not to your liking, I'll have them bring you something else," he says, and I feel myself blushing with a sudden shyness I haven't felt in years. Not since I was a girl. There's no place for shyness in a business career like mine. Adrian puts a hand to my face and runs his thumb over my cheek.

"You get to me, Adrian."

"That seems fair, since you get to me as well." Butterflies

stir and I can't help it. "Are you always like this?" I question but all I'm rewarded with is a charming, knowing smirk before we're interrupted.

The waiter reappears, and there's distance between us again. In his starched black uniform, the waiter sets out a wineglass. Then he shows Adrian the bottle, and at Adrian's nod he opens it and pours a sip or two. Adrian tastes it. The waiter watches him the same way I'm watching him. Probably too closely. He lets the wine linger on his tongue before swallowing it and giving the waiter a nod.

He fills my glass and places it in front of me, murmuring his replies to our thank-yous, and Adrian curls his fist around his own glass. Whiskey, on the rocks.

I watch him take the first sip and notice the way his shoulders relax.

"Is this how you are with all your employees?" I ask.

Adrian raises an eyebrow. "I haven't slept with an employee ever, actually."

"Why do I find that hard to believe?" I arch an eyebrow, leaning in, trying to flirt with him.

He answers me in an utterly serious tone. "Because you don't trust me and seem to hold a rather low opinion of me."

I jerk back a few inches, shock settling in. Is he really offended by this? We just had sex on his desk, in his office, at work. The only boundary was that it was slightly after 6:00 p.m. "I didn't mean to imply that I think poorly of you. And for the record, it's because you exude sex appeal so I imagine you could sleep with anyone you wanted."

Adrian chuckles, his rough short laugh a baritone rumble in his chest, and it breaks up the tension. "You do seem very hesitant around me. Is there something I can do to ease that?" His words fall slowly, drifting to the pressed and starched linen tablecloth as his eyes drop to my breasts. "To break the ice, perhaps?"

"You have a reputation, Adrian."

"Everyone does, Suzette. It doesn't mean that's who we are. One person could tell you I'm loyal to a fault, another that I'm a miserable asshole. Both could very well be honest impressions of me. So, believe them both."

Before I can even respond, we're interrupted yet again.

"Excuse me, sir." The waiter steps to the side of the table and passes a folded note to Adrian.

With Adrian's nod we're alone again, although I might as well not exist.

He reads it, tucks the thick white note card into his pocket, and checks his phone.

My stomach drops. "Is everything all right?"

His phone goes back into his pocket. "As all right as it always is."

My teeth sink into my bottom lip as I gather my courage for the next question, which I should have asked before I fucked him. "There isn't another woman, is there?"

"No." The answer comes quickly and decisively, and I believe him. "I haven't had a sexual partner for the better part of a year."

The handle of my fork rests in my fingertips, but I drop it back down to the empty small plate again. "No other man?" he questions in turn.

"No." It's a relief to hear that. A bigger relief than I would have thought.

"And we're to be discreet?" Adrian finishes.

"Yes," I say.

"Work during the day, and play at night?"

"Yes," I answer.

His eyes narrow. "I like when you answer me like that, a single word rushing out of your perfect, parted lips." His gaze burns. "I'd like to see those lips when I—"

Adrian gets another text and curses under his breath. He's not the only one. My phone buzzes too.

It's from Maddie: *Hey! Are you coming?*

"Oh … I'm so sorry." I push my hair back from my face and brace myself with both hands on the table. "I'm supposed to meet a friend tonight. I completely forgot."

Of the three women I'm closest to, Maddie is like my little sister. She's also going through a breakup and relying heavily on company to keep her from texting the asshole when she feels lonely.

"I can't believe I forgot."

"No time to eat?" he questions, not pressuring me in the least. His phone buzzes yet again before I can even answer, and he closes his eyes, visibly annoyed.

"I'm sorry, I really have to go. She's a good friend of mine and I don't know how it could have possibly slipped my mind that we had plans." I swallow down the horrible feeling of failing her, knowing exactly how I came to forget about anything other than the man seated in front of me. "I'm going to take a cab."

"If you insist."

"I'm afraid I do, Mr. Bradford." As I speak, I stand and he mirrors the motion.

"No longer Adrian?"

He holds his hand out to me and it takes me a minute to understand what he wants. "I'll walk you out."

It's almost unreal what a gentleman this man is after hours. "Will you be so kind to me tomorrow?" I question as if it's banter, but the truth is obviously buried there.

It only takes one motion from Adrian for the doorman to bring around a taxi for me. The night has fallen dark and the chill brings me closer to Adrian as the car pulls up.

"Phone." He says the one word and I hand him my phone without question. Adrian frowns down at the screen while he types something. It's his number. His fingers fly across the screen. I'll probably find out he's sent a text to himself with my number.

"I'll see you tomorrow," he says, handing it back to me. "Perhaps you'll give me the opportunity to play with you once the clock strikes six."

five

Adrian

I**T TAKES GREAT EFFORT NOT TO LET ON THAT MY PANTS** are tight from my little vixen's text messages. I'm certain Wyatt wouldn't appreciate that fact.

With that being said, it's my office. My meeting.

And if I want to read the filthy things she's messaging, I'll damn well do as I please.

I'll have to scold her when I see her. Not now, while she's working, when I'm not buried deep inside her and she has nowhere to go.

Scrolling through the last messages she sent, I have to readjust in my seat.

Suzette Parks has a very dirty mouth and I want to do very dirty things to it.

It's work hours, though, so I don't respond to the three she's sent me.

This morning was one thing, and technically I started the "sexting games" as she called it.

No panties today. I want to fuck you without having to rip them off.

Yes, sir.

That's my good girl.

You say that now but if you tell me to crawl under your desk, that will be a firm no from me.

Why do I think you're lying?

I remember when I sent the last message, I watched both the clock and the security monitors that kept track of her entering the elevator. It was nearly 9:00 a.m.

Tell me what you would do then, if I wanted you to keep me company in my office.

Did I set her up? Fucking right I did. Am I going to fuck her hard and rough to punish her for the unprofessional behavior she's displayed? Hell yes I am. And we're both going to enjoy it.

It's all talk from her. I know it is. So, scolding her will have to wait.

"I don't know, man," Wyatt says, nudging the container of lo mein closer to me. Piling the bit of it left on his plate onto a white plastic fork he tells me, "I prefer the place on Fifth."

"Shing Kwong?"

He nods, still shoveling the Chinese food into his mouth. Wyatt is tall, lean, and three years younger than me although it feels like there's a decade between us. He's naive, positive about far too much and riskier than he should be.

I didn't come from money. We were slightly well-off, but not like the Pattons, Wyatt's family. It shows. He makes deals like there will always be a safety net beneath him. I'd be lying if I said I wasn't resentful of it at one time in my life. As the end of a noodle slaps his chin, sauce dripping down his amber skin, the corners of my lips turn up.

Wyatt is a puppy dog in the elite groups I run in, but he's damn loyal.

"Yeah."

"Well, you're welcome to bring your own takeout next time you decide to swing by then, rather than having Andrea order it."

"So I'll have that contract for you in just a little bit."

My brow arches at the very sudden change in topics. "I knew you'd bring it up."

He smirks, not looking back at me, and says, "I can't help it; I'm excited."

"I haven't said I'll sign, and I'm still waiting on my lawyer to look over the clauses."

"It's been a year in the making," he comments, finally putting down his plate.

"I'm not sure it's the right time right now."

It's silent for a moment and Wyatt finally looks up at me, running his hand over his curly, jet-black hair. It's cropped close to his scalp with a slight fade on the sides. "'Cause of this," he says and motions behind him with his thumb.

Because of the eight-figure company I just bought? Yes. That would be why. Although I'd never admit it out loud. My funds aren't typically tied up in so many holdings. The timing was right for Holt & Hanover, though. He was desperate and I had the last bit of cash flow I could manage.

"You know I don't go into these things lightly."

One thick black brow raises as he leans back in the chair, pointing a finger at me. "You know this is a good deal."

"It *could* be a good deal," I respond, correcting him and before he can say any more, I tell him, "Let the lawyers talk out the details."

"They're minor," he presses, his insecurity showing as he grips the armrest of the lounge chair. "The merger is going to be a hit and I know you want in on it."

I mirror his posture, leaning back in my seat as I ball up my napkin and toss it onto my empty paper plate that's stained from lunch. "A number of events need to go accordingly." In this business, there are ebbs and flows. Some people can't handle the wild swings. Some don't prepare for the crashes.

"You sound like my father," Wyatt quips.

I merely grunt, checking my phone again and see she hasn't messaged any more. I'm tempted to send another text regardless.

My thumb taps on the desk, my attention very much focused on the last line she sent an hour ago.

"Who is she?" he asks and I stare back at him blankly.

"Of all the—" Just as a grin stretches across his face, ready to lay into me, there's a knock at the door.

"Come in." I'm grateful for the interruption.

"Mr. Bradford," Andrea says, stepping into the room. If it weren't for the faint wrinkles around her eyes and the corners of her mouth, she'd look two decades younger than she is.

"Andrea could look it over?" Wyatt suggests and then huffs a laugh.

"She looks over all my contracts," I'm quick to tell him. She may only hold the title of secretary, and she looks the part, but Andrea Anderson is sharp and has a legal background that could rival the best. Times were different back then and instead of a firm, or the head of an academic department, Andrea left law altogether and I was lucky enough to meet her before someone else got ahold of her.

"Sir." Andrea folds her hands in front of her pencil skirt. "Your one o'clock is seated in the conference room."

All traces of humor are gone and dread seeps in.

"Thank you, Andrea." As I stand, Wyatt watches me button my jacket and take a mint.

Everything feels stiff and uncomfortable.

The moment the door closes gently, Andrea disappearing behind it, Wyatt comments, "Uh-oh. I'm guessing someone is about to get a harsh scolding from their new CEO."

I huff a humorless laugh, striding around him and tossing what's left of lunch into the trash.

"Can you clean up on your way out?"

"Yeah, you all right?" he questions as I open the door and glance through to the conference room. There's a reason there's only one office up here and then that room.

I get a glimpse of some of the employees seated around a

table, my hand still on the doorknob. My hand is clenched so tight, my knuckles have gone white.

"You going to fire someone?" Wyatt makes another guess and this time he's right. I look over my shoulder to inform him, "An entire department. A very inefficient, very much *unneeded* department." I feel sick to my stomach just saying it. Knowing how in a single meeting I'll change their lives forever. But it's the right decision. The company is bleeding money with these cookie-cutter executives. Their pay increased while tasks were delegated and as the company grew, their roles diminished as new employees took on tasks that came with new demands. A dozen men and women walked into this building today over-looking tasks they barely comprehend.

"Shit," Wyatt says and he doesn't hold back on the misery. "I know if you're doing it, it must be done." His large brown eyes look sympathetic.

"Tell that to them."

six

Suzette

A DRIAN IS MOST OF THE REASON I COULDN'T SLEEP. Those dreams were too hot to forget and they made me twist and turn in the sheets until morning. There was plenty to keep my mind occupied between replaying what happened on his office desk and the way he treated me after. The man himself is a whirlwind and I can barely hold on. There's an ache between my thighs still, even though it's been hours and hours.

The tall macchiato does nothing to help the bags under my eyes, but with a deep breath in, I prepare to make my way to my office like nothing happened.

Stepping foot inside feels illicit in a way it never did before. I've always come in with my chin up, ready to do battle for another day. Today that kick-ass persona is nowhere to be found. It's somewhere between a childish puppy dog love and the feelings that accompany the walk of shame.

In all those hours of tossing and turning, I came to one conclusion: I have, what feels like, a crush. Back in high school I used to get this fluttering-heart feeling for some of the guys in my class … that ended less than well. Pining after men in college led to my ex-husband. So all of these feelings can fuck off. It's against everything I stand for to have that kind of feeling for Adrian. It's forbidden to have sex with your boss on his desk. It's wrong to daydream about it so much you lose focus on your work.

It's a no go. A hard pass. But I'll be damned if I didn't text him the second he messaged me. Those giddy little feelings are my kryptonite. I suppose there's always an exception to every rule and Adrian Bradford is just that: exempt from every boundary I've spent years defining. Even as I sit at my desk, the tapping of keys and hushed chatter around me, I can barely keep from looking toward the elevator. All I want to know is if he's up there. I want to know if he can't stop thinking about what happened on his desk either.

Hours pass slowly through the day until I get a text message from him at four. His name on my phone makes the temperature of my body kick up a notch. I swallow hard, trying to subdue it all.

Adrian: *Meet me at the elevator at six.*

The hours went by slowly before but now they drag on and on, each tick of the clock taking forever. I stare at my computer screen, rereading every email twice. Triple-checking my responses to clients and sending back nearly every design I'm given from the graphics department. Not because they need changing or that they don't fit the branding for said clients. But simply because I can't focus and there's no way in hell I'm approving anything when all I keep imagining is my boss's expression when he calls me good girl.

At four fifteen there's a meeting in one of the smaller conference rooms downstairs. It's all I can do not to stare at Adrian through the large paned windows. In the glances I do steal, he appears less than thrilled. Every expression is dour as they leave one by one, Adrian leaving last and not looking back.

At ten to five, half a dozen executive assistants and senior executive assistants, some of whom I know but most I don't, move through the office in a clump. It's a relief that something has happened to break up the routine of the day.

"Fired," Gail whispers to me. I nearly spill my coffee when she does. I didn't realize she was standing so close, also spying.

"What?" I question. I've known Gail for years now. She's a damn good resource for client retention, but also the lead watercooler gossip. "Did you say fired? Are you sure?"

Nodding, she sweeps her curly dark brown hair back over one shoulder and then holds her coffee cup with both hands. In heels and leaning against the wall, the modelesque Latina in her late twenties towers over me. "I bet there will be an email going out soon."

All of them? Fired? She leaves me with a sick feeling stirring in the pit of my stomach as she bids her farewell. "It's what he does. No one should be surprised."

I know he has a reputation, but how the hell can a company run if every executive is severed?

Not long after that, an assistant director, Daniel Prath, who I spotted in the conference room earlier, has a screaming fit at the elevators with another man I don't know. Including the phrases, "this company would have gone under without me" and "good luck staying in business."

They must be fired, then.

Although the whispers that spread, in part largely to Gail, include fears of the company running with so many leads laid off at once, most don't mind seeing them leave. I'm certain a few who were under the executive assistant in finance will cheer in celebration to that prick's departure. All I ever heard about him were complaints.

It doesn't take more than an hour to pass before there's a conclusion among the majority of whispers: Those men encompass all that is wrong with the corporate world. They let people go rather than compensating them in the manner they should have been paid. They hired new employees and paid them less, pushing more onto everyone else's plate. They demanded more and more from all of us, wanting everyone to take one for the team while increasing their bonuses every year.

It's not good for a business to run that way, and it's not

good for people to live that way. The management here uses up employees until they break, then fires them and starts over. They've never acknowledged or paid their respects to the employees who made the company what it is.

And now they're walking out the door.

Five o'clock comes and nearly everyone is gone already. Most taking the day off to "readjust" to new procedures from their higher-ups. I stay, like I always do. The last hour, when everyone's left and it's quiet, when the emails stop and calls go to voicemail, are my most productive. Judging by Adrian's statement yesterday, and his message from today, six is when the clock strikes midnight for him as well.

Somehow, that makes those giddy, girly feelings all the headier.

It's six on the dot when I press the silver button with the arrow icon pointing downward for the elevator. I don't know how I'm able to stand upright, with the nervousness that runs through me.

It isn't like me, none of this is. But I'd be lying if I said it wasn't thrilling.

When the doors open, my heart races at the sight in front of me. Adrian is already there waiting for me. Forcing myself to move slowly so he doesn't see my anxiousness, I move to his side and turn to face the doors. "I expect there will be a company-wide email shortly," I say to him as if it's casual conversation. We both stare straight ahead, the doors still open, making each second pass by at an achingly slow rate.

"Why is that?" He moves to press the button for the foyer and I note the way his bespoke suit wraps around his broad shoulders. And the way he fills the not-so-small cabin with his presence alone.

"I hear heads will be rolling."

As the elevator door closes, he smirks at me, a devilish look that brings an overwhelming heat to my cheeks. The elevator begins its descent and he asks, "Is that the talk at the watercooler?"

"More like the profanity Prath screamed on his way out."

He chuckles, then reaches for the button again. One strong knuckle pushes in the emergency stop button.

Tick, tick, tick, my heart rages in my chest. Desire fills me, moving over my skin and pinning me in place. I should know better than to do this but I don't. He's a fantasy come to life and I won't deny myself. How could a lowly sinner say no when the devil himself tempts her?

Confined in a small space together with no way out unless he decides and presses that button … all I feel is want and desire.

With one decisive stride, Adrian towers over me and personal space is nonexistent. My heel slips back half a step before I think better of it. He was calm and collected when I stepped onto the elevator, but now his eyes burn with a hunger I know all too well. With my next breath, the scent of his cologne fills my lungs.

"I've had a rather difficult day," he rasps. "And it's well after six p.m."

He pushes me against the wall all at once and it's just like when he put me on top of his desk. Reasoning becomes impossible and pushing him away is even more unlikely. Adrian slides my dress up, his hands hot and his touch sending every nerve ending beneath it into flames.

His hands roam in every place I've thought of him touching, of him claiming, since I left him last night. He's rough and commanding, gripping my curves and devouring my neck with openmouthed kisses. Every sensation is ignited and all I can do is hold on. With my arms around his shoulders, I can barely breathe, the heat suffocating me.

I don't doubt he's missed this as much as I have. Maybe he did spend his day like I did, obsessed with the idea of continuing what we started yesterday.

With ease he spreads my legs, standing between them and undoes his buckle. My back is pressed against the hard metal. I hook my knee around his hip and drop my head back against the elevator wall. "Suzette," he growls against my neck. It's even hotter now in the small space, because of how much I want him and because of the need in his voice.

He strokes his fingers between my legs, teasing me and I can barely stand it. "You were hot and bothered all night, weren't you?" he says, his piercing gaze staring deep into mine. He smirks while he asks the question, confident that he's right.

"No, I barely thought of you."

He chuckles at my response and then calls me a liar as two of his thick fingers push inside of me. "Tell me how much you want me."

"I want you," I moan, and rock as much as I can to feel more of him inside of me.

When he tsks, stilling his motions, I open my eyes. "Uh, uh, uh. If you're going to move your hips like that, it won't be for anything but me."

He takes his cock in his fist and lines it up with my wet slit, then thrusts in. The movement is so hard and controlling that it takes my breath away. I gasp at the size of him and he pauses, buried deep inside of me, as I adjust to his girth.

"That's my good girl," he says in a breathy voice against my neck. It doesn't take long for him to move again, and I meet him with every thrust, my heels digging into his ass.

"Yes," he coaxes. "You have no fucking idea how hot you are," he groans, pulling a strap of my dress down and kissing, nipping down my shoulder to my breast.

My voice deserts me and I can't reply other than to angle my hips to take him deeper. My nails scratch at his jacket, in an effort to hold on to him.

It's fast. It's dirty. And I want to remember every last detail.

The elevator door dings. I'm still trying to get my breathing to a normal rate, but at least my hair doesn't give anything away. My dress is as smooth as it can be, but there's no doubt that I'm a hue pinker than I ought to be given that the city has a chill in the air this late in April.

As I walk with him, keeping pace, I remind myself there are no obligations. This is nothing but a fling, or an office fuck buddy. Given that I haven't dated in the better part of a decade other than the one-night stands I had to celebrate leaving my piece of shit ex, I have no idea what we are.

But I want more of it.

The thought of whatever we are is both exciting and terrifying. Adrian makes me feel things, but I'm smart enough not to fall for him. I have to be, or this could end very badly. Hands to my hair, I smooth it down one more time and prepare to tell him a quick good night. My heels click on the marble floor of the lobby and I note that the place is nearly vacant. But not entirely. No one looks our way, though. I thank my lucky stars for that.

As we get to the large glass doors that lead to the bustling streets, I start what I think will be an acceptable farewell, "That was—"

"Come with me tonight." He's firm, businesslike as he stands toe to toe with me, waiting for an answer. His words reverberate through me, cutting off the farewell in addition to my thoughts.

"You don't need to buy me dinner."

"Do you eat?" he questions and there's not a trace of humor.

"Yes."

"Good." His eyes glint. "I want to feed you. Besides, we have things to discuss and we have—"

"You've made decisions regarding my department?" I question him, the sight from this afternoon putting me on edge instantly. "The only thing I've received from your team is a request for the client list."

That list is as good as gold. Everything they wanted in that email was essentially preparing paperwork so that another person could take over if need be. I'm not stupid, but I am under contract and not the only one with the list.

"We won't be discussing work at dinner."

"I can damn well discuss what I'd like."

"Watch that mouth of yours." His mouth quirks but he doesn't quite smile. More of a smirk. "It's after six," he whispers, and with the look he gives me, I glance over my shoulder to be sure no one is watching.

Adrian fixes his cuffs, readjusting his sleeves. "I have a late meeting with an associate. His wife wanted to do a tour of New York on a private ship. You could accompany me. The meeting will be short, and they're good company. I've heard the chef they hired for tonight is excellent as well."

The heat from the elevator is back, and all of it is on my face. "I thought we were just—"

"I want more than sex, Suzette. Although I enjoy that immensely."

"What exactly do you want, Mr. Bradford?"

"To get to know you," he says simply.

It throws me off. What we were doing in his office and the elevator is so forbidden that I'd assumed we would have strong boundaries and never cross them. Getting to know each other is definitely crossing them. "Well … the first thing I typically tell someone is I'm divorced and I hate the male species."

The lift of his brow is telling: *I wasn't acting like I hated him in the elevator.* "Surely there is more to you than your dating status."

I hesitate. "I'm not looking for anything serious."

"Having dinner after sex is serious?"

"Hanging on your arm as a date to an after-hours event? Being seen together … that's not discreet."

"I assure you, my evenings are discreet. Nearly everyone I speak to has signed an NDA with me at some point or another and it's all business."

"If you think you need to woo me or somehow …" I can't finish. I don't know how to say what I'm thinking.

"Or what?"

I decide to be blunt. "I don't mind just being a fuck toy," I admit to him, my voice low. "In fact, I enjoy it."

He groans as if I said it just to torture him. "Your fucking mouth, Suzette."

He must know how hot he is when he does that. When he speaks to me like that. It's not fair in the least. I have to bite down on my lip to keep from grinning. A genuine smile, different from the one I use in meetings or when I pass people in the hall at work.

He straightens and runs a hand over his mouth. "I'll make this very simple for you. I'm attracted to you. I'd like you to come with me tonight. Now say yes."

I try to read his expression. Unsettled and hot, I search for the meaning behind his words and the meaning behind his intentions. More importantly, what they'll do to me.

"Don't make me beg, Suzette," he states as if he really would. "Come. Say yes."

I answer without thinking, "Yes."

seven

Adrian

Suzette's phone rings the moment she gets into the car and she chooses not to answer it, texting instead. With a cocked brow, I glance at her phone and she shakes her head, her expression not hiding the humor. She holds up her phone and says, "My friend Maddie."

The texts read as follows:

Sorry, can't take the call, everything okay?
Fine. Any word on what Lucifer is planning to do?

Nothing yet.

Well come over and drink with me, we'll do a binge watch of Grey's or something.

I have to work.

Booooo. Well don't let Lucifer get you down.

"Lucifer?" I question, feeling the corners of my lips pull into a knowing smirk.

She clears her throat, crossing her legs in an attempt to look dignified. "When I heard Holt sold the company to some asshole with a reputation … We nicknamed him Lucifer."

My smile grows. "Hmm, sounds like a prick."

She has the decency to appear nervous under my gaze.

"Why is she asking about the company?"

"I outsource to her at times. And I've been … nervous and venting to her."

"You overthink things."

"I think them through as much as I need to, thank you for your concern, though," she responds with every ounce of the defiance I covet.

"Your smart mouth reminds me of something." My cock hardens as I pull out my phone and read her messages aloud.

"I'd like the wall first, fucking me midday so everyone could hear what you do to me." My tone is even as I read but when I pause, I make my desire obvious, readjusting in my seat. With a devilish grin I peek over at Suzette, finding her cheeks to be a scarlet red. A gruff chuckle escapes me as her lips part and her eyes widen.

"Adrian." The admonishment is hushed and it's only when her gaze darts to the front of the car that I understand why.

"Noah, would you put the divider up please," I call up to him and within seconds the dark partition is in place, granting us more privacy.

"You're blushing as badly as I am," she teases, joy clearly peppered in the statement. I can feel the heat in my cheeks.

"I'm sure he didn't hear anything," I tell her, although … I have no fucking clue. "He's signed a nondisclosure agreement," I add for good measure.

Before she can distract from the conversation anymore, I read the second text. "At night, I'd love for you to fuck me against the window, so I could feel the city beneath us and know every single one of them would trade places with us in a heartbeat." My words are spoken lowly, carefully but not in a whisper.

With her hands spearing through her hair that sits on her shoulders, she pulls the loose strands back as if she needs to feel the cool air against the back of her neck. "What?" she says and shrugs, her expression the picture-perfect resemblance of a minx.

"We have a work relationship during those hours, Ms Parks. I'm going to have to punish you for such … foul language and indiscretion."

Her brow arches, although she plays along with me. "Should I not respond to you then from nine to six?"

"It depends," I answer, "do you want me to play with you in the car on the way to dinner or not?"

Her simper grows wider. "That depends. What exactly do you have in mind for my punishment?"

Her chest rises with a heavy breath and her skin flushes as I unzip my pants and pull my cock through. At the sight of a bead of precum, Suzette licks her lower lip. I pat my lap. "Lay your head here and put your ass up on the seat so I can reach you."

Lying across the seat, her buckle still in place, she eagerly takes the head of my dick in her mouth, moaning and sending soft vibrations of lust to run through me.

I stifle the groan and press the intercom button for Noah. "Go round the block if we get there before I call up."

"Yes, sir," he answers back just in time for my little vixen to pull herself off my dick with a little pop. She works my length as she looks up at me, a perfect view of her breasts on full display.

"Back down, take your punishment like a good girl."

She asks breathlessly, her lips already reddened and slightly swollen, "This is my punishment?"

Smirking down at her, I take my time, pulling up her dress and feeling her bare pussy already wet. "My cock is to keep you quiet."

She eases herself back down my length and I palm one

globe of her ass before squeezing it and then the other, warming her ass up.

"You're going to take my cock as far down your throat as you can," I tell her, lowering my lips to be closer to her ear. "And I'm going to toy with you, spank you, and bring you to the edge."

Her gorgeous blue eyes look up at me through her thick lashes and I swear it's the most beautiful sight I've ever seen. "Don't you dare bite me," I warn her before slapping my hand against her ass. It's enough that my palm stings, her mouth opens wider and my cock drives deeper into the back of her throat.

She doesn't choke, but she sputters. The sensation of my cock being pressed against the back of her throat feels like heaven.

My middle finger drops lower, playing between her folds as I wait for her to readjust. With my toes curled, and her mouth already bringing me close, I spank her ass again and again. Two quick strikes and she cries out, whimpering and pulling off my cock.

Thank fuck.

Barely containing myself, I tsk her as if she isn't doing everything perfectly. Everything is just as I want.

"Adrian," she pleads, but doesn't object, taking a moment to readjust, the leather groaning beneath us.

"You're doing well," I say and comfort her, rubbing soothing circles against her heated skin. With her lips putting pressure on the head of my cock, she works her way down again and I'm quick to decide on the punishment in my head. There's no fucking way I can get through ten of these. "Two more," I barely get out, the pleasure building.

I make them harder than the first two, and the slaps resonate in the small cabin.

She groans, her cheeks hollowing and her brow pinched

until I massage the sensitized skin and then lean over more. With one hand splayed across her back, keeping her down, the other is in the perfect position to play with her pussy.

She jerks on my cock as I dip my middle finger inside her, curling it and finding that sweet spot. I know the moment I hit it because she writhes for me, unable to stay still.

Thank fuck. "I want to feel you come on my hand," I tell her and she mewls. She fucking mewls for me and then she moans my name as if she's already on edge.

I'm merciless as I finger fuck her, desperate for her to come before I do. She loses her composure, pulling off my cock and opting to pump me with her hand so she can breathe in short pants.

"Adrian." She says my name as if she's begging.

"Come for me. You're such a good fucking slut for me, taking whatever I give you."

"Oh my fuck," she says as her hands grip my thigh, her back arches and she cries out her pleasure into my suit pants, burying her head there and leaving my cock aching with need.

When she spasms around my fingers, I swear it takes all of me not to come undone with her.

"Good girl." The praise comes with deeper, calming breaths and she pushes herself up with chaotic ones of her own.

She glances down at my erection as I pull out a tissue to clean up after her release. I save my fingers for last.

The moment it looks like she's going to attend to me, I tell her to wait. "When we stop, I want my cock buried inside of you." Surprise lights her eyes. With her lips still parted, I run my thumb along her bottom lip. "As good as your mouth is, I think I'd rather bring you to the edge again."

And that's exactly what I do. I fuck her hard enough to rock the car in the dock's parking lot after asking Noah to take a walk so we could have a moment. I have her bite down on the leather to keep her as quiet as she can be.

It's much darker with the short hour it's taken to get to the dock, and cooler by the Hudson River. As I open the car door for Suzette, silently thanking Noah for parking in a rather private area of the lot, the breeze sweeps by us.

"I don't think I've ever taken a tour of New York at night on a cruise ship," Suzette comments softly as she steps out, her hand in mine. Her heels click on the pavement and she looks out toward the harbor.

I can barely focus on what she's said as the chill hits us. "Do you have a jacket?"

"I wasn't expecting to come out tonight."

"I'll have Noah deliver one." The moment I've shut the door, I slip off my jacket that's far too large for her and wrap it around her shoulders.

"You don't have to," she says as she shakes her head, her locks falling down her shoulders as she does. She smiles up at me with a sweet, sated look on her face. "But I appreciate it."

With my arm wrapped around her back, I hum in response and search the dock for Trent's ship.

From where we're standing, I'm not sure which ship is his and where we should start.

"And they say chivalry is dead," she teases.

Without thinking much of it, I murmur, "If I'm going to fuck you in the back of my car, I can at least make sure you're comfortable after."

"And to think I just called you a gentleman."

"Mr. Bradford," Noah says behind me, clearing his throat.

If I could experience shame, I'm certain I'd feel it at this moment. "Noah," I say and turn to face him, not missing the glee that shines in her devilish eyes. "I was just about to message you.

"If you could see to it, Ms. Parks doesn't have a jacket this evening. Very much my fault."

"Say no more, sir."

"Thank you."

"Thank you so much," Suzette speaks up, "but truly—"

"Truly you will be cold once we set off, and as much as I adore you in my jacket, I'm not sure it's the look you'll be going for."

There's a pause where Suzette stares back at me, and I wonder if my little vixen is going to fight me on something so simple.

"Mr. Weston is near the northern end, I believe," Noah speaks before she can object. "His wife Laura is hard to miss tonight. And I'll see to it that there's a jacket on your shoulders that's more suitable, Ms. Parks." With a nod, he's off before Suzette can object. I make a mental note to give Noah a bonus for his discretion.

"You don't have to buy me things."

"It's a jacket," I state as if it's nothing.

"Come, the Brooklyn Bridge and the Manhattan skyline are waiting for us."

"It's why I love the city," she says and there's an awe in her tone that draws me closer. With my hand on the small of her back, she leans in closer. I fucking love it. Those walls of hers are crumbling down.

"The skyline?"

"How bright it is at night. How beautiful and lively."

"It is the city that never sleeps." Walking toward the railing, we take a moment to appreciate the towering steel lit with shades of blue and yellow lights. "It's gorgeous, isn't it?"

"Mm-hmm," I hum in agreement, watching her take in the view as the water crashes beneath us.

"I've never taken a tour of the city via cruise either. If you weren't here, I wouldn't."

Peeking up at me, Suzette questions, "You wouldn't have come?"

"I would have, and I would have made the deal before the ship left. It's the same with the galas and charity balls and all of these … social gatherings. I stay at the bar, I meet and greet who I must and then I leave."

"All work and no play," she comments, her eyes locked on mine. There's a softness tonight I only got glimpses of before.

"Would you like to wait here for your jacket, or meet the hosts for the evening?"

"I think we should get on with it," she answers, shedding my jacket from her shoulders.

"That's not going to happen." I scold her lightly, slipping the jacket into place. "I wouldn't be caught dead wearing a jacket while you shiver."

"I won't shiver." The wind rushes by in that moment, as if to prove she's a liar.

A rough chuckle leaves me and I give her the option again. "We can wait here if you'd like or if you don't mind wearing my jacket for a moment, we can start the night."

"I think I don't mind either way," she says softly, staring up at me like she was before, although her gaze is ripped away the moment I hear my name in the distance.

"There you are!" Trent calls out.

"Well," Suzette whispers, "I suppose your jacket will do for now."

eight

THE BOAT CUTS THROUGH THE RIVER BELOW US AS the skyline rises above. The bright lights twinkle against the black sky. Up close, it's intimidating but there's still something elegant about those tall buildings.

The air at the bow of the boat is crisp and clean. With both of my hands holding the railing, I breathe in deep, grateful for a moment alone after the last hour of socializing. My cheeks hurt from the constant smiling. I laugh when it's appropriate and keep everything light. This isn't my first time at a gathering that's … out of my league.

I'm sure it's obvious that I don't quite fit in, but it's gone well as far as I can tell. Champagne flutes clinked as we worked through the crowd, and the small gathering of women mostly gossiped about social circles I'm not privy to.

Most notably, the view is stunning.

I grew up in New York, but not in the city. I knew the dream of it, breathed in the hope of what NYC offers. I believe in this city. It will never cease to amaze me.

New York City is freeing in the same way my divorce was liberating.

Admittedly, that freedom came from the fact that I had security in my job. I could make it on my own and live the dream I've had since I was a little girl without fear. That was then. My hands twist against the cold, smooth metal. This is now.

Apprehension spreads through my gut. I can't deny the fear

that my job might be on the line now. I've slept with Adrian and he's sending emails about gathering client lists like he wants to rearrange everything at the office. Or rather his "team" is. If I don't have that security anymore, then everything is at risk.

"You've been out here a while." The deep rumble from behind me is startling.

Adrian appears at my side by the railing, looking out with me. "I was spending time with my thoughts." Smiling at him, I step a bit closer. "Is your meeting done?"

"Yes."

"Did you seal the deal?" I ask him as he breathes in deep, looking over my shoulder to gaze at the skyline. He peers down at me, a charming smile at his lips. "Always, my little vixen."

With the heat in his eyes, I let out a nervous huff of a laugh and pull away.

"Dinner's about to start. Let me get you a drink."

It gives me a bit of relief that he's not pressing me about what's on my mind. I'm not sure how to talk about it with him yet. Adrian leads me back inside the cabin, the mood seeming a little more somber as more thoughts race through my mind. Thoughts of anxiety and anticipation about what's going to happen at work.

Adrian takes me by the elbow to guide me through the tables, stopping at the bar for a glass of wine. The ship is massive and spacious. It's obvious they spared no expense for this evening's outing. The group of women I was chatting with earlier are seated with their companions, dining on caviar as they overlook the river.

All the tables have been set with linen tablecloths and beautiful dishes. This is how the other half lives. It's elegance and convenience that will only ever be a dream for most.

"We're toward the stern ... for more privacy."

We reach our table, nestled in a corner with lit candles and the perfect view of the ship splitting the water that reflects the bright lights of the city. I stop at the edge, bracing myself, suddenly uncomfortable. With a firm hand he tilts up my chin. "What's wrong?"

"Just worried." The knot in my stomach ties tighter.

"About what?"

It takes great effort to keep my expression neutral, in case anyone may see when I say, "My job."

Light dances in his eyes. "It's after six."

"Unlike you, I can't just turn it off. I can't stop worrying about my responsibilities and wondering what's going to happen to my income … and what might happen between us."

There's a pause, a tension that gathers between us before Adrian pulls out my chair and tells me, "We can discuss it later, but I'm telling you, I don't want you to worry."

"As if I can just stop."

"You can. And you will."

"It's just hard to believe right now."

"Let me help you with that." His gentle smile is as confident as his touch. "You need to eat. Sit." He takes my wineglass from my hand, only a few sips gone, and helps me to my seat.

It's a bit chillier now than it was earlier and even with the beautiful double collar Mackage jacket Noah was gracious enough to have rush delivered before the boat set sail, it's brisk.

"May I?" Adrian asks, still standing as I take my seat. He moves the remaining chair around the table, dragging it to sit beside me.

"You'd rather sit next to me?"

"I'd rather have my arm around you."

There's comfort that's unexpected, in the way he simply wants to be with me. Next to me, with me, touching me. I crave it without realizing it.

The waiter comes by with appetizers: oysters on ice, bruschetta, and marinated olives with feta. Where we're seated, the chatter is muted and drowned out by the water, the breeze is comforting and it feels like the city has stayed awake just for us.

We're finished with our appetizers when Adrian orders two glasses of ice water.

"I'm all right with the wine," I tell him.

"I thought we could play a game," is his reply. "To keep your mind off work."

"What kind of game?" My cheeks are instantly flushed and hot, though no one seems to be paying attention to us, tucked away back here. "Would it be … discreet?"

"Very," he says and his gorgeous pale blue eyes rest on mine as he smirks, "as long as you can keep quiet."

"I have no problem with that." The suggestive game is enticing, and there's no doubt I would much rather get lost in this man's touch than ruminate on matters I cannot control.

Just as I rest my hand on Adrian's thigh, the waiter returns and a hot blush creeps to my cheeks realizing I'm the one caught. The waiter only offers a polite smile, not saying a word as he sets down the goblets of ice water and then uncovers dinner: filet mignon and lobster tail with mashed potatoes and asparagus, all neatly arranged in a tasteful way.

My mouth waters instantly.

Adrian's quiet and commanding as he tells me, "Pick up your fork and make sure you appear to be eating, no matter what I do."

"Appear to be eating or actually eat?" My fork hovers over the plate.

"You should eat," he decides. "I'll try to be fair and give you time to chew and swallow."

Adrian looks down at his own plate and says, "Enjoy dinner. That's all you need to do."

Small talk ensues. About the city, the ever-changing neighborhoods and real estate. Nothing heavy, yet it chips away at who each of us is and what we want.

"Why am I not surprised that you live in Tribeca," I comment offhandedly knowing how damn expensive it is. Yet another checkbox on tonight's elite list that I could never fulfill.

That's when I feel his hand on my thigh underneath the table, pushing my dress up. My fork scrapes against the porcelain, giving away my surprise until I can steady myself. His touch goes up and up until his knuckles brush against my clit through my panties.

Cold shocks me so suddenly, I gasp.

"With a sound like that escaping those lips of yours," Adrian scolds, his tone teasing, "people will wonder if something happened to you."

He doesn't let up with the pressure against my clit and I struggle to perfect my expression.

"Keep your thighs apart," he murmurs. "That's the only way to play this game."

Circular motions of his knuckles make me hotter, increasing the heat until all at once he removes his hand.

My initial reaction is to object, but that's quickly silenced as he plucks a piece of ice from his glass and, with his eyes on mine, his hand disappears under the table. My lips part with a hiss as the cold hits my inner thigh first. He doesn't stop, slowly trailing it up.

I let out a breathy laugh. "That's freezing," I admit. "It's so, so cold."

"Sensitizing, isn't it?" he says quietly and casually spears a stalk of asparagus with one hand, while his other slips the ice up and down my slit until slowly he presses it inside of me. Goosebumps dance along my skin as I focus on my breathing and simply staying still.

Adrian repeats this process, bringing me to the edge and then stopping me with the freeze of an ice cube. Abruptly, he stops.

"You're going to give us away," he warns lowly, his lips at the shell of my ear and his warm breath tickling my neck.

That's when I realize my fork is fisted in my hand and my eyes were closed tight.

"I know you can do it. My little slut knows how to hide it. Don't you?"

My breathing is rushed when another piece of ice slips along my skin, and my hand trembles. Adrian watches this with curiosity burning in his eyes.

"Oh my," I whisper and breathe, my eyes half-lidded.

"I want you to come for me."

"I don't think—" With two fingers he enters me, his fingers deft and knowing. As if he's memorized just how to get me off.

"I know you can. If you must, lay your head down on the table." The moment he suggests it, I obey, pushing the plate away and resting my head down.

He doesn't let up, not even when the waiter questions if I'm all right and he orders Dramamine for me.

The second his footsteps disappear, Adrian's touch becomes merciless and he whispers at my ear, "If you don't come for me right now, I swear to God I'll throw you over this table and fuck you until all of Manhattan hears you crying out my name. I couldn't care less about this deal if I can't even get my little whore to come on my hand."

My lips part, my warm breath heating my face still resting against the table and hidden by my arms. That's what does it. It's what brings me to the edge. I clench around him thinking of what he's just described.

The moment I'm granted my release, he removes his hand and it's only a moment after that his hand rests on my shoulder while rubbing soothing circles. Adrian informs the waiter that I will be fine.

"Take these, sweetheart," he says clear as day, without a trace of anything that's just happened in his voice.

"If she needs anything at all, let us know," the waiter says and I don't dare lift my head just yet. I'm flushed and shamelessly sated.

It's only once he's gone that I dare to peek up.

"Bad girl," Adrian admonishes me. "You'll do better for me next time, won't you?" he teases and I only blush harder.

Setting two small pills down on the napkin, he brings my plate back, placing it in front of me.

"The appetizers were … delicious," he comments.

"You're shameless," I counter, still breathless and gather my fork once again.

"I'm hard is what I am," he tells me, cutting into his steak.

"Do you want me—"

"No. No, not here." He considers me for a moment. "I want to make sure you know what you do to me. Watching you come undone for me … that's all I wanted."

I don't know what to make of him. He's ruthless. Confident. On the side of being arrogant. But the things he does to me make me forget everyone and everything else.

"You look like you want to say something," he comments, taking another bite. His food is quickly disappearing and mine's barely been touched.

"I thought you would be different."

"My reputation is not kind. I'm aware."

"They say you're an asshole and I thought it would be easy to hate you." It's the truth. And it slips out without censorship. Adrian smirks. "I've heard you're merciless."

"I am."

I guide my fork over my plate and lift a bite to my mouth. "Are you an asshole or are you merciless?"

"Both. I can be vicious." Adrian says this with a casual tone that makes me think he's telling the truth. Of course, I already know this about him. There's a reason the entire office is in a furor with him simply being in the building.

"I don't know what to make of you."

His eyes meet mine and his gaze lingers as if he's waiting for me to elaborate. My heart pounds with curiosity and fear that this will go badly and I won't have an office to go back to.

"There are people who earn big paychecks and then there are the people who write them," Adrian begins. "I wasn't born into wealth, but I watched my father work his way up to being one of those people who earned his paycheck. And then it was taken away from him after one wrong deal."

My body goes as cold as the ice he used to play with me earlier.

"I've looked into it since then," continues Adrian, "and it was a bad deal. He made a mistake. But that was after years of making the right decisions over and over, after working his way up only to be knocked down the second something went wrong. Not because it was deserved, but because he made too much and it would be too easy to give his tasks to someone else. Then the person who wrote the big check could simply make back that money by letting him go."

This is by far the most Adrian has ever shared with me, and my curiosity is piqued again. I don't know anything about his father, only what I've read about him, which is simple. He buys companies, breaks them apart, moves some departments around and eliminates others. He's the man writing the checks and doing the firing now.

"That company went under within two years," Adrian says quietly. Judging from his tone, this is important to him. The measured cadence of his words and the look in his eyes as he speaks.

"Without your father?" I manage to ask.

"Partially because of that. Partially because I bought the competitor. I hired my father. As the stock grew, I invested in other companies, including two crucial to my father's former employer … And I dismantled them."

Adrian uses a cool, almost bored tone to tell me this, and I'm even more afraid for my job now. He could do anything he wanted with the company. "Vindictive much?" I say, to cover the nervous pulse in my throat.

"He treated certain things, certain people, as if they were disposable. I showed him exactly what that meant. There are highs and lows in this business. Harsh decisions must be made. But the reasoning behind it is what matters. Is it for efficiency? For the bottom line? For power plays?"

"Why do you do it?"

Adrian's eyes flash. "Because if there isn't passion behind it, it shouldn't exist. It's a waste of time for everyone involved. It will fail, and the only ones who will benefit are the ones who are willing to sacrifice the purpose of it all." His deep voice is filled with conviction. Adrian believes what he's saying, and I imagine it's why he fired so many of the executives today and sent them all packing. He has a passion for this business, not simply an investment.

"I learned a hard lesson early on: if you can't beat them with morals and ethics, cut their throats and say that it's business."

A chill flows over my skin and numerous questions rest on the tip of my tongue. "I didn't buy Holt and Hanover to cut anyone's throat," he states before I can ask. "The numbers are still being run with slight changes." His tone is one of comfort, but the conversation is anything but. "When I know anything, you will as well. Do not worry."

I can only nod as a shiver runs down my shoulders and I realize we're back at the dock. The water is quieter and the chatter from the others much louder.

The waiter returns to check on me just then and he's relieved to hear I'm feeling better. If my head wasn't clouded with current topics, I would have blushed violently.

"Are you finished?" Adrian asks after time passes with easy

silence, with a patient tone that says I could sit here for another hour, if I wanted.

Once again, I tell him the truth. "Yes." I put my napkin on the table next to my plate.

"Good. When we get to the car I want you on your knees," he mutters beneath his breath, standing up at the same time I do. A shiver returns, but this one is heated and causes flutters in places I shouldn't be concerned with in public.

"So demanding."

Adrian's smile seems to light up the dining area. "Are you just now learning that, Ms. Parks?"

nine

THE CITY BLURS BY, A STREAK OF GRAYS WITH splashes of colors as Noah speeds up down the avenue. It's late, far too late given I have an early morning meeting with the executives of a company based overseas. There's no doubt in my mind that rescheduling it would not go over well.

Leaning forward, I spread my knees, resting my elbows there and stretch my back, feeling the pull of it in my spine. Without thinking, I stare at the empty seat beside me, where Suzette was yesterday. The corners of my lips pull up, remembering how she squirmed, how easily she gave in. How she melts for me. And how much she loved it.

Today was hell. Meeting after meeting and when she texted that she had plans tonight, I can't deny I felt loss. With her, I want every moment I can get. This evening held precisely none of them.

"Mr. Bradford?" Noah calls back, peering at me in the rearview although he doesn't use the intercom.

"Yes?" I answer him and then lean back in the seat, resting my head and meeting his gaze in the mirror.

"Shall I make it a habit of keeping the divider up between us when Ms. Parks joins you?"

The hum of the night surrounds us as I consider his question. There's no judgment; it's honest professionalism.

Something I've lacked today.

"I think it would serve us all well if you did, and I apologize if anything made you uncomfortable recently."

"Nothing at all, sir, just thinking of your lady."

Your lady. My brow rises, but my phone buzzes in my hand, interrupting my thoughts. There are only a few numbers I allow this late at night.

My father: *Did Wyatt send you the contract?*

My eyes roll back in my head as I inhale long and steady. My father is friends with his, and that's how we became acquainted nearly a decade ago.

My phone buzzes again: *Dale's here and we were wondering.*

Dale is Wyatt's father, rather protective but a supportive man.

I text him back quickly: *The lawyers have it atm.*

It occurs to me then that Suzette has yet to message. I'm quick to type a message but then I delete it. I try another that's less … domineering.

I prefer for that role to be played in person. Just as I finish typing her a message asking if she's home, a message comes through from my father, followed by one from her.

Suzette: *Just laying down for bed and thinking of you. Thank you again for last night.*

I ignore my father for a moment, choosing to message her: *The pleasure was all mine.*

She doesn't waste time replying: *You lie, Mr. Bradford. I enjoyed it immensely.*

With a satisfied hum, I sit back and see my father's messaged twice.

The lawyers will be fine with it.

Are you working this late? Please tell me you've cut back.

He's been on me for years now to work less. With the team in place and fewer projects, although they're costlier and more rides on their success, I've been able to slow down, little by little. Small steps toward a more "sustainable lifestyle," as my father refers to it.

Just got back from a date actually. I text him the white lie. It's not exactly truthful, but it will make him smile.

"Is that her?" Noah questions from the front. Again not using the intercom, and it takes me a moment to understand he means Suzette.

"Ms. Parks?"

"You have a smile for her. I can tell it's her. I have one that was just for my wife."

"Oh, calm down with that talk now, Noah," I joke with him. "We've only just met—"

"I told you Ann and I ... it was two weeks and then forever." His voice holds a hint of reverie.

"Yes, I know the story well." Noah's worked for me for the better part of a decade now. As my driver and at times my assistant when needed. "One day ... one day I'll have that," I say and then run my hand through my hair, thinking that *one day* seems to get farther and farther away as the years go by. "Ms. Parks is ... we are only getting to know each other."

"Is that what you kids call it nowadays?"

Letting out a brutish laugh, I turn my attention back to my phone.

There are emails and calendar notifications. My father messaged me about details of some buildings Wyatt is hoping to acquire, but he needs the capital first. My capital. As well as some questions about my date and whether it's serious.

Another message comes through, this time my mother, wanting to know about the date.

I debate on answering them, but I let my phone sit in my lap, thinking of Suzette at the dock yesterday and how easy it was. I haven't had that before. No one has ever fit so well, even if she fights me along the way.

As if she knows I'm thinking of her, a message comes through: *I need to sleep.*

Then you should sleep, my little minx.

I watch the phone with anticipation, knowing she's typing something, but then deletes it. A moment passes and she starts again. My phone buzzes, with the messenger open: *I like being your little minx, I think.*

I like it too.

The moment I send my response, it doesn't feel good enough. It doesn't carry the weight of just how much I enjoy her simply being there. I follow up with:

When you sleep, I want you to dream of me.

Yes, sir.

ten

Suzette

ADRIAN FILLS MY MIND EVERY HOUR THAT I'M awake, and most of the ones where I'm sleeping. His text messages make my pulse quicken with excitement.

I can hear how he would speak the words when I read them. It feels like falling. In only a week's time, I feel like I'm falling for him.

No one else at the office is fawning over him.

I'm often worked up and overheated, carefully avoiding him and the topic of him because everyone calls him the devil.

They complain about not knowing what's going to happen and how they think every task is in preparation for someone else to take over. Then there's me. I can't stop thinking of how he put that ice between my legs, and the soft groans that he makes when he fucks me on his desk. Purposefully avoiding the obvious and doing everything I can not to worry. Because he told me not to, even though all signs point to the company being sold off.

It's all ridiculous and overwhelming. If I wasn't fucking him, I might have quit already … well, not if I couldn't take the clients with me. Maybe. I don't know. Like I said, it's all too overwhelming, so I choose to believe him. I'm doing everything I can to listen and not worry.

With my fingers tapping aimlessly on the keys, I have to snap myself out of it. Not that it matters; we're on a freeze with clients this week. I could lose my shit and it wouldn't make a difference in productivity. The only work that's getting done is paperwork and severance packages. I could be a nervous wreck like the rest of the office, or I can fantasize about the clock turning six.

Every day, I rock back and forth between the two of them.

A light knock at my door takes me out of my thoughts. A young brunette in joggers and a flowy tank stands in my doorway.

"Maddie," I say, greeting my friend for lunch. "I was wondering when you were going to get here." My chair rolls to the left as I push my keyboard to the side to make room for takeout.

Passing me a brown paper bag she sighs and says, "Sorry. Traffic was hell."

She's gorgeous, as she always is, but there's a sad curve to her mouth. "You okay?"

She takes the seat across the desk from me and opens her bag in her lap, waving me off with the other hand. "I think I need a man or a really good vibrator."

"I vote vibrator," I joke with a short laugh, unrolling the top of the bag without taking my eyes off Maddie. She's young, naive, and a romantic. A.k.a. the prime suspect for assholes. She barely cracks a smile. "Is that dipshit Daniel still on your mind?"

Maddie groans. "He's always on my mind, and I can't get him off of it. It's not fair. Why did such a shitty person have to get so far into my head?"

"That's how it always seems to be. The worse the person is for you, the more you think about them."

"Let's go out and go man shopping tonight. There's a new club down on Madison Avenue. It's like my grandmom always said, get over one by getting under another." She takes a bite out of her turkey club and guilt washes over me.

I haven't told Maddie about Adrian yet, and it seems like

a betrayal of our friendship, almost. Suddenly I have no appetite. The chicken caesar wrap stays at the bottom of the bag.

I'm not sure what I would tell her. Being discreet means not blabbing your business to anyone who'd listen. I wince at the thought. Maddie's not just a random person. She's my friend, one of very few, and she's been my friend for far longer than I've known Adrian.

"I've looked up Lucifer," I joke. "He's hot as hell."

"Why don't you cuddle up to him?" Maddie half teases although her tone is dull. Her large doe eyes twinkle as she grins, pausing between bites to say, "Get a little action. Save the day. You'd be the office hero."

"The office needs a hero," I comment, keeping my tone light. "Everyone's nervous about their jobs now that entire divisions have been laid off."

My department has kept the same workload, but four people have been taken for interviews. Not by Adrian himself, but by some team he hired.

"Speaking of heroes," Maddie says, and then she talks about the new TV show she's been watching on HBO for the rest of the time we're eating. I'm grateful for the change in subject and somehow I've gotten out of going to the club with her this weekend. It's pleasant conversation and a much-needed break in the day. The wrap was decent too although I barely tasted it.

All I could think is that I should tell her. Maddie would keep my secrets and maybe she would smack some sense into me.

I know part of the reason I don't is because of that very fact: She would give her opinion, and what if it's to stop seeing him? What if she says it's wrong and it's going to end in failure and heartbreak? She's the romantic of the group, and yet I don't even have faith she would approve.

When she's gone, there's a small fire under my ass. A need to prove there's nothing at all wrong with it. We work during the day, play at night. I haven't changed who I am and there's nothing wrong with it.

This feeling that everything's up in the air isn't good for my productivity or anyone else's, and the only way to know what's going to happen is to ask him directly. And it's not six yet, so business is business.

Every single time I gather the courage to demand answers or terms, to know what the hell is going on so I have something I can tell everyone who needs answers, there are people in his office.

Adrian's secretary furrows her brow whenever I pass close to her desk. On my third trip, I decide to ask her what she knows. I imagine she's got to know something, given how close she works to Adrian. And any little piece of info I can bring back would be a win. "Hi there," I say, greeting her with a smile. Laying on the charm. "I'm Suzette. You're new to the company." My hip rests against her desk.

"That's right," she says with a tight smile. "Not new to Mr. Bradford, though. I'm Andrea."

There's a tinge that runs through me. It's a feeling I don't like. My gaze slips to this woman's hand, a woman who could be my mother, and I find a wedding ring back there. Jealousy is unbecoming and I can't believe I felt it for a second. In her white flowy blouse and pencil skirt, Andrea most certainly takes care of herself.

"How long have you been his secretary?"

"Oh, years and years. You know how it is with a good job. You stick with it."

"I do know about that." My stomach turns over. That's exactly why I'm here—to talk to Adrian about the future. This job saved me after my divorce and made it possible to have the freedom I gained, but if I'm let go, I'll be in an even worse position. "Sticking with it is usually for the best. I've heard he can be …" I deliberately let my voice trail, waiting for Andrea to pick up where I left off.

She gives me nothing, tilting her head with her perfectly plucked brow raised and her hands folded in her lap. Touché. I finish it myself. "A bit … ruthless."

"I would agree with that at times."

She nods and I do as well … neither of us giving the other anything.

"If you've worked for him for that many years, you must have seen him take over a number of companies like this."

Her eyes widen. "Oh, yes. It can be unsettling for the people who have been there the longest. Adrian insists on changing things where they need to be changed instead of sticking with the status quo. It means a lot of shuffling around at the beginning."

I wince. "That's what I've heard … the shuffling, though, that's—"

"Ruthless." Now she finishes it.

Hearing about a powerful man like Adrian shuffling people around doesn't soothe me when it comes to my own job. He's merciless when we have sex, and he must be the same way when it comes to business. He won't keep me on if it's not the right thing for the company. My throat tightens at the thought of being let go by him. Stomach turning, I breathe deeply to keep myself in check. I've had to do this many times over the years, working with men who didn't know how to listen to a woman.

Oddly, the thought of being fired from my job isn't the only thing at the forefront of my mind. Adrian is there as well. If I'm let go from this position, there will be no more meeting up at six for discreet activities. So his secretary's words aren't very reassuring. I hadn't considered how I might lose my job and Adrian at the same time. Though it's a bit presumptuous to think there's such a thing as losing Adrian when what we have is a fuck-buddy agreement.

"You work till six," she comments and now it's my turn for my expression to pinch.

"I do."

"I only noticed because of the submissions."

I pause, nodding but not contributing; it's her turn to show her cards.

"Mr. Bradford seems to have changed his habits," she says and leans back in her chair. "He never used to stay late. Once it was five o'clock, he went home. But it seems his preference, for this company only, is now six."

"Oh?" The back of my neck tingles.

"Mm-hmm," she hums.

"Well, that's something." Does she know? It's all I can think as she stares up at me. She's older, wiser maybe. I don't know. But everything in me is screaming that she knows.

"I'm sure he won't let you go," the secretary says, her expression innocent. "Seems to me you've been doing quite a bit for this company."

"I've done a lot of work," is my distracted reply. She might not let me in to see him, but that doesn't mean I'm any less hungry for information. I'm not sure how to phrase it, though.

"Can I tell you something?" she asks.

"Of course," I reply and my nervous voice betrays me.

"He seems to be distracted lately."

"Oh? I'm sure I wouldn't know anything about that."

She takes in my red cheeks. "Hmm. I think you might. I'm good friends with his driver."

I blush deeper. "I see."

Reaching for her glasses, she barely contains her cat-ate-the-canary grin. "If it were up to me, I'd let you in there, love, but I can't."

"Oh, I'm not—I don't do this kind of thing." A numbness creeps through me. How long have I worked here, only to potentially have my reputation ruined by the rumor mill? I have no idea if I can trust this woman in the least, although she seems friendly. I did just lie to her face, though.

Restlessly, I shift my weight from one foot to the next. I stop as soon as the secretary notices. "I really don't do this," I say again.

"Neither does he," she says, leaning in, her tone friendly still. It eases something in me. "I mean it. I've worked with him for over a decade now. Mr. Bradford … he doesn't behave like this. He's strict with his regimen and occasionally a woman has come in to speak with him. But it's never … like this."

eleven

Adrian

"YOU KNOW HOW I KNOW YOU WANT TO PUSH me today and not in a good way?" I question the vixen at my side. Her cherry-red heels clip on the pavement as I open the door, waving toward Noah that I've got it. The spring day is a cloudy one, with gray skies and the threat of rain clouds.

"How's that?" she asks, gripping the door frame, one shoe inside the car, the other firmly planted on the curb. She stares at me from over her shoulders, the wool coat perfectly hugging her frame.

"Because you're eager to get me alone in this car. I didn't have to fight you."

Her smile is wicked, her rose petal lips trying all they can to stay pursed, but they fail. "Inside," I command her and she obeys, properly and politely as I shut her door for her, knowing damn well she's going to try to get information out of me. While I sat through meeting after meeting, she came looking for me. Andrea let me know. She suggested I order flowers, of all things.

I'm not sure what exactly she thought Suzette was coming to see me for, but if I had to guess, with the cars buzzing by us and the nightlife of the city turning vibrant, it's about her department and the upcoming meetings.

With a steadying inhale, I climb into the back seat and shut the door.

"I tried to speak to you all day." She doesn't waste a second.

She peeled her coat off, laying it across her lap and at first glance, I'm given a damn good look of her breasts. Whatever contraption she's wearing has pushed them to the top of her blouse which hangs low, I presume to display cleavage.

Not fair.

Reaching for my seat belt, I prepare myself.

"I had roundtables with my team." The belt clicks into place and the tick of the blinker is barely heard as Noah rolls up the partition, allowing us privacy.

"Your team who's talking to *my* team," Suzette stresses and I can't help but to let out a chuckle.

Leaning my head back, I turn to face her.

"I don't find it funny," she tells me and there's a hint of hurt there.

"Because you aren't in control," I tell her honestly.

With her hands in her lap, she fidgets with her fingers and tells me, "I just need to know what your plans are."

"It's after six, Suzette." I'm soft with the reminder.

"I don't like this." She's equally soft with her disappointment. It's unsettling. Not anger; she's genuinely upset.

"It's okay to be uncomfortable. That's how progress is made," I tell her, in an attempt to ease her mind.

"I suppose I could leave you uncomfortable then?" It's not quite a tease or a threat, but some combination of the two.

My response is firm. "Don't tempt me to punish that mouth of yours before we've had dinner." She swallows, the threat coming through as it should. To remind her that she loves what I do to her, that right now the office is behind us and we're to get lost in each other.

Her posture remains stiff, though, and her gaze guarded.

In an attempt at a truce, I rest my hand on hers, and she reciprocates by turning her small hand to hold mine. "Thank you," I murmur and then run my thumb along her soft skin.

"Please, answer me one thing," she presses and I close my eyes to respond with a short nod.

"What are you going to do with it?"

"With what?"

"The company?"

I remain silent. As if it were so simple to have a one-sentence answer, or to even know what would be best so early on.

"A split-up? Go public for shares? I looked into the other companies under your LLC, so I doubt you have a merger in mind."

When I finally open my eyes and look back at her, fear lingers in every nuance.

I debate on confiding in her, knowing how quick office rumors are to spread and the chaos that little bits of information can create. But then she utters a single word, staring back at me like I could make every little worry she has vanish. "Please."

"The plan is a split-up and the merger of the new entity and another company I have in mind … if possible."

She doesn't hesitate to question, "And what about the other? The original entity? The departments that aren't useful for the merger?"

I'm silent, half wondering if she's playing me. If all of this was a setup and she's pumping me for information. "There are inefficiencies that cannot be overlooked."

"Where does my department—"

My tone is harsher than I'd like as I interrupt her. "Not everything has been decided." Gentling it, I add, "You don't need to worry."

"As your lover or as your employee?"

"When I tell you that you don't need to worry, I need you to believe it. I need you to trust me."

She's silent, and every second that passes feels as if another weight has been added to my chest. It's obvious I haven't eased her concerns in the least. She wants a definitive answer and I can't give her one. I can't say anything with certainty.

"No more. It's after six and I promise, I will make time for you at work. As your boss. Right now I only want to be your lover, as you put it."

It seems for a moment that she'll say something; her lips part and she inhales, but then her gaze falls and she merely nods. Not looking back at me.

"Thank you for respecting the boundary."

"I don't like it," she whispers, at first looking out the window but then she meets my gaze.

"You look gorgeous squirming, though." I pick up her hand and kiss the back of it, our fingers laced together. "It would please me if you wouldn't worry."

In a breath she laughs, as if it's the most ridiculous thing she's heard. "Is that all you need, for me to just not worry?"

Softly, I repeat the reassurance, "You will be all right."

She's quick to tell me, "It's not just me." She shakes her head. "I'm sorry. I'm done. I'm done for right now. I won't bring it up again."

"I want you to confide in me, I do. I wish I had the answers for you, but I don't."

"When you do, will you tell me?" There's hesitancy in her tone, but also hope.

"The second I know, I will tell you everything."

Her shoulders drop slightly and she sinks deeper into the seat, not responding other than a nod and a soft, "Thank you."

A moment passes, and the tension lessens.

"I had a hard day today," I confide in her, our fingers still intertwined.

"I did too," she speaks softly. "Fridays are long days, but at least we have the weekend." Just when I think that's all she'll say, she offers, "Can I do anything?"

"Do anything?"

"To make anything better."

"Not with work—"

"No, with you. Can I …" she trails off and tosses her hand in the air, the one I was holding. "Can I yell at someone, or massage your shoulders? I could …" she pauses and rolls her eyes. "I don't know, write an angry email or order us takeout for dinner." In my silence, her tone is laced with exasperation when she says, "I could … I don't know. What would make it better?"

"You could kiss me."

"Would that make it better?" she questions, the hint of a smile on her lips.

"Yes. If you kissed me, it would."

She doesn't waste a moment, and when she kisses me, her hands wrapped around my face, I can feel her smile.

twelve

Suzette

THE NEW YORK SKYLINE IS MUCH DIFFERENT FROM the windows of Adrian's penthouse. I'm used to feeling as if it's towering over me, but in his living room we're a part of it. In the heart of Tribeca surrounded by historic industrial buildings and new construction that's all steel and glass.

It's the epitome of New York.

It almost seems like a movie backdrop is wrapped around the entire room. Floor-to-ceiling windows that, with a touch of a button, darken for privacy surround us. Every other day, Adrian introduces me to more wealth than I've experienced in the years I've planted roots in this city.

Behind me, he busies himself in the foyer answering a call. The design is open concept but so far away, I feel lost in the view. Even his furniture seems to play a part in the city.

It's the perfect layout for a home with so much luxury. Hardwood floors shine under my feet and the neutral color scheme is fresh and strong. He has high ceilings and windows that kiss those ceilings, and beneath is a living room with sumptuous leather furniture that looks like it cost a mint.

Nothing in his home is out of place. There's not a single ounce of clutter, which adds to the masculine energy. It even smells like wealth, if ever there was a scent, one so clean it makes me a little jealous. I can imagine the people it would take to make a home look like this. A housekeeper at least, and others to make sure the walls and furniture stay perfect. The view alone is worth millions.

I can hardly keep my mouth closed as he gives me the tour, passing quickly by his bedroom and ending up back in the living room. "I didn't realize just how wealthy you are." I swallow thickly, my fingers playing at the hems of my silk sleeves.

The last time I felt awe like this was when I was flying into New York City for the first time. I couldn't believe I was finally going to live here, in a place I'd dreamed about for so long.

Adrian grins, slipping his arm around my waist. "I'm certainly not the richest man in New York."

"How very modest of you," I teasingly respond although my normal bite is lost.

There's a deep rumble from his chest, a short hum. I've noticed him do it a few times now and with it, his hand drops lower, to the side of my hip and his thumb rubs soothing circles there.

It causes a tension, a nervousness inside of me. It's more *serious*. Because I crave it. I want more of that masculine hum of satisfaction.

Being in his personal space and seeing his things and furniture is way beyond what I ever thought I'd do with him. I'm nervous to get it right and keep my cool, but I'm a strange mixture of giddy and hot. The more I learn about Adrian, the harder it will be when things end between us. I'm not sure I want things to end between us. Which only adds more to the feeling of not having the upper hand.

I certainly don't want them to end here, in his beautiful penthouse with all his fancy furniture and Adrian in his suit from the office. Despite working all day it's still crisp. I'd like for him to take it off, or to play the game we always play … but in his home, we don't have to rush.

"Are you all right?" he asks, his voice low.

"I'm fine."

"Do you want a drink?"

I nod. A drink would be good. Something to hold in my hands and busy myself with.

"Let's step into the kitchen, then." In Adrian's kitchen, which is an elegant, masculine space with dark marble countertops and tall reclaimed wood shelves, he takes down two cut glass tumblers. Light bends through them, refracting as he cradles them in his large palms. Even his tumblers reek of wealth. "What would you like?" he asks.

"You choose," I offer, not knowing what's in his kitchen.

"Whiskey?" he questions. "I have a favorite you may not have tried before."

"I don't mind whiskey."

"Chocolate cream cold brew whiskey," he speaks clearly, opening cabinets and leaving me alone by the kitchen island, standing quite alone in the expansive space.

Once he has what he needs, the bottles lined up and large spherical ice cubes taking up space in the tumblers, he strips off his jacket so he's just in his shirt from the office. Like his suit, his dress shirt is still pristine after a day of sitting in meetings and restructuring the company. My mouth waters at the thought of what's hidden under the belt around his waist and the white shirt above.

How did we come to be here? How did I find myself in this penthouse, with a man like him?

"If you don't care for it, I'll happily drink both and get you something else," he offers and I nod a thanks, deciding I should take that seat at the island after all.

He's capable in the kitchen, mixing this drink like he's made it a thousand times before. I have another flash of jealousy. Maybe he has, for some other woman, though it's none of my business who he brings here or who he makes drinks for. It comes and goes, leaving me questioning how much he's gotten to me. We've both been with other partners. And this, whatever is between us, is mutual.

Evening light glows around him as he tells me, "Let me know what you think."

"Thank you," I tell him as he hands me the heavy glass. The first sip goes down smooth. "Wow." I never would have guessed chocolate and whiskey would be a combination so easy and delectable. He's made it better than any bartender could have. It overwhelms me, how good it is.

"You like?" he questions, standing and leaning against the island.

"I do."

"Now that you've seen mine, I'm wondering about yours," he says, sipping his whiskey.

"My place is nothing like this," I comment, a bit worried, but also blunt. I'm sure he's aware. I don't come from *this* kind of money and my position certainly doesn't pay a salary where I could afford anything close to this in my lifetime.

Adrian sips his own whiskey, which he takes straight.

"I imagine you bring work home?" he asks.

"I prefer to stay at the office, but yes. My apartment is small. When I split with my ex, I sold off everything and bought a place in the West Village that I'd wanted for so long."

"Hell's Kitchen is fitting for you." I nearly tell him I'm barely there anymore, although I still love the neighborhood, but then I realize what he's revealed and discussing my apartment location seems unimportant.

"How did you know where I live?" I question and then answer for myself. "Did you snoop in the company files?"

"Of course I did. When I saw you that first day staring at me across the conference table, I already had your number."

"Well, that's not fair," I say with a pout, although it comes out a lust-filled whisper.

"I don't play fair."

"So you liked me while I hated the thought of you?"

He nods. "It's easy to hate the devil. So no offense taken."

I laugh, the nervousness dissipating. The drink Adrian made for me is helping. His expression intensifies, though, and he takes another sip of whiskey. "If it makes you feel any better, I don't think you're the devil anymore." Without thinking much of it, I raise my drink and confide in him, "That name is solely reserved for my ex-husband now."

His next question is casual: "What happened between you and your ex?"

Immediately I regret bringing Carl up in conversation at all. His name is the equivalent to an ice water bath.

I'm over that man, and I'll never want him again, but it still causes an old pain in my heart to talk about it. Luckily, the pang of betrayal is over quickly, and I can answer Adrian honestly. "He cheated … with the company secretary."

Anger darkens his features. "So he was a fucking idiot. Got it."

"No. Not an idiot. He was a manipulative bastard and damn good at it." My throat is tight as I correct him, once again feeling like a fool. "It wasn't just once, either. He had an affair for over two years. He used her to get details he shouldn't have been privy to."

Adrian takes a step closer and puts a hand on my shoulder. "I'm sorry," he says, his voice rumbling through me. "I'm sorry he hurt you and took advantage of you." He seems to make a decision. "My last ex was somewhat similar when it came to dishonesty."

Setting the glass down I admit to him, "I googled your name and love interest."

"You tried to look up my dating history?" He grins at me as if it's comical. "Did you find anything?"

"No," I state and he chuckles at my pursed lips.

There's almost no information online about Adrian's love

life, as if it's been purposefully kept offline or scrubbed from the internet. There are companies that will do that for a person, and Adrian has enough money to hire them. Though most people don't care so much about erasing their exes from history.

"What happened with your ex?"

He drains his glass and pours another, taking in a deep breath. Just then, the intercom at his door rings, stealing his attention.

"One moment," he tells me and Adrian goes to answer.

"Food's here, Mr. Bradford."

"Bring it up."

It's quiet as he pours his whiskey, and I attempt a bit of small talk thanking him for dinner.

A doorman appears a minute later, in gray slacks with a shiny black name tag on his crisp white shirt, and two bags in hand. I cling to the tumbler, feeling out of place once again.

Adrian takes the bags out to the living room, where there's a massive sofa and a coffee table large enough to dine on.

As I slip off the stool, he opens the bags and lays out the containers on the table.

"The view is better in here," he tells me and when I reach the sofa, my hand on the soft leather, he peeks up at me to add, "and touching you will be far easier here."

A blush creeps up into my cheeks and I take the seat next to him. The savory smells of basil and marinara waft toward me.

"Italian?"

"Have you had Scalini Fedeli before?"

I shake my head gently, glass still in hand. "I haven't."

There's that hum again, that satisfied hum coming just before he balls up the paper bags. Rising from his seat, he tells me I'm going to love it.

As he plates the food, capellini with prosecco, porcini ravioli and arugula and buffalo mozzarella salad, my mouth waters.

I do however notice that the conversation from the kitchen has stopped altogether.

Maybe he's not going to tell me. It's obviously a painful subject if he's just going to move on from it. Curiosity flares again, but I don't want to ask the question. I'd rather sit with him, enjoy this meal and wait for more of those deep rumbles from him.

"She never loved me," Adrian says, breaking the silence after the food is plated. "She never even wanted to be with me. She was with someone else the entire time."

"Oh my God." My heart breaks for him. I know this feeling so well. I wish I didn't, because it means my ex was a horrible person who wasted my time, but I know the betrayal that's coursing through his veins. It makes you feel so sick and stupid. Like you should have known all along what was happening, but you didn't.

"He told her to sleep with me because he wanted her to persuade me into certain deals."

"That is …" Horrible. Worse than horrible. Devastating. It would make it hard to continue trusting people in business after that. Almost impossible. No wonder Adrian rearranges companies to such an extent. He doesn't truly trust anyone to be what they say they are.

"We were together for nearly six months before I realized."

"I'm sorry." I set the tumbler into my lap, both hands cradled around it. His focus is on his plate. His fork twirls the pasta around but he doesn't eat.

His eyes find mine and he offers me a smile that doesn't reach his eyes when he says, "Maybe it's not polite dinner conversation."

"It's fine. I want to know more about you."

He gestures at the food on the coffee table. "You must be hungry," he says, and I know this part of the conversation is over.

My appetite has vanished, though, apart from small bites, which are delicious. We eat in relative silence. I'm sick on his behalf, and on mine. I never thought Adrian Bradford and I would have something like this in common—such complete betrayal by an ex. I guess betrayal doesn't care if you're rich. It can find you anywhere.

"What do you think?" he questions.

"About what?"

He huffs a small laugh, taking another bite before glancing at my half-eaten plate.

"Oh, it's delicious. I—You were right. It's delicious."

He's barely touched his plate as well. "I'm not as hungry for dinner as I thought I'd be."

"Me either."

A moment passes as he leans back, the sofa groaning under his weight. The plates stay where they are on the table, the empty tumblers of whiskey next to them.

"I'll never do that to you," he murmurs, his gaze drifting to my lips.

I turn onto my side, lifting my knees up and letting my heels fall to the floor so I can rest my legs on the edge of the sofa. "I won't either. Cheating and lying are—"

"For assholes who can live with their misery," he says, finishing the statement for me.

I rest my cheek on the back of the sofa, and my hand slips into his. "Yeah."

As if he senses my thoughts, he says, "I want to get lost in you."

I don't have a chance to respond, only to part my lips as he crashes against them.

As soon as he touches me it's like we're back in the office, frantic for each other. He strips off my clothes with brutal efficiency. A gasp leaves me as he lifts me, forcing my legs to wrap around his hips.

I think he might take the floor, but instead he takes me to

the windows looking out over the city. He's still fully clothed, save for the top buttons undone from my efforts a moment ago.

My stomach drops at the height of the building but Adrian murmurs in my ear, "You're safe here, safe from everything except being my fuck toy. Isn't that what you said you wanted?"

I wonder if they can see me. There's no other building this tall, but it would only take someone craning their neck to see me bared to the powerful man behind me.

My answer is a moan. He puts both my hands on the cool glass. "Keep your hands up," he commands me. "And spread your legs." My breasts press against the glass as my hips are pulled against his crotch. His erection pushes against my ass.

His hand dips down between my thighs and teases up until he's stroking my clit, alternating it with pushing his fingers inside me until I whimper for more. Then he focuses relentlessly on my clit until I come on his fingers with a cry, shaking against the windowpane. My legs nearly give out and I cling to Adrian as best I can, holding on to him to keep my balance. His lips trail down my neck as he toys with me, bringing me closer and hotter to yet another release. It's hot and my pulse races, for the sheer force of my orgasm and from the view. The chill of the glass is at odds with how my body hums. He plays me like he knows every inch of me, and I fucking love it. I love what he does to me.

He tells me, "I think I'll fuck you here." His fingers slip lower, to a place I've only experimented with once. My eyes widen slowly and my lips part in an O. "Have you had anal before?"

I swallow thickly before answering, "Not in a long while."

"Did you enjoy it?" he questions and I rest my head back, staring down at the city. "It was … different. We didn't get far," I admit. A college fling once tried … we were drunk and lube was scarce. "It was a no go for lack of … preparation."

A deep rumble of consideration comes from his chest as he seems to consider what I've told him. "Are you curious?" he asks.

"Yes," I admit, my heart racing.

"And you would you trust me to do my due diligence?" he questions and I can feel his smile against my neck. His fingers play at my clit again and my "yes" becomes a moan of approval. The thought instantly makes me nervous, but I would let Adrian do anything. I trust him.

"Lie down for me over here," he says, picking me up and taking me to his sofa. At first I yelp in surprise, clinging to him, but it quickly turns into a short laugh, smiling into the crook of his neck.

He's gentle as he sets me down on the soft leather cushion. "Wait here."

He comes back a moment later and puts me into position on his couch, on my belly, knees bent slightly. I'm quick to grab a pillow, laying my cheek against it and wondering what he'll feel like ... *there*.

Adrian kneels behind me and spreads me wide, his fingers playing at that place, cool and slick with lube. He pushes one finger inside, then two. It's an odd pressure and it makes me tense slightly before relaxing. The simple act heats my entire body and with it, my head thrashes and I moan gently into the pillow.

"How does it feel?" he questions.

"Good," I respond in a groan as his other hand finds my clit, his fingers still in my ass. "Fuck," I moan into the pillow.

"Tell me if anything feels uncomfortable," he tells me. "This shouldn't hurt, Suzette. It should feel good." All I can do is nod with my eyes closed. The sensation is all consuming, tingling every inch of me. With a whimper, I swear it's more sensitive and more illicit to be fucked like this.

He shifts us to the floor, which gives me a sensation of stability that the couch didn't, and I feel the head of him against me. I take in a quick breath.

"Push back," he orders, and I do. My body goes hot as he presses inside.

My hands fist the pillows and he tells me to relax.

"I want you to enjoy this," he whispers at the shell of my ear, his warm breath and gentle kisses adding to the overwhelming sensation.

With my eyes half-lidded, my lips part and I push back. Strangled moans pour from me. "That's my good girl," he urges me on, slowly pulling out and then pushing back in. Adrian murmurs things behind me but doesn't rush. It's very slow, and it makes me all the hotter. The full sensation turns to something else, something needy and undeniably pleasurable. Inch by inch I push myself back on him until he's fully inside me.

It's that last thrust that seems to shock my system. My eyes go wide and it feels too much, too hot, too full. Just too much.

"Oh," I gasp. Biting down on my lip, I utter a small grievance. "Stop, no. I don't know." It happened too fast, out of nowhere. He stops at once, stilling and my hand grabs the top of his.

"It's all right. How do you feel?" he questions. Fuck, it's just so much. I want it, I want him. *I want this.* It's a sweet mix of pleasure and pain.

"Scared," I admit to him, remembering how much it hurt before. It was nothing like this. Not at all, but with a cold sweat on the back of my neck, I swallow down the unwanted memory.

"Just breathe," he says softly. "Give me a word that means stop."

"Whiskey," I say, the first thing that comes to mind.

"I'm going to move, Suzette."

He does, and it feels overwhelming to the point of paralyzing. There's not an ounce of control left for me; all I can do is hold on. I've never been taken in such a forbidden way before. Adrian is slow at first, then faster and deeper. I clutch a blanket he's thrown on the floor beneath us. With one hand on my clit, he takes full advantage of pushing me to the edge.

His thrusts get harder and deeper still and if it weren't for his lips on my neck that beg me to kiss him, I would be writhing beneath him.

"What's your word, Suzette?"

"Whiskey," I whisper, feeling the pleasure build and build.

"Good. I need you to remember that."

I almost ask him why, but he doesn't give me enough time. Adrian holds me down and fucks me ruthlessly. With deep strokes, he takes me like I'm his fuck toy.

I come instantly, his name on my lips and pleasure like I've never felt before rocking through me.

thirteen

Adrian

EXHAUSTION LAYS HEAVY AGAINST ME, IN THE BEST of ways. The city lights creep through the edge of the curtain and cast a soft glow in the bedroom. The bed is warm and Suzette's body is molded to mine under the sheets. Her back to my front, my hand over hers. She makes this little humming sound every time I kiss her just beneath her ear. It's addictive. And when I sleep, I pray I hear it. The contentment, the satisfaction. I could see myself devoted to that soft sound.

"Did you enjoy it?" I question in a whisper at the shell of her ear.

Her response is a hum, a sated one cloaked in sated fatigue. My cock twitches at the memory.

"You'll tell me if it hurts," I whisper, bringing my hand to her hip as she presses her ass against me.

"Mm-hmm," she murmurs. She's quick to take my hand back, slipping her fingers through mine. Her eyes stay closed. She's well and thoroughly fucked, and after the night we've had, sleep should come easy.

All I can think is that I didn't ask to fall for her. It wasn't a part of any plan.

Every detail in the beginning was something I had planned. But she was unexpected, and *this* is entirely unexpected. Falling for her feels like it changes everything. I don't know what exactly changed, but everything feels different.

"I'll dream of you," she says.

"As you should," is what I reply. I bite my tongue before I let slip, *I'll dream of you too.*

If you're reading this, put your phone down and listen to your father.

My mother's text shows on the screen as I pick up my BlackBerry. I can't help but huff out a humorless laugh before setting it back down and tending to the pan on the stove.

The smell of bacon fills the kitchen as I flip the pancake one last time before slipping it off the skillet and onto the pile of six on the plate.

The fresh fruit was already sliced and prepared. All I had to do was pour the mix of cantaloupe, berries, and watermelon into the small bowl.

I'm not a chef by any means, but I can manage a simple breakfast.

The stack of pancakes joins the table next to the syrup and butter. Deeming it acceptable, I glance behind me toward the stairs deciding to wait until Suzette is up so she can join me. My BlackBerry buzzes again and I'm not certain if it's my father, telling me I need to take the weekend off, or my mother, agreeing with him. It could also be a work email, calendar notification or someone else who needs something from me.

With a black coffee in hand, I stalk to the adjacent living room and peer out of the windows overlooking the early morning in the city. It's already bustling beneath us.

This city never sleeps and, if you want to keep up with it, you can't either. The only thing that stops me from heading to my office is the knock on my door.

"Come in," I call out, knowing exactly who it is.

"Mr. Bradford," Noah greets me, carrying a variety of large

department store bags in different colors, half of them with tissue paper peeking out. "This should do, I hope."

"Have you got everything?" I question, very much focused on the details beneath Suzette's clothing.

The older man nods, professional but with a knowing look as he sets the bags down. "Ann selected the delicates." His sport coat and dark jeans are evidence that he has plans, more than likely with his wife.

"I appreciate it. Please let her know I am grateful."

"Is there anything else, sir?"

"Not at the moment."

"I'll be off then," he says and waves a short goodbye before glancing around the room, I imagine to spot the lady these clothes are intended for.

Much to my gratitude, the front door closes before Suzette quietly makes her way into the room. Her bare feet padding softly on the hardwood floor give her away. With her hair a messy halo, and dressed only in one of my undershirts, she could not possibly look more fuckable.

My grip on the mug in my hands tightens as I suppress a groan.

"Good morning," she offers, brushing her hair from her face. As her arms fold in front of her she gets reacquainted with my penthouse, glancing around before stopping in front of the set table.

"Good morning. Your clothes arrived." I motion toward the bags with the mug. "Coffee's on as well. Should I make you a cup?"

With surprise lightening her gaze, it dances between the bags and myself. "I'm sorry, did you say clothes arrived?"

"I think you could use some caffeine," I state rather than answering her. As I make my way to the kitchen, the tissue paper crinkles behind me.

"You ordered these for me?"

I pour her a cup, listening to the sounds of her opening each bag. "You needed something to wear home. Cream and sugar?"

"Please." Tentatively, I take in her posture. She's not unfamiliar with wealth, but I imagine it can be difficult for a woman like Suzette to readily accept.

"I should pay you back," she murmurs. I imagine she's attempting to tally the total.

"It's a gift."

"You didn't have to," she tells me, still holding an crimson silk shift dress with both of her hands.

"You keep saying that and I'll keep reminding you, it's because I want to." Setting her coffee on the table, I add, "Besides, I will very much enjoy seeing you in that dress." It's that deep red shade she seems to love so much. "I just hope it fits you."

"You're too much," she tells me, and I catch her gaze. "Thank you."

Good. That's all she needs to say.

"And breakfast?" She finally sets the dress back into the shopping bag, careful with the fabric, and gives me a simper. "You made breakfast?" She selects a small chunk of fruit.

"I thought you might have an appetite this morning.

"You would be right. I'm famished."

"I was thinking breakfast and then a shower?"

"As much as I like the smell of you and your body wash, I don't have anything to shower with."

"Everything you need should be in one of those." I motion toward the bags.

"Toiletries?" Again she seems surprised. Nodding, I take the seat across from her, making my plate of bacon and pancakes.

She seems shy as she speaks. "Thank you for letting me stay overnight ... and for all of this."

What kind of men has she been with? Did she think I'd fuck her and then send her home in a taxi?

Her apprehension fades as we eat.

"What are your plans for the day?"

"I'm behind on a contract for—" she starts, picking up a slice of bacon and then pauses. "What are the rules for the weekend?"

A short chuckle leaves me and I smirk at her. "We can negotiate those terms, Ms. Parks."

There it is. Her gorgeous smile and lightheartedness.

"I would like to spend the day with you, but I'm a bit behind with work." She sighs dreamily and adds, "A man has been distracting me."

I hum in agreement. "I know what you mean. There's an exceptionally beautiful and stubborn woman who's been distracting me as well."

Her simper widens and she rocks slightly in her seat.

"You look gorgeous, by the way." She blushes, as if she's a shy little thing. Does she know how all of these facets of her have me more and more addicted?

I offer, "We could plan on working and fucking, fucking and working. Occasionally we must eat, though."

The smile dims as she lays her arms on the table, slightly more serious. "As much as that sounds exactly like the productive weekend I'd enjoy, I'm a little sore and I think I'd like to work from home."

I can't help that the corner of my lips tips up in an asymmetric smile. "Sore?"

She blushes again. "I think I may need to rest for the day, if you don't mind."

Before I can feel any kind of disappointment she questions, "What are your plans for tonight?"

"Wide open, Ms. Parks."

"Would you like to go on a date with me?"

"You're asking me out?"

"Officially. Yes. I think the weekends … maybe we could date on the weekends?"

My smile matches hers. "I think I'd like that."

fourteen

Suzette

It's difficult, and unladylike, to eat yogurt and talk at the same time, but I'm managing it. Gail shovels a handful of almonds and raisins into her mouth as well, completely unfazed. We're both rushing through lunch and it's not uncommon in the least. Today is different, though. It feels as if everything is riding on this one task delegated from the "team."

Projected profits and client referrals based on previous numbers. A.k.a., how profitable is our division on its own? I'm more than certain we'll impress. Perhaps it's cocky or arrogant, but I know we're damn good at what we do and, as Gail so eloquently put it, it's time to whip our dicks out.

Lunch break be damned.

Maddie sits on one end of my desk, watching the conversation as she eats her caesar salad, and another of our coworkers is at her side. His name is Dale and Dale is … well, he's Dale. He's got a sharp eye for marketing but his social skills are subpar. So he stays in his cubicle avoiding us as much as he can.

Today, I wish he'd done just that. There's an uneasiness about him and it puts a damper on the atmosphere that would otherwise be motivating.

"No, listen," I say to Dale. "I have an idea I want to pitch to you before we part ways again and you leave us to the figures."

"I'm not sure you should be pitching any ideas." He gives me a look that definitely means something and my face goes hot.

"What do you mean? I always pitch you ideas. It's no different for me to do it right now."

He arches an eyebrow. "Even with all the rumors flying around the office?" At once, my ears turn red hot. Gail pauses mid-chew, her dark brown eyes going wide and Maddie peeks up from her salad.

My heart drops in nervousness. "What rumors?"

"People have seen you with a certain someone," Dale says, his gaze darting toward the elevator.

"Who?" Maddie asks. *Fuck. Fuck, fuck, fuck.* With numb fingers I drop the mostly eaten yogurt to the small trash can.

As I do, I shoot her a look that gives her all the information she needs to know. Betrayal doesn't pair well with the sweet yogurt. It tastes far too sour.

Her mouth drops open. Two weeks of seeing Adrian nearly every day, and it was bound to happen. Shakily, I sip my water and take a few deep breaths to calm down, not responding at all to Dale.

"You're seeing him, aren't you?" Gail questions to my left. All eyes are on me and I fucking hate it. I knew this would happen. Office trysts *always* get out. I just wish it wasn't today of all freaking days.

Dale watches me carefully, as if he's not sure he can trust me anymore. I don't like that feeling. It's a sensation of being accused of something, though he is right that I'm seeing Adrian.

I nod in confirmation. The corners of Dale's mouth turn down. "So he sleeps with you on the weekend and then fires your coworkers on Monday."

A chill runs through me at his bluntness, but my back straightens.

Sighing, I put the bottle of water down on my desk. "That's pretty much how it is." My tone is bitchy yet stern as I meet his gaze head-on.

"And none of that has anything to do with the last decade

of work I've put into this client list. So," I say and glance over my shoulder at Gail, "back to putting together this presentation because as much as I wish fucking Adrian would save our asses, we both made it very clear that lines would not blur." I pause, waiting for Dale to say anything at all. For Maddie or Gail to pipe up.

A long moment passes with a heat tingling at the back of my neck.

"What if you tried blow jobs too?" Maddie says, then shrugs and Dale shakes his head although there's a hint of his smile showing.

Gail is less than impressed. "I need a moment," is all she says before walking out, leaving that pit in my stomach to weigh heavier.

That particular feeling only grows as the day progresses. Each time, it grows and grows until I feel like I could throw up.

The rumor is confirmed within minutes. It's easy to tell when each of them know.

Dale was correct that Adrian does the firing, and not me, but it's me who my coworkers come to for answers when it's done. All of them are upset, and nothing I can say offers them any comfort.

It's as if my office becomes the place to vent. The place for them to safely unleash their anger. Unfortunately for me, it also appears to be the day the graphics department is getting culled.

So one after the other pass snide looks my way before heading to their office with empty boxes to clear out their things.

They just lost their jobs. I feel compassion for them, even the ones I didn't get along with very well. Frustration mounts and I'm more upset than ever toward the end of the day.

A woman who's just been let go comes into my office at three. "What the hell, Suzette?" Her face is almost white, and her voice shakes from how upset she is. "Half of the department was just let go."

"He's rearranging things," I say helplessly. "I'm so sorry."

"Let me guess, there's nothing you can do."

"I'm sorry," is my only reply. I can't give her anything else. I'm not the owner of the company; Adrian is, and I'm not even the second step down in the company. "I have no input or authority."

"Wonderful," she says sarcastically. "Goodbye, Suzette."

A few minutes later, another person who has been fired storms across the hall. He turns his head and stares at me on his way past, but doesn't say a word.

It's not until Gail comes back, taking her seat and appearing on the verge of tears. "If you knew something, you would tell me, right?" We've worked together for years and I've never seen her like this. Her tan skin is flushed. "If I'm going to lose my job, I just need to know so—" her voice cracks and I can't take it.

"The second I know anything—"

"Could you ask him?" She stresses, "Please?" Her dark brown eyes are rimmed in red and I know she's a mess witnessing so many layoffs so quickly and with whispers of a merger, where our jobs would no doubt overlap with others and thus, more layoffs.

"Please," she begs me. With a nod, and a tight swallow, I agree.

"I can ask him," I tell her and then I firm up my response. "I'll ask him today."

Sitting here and waiting for an answer isn't enough, not for me and not for the team members I have left. I've worked far too hard for this company to let it all go to shit like this. If we lose Gail, the report we put together today is irrelevant. Clients stay with us because of the team. We can't break down like this.

I won't let it happen.

At five forty-five, I knock on the door to Adrian's office. Shaking out my hands, I prepare myself. Not the version of me he sees after six. But the version who existed before that man dared to walk through the doors to this building. The badass businesswoman who doesn't take any shit.

It's a small blessing that his secretary is gone for the day and her desk is empty now. Most of the building is cleared out, but not everyone. And I have fifteen minutes. He can offer me fifteen minutes if it means saving the most profitable department in this company.

"Come in," Adrian calls from inside the office.

Steeling myself, I open the door and go in, then close it behind me. The move is fast and I say a silent *thank you* that his door was unlocked.

Before he can say a word, I approach his desk. It seems to take forever and the scent of people's fear as they got fired today hangs in the air. His large, spacious office must have seemed like an awful joke to the people who lost their jobs. I could be one of them, and Adrian is the only one who can confirm my fear or dismiss it. That's why I'm here. This conversation is needed, because I can't sit at my desk for another day with nothing to say to the people I've worked with for years as they file out past me. I handpicked my department. They should be able to rely on me.

"My department is essential to what our company does," I begin, without waiting for his permission. I don't need it outside of the games we play. "If you want to keep the company going, you'll need to keep the core team intact. Every single one of them is essential, and I can vouch for them and their work."

Adrian shifts in his seat, his dark suit crisp, his expression inscrutable. As he leans back, his hands relaxed on the armrests, I wait for any reaction at all, but I'm given nothing.

"Almost everyone I could part with is already gone, and my team won't be able to keep functioning if we lose any more people. We've brought in the most revenue of any other department over the last few years, and you can expect more of the same over the next five years. We're projected to triple our profits by then."

Adrenaline rages through me at the very fact that we will

triple in only five years. There's not a damn word I've said that's exaggerated. My heart hammers in my chest as I stare back at Adrian's cool gaze. Again, he doesn't react other than to gesture to continue.

"I'm damn good at my job, and I have good people, and we're going to keep striving for excellence."

"Are you done?" he questions.

"There's no one who can do what we do and keep those clients. No one has the relationships we do. No one has the word of mouth that we do. Replacing any of us would be a mistake."

I swallow so hard, it's audible and still, I'm given nothing.

"Adrian." I whisper his name, on the verge of breaking. Anger simmers but also a hurt I can't describe.

"We're on the clock, Suzette," he warns, the first sign of compassion noted in my name on his lips.

"If you're going to lay them off," I say and swallow, "I need to be able to tell them. I need to know what's going on."

"That's what you came here for? To figure out who's getting fired next?" His tone is unimpressed.

"I want you to keep in mind that we're a team. We work efficiently and our plan is solid; our performance speaks for itself."

He eyes me from across his desk, lips pursed. "You'll have an answer when the team is ready."

Frustrated, I look him in the eye. "You could at least say you'll consider it. You can at least tell me you'll let me know if anyone is in danger."

"I won't. It doesn't matter, Suzette. The team is running the numbers. The numbers are what guide my decision, not emotions. Not a plan, but what has been done and what is comparable. You're aware you have a list of clients, but they aren't the only clients and even that list is sellable."

Heat spreads over the back of my neck. I'm burning with frustration and anger, tears stinging the corners of my eyes. "You're heartless. You know what this means."

"And you know I bought this company for profit, and it's been bleeding money for far too long."

I'm left speechless, staring at him with nothing but resentment.

He won't give in, and somehow it shocks me. I should have known this about Adrian Bradford. He takes what he wants and does what he wants.

I knew that all too well when he fucked me on this desk the very first day we met. My heart hurts and I put my hand up to cover it, but it's too late. The damage is already done. "I can't believe you won't even give me the respect of letting me know if my team is at risk of losing their livelihoods. If you're just going to sell off the list, you could tell me that. I'm not fucking stupid. You would know if you already had a buyer."

Adrian folds his arms over his chest. "I listen because it means something to you. Do you think I would have let anyone else barge in here without a meeting?"

That same sickness from earlier stirs and I say nothing, knowing he's the one who's caused it.

"There needs to be a … separation for us."

"How the hell am I supposed to separate this?" is all I can respond, my voice shaky.

"I want you to be happy," Adrian says simply, unfolding his arms and pushing the chair out from his desk slightly. "I want you to know I care for you."

There's a pause, and my frustration grows again. He cares for me? But can't answer a simple question? "They need to know as soon as possible so they can prepare," I press further and Adrian doesn't budge, his lips pressing into a thin line.

"Would you really sleep with me one night and then fire me in the morning?" I question with my voice tight.

"Suzette," he says, his voice carrying a note of warning. He doesn't say no.

Betrayal seems to push out every other feeling I have,

making my face hot and my chest hurt. I know a losing argument when I see one and I know Adrian won't be convinced right now, but I can't help myself. "The company—"

"It's after six, Suzette," he replies, cutting me off. "You'll have your answer when the team has consolidated numbers and risks."

"Oh," I say with a bitter tone. "You can't tell me now because you're off the clock. Because it's six, so now I'm just a lowly fuck toy for you to come in?" Even as the words escape my mouth, I know they cross the line.

"You know that's not why." His statement is a string of carefully restrained anger, his grip tightening on the armrests, turning his knuckles white. Good. I hope he's pissed off. I hope he's upset like I am.

"I would never speak to you like that," he continues. "I would never treat you like you didn't matter. You know that," he tells me, his tone softening, his pale blue gaze pinning me. "And I don't like you talking about yourself like that."

"How am I supposed to—"

"You told me you could separate the two—" I cut him off before he can finish.

"I'm trying to compartmentalize," I argue back. He's gripping the desk, obviously upset now. "I'm sorry. I need a moment and I think—" Just as I turn my back to him, ready to get the hell out of here so I can lose it alone in a bathroom stall, he speaks up.

"No. We need to get out of here. We have dinner plans."

How am I supposed to sit through dinner like this with my stomach in knots and my face burning? I don't think I can do it. "Maybe we shouldn't tonight."

All my emotions tumble over me, filling my body and seeming to spill over into the room. Tears fill my eyes, but I don't want to cry in front of Adrian. I don't want to cry here in the office, where we've done so many things and where he keeps chipping away at my department and the company I've worked so hard to build.

"Maybe we shouldn't," I say again weakly, and start to leave.

His voice comes immediately, so deep and commanding that it stops me in my tracks. "Don't you dare walk out that door."

fifteen

Adrian

I'M MORE THAN AWARE THAT THERE ARE EMPLOYEES STILL in the building. A few might be close enough to hear as Suzette bites out, "What the hell did you just say to me?"

She's visibly upset and spiraling. I've seen it before. A hundred times at least. Crying, cursing, screaming at me. I've been struck more than once.

My skin blazes with both indignation and embarrassment. I don't do squabbles in the office, I don't have shouting matches with employees. Then again, I've never slept with anyone at the office before either. This is why. This is exactly why it was a mistake.

With daggers in her eyes, Suzette stares back at me and says, "Did you just say, 'don't you dare?'" Her voice is deathly low and her gaze narrowed.

Her breasts rise and fall, peeking through her blouse as she breathes in deeply, stalking back toward me.

"I'd like you to calm down," I say, keeping my tone gentle. The last thing I need is publicity or a lawsuit.

Her eyes widen. "Calm down?" Outrage coats the two words. *Fuck.* I can't do anything right by her. This is a lose-lose situation and she sure as hell knew it when she walked in those doors.

I take in a steadying breath, standing from my seat, my dick hard, needing to fuck the anger out of both of us.

"Suzette." I speak her name as she stalks toward me.

"I am struggling today." Her words are frantic. "Watching coworkers pack up their offices, while others didn't even come in. Do you know how many people have given their notice?"

"Fourteen so far," I answer without hesitation. "Change is difficult, uncertainty is difficult, doing *my fucking job* is difficult," I stress, feeling the frustration rise.

"What am I supposed to tell them, Adrian? Rumors are going around about us and they're coming to me like I'm the one who did this," she starts and before she can continue, I stop her in her tracks. Toe to toe I stand apart from her.

"I am doing my best. If my best isn't good enough, then they can go find better." My words are stern and she acts as if they've struck her. Gripping her hips in both of my hands, I lower my lips to hers to say, "And if any of them have a problem with the two of us, tell them I want you more than anything. More than this company. More than profit, more than any fucking thing. I want you."

She's silent, her wide blue eyes brimming with a mix of emotions. Her hands on my chest put distance between us, so I take them in my own.

"I want you," I repeat, my voice strained and the words raw. "I want you," I tell her a third time, letting it sink in. "This will all be over soon, and when it is, I will still want you."

"Adrian," she says and my name is a plea on her lips, like I'm begging her for something she can't give me. Panic sets in, something I haven't felt in a long damn time.

She knew this was a possibility. I will vouch for her if something happens, but her résumé is impeccable. She will survive. I'll make sure of it. But I cannot guarantee an entire department. I can't promise her the things she's asking for.

"Tell me you want me."

"Adrian," she whispers and her voice is pained. It's unexpected and feels as if she's struck me. I can't remember a time when I've given her a command and she hasn't obeyed.

Moving my hands to hold her, one spearing through her hair and the other on the small of her back, I whisper in her hair before kissing her temple. "Tell me that you want me and I'll make sure you get everything you need."

All I can hear is the sound of her swallowing. I can't lose her over something like this. Something so insignificant. *It's significant to her, though.*

"It's after six," I remind her. "Come here, let me fuck the memory of that prick boss out of that pretty head of yours."

"Don't," she warns me and uncertainty clouds my judgment. Every inch of my skin is hot, anxiousness quickening my pulse.

"Let it rest for one more night. I promise your department will be the priority tomorrow." I shouldn't have said that. The second the words are out of my mouth, I know I shouldn't have spoken them.

"You promise?"

And still, I double down at the thought that it's what she needed to hear. "I promise."

She pulls back, staring into my eyes. "You promise? Because I don't think I can take much more of what happened today and as much as—"

"I told you, you have my word." With my pulse hammering, I bend to kiss her, deeply and desperately. I've lost the upper hand and I couldn't care less. Her lips mold to mine, but she's quick to break them.

"I'm sorry," she whispers between us. Picking her ass up, I move her to the desk, her legs spread as I stand between them.

She repeats, "I'm sorry, I shouldn't have come in when I was—"

"Stop," I say and then kiss her again.

"No." She pushes me back, breaking my hold on her and heaving in a breath. "I'm sorry I didn't tell you that I want you too. I do. I do, Adrian, and I'm sor—"

With my finger pressed against her lips, I give her the

command, "I said quiet." Heat dances along my skin. Both of us pent up, both of us suffering from the way we came to be.

Working the knot of my tie, I order her, "Lie back, with your hands by my chair."

She doesn't hesitate, eager to make it up to me.

My mind whirls with the implications of what's happened in the last hour, but I can barely focus on anything other than taking back control.

"You'll be quiet," I tell her in a whisper, steadying my breath as I use my tie to form a handcuff knot and stalk around to the other side of the desk. Slipping both of her hands through, I tighten them and then order, "Above your head."

She doesn't object and although the loose end is short, I'm able to tie it to the drawer handle. Lying flat on her back across the desk, her hands above her head, she has to bend her knees so her heels balance on the edge of the desk.

"What am I going to do to you?" I round the desk, loving how she looks.

This is better. This is how she should be.

With a hand on each of her hips, I drag her so her ass is at the edge of the desk. Her gasp fuels me further. Reaching up her skirt, I bunch it and drag her panties down her ass until they're free from her and a pile of lace on the floor.

"Spread your legs," I command and she obeys.

I position her heels how I want them, her legs spread as wide as she can. Fucking gorgeous. Her cunt is right there for the taking. Standing between her thighs, I unbutton her blouse one button at a time, exposing her blush-colored bra. I wish I'd taken it off before I thought to have her lie down. Her breathy pants are additive.

"This is how I want you in this office after hours."

Dipping the cups down, I free each breast, plucking and pinching her nipples and taking my time to play with them.

"My plaything, mewling for me."

"Adrian—"

"You'll be silent or I'll gag you, my little vixen. Do you understand?"

She starts to answer and thinking better of it, she swallows thickly and nods. The cords around her neck tighten, and I lean down, trailing kisses there as my hand slips to her slit.

"So fucking wet already," I murmur against her neck. "My greedy little whore … let's see how much you can take." With my lips on hers, I keep her quiet as I slip two fingers inside of her, curling them and quickly finding the bundle of nerves that has her sucking in a breath and arching her neck. My thumb moves to her clit and I'm ruthless as I force the first orgasm from her. It doesn't take long at all, her heels slipping from the edge of the desk, her muted cries of pleasure silenced as I devour her mouth with my own.

When she clenches around me, I only pause for a moment, wetting a third finger with her arousal before doing it all again. I don't kiss her this time, I stare down at her as she closes her and her head thrashes.

"Adrian." My name is hardly recognizable as it mixes with a tortured cry of pleasure.

Pulling my hand from her I smack her pussy, my middle finger landing directly on her clit.

Her arms pull back, the tie keeping her restrained, and her back bows as she cries out a beautiful sound of desperation.

"Quiet now, my little vixen," I tell her and her darkened gaze finds mine. Once she's regained her composure, I do it again, fucking her with three fingers until she comes undone.

My cock is hard watching her skin flush. When I finally thrust inside of her, I'm not merciful in the least. The desk allows me to fuck her deeply and roughly. Punishingly so.

She thought she was sore two days ago … she won't be able to walk out of here when I'm done with her.

sixteen

THE ONLY THING ALLOWING ME TO CALM DOWN LAST night was, ironically, Adrian. If he hadn't taken me in his office, I don't think I would have been able to sleep. After being taken so thoroughly all I could think about was a hot bath, pajamas, and a glass of wine. My worries couldn't keep me awake long after that and I took my well-fucked body to bed.

A part of me is convinced he only said those things to pacify me. That he told me tomorrow he would give me a straight answer so I would calm down. The other part of me knows he hasn't given me a reason to think he'd lie to me. He's many things, but he hasn't lied to me. All of me, though, every single part of me is embarrassed for losing it on him. It wasn't professional and it crossed the lines we agreed upon.

With all of those thoughts fighting for the center stage of my insecurity, sleep wasn't as restful as I'd hoped it would be. My light dreams were far too real. Coworkers glared at me from outside my office door. No one would tell me what was happening, though. They wouldn't give a reason why they were so angry. "We're transitioning," I said, and I knew it didn't make any difference. Eventually, the dreams stopped and I fell into a deep sleep for all of a handful of hours.

I think it's safe to say the reality of my position at work is catching up to me.

My outfit for today was a decisive choice. It consists of a pencil skirt and blouse that is the epitome of attire for head bitches in charge. Selecting my accessories carefully, I went with classic pearl studs and paired them with a triple strand of pearls.

Giving myself a once-over, I nod. My outfit is perfect, and I'm calm enough from last night to face whatever Adrian says this morning. Although I'm exhausted with bags under my eyes, I'm a professional and I'll act accordingly.

None of it explains how my hands go numb and my stomach turns over every time I think of Adrian, though. This is exactly why they say not to fuck your boss. Every instinct I have tells me that today is our last day and potentially my last day at work as well.

He's taken over my mind and my emotions. How the hell did I let that happen?

I can lie to myself all I want as I smooth my skirt down, but he's still lingering behind every one of my thoughts.

I reassure myself on the trip into the office that I'll be professional and that whatever happens, I will survive. And that these emotions are warranted. It's perfectly normal to experience insecurities around something as intimate as sex, and something as forbidden as sex with the man who holds your future in his hands. Not just your future, either, but that of everyone you work with.

The thoughts marinate all throughout my morning routine. From paying for my morning coffee at the stand on the corner, to nodding at colleagues on my way to the elevator. These feelings and thoughts don't leave me. Dwelling on it all won't help. All I want to do is rip the fucking bandage off.

My thoughts will only get more complicated, and what can simplify them is answers. The email went out this morning, and four people have already texted me. The only one I replied to was Gail, who's waiting for me so we can head to the conference room together. Three departments are meeting at once this morning. The last three. Just the thought sends unease washing through me again.

"You ready?" Gail asks me, a notebook tucked under her arm as she pulls the hem of her dress down. It's a dark red number with three-quarter sleeves, and it hugs her curves all the way down to her thighs.

Red is a confident color. Nodding, I lift my coffee to her. "Let's do this."

It's quiet as we take the elevator up. "At least we'll know," Gail murmurs and I nod, choosing not to say anything at all. Her nervousness is as obvious as mine.

I hate this. I hate every bit of it and that's all I can think as we settle into the room, all twenty chairs filled and three men standing in the back corner.

The conversation swells from soft murmurs and gossip to one man speaking far too loudly in the room and then all at once stops.

Adrian strides to the head of the table to address everyone. If I hadn't spent so much time with him, knowing the curve of his jaw, the strength in his stance, I might not notice the subtle darkness under his eyes, as if he hasn't slept either.

His suit is crisp, though, custom fitted no doubt, and his shoulders set back, the air seeming to bend around him.

"Good morning," he says, and my body instantly heats. He has all the power to turn our lives upside down, but I still crave the sound of his voice. "I'm not going to waste any time. As part of this company's restructuring, some departments will be dissolved."

Sucking in a breath, I prepare myself.

"Your applications will be suggested to a competitor who will need to hire a number of positions after a merger." His eyes meet mine. "The only department that stays is brand positioning and marketing. It will stay in its entirety."

Mutters fill the room instantly, but Adrian cuts them off with a gesture.

"Did he say our department?" Gail whispers. And I nod

without thinking. It's what he said, isn't it? He said brand positioning and marketing?

Gail lets out a not-so-subtle sigh and grabs my hand, squeezing so tight that my knuckles hurt. My department is safe. I can barely breathe, let alone sit here and absorb everything else he said.

There will be a merger.

He said there will be a merger.

We are safe, but what are the details of the merger? What exactly is happening? A split-up? He continues, fielding questions and a few men file out without a single word. They're pissed, dealing with the gravity of the situation. Everything seems to happen around me in a whirl. I have a million questions for Adrian. If the other sectors are being merged, what does that mean for my department? I rely on finance and purchasing and production to do what I do. Our department is all about ideas and relationships, but bringing those ideas to life relies on others. Does this mean I'll have to outsource? To the new company, even?

It's not long before I feel lingering stares on the back of my neck, and my ears go hot. They're all stealing glances at me, one by one. The corners of their mouths are turned down in disapproving frowns.

They know. This looks bad. So fucking bad. And yet, it's what I asked for. The reality of their assumptions hits me.

Everyone here knows I've been sleeping with Adrian, and they think he's keeping my department because I couldn't keep my legs closed. It will never matter to them that I took my own power in being fucked by him. All they see is a woman who went behind everyone's back to sleep with the boss and guarantee her department would stay intact.

That sickening feeling takes over again. Every part of me is on edge and Gail seems to catch on, squeezing my hand again and whispering, "Fuck them."

Frustration clenches my jaw. For so many years, I've thrown myself into this work and made tough calls and spoken my mind to my superiors even though I knew it would be risky to do it. I've been the one on the line many times, all in service of building this company into something worthwhile. Now everyone in the room thinks I slept my way to the top. Not even to the top. They think I slept my way to keeping my job.

My discomfort grows with the silence. I'm not sure what Adrian is waiting for, but no one does anything. No one pretends to have another meeting or rushes out with their cell phone to their ear.

It hits me then, that he's reading the room the same as I am. He knows exactly what they think and why they're all looking at me. Not Gail or anyone else from my department. Only at me. His gaze slips to mine and the back of my eyes prick. I can take it. I'll deal with the fallout and whatever damage is done to my reputation.

Adrian is handsome and stone faced at the front of the room. He's a defensive, arrogant asshole, that's what he is. Adrian has a strong jaw and an even better smile, but the expression he wears now is hardly encouraging.

"Not one of you came to pitch to me," he says finally in a deadly tone, and the room holds its breath. They've been waiting for the release of finally knowing what's going to happen, and now Adrian's dragging it out. "Not a single one of you but the lead for brand positioning and marketing. One of you came to me with a plan, and I may be a heartless prick, but if there is value and a potential profit ..." He's looking deeply into my eyes now, in front of all my colleagues. Every eye in the room is on us. "I do consider it."

seventeen

Adrian

TODAY WAS LESS THAN IDEAL. I'VE NEVER FELT SO conflicted when it comes to business.

Because she's a factor now. The moment the meeting ended, I left first and I'm ashamed to admit, I closed the door to my office to avoid it all. Especially Suzette and all the questions written in her expression in that conference room.

There's not a doubt in my mind word will get out.

Wyatt clears his throat across from me, and I wish I'd canceled this meeting, but in truth, I'd forgotten about it until he walked through the door.

"Whatever's going on, just tell me," he comments from across my desk. A stack of papers, or more specifically, the contract he wants me to sign sits in front of him. To-go bags from a sushi place are in the other lounge chair beside him.

"We don't have to discuss business," he offers. He's dressed in his lucky dove gray suit. He's worn it to every wedding and every business meeting I've accompanied him to. He told me once that it's his lucky charm. But as he fiddles with the thin pale pink tie, he leans forward, and his eyes search mine. "Whatever it is, you can tell me."

"You didn't come here to be my therapist."

"No, but I'm always your friend. Business aside, you look wrecked." He leans back, his tie wrapped up in one fist that lays on his chest. His brow's pinched as he speaks with concern. "Like, is it a chick, is it your parents? What's going on with you?"

"A chick," I utter before I can stop myself and then I hate it. I hate the description. "She's not just some woman."

"Oh shit." Wyatt elongates the words, pushing the contract out of the way to make room for the sushi.

"I'm not hungry," I tell him and he only pauses to tell me, "Look, I need to eat. You pour your heart out, I'll stuff my face. Whatever's left you can have later." The plastic bag crinkles as he digs out his carton of choice. "So, what'd she do?"

"Nothing that I shouldn't have known was coming." It was written on the walls. Before I even stepped foot in this building, without even looking at the security footage to detail employees, I knew Suzette Parks was going to fight me. It was written on the fucking walls.

"You're going to have to elaborate," he states, opening up a small container of soy sauce. "She cheat on you?"

"No. No. She wouldn't do that."

"Do we hate her? Want to date her? You haven't given me anything at all, so I'm going to need you to fill me in."

I stare across the desk at Wyatt. He's young, a player, never held on to a woman for more than a few weeks. There isn't shit he could tell me that would help in the least.

"You can vent to me," he assures me, separating a pair of disposable chopsticks and giving me an exasperated look. "Whoever she is, she's gotten to you. You were distracted last time I was here; you're obsessed to—"

"I have feelings for her," I admit to him rather than listen to him continue. "I like her … a lot and because of that, I compromised a business."

The California roll stops midair. "What business?"

Tapping my two fingers on the desk, I point to the door. "This one."

"What do you mean? You okay moneywise? You need help or something? You know my father—"

"I don't—No. No. It's fine moneywise. It's just …"

"Oh thank God," he mutters, far more relaxed as he leans back with the container in one hand and the chopsticks in the other.

"It's just, I'm taking a risk I wouldn't, if it weren't for her."

"It's not so bad," he says after an exaggerated swallow. "You've done it before," he reminds me.

"And I nearly lost it all before."

"Passion outweighs statistics." He tells me something I've told him years ago. Pointing the chopsticks at me he adds, "You know that."

I can only nod, feeling the anxiousness of this morning come back to me. "She knows what she's doing and I think this would be best for her," I tell him.

"But not for you?" he guesses.

"… It would be much easier to merge, which means she could lose her job, her entire department even. It would mean uncertainty for her."

"So what, you're keeping her out of it?"

"I'm forming a business for her and her department alone. Allowing her to keep the clients while the remainder of the business is merged with another company."

He arches a brow, surprised. "One of your other companies?"

I shake my head. "I'll profit quickly and be done as far as the merger goes. The investment goes into her business, though."

"Does she know that it's her business?"

"She'll find out soon enough."

"Is she ready for that? That's kind of," he says and repositions himself, more serious now. "It's kind of a lot."

"It was that or the alternative, giving her passion to someone else to control."

Wyatt shakes his head, his brow still raised as if it's stuck there now. "Well okay, so … now I see why your mind is occupied." He aims for another piece of sushi but stops before picking it up. "Wait, you're screwing someone here?" he questions.

"Like you're sleeping with the head of a department and because of that, you're forming a company for her to protect her from the obviously correct business decision?"

My stomach drops as I nod. "More or less."

"How long have you been with her? It's got to be serious."

"Less than a month, but yes. I'm serious when it comes to her."

If I thought his brow couldn't raise any higher, I thought wrong. It's quiet a moment, and the weight of my decision settles against my chest, uncomfortable and heavy.

"So, you're telling me," Wyatt pipes up, chopsticks once again aimed at me, "all I have to do to get you to sign these papers is sleep with you?"

The laughter is unexpected and if there was anything on my desk, I'd toss it at him. It's the first time I've smiled all day. "You're an ass, you know that?"

"I'm an ass who's happy you're in love," he comments and everything stops. "Men in love do stupid things but, if she's worth it, she's worth it."

"She's worth it," I tell him quickly. Ignoring the cold sweat that slips down the back of my neck at the thought of being in love with her.

"Good, maybe marry her or something. In case the company takes off."

"Marriage is not a business deal."

Wyatt shrugs. "It could be."

The knock at my office door is discreet and Andrea reveals herself. "Mr. Bradford, I just wanted to let you know the next meeting is seating now."

"Thank you, Andrea."

"All right, I'll get going then." Wyatt stands to leave. He takes in a deep breath and pushes the contract my way. "While you're a little puppy dog in love, could you take a look at that and sign it, please?"

Picking up the contract, I tell him, "You got it." I decide then and there that I'll sign it tonight.

Andrea watches our exchange from the threshold of the door.

"Give me five, and then can you scan this in for me?"

"Of course," she says warily and I look up at her.

"Everything all right?"

"Just checking on you. I know things are a bit tense at the moment."

"It's nothing I haven't dealt with before."

She stares back, her glasses slipping slightly from the bridge of her nose and her brow rises just as Wyatt's did. "Is there something else? Something you want to say?"

She shakes her head softly, the corners of her lips turning down. "No, sir."

"You can tell me," I say. "If there's something on your mind, speak freely."

"If Ms. Parks asks to meet with you, would you like me to let her up still?"

"Of course," I'm quick to answer.

"Good, good." Relief colors her face.

"Why would you ask?"

"She seemed upset yesterday, and so did you this morning. I just … I'm glad to hear that, is all."

eighteen

Suzette

GUILT AND NERVOUSNESS AND GRATEFULNESS SPIN through my mind for the rest of the day at work. All I can do is count down the minutes until 6:00 p.m. when I know Adrian will step into that elevator and I can be raw with him and let everything out. It's a gray area regarding the boundaries we set, but I have to get it out of me.

It's a mix of every emotion, so intense I have trouble concentrating on anything at all. My office door stays closed and I ignore every text and email and knock. I rescheduled several meetings and give myself the day to gather my composure.

This is what I wanted. It's exactly what I was hoping he would tell me was going to happen when I stormed into his office yesterday. Keeping my department whole is security and yet I feel nothing but insecure.

It all feels wrong. Just then my inbox pings with a new email notification and the subject line encompasses exactly what plays on repeat in my mind: *If you weren't sleeping with him, you'd have to fight for your job like the rest of us after the merger.*

There's a sinking feeling in my chest and when I click on the email header, the address is one I don't recognize. More than likely it's a throwaway account.

"Fuck you," I mutter and click delete although I can't say that they're wrong.

For the last hour, I do what I can, making plans for

reassuring our clients and reaching out to other department heads to ensure we have what we need to continue.

If we don't, we will. I won't let us miss a beat. It's critical for our clients to know we're stable and there won't be any delays.

If Adrian is keeping our entire department, I have to make sure we have something to show for it. We have to be the best, now that he's singled us out.

I feel guilty that my department is staying because of what Adrian and I have done together ... but not guilty enough to stop doing it.

I'm nervous that he'll change his mind and even more nervous that he'd be right to do it. And I'm grateful to him for announcing in front of everyone that he would be keeping our department. It saves me an untold amount of time trying to reply to questions when I don't have any firm answers.

I shake off the nervousness as best I can when it's finally time to get into the elevator. The office has been emptying out for a while now, and there's no one to see me step in. Adrian is already there waiting, occupied with his phone. When he glances up at me, my heart races. All the jitters rev up and I forget everything I was going to say.

"I can't do dinner tonight. I have a number of things that have piled up and arrangements that need to be finalized." My heels click as I step into the elevator, pretending like that's all right. Like it doesn't feel as if he's struck me and confirmed that everything is wrong and off between us.

"Okay," I say softly, staring straight ahead as the doors close.

"I can drop you off at your place if you'd like," he says briskly. It's cold and I stand a little further away from him as the elevator moves. He puts his phone in his pocket and presses the button for the first floor.

"Are we okay?" Now what I'm feeling is all nerves. It's tense between us, and different. There's none of the hot playfulness that's been part of every meeting we've had, and I can't help but wonder if it's because of what he did earlier. I know Adrian made that choice because of me. Guilt comes roaring back.

Adrian lets out a sharp breath and punches the emergency stop button on the elevator. "I need us to be—" he begins, and then he grabs me, pulling me commandingly across the space and into his arms. He lifts my face to his and kisses me hard and passionately, his tongue seeking entry into my mouth, and I part my lips for him with a moan. Heat blazes between us in an instant. It's unexpected but oh so needed.

Relief and desperation stir inside of me as I cling to him. My back hits the wall of the elevator and everything else slips away, fading to black and blurring into nothing.

My breathing is chaotic and my eyes stay closed as Adrian pulls back. His plea is what forces my eyes open. "What do you need from me to prove to you that you matter to me? That I want you happy and I want you mine and I couldn't give two shits about anything else?"

Gripping his collar, my fingers grazing against his stubble, I selfishly pull him in for another kiss, soft, slow and deliberate. He tastes minty and every bit of the man I know him to be. I could live here in this elevator if it meant kissing him forever.

Staring back into his pale blue gaze, I stop myself from the response that begs to be heard. The words are on the tip of my tongue. *I love you, Adrian.* Instead, I kiss him again, needing the stability of his body, until he pulls back to catch his breath. "Will you text me tonight when you're done?" I attempt to make it sound casual, but I'm not sure if it works. "I'm sorry I'm so needy right now."

He takes my face in his hands and looks me in the eye. "Stop saying you're sorry. I will text you." Adrian leans down and presses a kiss to my cheek. "Do you want Noah to take you home?"

I shake my head. "I can spend the evening with Maddie."

Adrian reaches for another button on the elevator's panel,

and then we're moving down again. He kisses me all the way to the bottom. "I'll text you," he promises again. One more kiss and the elevator doors open. Adrian is completely self-possessed and put together by the time he steps out of those silver doors and disappears into the lobby.

If only I could be the same.

Maddie's apartment is a cute, small place in SoHo. By small, I mean teeny tiny. It's a one bedroom with a decent-sized living room. A crocheted blanket from her grandmother rests on the back of her sofa and our takeout containers are spread out on the coffee table. The comparison of her place to Adrian's is unavoidable. They are complete contrasts. From the view to the flooring, even the light fixtures. All Maddie has is a single lamp in the corner and ceiling lights in the kitchen. Maddie's fridge hums in the little kitchen off the living room and every so often the radiator makes a clicking sound. Even if it is small, it's comforting to be here. It reminds me of when I first moved here. Before my ex, before this job. Over a decade ago now.

Curled up on the other side of the couch, Maddie works her way through the Chinese I picked up on the way here and groans about her latest hellish dating experience.

"He wanted me to pay for everything, including his dinner, after he was such a dick because, quote unquote, 'If you don't want to see me again, that's on you and you wasted my time,'" she says. Her eyes widen just as mine do, with disbelief. "I shit you not."

"That is … exceptionally … like, I don't even have words."

"I would have been happy to split the bill, but are you kidding me? I'm not going to pay a fee for not liking the guy."

"That sounds awful," I say, commiserating. "It's bullshit that you even have to put up with guys like that."

"I don't," Maddie tells me and laughs. "I left him in that restaurant. I just wish there were more good guys on this freaking app, you know? It's so exhausting to have to search through all of them. Like I'm obviously not good at picking, could someone else do it for me?" A titter leaves her, but I know she's less than happy and there's truth to the statement.

"I haven't looked at a dating app in a long time now." Stirring the lo mein with my fork, I add, "Not for … months now?" I surmise, "Not since those first few weeks of the separation."

Chewing my inner cheek, I keep my next thoughts to myself. I never would have found a man like Adrian on an app. My throat is tight with how much I miss him, and how I want things to be normal between us. It's been a long damn time since I've missed someone. Truly missed them, and that realization toys with me as well as Adrian himself does.

"Men are trash," Maddie says and sighs, and that's what does it.

I break down crying over my Chinese food. What the hell is wrong with me? "I swear I better be getting my period or something because I am nothing but an emotional wreck today." I create the excuse, pushing it out the moment I lose it. The small napkins from the restaurant make for perfect tissues.

"Oh my God." Maddie places her container onto the coffee table and scoots over next to me, slinging an arm around my shoulders. "What happened? It's okay to cry," she tells me. Of course she would say that. She's the emotional one. I'm not. This isn't me. It's not who I am.

"You know about Adrian," I barely manage to get out. "You heard the gossip at lunch, and you know what those rumors say and you know it's true but … it's not just sex."

Maddie's eyes are wide. She keeps giving me little nods, like she's following along, but when the pause comes her mouth drops open. She cracks a bright smile. "It's not just sex? Is it—"

"No," I cut her off. "It's more than that." Another sob wracks me and it only frustrates me more. "I think I'm falling for him."

nineteen

Adrian

SITTING IN THE OFFICE, OVERLOOKING THE CITY, I come to one conclusion. There's only one reason I would negotiate everything like I have the past three days. Every meeting, the marketing department and client list was mentioned. Every deal, the number went up, with the condition it was included in the acquisition of the company … and I turned all of them down. Settling for less. Barely breaking even on a deal I spent months pursuing.

It was all to her and compromising every other deal.

Of course they took what I offered, though. Everyone who needed to sign, did so. Ending the majority of their competition was a worthwhile deal for them. Even if the coveted list remains with Suzette. Her job is secure. It will be unsteady for a while I imagine as she adjusts. She will, though, she will survive and she will thrive. There's no doubt in my mind, even from the numbers' side, and the team agrees. It's not cost-effective and it's a risk to float the company, but for her, knowing that there's not a chance in hell her position will be in jeopardy, it's worth it.

And there's only one conclusion I can make of that. It would have been a quick few million, freeing up my cash flow, ending one project and moving on to the next. Instead, I'll be supporting a company who may lose clients, whose stock will plummet once the split is finalized. A company that will have to prove themselves … a company run by her.

I think I love her.
I think I want to propose to her.

My phone rests in my lap and I stare down at the messages I typed out. I delete the two texts. It's insanity. Running my hand through my hair, I groan at the ridiculousness of it all.

I haven't a clue how Suzette will even react once reality hits her. I've gifted her a company. Technically the board will meet and vote on the positions needed to be filled to move forward. She will be nominated and everything she worked for, will come to fruition.

Heat tingles along my skin, not knowing how she will take it.

The meeting is set for next week and my instinct screams to secure her before then. To propose, to woo her, so that when the time comes and it dawns on her, she'll already be mine.

All of that doubt and insecurity will be worthless if she's already wearing my ring.

It's one thing for a man infatuated to shower a lover with wealth, a lover with trust issues and one that seems to be ready to run any minute. It's another for a future husband to secure his fiancée's livelihood.

The only question that remains is whether or not she'll say yes. Whether she wants me like I want her.

I'm infatuated. I've lost my fucking mind over her.

I think I'll propose to her. I type it out to Wyatt and wait a moment, debating on whether I should do it without telling anyone. I could take her to any jewelry store she wanted, let her choose the ring she wants most and do it then and there.

My thumb hovers over the message.

I already know Wyatt is going to try to talk me out of it. That's what I would do, if he texted me out of nowhere that he wanted to propose to a woman he just met last month.

A woman who's gotten into his head and clouded everything.

But isn't that what love is?

I don't have a moment to send it. Wyatt and my father message me at once.

Wyatt's message asks if he can see me.

He adds: *It's important. As soon as you can, I need to see you.*

An anxiousness comes with my father's message: *You didn't sign that contract, did you?*

My gut drops and Wyatt messages: *Where are you? I'll come to you now. I fucked up. It's all fucked up.*

There's a prick at the back of my neck, a numbness that flows through my veins.

I respond to them both immediately. To my father: *I signed it.*

To Wyatt: *At the office.*

My father: *Fuck. Call me now.*

Wyatt texts back at the same time that my father calls. Clearing my throat, I glance at the closed office door and then turn my back to it, facing the office windows.

"Adrian." My father greets me and before I can do the same he says, "Tell me you didn't sign it."

"I already told you I did."

The tone in his voice is unsettling, enough so that my entire body tenses. There's desperation I can't help but to feel pulling at me through the line.

"Whatever he's gotten himself into, I'll help him out."

"It's not just him," my father grits out between his teeth. "Did your lawyers not change the fucking clause? You're on the hook for his investment in the building."

"What?" My pulse races and I'm quick to open up the drawer, pulling out an unsigned copy, a previous version Wyatt had given me. Andrea has the signed copy. Signed, sealed, delivered.

"He made the purchase this weekend for the real estate

not two days before the city announced the fucking highway would be built across the street."

Wyatt's deal, his big idea, was high-end residential builds. It's what his father made his name doing. They're builders and damn good. "A highway?" I can't fucking believe it. "How did he not know?"

"The more important question is, how the fuck does he sell it now and how the hell do you get out of this contract? If not, you're going to have to sell as much as you can. It's to the tune of twenty million."

"Twenty million," I repeat, bracing myself on the desk. The numbers run in my mind, all of the companies, all of the holdings and deals I could maneuver just to cover a short like that.

"Twenty fucking million." Every way I look at it, one company stands out above the rest. Worth eight million for a single client list.

I could fucking throw up.

"You'll sell if you have to, hold on to the best investments only. I'll help where I can, but I don't see a way out. You're going to have to shift money and hold out for the right timing."

"I need at least a hundred grand a month for a different investment." All the numbers for payroll and transitions tally in my mind. The company will earn it back, but not in the first quarter. Probably not for the first year. It has to float.

"For what?" My father's tone is exasperated. "You'll be lucky if you have enough for your personal expenses."

"I'll leave those numbers to my financial manager," I bite out, irritated but also fucking terrified. I saw what happened to my family years ago when my father lost it all.

As if reading my mind he states clearly, "You might be fucked, but you'll survive this. You're going to have to sacrifice a number of things, but I'm calling the lawyers, I'm calling everyone. I will do everything I can, but I'm not sure there's much we can do but sell. Take the hit. Reinvest when there's time. At least it's only twenty million lost."

I can barely swallow, my eyes closed as I realize what I would do if things were different. A quick eight million is right there.

"Fuck," I say and breathe out. I promised her. I promised her she didn't have to worry.

"I can't fucking believe I signed."

"I can't believe he was that fucking stupid."

"It's his first on his own."

"Even still, he should have fucking known to talk. He could have made fucking sure there weren't whispers and deals in the making. If he'd told his father, at the very least, he could have been given a heads-up."

Investors talk. Politicians are paid. Deals are made. It's how this business is run. But only those in certain circles are privy to high-level information. Wyatt's father would have known. He would have stopped him from buying property whose value was days away from plummeting.

"If the sellers knew—"

"Do you know how long litigation would take? And that's if you can prove it." I swallow thickly. There's a reason they say the business world is run by crooks.

He got fucked over. And I signed the dotted line to come along for the ride.

Just then, the office door opens, Andrea calling out behind Wyatt.

With my phone pressed to my ear, my father cursing and repeating lines of the contract. Wyatt stares back at me, his eyes rimmed in red and looking like hell. His light tan skin is blotchy like he's barely keeping it together.

"I fucked up. It's a lot of fucking money."

"Sir," Andrea starts, a nervous energy around her.

"It's fine, Andrea." I wave her away as Wyatt takes hesitant steps inside the barren office, his hand running down his face. "I'll call you back," is all I say to my father without taking my eyes off my good friend, who just made a horrific deal … one for the both of us.

twenty

Suzette

I KNOCK SOFTLY AT ADRIAN'S DOOR AND GO IN. IT'S THE latest I've ever visited him, but he's been busy all day and evening. As it stands I've barely seen him the last two days, and when I do, he's reserved with me and soft in a way he hasn't been before. I nearly left, thinking maybe he just needed space and wasn't telling me, but I thought better of it.

I messaged: *I have work I can do too, do you mind if I stop by later tonight?*

His response told me everything I needed to know: *I'd love it if you did.*

So with all these nerves still wreaking havoc inside of me, and the realization that I'm head over heels for a man and I think he may be head over heels for me too, I crack open the door to his office.

"Adrian," I call out, saying his name as if to gauge whether or not he's done even though he told me if I came up at nine he should be finished.

Sitting at his desk, Adrian runs his hands over his hair. "Suzette," he responds, my name a murmur on his lips. His stress is apparent even from the door.

"Come have a drink with me," he offers and I instantly relax.

I go around his desk and fold my arms around him from behind, resting my chin on his shoulder. He leans into me for a kiss on the cheek and I feel like I could burst with all the things that threaten to spill out of me. There are so many things that I can't decide what to say first. That I love him? That I'm in love with him? It feels almost childish, raw and vulnerable. It doesn't escape me that I'm insecure and he hasn't given me a reason not to be. I'm holding back and he hasn't as far as I know. This is the part of the relationship where it doesn't feel even.

He may be my boss, the devil in a suit, rich and powerful and I'm lowly compared to him on the surface of it all, but I've never felt inferior. Not until now. Not until I've realized how I feel and that I'm terrified to admit it, just in case he doesn't feel the same.

Adrian turns his face to mine and stands up, pushing his chair out of the way before I can speak. I can taste alcohol on him. He's been drinking, no doubt to get rid of the stresses of the day, though it's a good stress. At least I thought it was. The numbers are good and I'm excited for our meeting next week. I'm not sure what it will entail but I already have a business plan laid out. It'll be wonderful, I can reassure him of that.

"I need you," he whispers against the crook of my neck and the warmth of his breath forces my head to fall back and desire spreads through me like wildfire.

He's almost frantic at my clothes, pushing my skirt up and lifting me onto the desk. A gasp leaves me and it's all too welcomed. Maybe he needs this as much as I do. Adrian strips off my panties with an efficient movement as he looks me in the eyes, his emotions running through them too fast for me to name them all. He undoes his belt and zipper and pushes into me with the same ferocity he used that first day. He's not shy about putting his hands on my body wherever he wants them. He touches me everywhere he can reach, with a firm grip on my thighs and my hips. Adrian fucks me in the way I love him to, with possessive strokes. Pleasure pools between my legs at how close he is and how intimate it is to be used like this.

My nails dig into his shoulder as I moan his name. His

thrusts are merciless and the pleasure builds and builds without warning.

We're in danger of knocking things off the desk now and it's so hot to see him unraveling like this.

All too soon, I come first and then he follows. It's only when he leaves me, both of us still catching our breath that I realize he's fully clothed.

"Would you want me still if I couldn't afford it?" His question came out of nowhere.

"What?" My head is cloudy with lust and my legs still tremble as I try to gather what he's said. "Afford what?"

"To support the split. To fund the company during the changes."

I pull back so I can look into his eyes, following his movements as he undoes his tie and then reaches into his desk for tissues, no doubt to clean up. I'm surprised that he's talking business after six, let alone the second he finished inside of me. Of all the things I want to respond, I want to tease him about it, to lighten it and allay any worries he has.

Before any words can leave me, his gaze pins me. It's one of a wounded man. The same vulnerability that plagued me all day stares back at me.

"I couldn't give two shits if you have money. I don't care." The last couple of days play through my mind. "Is that what's been bothering you?" I ask. "Is it because of my department? I mean it, Adrian." I lick my lips, rushing my words out and praying he understands just how much I mean it. "If you don't want to save the department, if it has to go … I would still want you."

His pace has slowed, but it's as if he can't bring himself to end this conversation. Adrian looks down and I swallow hard.

"Adrian. I swear to you. If you need to tell me something, it's okay." Reaching for the box of tissues and taking it from him, I attempt to convince him. "If you need to tell me something, you can." There's an ache that starts in my chest, but it works its way outward. "I'll still want you."

His pale blue eyes come back to mine again. "Suzette."

"Jobs come and go." I get a lump in my throat from unshed tears and my love for him. *How did this even happen?* I've never wanted to cover myself more, but I'm on his desk and my clothes are on the floor. "Just like clients. I love my job. I love what I do, and I believe in it. But if something were to happen …" Feeling his eyes on my naked body like this makes me even more emotional. Adrian is so connected to this job for me. I met him here, even though he came to change everything. I don't know whether I'm just clinging to those memories or if I'm genuinely afraid to lose my job. "If funding fell through …" He doesn't react at all, other than to pull my hips to the edge of the desk and rest his forehead against mine. "If it all fell to shit and was taken away …"

"Hush."

I do hush, because I can tell what he wants right now is to lose ourselves in the pleasure of this moment.

"I need you again," he whispers and I'm shocked as he pushes me back. Still hard, still demanding and as rough as he was earlier.

"I want you and I'll always want you," he tells me between thrusts, his voice thick with emotion. My lips crash against his and a wave of emotion spreads through me.

I want to tell him, "That's all that matters." But words fail me and strangled moans are all I can offer him.

He groans, "I need more of you."

I spread my legs wide for him and brace my hands on the desk so he can fuck me as hard as he likes. "Come for me," he whispers in my ear, and heat explodes between my thighs in clenching pulses that make him groan and pulse. When he's finished he pulls me off the desk and into his chair. I'm straddling him now, his hands on my waist, and I try to catch my breath so I can continue our conversation.

Even if he doesn't want to. Even if it means being too open, too raw, too needy. I just need him to know exactly how I feel.

"Listen to me." I take his hand and put it to my chest. "I would survive. I could start my company from scratch. I might not be able to keep the clients, but I would find more. I don't want you because you can support me, if that's what you're worried about. I want you for you. God knows I hated the idea of you when I first saw you but I—" I swallow, and chicken out, backing away from the truth I'm too scared to voice. "I want you." It's all that I can say.

It's true. If I learned one thing from my divorce, it's that I'll always be able to find a way to support myself. I might worry about it but if the occasion arises, I'll handle it. That's what it means to be a woman in the world. You always have to be able to find a way.

I put both my hands on the sides of his face. "Are you all right?"

He strokes my cheek. "It was only a question. I didn't mean to make you worry."

"If I should worry, you would tell me, wouldn't you?"

He looks deep into my eyes and pulls me in for another kiss. This one is deep and slow and it's like he wants to memorize every part of me. "You don't have to worry," Adrian whispers against my lips. "I want you."

"I want you too." I pull his lip between my teeth and add a little pressure so he can feel it. His deep groan is everything I needed to hear.

Adrian's already hard beneath me again, so it takes nothing to lift myself up and ease back down on his thick length. It's a sweeter connection this time, though he's just as possessive with me. I lean down and kiss him while we move together. Adrian can't help but take control, making his thrusts deeper and harder, and it feels so good that it brings on another orgasm. It moves through my body and makes me tip my head back with the kind of ecstasy I've been looking for all this time for so long. I never thought I'd find it again and I found it here in Adrian. Here in this most forbidden of arrangements.

When it's over I open my eyes and look into his. He's watching me with heat in his expression and love too. "I love you," I tell him.

He groans and pulls me down onto his cock, fucking me as deep as he ever has. He holds on tightly, as if he never wants to let me go, but he doesn't say it back.

twenty-one

Adrian

"The penthouse in Tribeca is five million," I speak clearly, standing in the office and imagining how this office in the high-rise could easily double for temporary housing. I'll take the meetings in the conference room. "I'll sell the furniture with it, that should bring it up another million."

"Business shouldn't affect your personal—"

"We tallied the numbers with the other assets," I repeat to my father. My financial advisor is on the phone as well. He's seen the contract, he knows what deals went down. More importantly, he has a tally of every investment I have. I simply can't lose the majority of them. If I sell now, I'll lose so much more than the current value. There is only so much that can give. "I'll find somewhere cheaper, and that's far better than losing investments or paying the interest."

My financial manager, Sean, speaks through the line, "I agree and there are plenty of other markets on the upswing. It could be beneficial in the long run."

"There's no reason not to sell the list and dissolve the—" My father attempts to chime in. If I didn't respect him as much as I do, I'd tell him to fuck off. To get off the line. To get out of my business. But as it stands, he's my father. He's just as involved in this deal as he has been in the others. He's my mentor and I know he means well. That list and Suzette's departments are nonnegotiable.

I told her I would protect her. And I meant it.

"Yes, there is."

"I saw the deals, Adrian. Why the hell are you doing this? I didn't raise you to—"

"Because she'll hate me," I bite out, forming a fist as my muscles coil. "This is a business call. If you cannot remain professional, I will take the call alone as I would have preferred to do."

"Who is she?"

"It's personal. I'm keeping that investment and I want you to respect that."

"It's worth you losing your home?"

"It's worth me losing everything." The amount of rage is equal to my desperation. Chaos swarms in my blood. "I cannot lose her."

There's silence on the line before an awkward cough from my advisor. Sean states the numbers we've gone over a hundred times in the last six hours.

"If she would hate you for it, then she's not the one for you." My father's tone is somber and before I can say anything else, there's a click on the line.

"Adrian?" Sean questions, "Are you still there?"

"Yes, it was my father who left." There's a hollowness in my chest that fills with a mix of emotions. "Where were we?" I say and then sit back down in the chair.

The money, the power—none of it means anything if I can't have her.

Keeping Sean on speaker, I text my father: *She doesn't know any of this and I don't want her to. I love her and you will too when you meet her.*

I know it's the right thing to do by her. I can make this work. I can have it all.

I text him again before he responds. *Maybe hate was strong. She would be upset, but she wouldn't hate me. I want to do everything I can for her. You need to trust me on this.*

All she needs is this chance. I believe in her and I'll make the money back. I'll be a man worthy of a woman like her.

I just don't know how to tell her or if I even should.

"If we could touch base about the article today," my advisor starts, "it does not seem to be as telling as we were led to believe." I was given a heads-up yesterday that Wyatt's dealing would make headlines. It's a scandal in the making given how the property deal went down.

"I was able to pull some strings," I tell him.

"Have you gotten any pushback from investors? Any concerned calls?"

"A few." My brow pinches at remembering the early calls and emails this morning, wanting to know whether or not the deals would still be going through. "As far as I know, everyone is satisfied."

"Excellent. I know this isn't ideal, but this is manageable. I do, however, recommend not signing any contracts of that magnitude until the lawyers have approved. I spoke with Carly and she told me she had not finished negotiations."

I can only nod, remembering how light I felt, signing that contract … with Suzette on my mind. With Wyatt's approval, about her. Coming to terms with how I'd fallen for her.

"I was distracted," I admit to him.

"Whatever it was, see to it that this doesn't happen again. There's only so much we can do and next time it may not be salvageable."

The knock at my door is hesitant and then Andrea opens it without waiting for a response. It comes at the same time that a text comes through.

"Not now," I tell Andrea who nods and closes the door softly.

I thought it would be my father, but it's Suzette.

I want you. I love you for you. I don't need your money, and I wouldn't think less of you if you weren't in the position you're in.

As if this day could get any harder. I know she loves me. And I'm going to prove to her that I love her back. Words aren't enough.

"It will be tight for a few months unless something breaks. We can file for a few extensions. It will get you through and we can keep it discreet, but you do not have leverage to spend for the time being."

"I understand." A heat tingles the back of my neck. This position I'm in is less than ideal. I can't blame Wyatt. The blame squarely falls on my shoulders.

Sean twists the knife even more. "For all intents and purposes, you are broke."

"I know, Sean. I know what it means."

There's another knock on my door, more forceful than before.

"Mr. Bradford," Andrea speaks up and her tone makes it evident that whatever it is, it needs to be said now.

"I'll call you back shortly," I tell Sean and hang up before he can respond as Andrea walks in. The door closes behind her. Dressed in loose gray pants and a billowy white top, she's nothing but professional.

"What is it?" I question.

"I made a mistake," she tells me, not taking the seat she stands behind.

"We all do," I say, attempting to ease any worries she has, but her expression doesn't appear to reflect that. There's not a worry line in sight.

"The error in the contract with Mr. Wyatt Patton's—" she starts.

I still, my blood going cold. "What about it? What error?"

"I sent in half of the contract signed, but the second half ... Somehow," she says and gestures in the air, a shrug rolling from her shoulders, "I faxed it over unsigned." Her lips quirk up at the end. As if she knows.

Of course she does.

"Andrea." My head falls into my hands for only a moment, the relief waning as if this isn't real. "Could you repeat that, please?" I swallow thickly, praying that what I heard her say is exactly what she did say.

"From what I can tell," she tells me, now taking the seat slowly, "I must have had some questions and somehow I mixed up the paperwork."

"I have to call my lawyer," I tell her, still in a state of disbelief, my hands nearly trembling. If she's serious, if she didn't send it … It's twenty million that she saved me.

"I thought you might say that." She pats the desk before standing. "She distracts you, but like I've always told you, I've got your back."

"I could kiss you—"

"Please don't," she says jokingly.

"I don't know how to repay you," I tell her softly before she can leave, still not truly believing. Not until I see it myself and not until it's confirmed.

twenty-two

Suzette

I DON'T THINK I'VE EVER BEEN SO NERVOUS FOR A dinner date. This man has fucked every part of me, he's seen me break down and punished me in ways a younger me wouldn't understand.

He knows me and every inch of me. And that's what scares me. He could crush me so very easily and it would take far more than a bottle of rosé at Maddie's to get over him.

In the back of his car, with Adrian's driver taking me through the city, I sit alone. According to Noah, he's to take me to dinner and Adrian is meeting me there.

I play it off as if I'm not nervous at all. As if tonight doesn't feel different. As if that's a perfectly normal thing to happen. It's a perfect New York City evening. The sunset is a watercolor painting above the buildings, slowly growing darker as the few stars we can see appear high above us.

I'm in love with him, and no matter what he says, I think he loves me too. My heart beats faster with every minute that passes on the drive, and I can't concentrate on my phone. Finally, I put it in my purse and ignore it completely. All the emails I need to send can wait.

I don't miss Noah's eyes peeking back at me and the third time I meet them, I cave.

"Is he going to break up with me?" I question, my voice

squeakier than I'd have liked, though I know he's not the person I should be asking.

His head tilts a bit and if I'm not mistaken, the wrinkles that form around his eyes indicate that he's smiling although I can't see that part of his face. "I didn't think you were dating, Ms. Parks."

I laugh, feeling a little less nervous. "Very funny." My fingers fidget among themselves.

He laughs back at me. "He would be a fool to do such a thing. And Mr. Bradford isn't a fool." I can only nod in agreement although I don't feel entirely reassured.

"Besides, we're here so it's a little too late to run."

Peeking out through the tinted window, my gaze focuses on a tempting man in a suit. Heat flows through me seeing Adrian's waiting for me on the sidewalk. He pulls the door open for me before I know what's happening. I step out, slipping my hand into his to keep my balance.

"I'll take it from here," he tells Noah, and that's when I see we're at the Waldorf again. Glancing down at my office attire, I give Adrian a look and he only smirks back.

"If you'd like to go shopping first," he offers although I'm certain it's more for comic relief than anything else.

"You are a devilish man," I comment, and move to stand beside him, his hand still holding mine.

His rough chuckle is a soothing balm. "You look gorgeous," he reassures me.

With every step, the nervousness lingers but it's different now that I'm with him. Maybe it's the way he holds me, or the way he peers down at me. The way his hand splays against my back as we walk in or how he helps me into the booth. I'm not sure what it is, but I want it all.

I would give him everything I have today, for him to simply want me tomorrow.

Adrian

"Sir, another?" the waiter asks, politely gathering my attention. If I recall correctly, he's the same waiter we had our first night at the Waldorf, our dinner that never came to be.

The same tucked away booth as well.

I shake my head once. "Thank you, though."

"And for you?" he asks Suzette.

"I'd like dessert I think," she says and gazes back at me as if asking if I'd like to join her.

I only smile back, feeling the nerves heat.

"Maybe the dark chocolate tart?" the waiter suggests and I pray I don't show my reaction in the least.

When the plate comes out, her diamond will be on it. My composure threatens to break when she agrees.

I've gone over every response she could have.

If she says it's too soon, I'll respond, if not now, then when?

If she thinks I've gone crazy, I'll agree, I am losing it be-cause of her.

It doesn't matter what she thinks of it, so long as she says yes. So long as she's mine to have and to hold, to be with me forever. For fuck's sake, if she thinks it has to do with work, I'll tell her how I signed a damn contract I shouldn't have because I couldn't get her off my mind. That alone should convince a businesswoman like her that she should say yes before I go broke drowning in thoughts of her all day.

"Are you all right?" Suzette questions and it's only when I look up to see her glancing at the cocktail napkin in my hand that I realize I've twisted and pulled and creased it to death.

"Fine," I answer her and in my periphery I see the waiter slipping the plate down in front of her.

My heart races and I tell her that I'm perfectly fine and wait.

Her gaze doesn't leave mine. Even when I motion to her dessert, spotting the four-carat diamond sparking from where it sits in the red velvet box.

"I just—" Suzette starts and then licks her lips. "I know I'm … I know that I—" she hesitates. This gorgeous, intelligent, strong-willed woman hesitates, because of me.

Because I didn't say *I love you* back. I know damn well that's why.

"I want you to marry me," I murmur, unable to hold it back any longer.

Her kissable lips part and her light blue eyes widen. "Adrian."

I motion to the ring on her plate and she gasps, a loud yelp of a gasp, covering her mouth and jumping back slightly.

She stares at it, as if I'm not waiting, unable to breathe and desperate for her to answer me.

"Marry me," I tell her, a command this time and that gets her attention. Her hands lower, although she still stares at me as if she's in shock.

"For the love of all things holy, if you don't say yes right now, I swear to God I'll throw you over this table."

When she smiles, this beautiful smile that reaches all the way up to her eyes, I know it'll be all right.

"I love you," she tells me, her cadence soothing.

"That isn't a yes and I'm going to need you to say—"

"Yes," she says in a breathy voice and it takes everything in me not to topple the table as I rush to her.

To kiss her. To hold her. "I love you too," I tell her the moment she breaks our kiss. "I love you and I need you with me."

Her eyes shine back with every emotion I feel stirring inside of me.

"I love you and I want you, and I need you too."

epilogue

THE CITY NEVER SLEEPS. IT PROVIDES A CONSTANT light as it slips into the office. Even at nearly 1:00 a.m. With a deep breath in, I lie back, nestling beside Adrian on the pullout sofa. His smell surrounds me, fresh and clean with a hint of sandalwood, and so do his arms as he wraps them around me, planting a kiss on my forehead.

This is how we've slept for the last two weeks nearly. He stays with me, working and taking calls, while I do the same.

The numbers are promising, but not guaranteed.

"Was it a good day?" he asks me, his chest rumbling as his hand runs down my back.

"A great day. Gail secured the final client."

"That makes me happy to hear," he comments and although exhaustion coats his tone, I know he truly is happy. It was shaky at first. A number of clients debated on leaving, and they all wanted to renegotiate. Gail took the brunt of it.

"Me too," I say and then ask him, "And what about you? Any updates from Wyatt?"

His friend got into a bad deal. I'm not certain of the details but I know it's been rough on him and it involves politicians and a lawsuit and some other developer.

I was nervous at first that it might involve my friend's husband, Mason. He's a developer and I've heard whispers about the depths of corruption that surround him and his family.

He loves Jules, though, and she swears he's one of the good ones. Thankfully, he wasn't involved.

"He'll be all right, but the next few years will be difficult for him. The loan I gave him will help, but he's in for a hellish year if not longer."

"And what about the contract?" Again, the details are murky, but I know at some point, Adrian had signed on to some piece of this shit show.

"It's null and void. Even if I'd signed, he said it was his mistake, we'd never discussed it and he would deal with the fallout."

"He's a good friend."

"He's a good man. Not everyone survives the lows, but he will."

"You still seem down," I comment.

"Just a long day," he says and settles higher up on the bed, "and my little whore has been ignoring me at work."

"It's after six, we're not supposed to talk about work," I tease him, sitting up slightly to nip his bottom lip. He gives me a gruff groan and I love it.

"Hey," I whisper and nudge my nose against his, "I want you."

He hums, that sound I crave before giving me the command, "Roll over."

Heat rushes to my cheeks and I do as he says, laying on my stomach and watching him pull the white T-shirt over his head. This sexy powerful man who comes undone just for me. It's heady, and I'll never get enough of it.

My eyes close when he kisses my neck with the same passion we had the first day.

"Be a good little slut for me, and get on your knees."

I fuck my boss every night in his office.

And I love it.

I love him.

about the author

Thank you so much for reading my romances. I'm just a stay at home mom and avid reader turned author and I couldn't be happier.

I hope you love my books as much as I do!

More by Willow Winters
www.WillowWintersWrites.com/books

Enjoy a sneak peek from our co-written work together.

come here and
KISS ME

prologue

Ronan

I BRUSH THE GLASS EDGE OF THE WHISKEY BOTTLE against her swollen nub and she writhes on the bartop as much as she can.

The silk ties at her wrists don't allow much movement. She's bound to draft pours with another tie blindfolding her.

Those gorgeous legs of hers are spread so her ass sits on the edge. Her red bottomed heels perched on the bar and delicious cunt just inches from my face.

I take another swig and then wipe my mouth with the back of my hand. She tastes of expensive sin that could cost me everything and all at once. Brooklynn's dirty blonde hair tosses carelessly as I pluck her nipple just because I fucking want to see those plump lips part again. Give me those little moans and strangled sighs of pleasure.

Light filters through the bar, highlighting the rows of colored glass and dark amber woods. A passing car doesn't stop and my heart races at the thought of someone seeing us in this predicament. Looking over my shoulder, I check once more that the blinds are closed as best as they can be. No one should come here when the bar closed over an hour ago.

I take another swig then let a bit of the whiskey drip down her clit to the opening of her cunt and take a languid lick. Sliding two fingers into her warmth, I curve them and finger fuck her until her thighs shake and hips buck.

"Stay fucking still and take what I give you my little whore,"

I murmur as I press the weight of my body against hers to keep her pinned. She obeys like the good girl she is for me.

Ever since I first laid eyes on her, I've wanted to fuck those sounds out of her until she's screaming my name and surrendering to me. The sound of my zipper fills the silence and I let my suit pants fall to the floor. She swallows, the cords in her throat tightening and the blush in her chest creeping up her neck all the way to her high cheekbones and then to her temples. I'm silent as I watch her, knowing if we do this, there's no fucking way anyone can know.

She may think she's rebelling from her rich prick of a father by having a sordid night and forbidden affair. But they can never find out.

And it can never happen again.

The stolen glances that last too long. The way her lips tilt up when she says my name as if teasing me. Every little touch she's tempted me with over the years that no one else sees can never happen again after what we did tonight.

"Ro," she moans my name as her body trembles with pleasure. Her back arches slightly and her hair turns into a messy halo on the bartop as her head falls back with those sweet sounds uttered from her lips.

With the last of the whiskey, I toss back half then savor the other half, staring down at her gorgeous body laid bare in front of me. Swishing the expensive liquor once, I hover over her, nudging her nose with mine and then let the whiskey fall to her lips. She's such a good fucking girl, taking what I offer her. Our lips meet and I kiss her with the desire that's built up over the years.

The bottle slams to the table as I lose myself in her kiss. With one hand on her hip, keeping her where I need her, the other stroking my cock and then lining myself up, I plunge into her in a single stroke, taking everything I've always wanted.

And the one thing I could never afford.

I'm reckless as I fuck her.

She didn't come here for me tonight.

None of this should have ever happened.

But I'll be damned if I don't give in to a temptation I had for years when it's presented so easily, so willingly… a fucking gorgeous enticement.

It's not until the email I'm sent in the morning that I realize they saw everything. I don't know who was watching or how the fuck it happened. But as I press the play button on the anonymous email, I know damn well someone saw and exactly what they're going to do with the recording. Fuck!